The snare drum plunged downwa through the priso wooden block, th widely, mouth still gaping in an unfinished cry, the prisoner's head rolled off the edge of the platform and fell with a wet sound into the mud below. As if freed from a spell, the peasants breathed once more, tasting air thick with blood and fear and death.

In the summit of the bell tower, the hunchback turned from the grisly scene below and dashed to the dangling ropes. It was time for him to play out his role in this dark charade. His powerfully muscled arms flexing, the hunchback pulled on the ropes. The bells swung in the shadows above, ringing out a mournful dirge for the dead man. The pigeons erupted in a gray, fluttering cloud, winging from rafter to rafter as the sound thrummed through the very stones of the tower. The tolling of the bells was deafening, but the hunchback only grinned, closing his bulging eyes in an expression of sublime joy. To him it was not the grim song of death, but the sweet music of release.

Ravenloft is a netherworld of evil, a place of darkness that can be reached from any world—escape is a different matter entirely. The unlucky who stumble into the Dark Domains find themselves trapped in lands filled with vampires, werebeasts, zombies, and worse.

Each novel in the series is a complete story in itself, revealing the chilling tales of the beleaguered heroes and powerful evil lords who populate the Dark Domains.

RAVENLOFT BOOKS

BOOKS

Tower
of
Doom

Mark Anthony

**For my own wonderfully twisted brother, Shane.
(You were *too* at the bottom of the stairs!)**

TOWER OF DOOM

Random House and its affiliate companies have worldwide distribution rights in the book trade for English language products of TSR, Inc.

Distributed to the book and hobby trade in the United Kingdom by TSR Ltd.

Distributed to the toy and hobby trade by regional distributors.

Cover art by Bruce Eagle.

First Printing: November 1994
Printed in the United States of America
Library of Congress Catalog Card Number: 94-60210

9 8 7 6 5 4 3 2 1

ISBN: 0-7869-0062-8

TSR, Inc.   TSR Ltd.
P.O. Box 756   120 Church End, Cherry Hinton
Lake Geneva, WI 53147   Cambridge CB1 3LB
United States of America   United Kingdom

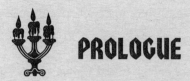

PROLOGUE

The last tatters of the storm that had lashed Nartok Keep during the night finally broke and fled before the violent crimson dawn. Sunlight spilled across the ancient stone of the keep, thick and heavy as blood, illuminating high walls that seemed to sag under their own ponderous bulk and a motley collection of towers that reached up to rake the underbelly of the sky. In the dark before the dawn, a throng of folk had climbed from the village below to the summit of the crag upon which the keep perched. They gathered now in the churned mud of the courtyard, huddling silently before a skeletal wooden scaffold.

They had come for an execution.

From a window high in the spindly bell tower of Nartok Keep, a lone figure watched the grim scene unfold below. The watcher was swathed in a frayed black cloak that covered him from head to toe. Beneath the garment, a peculiar mass protruded from the figure's stooped back. He looked much like a man bent under the burden of a heavy pack.

"Come, my friends," the man said softly. "We must not be late."

Had anyone been there to hear his voice, he might have thought it beautiful. It was deep and resonant, like the tolling of a bell. But the only reply was the soft trilling of the mist-gray pigeons perched upon the crumbling window ledge. He stroked the birds fondly with a gnarled hand. The creatures ruffled their feathers and stared up at him, their eyes like dark jewels.

The man turned and moved with an odd, lurching gait across the small chamber. It was a dreary room. Only a feeble light managed to find its way through the narrow slit of the window, and it was not kind to the scant objects it found within. Moldy straw covered the stone floor, and chill draughts whistled unceasingly through chinks in the mortar. A musty pallet and worm-eaten chest were the only furnishings.

The cloaked man scrambled up a rickety wooden ladder and climbed through a trapdoor into a lofty chamber filled with dappled brilliance. Wind and sunlight streamed through the intricate wrought-iron gratings that covered the high arched windows. From stout oaken rafters above hung a dozen massive bells, each trailing a rope through a series of pulleys.

A pigeon fluttered down to land on the man's outstretched arm, followed by another, and another.

"Yes, Lisenne, I will play your favorite harmonic today." He caressed a bird whose feathers glowed with faint green iridescence. "Now, there will be no pecking, Oratio," he chided gently. "You have no cause to be jealous. And you, Armond, shall have your choice next time. Go to your places now, my friends." The birds winged away to their high perches.

The sound of a snare drum drifted on the air. The cloaked man shuffled to one of the arched openings and peered through. In the courtyard below, a pair of the baron's knights, handsome in their brass-buttoned coats of blue wool, pushed a ragged old man up the steps of the scaffold. The prisoner's gaunt face was the color of clay, and mad terror shone in his eyes. He looked like one who had already gazed into the dark abyss of death. A black-hooded executioner forced the prisoner to his knees, pushing his head down upon a block of wood. The block's surface was stained a dark, rusty color and scarred by deep gouges. Next to the block lay an object draped by a black cloth.

One of the knights glared at the crowd. "The lord inquisitor has found this man guilty of treason against Baron Caidin of Nartok!" The fearful villagers cringed in a knot. "See that he does not find any of you guilty of the same!"

High in the bell tower, the cloaked man whispered excitedly. "Be ready, my friends! The moment approaches."

As the pigeons bobbed their heads, the man cast off his heavy cloak. Beneath was a form that could only be called hideous. The man might have been tall were his back not bent nearly double upon itself, twisting his shoulders into an agonizingly humped shape. His legs were unnaturally bowed, and his hunched torso made his arms seem horribly long for his body. Worst of all was his visage. Countless years of craning his neck and peering upward at queer angles had twisted his face into a grotesque mask. His blue eyes bulged disconcertingly in their sockets, and his mouth was drawn up in a perpetual, yellow-toothed grimace.

In the courtyard below, the snare drum rose in crescendo. The executioner lifted the black cloth from the object beside the block. Beneath was a half-moon blade. Intricate runes and sinister sigils coiled like serpents across the smooth steel. The blade was so massive that, had it been hafted to the end of an axe, no man could possibly have lifted it. The prisoner gaped fearfully at the blade. A gasp rose from the crowd.

The half-moon blade began to rise, as if lifted by an unseen hand. Thick red sunlight dripped blood-like from its edge. The blade rose higher, propelled by some unspeakable force, or perhaps by its own volition, a living thing fueled by an inherent will to slay. At last the blade halted. It hovered high above the scaffold, shining like a crimson moon against the dome of the sky. The prisoner, who apparently could bear the atmosphere of portent no longer, struggled, craning his head to gaze upward.

"Come, be done with it!" he shrieked. "What does it matter to me now?" Insane cackling rose from deep in his throat. "I am already—"

The snare drum ceased. The half-moon blade plunged downward. It flared brilliantly as it bit deeply into the wooden block, then went dark. Eyes still staring widely, mouth still gaping in an unfinished cry, the prisoner's head rolled off the edge of the platform and fell with a wet sound into the mud below. As if freed from a spell, the peasants breathed once more, tasting air thick with blood and fear and death.

In the summit of the bell tower, the hunchback turned from the grisly scene below and dashed to the dangling ropes. It was time for him to play out his role in this dark charade. His powerfully muscled arms flexing, the hunchback pulled on the ropes. The bells swung in the shadows above, ringing out a mournful dirge for the dead man. The pigeons erupted in a gray, fluttering cloud, winging from rafter to rafter as the sound thrummed through the very stones of the tower. The tolling of the bells was deafening, but the hunchback only grinned, closing his bulging eyes in an expression of sublime joy. To him it was not the grim song of death, but the sweet music of release.

PART I

The Monster in the Tower

ONE

Wort had lost count of how many years he had lived alone with the pigeons in the old bell tower.

These days, few in Nartok Keep knew who rang the bells each time there was a death in the keep or village. Some spoke of a ghost that lived in the tower. Others believed that the bells themselves were enchanted. Sometimes—when a funeral procession marched through the gates of the keep or when an execution was about to take place—a passerby might glance upward at just the right moment to see a shadow move high in the dilapidated spire. So it was most often whispered that it was neither ghost nor enchantment that animated the bell tower. No, it was a monster.

Wort did not mind the dark superstitions that surrounded the tower. They helped maintain the solitude he favored. No one ever dared come to the spire—except for the unlucky scullery boy who, every third day, was forced to tread alone down a dim corridor to leave a sack of food and a jug of water beside the door that led into the tower. The kitchenwife did not know why these actions were to be carried out, only that the order had come from Baron Caidin himself years ago.

Only rarely did Wort set foot outside the demesne

of his tower. It had been months since the last occasion.

"It is better here with you, my friends," he said softly to the pale pigeons that drifted down out of the darkness like ghosts to perch upon his hunched shoulder. "You are not afraid of me. Besides, here we have our books."

He hobbled to the battered chest next to his mouse-eaten pallet and threw back the lid. Inside were myriad volumes, some bound in oiled leather, others in purple cloth. Gingerly he picked up one of the books, and began to read aloud from its crackling parchment pages.

" 'As the prince journeyed deeper into the greenwood, he came upon a clear silver font, and being thirsty, he knelt to drink. Even as the first drops of cool water touched his lips, the sky darkened, and thunder rent the air. In moments, a dozen rose vines wove themselves about the prince, trapping him in a thorny cage. He tried to break free, but the thorns pierced his flesh, and blood fell upon the roses, changing the blooms from white to crimson.' "

Wort turned the page, and suddenly a handful of pale red rose petals fell from the book. Laughing, he caught some as they fluttered toward the floor. As quickly as they had come, the petals vanished in a silver flash, leaving only a faint, sweet fragrance to drift upon the air. He read on.

" 'As the prince watched, the font glimmered with magic. Like a mirror reflecting some distant place, the image of a beautiful woman appeared on its surface. "You have dared to drink from my pool!" the woman spoke in rage. "Know then that the price for such a drink is death. . . ." ' "

Slowly, Wort shut the enchanted book and placed it back in the chest. The birds about him cooed expectantly.

"No, I will read no more until tonight, my friends. We will learn what happens to our good prince then."

Wort had discovered the magical book in one of the keep's many forgotten rooms. Sometimes the stories seemed so real that Wort imagined he was the handsome prince or noble knight who was the hero. That helped him to forget. There were times when the thoughts in Wort's mind seemed more twisted and painful than his deformed back, but the books quieted such thoughts. Of course, nothing was so good as the bells. Their thunderous music seemed to blast the dark memories right out of his head, until all his senses were flooded by their glorious tolling. No, nothing could make him forget like the bells.

There was a time when Wort had lived in the keep with the rest of the baron's court. That had been before Caidin, when the Old Baron had ruled Nartok, when Wort himself had been only a boy. Even then, servants and nobles alike had regarded him with disgust, muttering charms against the Evil Eye as they passed him. As a boy, Wort had never understood why. Then one day the steward had given him the task of polishing a tarnished silver bowl. When he had cleared away the dark grime, Wort had been so startled to see a hideous face staring back at him that he had dropped the bowl, denting it.

"You are as stupid as you are ugly, Wort!" the steward had berated him, boxing his ears. "Don't you even recognize your own reflection, boy?"

Wort had always known that he was different than other children, that he had been so from birth. Now he knew that he was not merely different. He was horrible. From that time on, he had done his best to conceal his appearance to avoid troubling others. For a time it seemed to work. But he could not keep his twisted form covered every moment, and as he grew older, those who glimpsed it regarded him with growing fear.

One day, when Wort was trying to help an ashwife clean the hearth in the Grand Hall, his hood had slipped back. When she saw his twisted face, the ashwife had screamed. In her haste to get away she had fallen into the fire and was badly burned. Several servants came to carry the woman away on a makeshift stretcher. Wort would never forget what one of them—a young man whose eyes had been filled with hate—had hissed at him.

"Look what you've done, you monster."

"I was only trying to help," Wort had choked pitifully.

After that, the steward had forbidden Wort to assist any of the other servants. In the end, it seemed the only way Wort could truly help people was by leaving them alone. With nothing else to occupy his time, he had taken to exploring the sprawling bulk of the keep, making his way down shadowy corridors and through dusty chambers where none had set foot in centuries.

One day he had stumbled upon an entrance into the abandoned bell tower. The bell ropes had rotted away, and the bells themselves had been covered with filth, but despite the tower's dreariness it became Wort's secret retreat. Here there was no one save the pigeons that roosted in the belfry, and—miraculously—they did not seem to fear him. Here there was the power of the bells. The tower had become his only home, as a boy. Now, in the autumn of his thirty-third year, few remembered the hunchback who had disappeared long ago from the corridors of the keep. It was just as well. Wort knew that it was better to be forgotten than feared.

"But today, I must do a dangerous thing—I must go down into the keep, Celia," he said to a pigeon now perched upon his wrist, pecking at the crumbs of bread in his cupped palm. "I must ask Baron Caidin for a new bell. One of old bells has cracked, I fear, and it is causing a dissonance in the minor harmonic."

The bird seemed almost to nod its head, ruffling its feathers in apparent disdain.

"Ah, yes, I see you heard it as well as I. It simply will not do, will it?" The music of the bells had to be perfect to drive the black thoughts away. Wort had to get a new bell, and soon, lest he be overcome by his twisted memories.

Wort tossed the pigeon into the air and watched it flutter up to the rafters. Wrapping himself in his heavy cloak, he lumbered down the cracked steps of a spiral staircase, then locked the tower's oaken door behind him with a heavy brass key. Lurching, he made his way down a twisting corridor. Only a faint gloom filtered its way in through the ivy-choked windows, illuminating thick strands of cobweb and mold-stained walls. Like many parts of the vast keep, these passageways had fallen into disuse over the last hundred years. The number of people who dwelt in Nartok dwindled with each passing year, as if a dark blight was gradually draining the life from the barony. One could almost smell it in the air, pungent and disconcertingly sweet, like the scent of rotting meat. Nartok was dying. However, it had been dying for centuries, and no doubt it would continue to die its slow death for centuries to come.

In his time Wort had explored all of the chambers that lined the corridor, and he found many forgotten treasures—like the enchanted book—within. Most wondrous of them all was the tapestry. He had discovered it hanging on the wall of a musty storeroom. The weaving was moth-eaten and rotting in places, its images obscured by grime. But in the center of the tapestry, shining through the dark tarnish of uncounted years, Wort spotted an angel. Though he could barely make out the garden in which she floated, the angel herself seemed to glow, as if no amount of dust and dirt could dim the inner light of her timeless beauty. Time and again, Wort had gone to the room to gaze upon the angel, for she seemed so peaceful, so gentle. There was so much love in her purple eyes that sometimes he dared to imagine that there might be enough for him.

Wort shook his head. Those were dangerous thoughts. No one could love someone as hideous as he. Pushing the image of the angel out of his mind, he hurried on his errand. Making certain the hood of his thick cloak cast his face in shadow, he stepped through an archway into a torchlit corridor. He had reached an inhabited portion of the keep. Cautiously, he made his way from chamber to chamber.

Despite the decay, Nartok Keep was still the heart of one of the richest fiefdoms in all of Darkon. It was particularly famous for its ruby-colored wines, which sold at exorbitant prices in the great city of Il Aluk to the north. The barony's vast wealth was ostentatiously displayed in every chamber. Chairs of crushed velvet sat next to tables of glossy wood, laden with silver candelabra and crystal vases. Soot-darkened portraits of long-dead nobles stared down from the walls, their hungry, jealous eyes glaring at the descendants who now possessed what had once been theirs.

Finally Wort reached the gilded doors that led into the Grand Hall. The young page given the task of guarding the portal had fallen asleep in his chair. Wort glided with uncanny silence past the sleeping boy. Carefully, he opened one of the gilded doors just enough to slip through, then pushed it shut behind him.

". . . and the inquisition continues to uncover traitors in your fiefdom, Baron," a sibilant voice spoke.

Wort quickly ducked into the pool of shadow behind a grotesque marble statue—a dying stag, its neck pierced by a steel arrow. Baron Caidin was in the midst of a meeting. Wort craned his neck to peer through the stag's antlers. Three men stood in the center of the vast, marbled Grand Hall. Beneath their feet was an intricate mosaic embedded in the surface of the floor. Rendered in bits of colored tile, the mosaic depicted an ancient, forgotten battle in gory detail.

"Indeed, my lord baron," said another voice. "I suspect your lord inquisitor could find traitors under a stone if he attempted the feat." The second speaker was a stout, broad-shouldered man with sharp eyes and iron-gray mustaches. He wore the midnight blue military coat of the baron's knights, but the golden braid coiled about his right shoulder indicated his superior rank. "Lord Inquisitor Sirraun appears to have a talent for finding treachery in the most unlikely places."

"And does that disturb you, Castellan Domeck?" Sirraun turned upon the muscular, gray-haired knight. The lord inquisitor was a gaunt man with small eyes and a mocking, almost lipless mouth. His tight-fitting garb of coal black accentuated the unhealthy color of his sallow visage. "Perhaps you have something you wish to hide. I wonder what secrets you might reveal, good castellan, given the encouragement of a skillfully placed hot iron or a few judicious turns of a thumbscrew."

Domeck gave Sirraun a look of open disgust. "I have found that those most interested in discovering the secrets of others usually have the most to hide themselves." He clenched a fist. "No, the best way to avert betrayal is to defend ourselves with sabers, not with lies."

Sirraun shot Domeck a poisonous look, but before the castellan could respond, the third man interposed himself between the two.

"As usual, your squabbling grows tedious," he said sourly. He was a tall man of graceful yet imposing bearing, dark haired and uncommonly handsome. His short, carefully trimmed beard was glossy with expensive oils, and his eyes glittered like emeralds above a proud nose. He wore a long coat not unlike the castellan's, but far richer. The garment was fashioned of purple velvet with silver trim, its sleeves gashed to reveal crimson silk underneath.

"I am sorry, my lord baron," Domeck grumbled.

"Begging your forgiveness, Baron Caidin," Sirraun fawned obsequiously. "You know that I live only to serve Your Grace."

"Yes, you do," Caidin said darkly.

Sirraun's eyes bulged in alarm. The castellan shot him a satisfied smirk.

"Here is my will," Caidin went on in an authoritative tone. "Sirraun, do what you must in the name of the inquisition. A plot to assassinate me festers in my barony—we know that from the prisoners you tortured—and I want every trace of it found and excised." He raised a hand before Domeck could protest. "And you, my loyal castellan, will make certain my knights are prepared to defend me should an attempt be made upon my life. Understood?"

Sirraun and Domeck exchanged looks of loathing, then nodded reluctantly.

"Excellent," Caidin pronounced with satisfaction. "Then I shall expect—"

A sudden cry echoed about the vaulted Grand Hall. The three men looked up in surprise. Wort lurched from his hiding place, reaching behind himself to grab the creature that had leapt on him without warning. A sharp pain bit into his neck. With his powerful arms, he managed to yank the thing off and fling it across the hall.

"Baron Caidin," the creature squeaked as it flew through the air. "I have found an—"

Abruptly it struck a gilded stone column and slid slowly to the floor.

"—intruder," the creature finished dizzily.

Wort could see now that the creature that had attacked him was a small, wizened being with purple skin and large, pale eyes. A gnome. It was clad in a frilly white shirt and a frock coat of purple and silver, styled in miniature imitation of the baron's garb. The gnome still clutched the small stiletto with which it had scratched Wort's neck.

"Good work, Pock," Caidin said with a wolfish grin.

"Thank you, Your Grace," the gnome said in a croaking voice. He struggled to his feet, wobbled, then fell back down. "I've always excelled at being thrown."

Wort watched apprehensively as the three men advanced on him. He wondered if he should run. Too late, he saw Castellan Domeck reach out to jerk back the hood of his black cloak. Wort cringed, holding up a malformed hand to shade his eyes from the dazzling brilliance of the Grand Hall's many-candled chandeliers. Domeck stepped back, taking in a hissing breath of revulsion.

"Wort," Caidin said between gritted teeth.

"You know this grotesque creature, Your Grace?" Sirraun said in amazement, gazing at Wort as if he were a fascinating new species of insect.

Pock gained his feet and tottered toward the others. "Do you take the baron for a fool, Sirraun?" he demanded pompously. "Of course he knows his own *brother*."

"Brother?" Domeck asked in curious disgust.

Caidin glared murderously at Pock. A hint of green

colored the gnome's purple skin. He swallowed hard. "Er, I think I had better go lie down, Your Grace. The blow to my head must have addled my brains, which isn't all that hard, mind you." Quickly he scurried away, vanishing through an archway.

A knowing smile twisted Sirraun's mouth. "I have heard rumors that the Old Baron sired a bastard or two. Of course, I cannot blame him for keeping such a wretched thing as this a secret."

Wort tried to shrink away from the brutal stares of the others. He found himself backing up against the sharp stone antlers of the statue.

"Leave us," Caidin told the castellan and lord inquisitor. Knowing better than to protest, they retreated from the Grand Hall, though not without casting a few more contemptuous glances at the hunchback who had been revealed as the baron's half brother.

"I should have you beheaded for this, Wort," Caidin said casually.

Wort tried to sketch a bow, but his twisted form made the action a mockery. "Forgive me, Caidin. I did not mean to disturb you. I leave my tower so seldomly. I forget . . . I forget sometimes how things work outside."

"Then do not forget again." Caidin moved to a table and poured himself a glass of blood-red wine, draining it in one draught. He did not offer any to Wort. "Why have you come this time?"

Wort took a trembling step forward. "A small thing, Brother. One of the bells in the tower has cracked, I fear. It causes a dissonance in the harmonics. I would like . . . I would like a new bell."

Caidin laughed. The sound was harsh and sneering, a strange contrast to the baron's handsome face. "*You* want something from *me?*"

"Please, Brother . . ." Wort stuttered.

"Do not call me that," Caidin warned. "I suffer you to live in the tower, Wort. In my kindness, I have food brought to you so that you need not leave to face the cruel jeers of others. Do you think the debt I owed you once has not been paid many times over? You would do well not to press my generosity. Otherwise . . ."

Caidin dropped the empty wine glass. It shattered, and several drops of crimson wine spilled upon the mosaic embedded in the floor. Suddenly the wine vanished, as if sucked into the mosaic, and as it did so the images formed by the shards of colored tile began to shimmer and move. With eerie silence, the battle played itself out beneath the baron's boots. The two armies clashed. Swords bit deeply, arrows flew, blood flowed in streams of undulating red-ochre tiles. Wort watched in dread fascination, sickened at the carnage played out in the swirling mosaic. At last the images grew still once more.

"What, don't you care for the mosaic, Wort?" Caidin said mockingly. "Its enchantment is quite old, and quite rare."

Jerkily, Wort shook his head.

"Truly? I find it . . . compelling." A vicious smile curled itself about his lips. "Now leave. And do not disturb me again. *Brother*."

With a heavy sigh, Wort turned away. He pulled up the hood of his cloak once more and left the Grand Hall, passing servants and courtiers as he shuffled through the keep's corridors. It had been more than a year since he had last spoken to Caidin. He should have known his brother would have, as usual, grown crueler in the meantime. Why that was, Wort could never understand. Caidin had everything—a strong body, a handsome face, a rich fiefdom to rule. Could he not spare his unfortunate brother the cost of a single bell?

As he stepped into the courtyard, Wort saw Castellan Domeck moving across the open square. Quickly, Wort lumbered forward, kneeling in the cold mud and grasping the castellan's black-gloved hand before the surprised man could recoil.

"Please, Castellan Domeck," Wort begged. "You must speak to my brother. . . ."

Domeck's lip curled back. "Get away from me," he snarled. He jerked his hand away, leaving the empty glove in Wort's grip, and strode across the courtyard. Wort stared at the glove as hope died in his heart. Nearby, a flock of pigeons pecked at the mud. "What will I do, my friends?" he whispered sadly. They offered no answer.

A horse clopped by, spattering Wort with mud. As he gazed at the horse's steel-shod hooves, an idea struck him. Perhaps the blacksmith in the village could help him. A smith might be able to fix the broken bell. Wort hastily stood, absently tucking the castellan's glove into his pocket, then hobbled through the gate of the keep.

It had been years since Wort had been down to the village. He picked his way slowly along the winding road carved into the crag upon which Nartok Keep stood. Far below, the motley collection of thatch-roofed buildings that made up the village lay clustered haphazardly at the foot of the tor. It looked almost as if the meager dwellings were huddled together in fear against the endless landscape of bog, thicket, and dun-colored heath. Perhaps a league west of the village, Wort could see the jagged stump of what seemed to be a tower rising up in the midst of the windswept moor. No road led to the half-finished tower, and no buildings stood near it. It loomed dark and lonely on the horizon like a giant's tombstone.

That must be the tower the folk in the courtyard spoke of, Wort thought.

Often, when the wind was still, the voices of people standing in the courtyard below drifted clearly through the window of Wort's chamber in the bell tower. That was how he first learned that folk believed it was a monster who rang the bells each time the soul of someone in the keep passed on to the Gray Kingdom of the Dead. Of late, the thing he had overheard people down in the courtyard whispering about most was this forbidding tower.

Rumor told how, one night, the ring of stones had appeared without explanation far out on the grassy moor. A shepherd was the first to discover it. He found three of his flock inside the ring of stones, all dead. Afterward, other shepherds told similar tales. Soon it was whispered that the place was blighted. Some said that the ring stood upon a spot known to have been cursed by Vistani after one of their gypsy kindred was robbed and murdered there by a village man. One day several curious boys ventured to the circle on a dare. Inside they discovered Jurgin, the village drunkard, or at least the remains of him. It appeared that much of his body had been consumed by some beast. After that, no one ventured near the circle. Yet each night the ring seemed to grow inexplicably, for each morning when the folk of the village awoke and gazed out their windows, they saw that another layer of stones had been added to the mysterious tower.

So it had gone on, night after night, until now the half-finished tower loomed over the moor, and at sunset its giant shadow stretched like a sinister finger toward the village. What force was raising the tower none could say, nor was it known what would happen when it was finally completed.

The bloodshot eye of the sun was falling toward the horizon as Wort hobbled into the village. Foul-smelling water ran in rivulets down the muddy street

before him, its breadth crowded with peasants clad
in severe garb of dull gray. A scrawny dog growled
as Wort passed by. Gathering his cloak more tightly
about him, he hurried on.

He wasn't certain where the blacksmith's shop
was, but he listened for the ringing of a hammer.
Clumsily, he wended his way through the throng of
villagers who pushed carts of radishes and turnips or
carried straw baskets filled with eggs. The viscous
mud of the street let off a sickening stench. A chill
sweat slickened Wort's skin. He wasn't used to being
this close to other people. It was almost frightening.
Every moment he expected the folk around him to
stop in their tracks and point at him. Clad as he was
in his thick cloak, however, they paid him no heed.

A puff of acrid smoke filled Wort's nostrils. Up
ahead he glimpsed a wooden sign with a horseshoe
nailed to it. There! He quickened his pace. Surely the
blacksmith would be able to help him.

The crack of a whip sundered the air.

"Make way!" a voice shouted roughly. "Make way,
vermin!"

The crowd of villagers abruptly parted as a wagon
drawn by four black horses careened down the street.
The eyes of the beasts showed white, their sides
flecked with foam. The driver cracked his whip again.
Wort found himself pulled along with the crowd and
crushed up against a building. Panic clawed at his
throat as bodies pressed all around him.

That was when he saw the girl.

She was standing in the middle of the street,
apparently forgotten by her mother or father, a
golden-haired child drawing patterns in the mud with
a stick. Her back was to the approaching wagon.
She did not seem to hear it.

"She'll be crushed," Wort muttered in alarm. "Why
doesn't someone help her?"

The peasants only stared with blank eyes, as if they saw nothing. The galloping horses bore down on the girl. Apparently the driver did not see her either. Or did not care if he did. Without stopping to think what he was doing, Wort forced his way through the tightly packed crowd. People muttered curses at him as he shoved by. He ignored them and fought his way to the fore. The girl in the street dropped her stick. She turned about to face the wagon, freezing in terror.

With a cry, Wort hurled himself through the ranks of the villagers. There was a sound of rending cloth. Dimly he realized his cloak had been torn off. He lunged forward and crashed into the child. She screamed as he fell with her into the muck. The horses and wagon hurtled by, scant inches from Wort and the child whom he protected with his massive arms. Then, with one last crack of the whip, the wagon was gone. A dead silence descended over the street. Slowly Wort stood, pulling the girl to her feet.

"Are you all right, child?" he croaked. She only regarded him silently with grave blue eyes.

Then someone screamed.

"The monster! He has the child!"

Wort looked up in shock. He saw a sea of faces staring at him with disgust, horror, and . . . hatred. He felt naked without his heavy cloak.

A pale-faced woman rushed toward Wort. "Get away from her, you monster!" she shrieked, snatching the girl roughly from his hands. She dashed away, clutching the girl tightly. The child looked back at Wort, her blue eyes strangely hurt. Then the woman was lost in the crowd. But the throng was not done with him.

"Look at the freak!" someone shouted.

"You should be ashamed!" another screamed.

"Get out of here, you beast!"

Wort reeled as a clod of mud struck him on the back of his head. "I was only trying . . ." another cold lump of mud hit him in the chest ". . . trying to help her." The crowd closed in on him. Shouts of fear and anger bore into him like knives.

"Begone from our village, monster!"

"The monster tried to kill the girl, did you see?"

"Kill the monster!"

More mud clods struck Wort. He spun around, trying to protect himself, but the blows hailed from every direction. With each blow, the word resonated in his head. *Monster. Monster. MONSTER!*

Suddenly a fearsome voice let out a bellow of rage. "I wanted to *help!*" Only dimly did Wort realize the voice was his own. A terrible image flashed before his mind—the burnt ashwife from his boyhood, shrieking as fire licked at her hands, her arms, her bubbling, cracking face. Didn't she understand that he had wanted to help her? Couldn't any of them understand that? It was *her* fault she had been hurt. Not *his.* Blinded by mud and hot tears, Wort broke into a clumsy run. Peasants screamed as they scrambled to get out of his way. He did not see them or the horrified looks on their faces. Sobbing, he ran on, leaving the shouts and jeers behind him.

Wort wasn't certain how he made it to the bell tower. He did not remember how many townsfolk had shrunk from him in horror as he climbed the twisting road to the keep and stumbled across the courtyard. The next thing he knew, he burst into his chamber.

"Curse them!" he shouted. Rage ignited in his chest, searing his heart, burning away the self-pity that had dwelt there. "Curse them all!" A cloud of pigeons erupted into flight before him. "Only I would help the girl. Only I! Yet how do they reward me?"

Wort flung open the lid of his trunk of books. He

grabbed the enchanted storybook he had been reading, then ripped it in half with the brutal strength of his bare hands. With a silver flash its magic shattered. White-hot fire consumed its crackling pages. Wort had been wrong. All these long years, he had been so terribly wrong.

"I am no hero," he snarled. "No brave knight or handsome prince!"

Swiftly he climbed the ladder into the belfry. The last crimson rays of the sun dripped like blood through the iron gratings.

"If people wish me to be a monster, then that is what I will be!" He grabbed the ropes of the bells. "Beware Nartok," he shouted. "For on this day you have created a monster!"

The bells rang in a darkly dissonant cacophony as a storm of ghost-pale birds filled the air.

 **TWO**

When King Azalin of Darkon announced a masquerade at the royal castle of Avernus, each of the countesses, dukes, and petty nobles of the grand city of Il Aluk waited breathlessly to learn whether he or she had been invited. Soon after the announcement, mysteriously hooded messengers began appearing at the doors of hilltop mansions and fashionable city redstones to deliver the coveted black and gold invitations to the lucky, while the less fortunate looked on with no small amount of envy. The invitations themselves were exquisite and wonderful things, which strangely and somewhat startlingly vanished in a puff of cool flame after being delivered, leaving only a small disk of thick gold foil, engraved with the Fiery Eye that was Azalin's personal signet. The precious gold tokens were the only means of admittance to what would certainly be the year's most talked-about social event.

Finally, the much-anticipated occasion arrived. As the pale orb of the moon lifted over the turgid waters of the Vuchar River, the favored nobility of Il Aluk streamed from the city in gilded carriages and undertook the brief journey to Avernus—an imposing castle that loomed on a rocky hill just south of the capitol. No one ever knew what to expect at one of Azalin's masquerades, but it was widely thought that the king was a great wizard, so everybody anticipated something fantastical. One by one the carriages rode the twisting avenue to the castle and were swallowed by the arched gateway. The party had begun.

A woman clad in a gown of emerald-green silk moved with smooth grace through the throng of revelers that filled the vast ballroom. Her coal-black hair was coiled about her head in an intricate arrangement, and a single, uncommonly large pearl rested gently in the cleft of her bosom, glowing like a tiny moon against the luster of her dark copper skin. With a gloved hand, she held a mask with tilted cat eyes before her face. Behind the false face, her own green-gold eyes glittered with contempt.

The woman was Jadis, and unlike those around her, she was not one of Il Aluk's pretentious nobles. She had not come seeking favor from the king, nor entertainment, nor even a fleeting lover. She was Kargat—one of King Azalin's personal spies—and she had come to be assigned her new mission.

Jadis ascended a wide stairway to the promenade that encircled the ballroom. Hundreds of masked lords and ladies danced below in the cavernous chamber, bathed in the crystal-refracted luminescence of countless candles. There was something out of the ordinary about the dancers. They moved in the same complex patterns favored in all of the city's fashionable ballrooms, but Jadis knew this was a dance like none ever witnessed in Il Aluk.

The dancers careened about the red-veined marble floor with wild, jerky movements, like marionettes controlled by a drunken puppeteer. Their heads lolled strangely from side to side as they whirled and spun. The ceaseless smiles plastered to their faces were garish, even grotesque. It was the wine, of course. Dozens of pretty, golden-haired boys moved with fluidity through the throng, bearing trays of goblets filled with the glistening ruby liquid. It was no mundane vintage. The more wine the revelers drank, the more their eyes stared wide, dark, and unseeing behind their masks, as if each were gazing into some secret dream invisible to all the others.

Bored, Jadis turned from the wild dance below, wondering when the summons for her would come. "Patience, love," she whispered to herself. She moved along the marble walkway, letting her gloved hand slip sensually over the golden balustrade. Wicked laughter and wordless sounds of pleasure drifted from sheer-curtained alcoves and dim grottos that lined the promenade. Jadis caught interesting glimpses of activity in each as she passed by.

In one of the grottos, nobles lounged on velvet chaises while handsome attendants—their bare, muscular flesh slick with oil—placed crimson fruits into open mouths. The patrons wore heavy-lidded expressions, sated yet strangely hungry, their lips stained scarlet from the dark juices of the fruit. Within another alcove, men and women clad only in the skins of animals crawled about on all fours, barking, howling, and purring as though they were beasts.

Without warning, an obese man wearing a ridiculous mask concocted of feathers and jewels rushed from a torchlit grotto and held something out toward Jadis.

"You simply must try this," the nobleman said in a gasping voice. "I have never tasted anything so delicious in all my life."

Jadis arched a dark eyebrow. In the man's hands was a raw, quivering heart. His chin dripped blood. She gazed past him into the grotto and saw that a score of other revelers were feasting in delight upon a white unicorn they had killed with their bare hands. Now they tore meat off the carcass with their teeth, their silken gowns and rich velvet coats soaked with blood.

"No, it's all yours. Enjoy yourself," Jadis crooned indulgently.

"Thank you, my lady," the man whispered tremblingly. "I will." He hurried back to the gory feast.

As Jadis watched, a young nobleman wrenched the unicorn's spiral horn from its head. The horn began to glow with pearlescent radiance. Tendrils of moon-pale light reached outward, spiraling around the man's body. He threw his head back, trembling as if caught in the throes of deepest pleasure. Back arched, he rose to his toes. The magical radiance from the horn was lifting his body from the ground. Abruptly his trembling turned into violent convulsions. Blood trickled from his ears and mouth. Yet the look of rapture on his face did not lessen. The horn flared brilliantly, then went dim. Like a rag doll, the nobleman collapsed to the floor, stone dead. The horn rolled away. Of course, Jadis thought—only one who is pure of heart should dare touch a unicorn's horn. In moments, several other nobles bent over the fresh corpse to feed.

A low sound of mirth escaped Jadis's throat. Azalin was brilliant. The pretentious nobles who had come here this night seeking to curry the king's favor or to hatch plots of intrigue against him would soon forget their subversive intentions as they drowned themselves in the sea of dark pleasures that filled the ballroom. Even after the revel was over, and after the party-goers returned to the city with only dim memories of what had occurred here, they would find themselves filled with strange, longing hungers, the pursuit of which would consume their energies in the year ahead, so that they would have neither time nor will to scheme against the king. Then would come another ball, and the sinister cycle would begin again. With his extraordinary masquerades, Azalin kept the nobility of Il Aluk utterly in his thrall.

Then again, as Jadis knew well, the Kargat played its crucial role in the king's perfect domination of Darkon. Few of the ordinary citizens knew of the Kargat, or at least few lived long with such dread knowledge. The secret society of spies and assassins to which Jadis belonged wove itself throughout the entire realm of Darkon, like a vast spider's web in which all threads led back to the center—to the master spider, Azalin himself. The Kargat had plucked Jadis as an orphan child from the streets of Il Aluk and raised her to serve the order. Though given no choice in the matter, she did adore her work. There was nothing she would not do to serve the king.

A boy clad in a coat of golden brocade silently held out a tray of goblets toward Jadis. She took one of the glasses and raised it high.

"To you, my great king."

She lowered the goblet to her lips, then thought better of it. Not for her the dark rapture that seized the revelers. She poured the wine on the floor.

Jadis turned to find herself facing a broad-shouldered man, his face concealed by a fanciful lion mask. For a moment, she wondered if he had been sent to take her to the Kargat lord for her next mission. But no, the man's eyes were empty and ravenous behind his mask. He was simply another noble caught in the tide of lust that surged through the ballroom.

"Come with me, my lady," he said hoarsely, gesturing toward an alcove where Jadis glimpsed dozens of writhing, naked forms.

"I think not," she replied coldly. She stretched a hand before her, like a cat extending its claws, and absently examined her scarlet fingernails.

The man shook his lion's mane of long golden hair. "But I have never before seen a lady as beautiful as you. I must have you." He reached out and luxuriantly ran the back of his hand over the smoothness of her throat.

Jadis's eyes glittered. The man's body was strong and attractive beneath his tight-fitting coat and breeches, but she had no time for such diversions. Swiftly, she reached up and grasped the man's wrist, twisting it sharply. He cried out in pain.

"Find yourself different prey to feast upon, my lord," she said sharply, then whirled to move away through the throng.

The summons came just as she descended from the promenade and stepped onto the ballroom floor. She felt something pressed into her gloved hand and turned in time to see a hooded figure disappearing through the crowd. She looked down at her hand to see a small square of crisp golden parchment. Written upon it in flowing script were the words, *Seek me in the northernmost antechamber.* Even as she read the message the card was consumed by a puff of crimson flame, leaving only a small disk of gold foil in her palm, engraved with the symbol of an eye surrounded by tongues of fire. Jadis's heart fluttered. The Fiery Eye was Azalin's personal intaglio. The card had come from him! She hadn't hoped to meet him directly. Truly, she had risen high in the Kargat.

Swiftly wending her way across the crowded dance floor, Jadis approached an iron door set in the north wall of the ballroom. A pair of crimson-uniformed guards stood to either side, but neither glanced at her as she opened the portal. She stepped through and pressed the door shut behind her. The octagonal chamber beyond was empty save for a single, ornately carved mahogany chair. Jadis supposed there was nothing to do but wait. She sat down and smoothed her gown, trying to calm the rapid beating of her heart.

Without warning, the armrests of the chair swung inward, pinning her tightly against the chair's back. She let out a gasp as the silver piping that trimmed the chair's cushions snaked out, coiling around her wrists and ankles, binding her to the wooden frame. Suddenly the chair itself lurched into motion, its four legs creaking and bending, and it walked like a living thing toward a roaring fireplace. Jadis struggled to free herself, but the silver cords held her fast. Sweat beaded on her forehead as the chair approached the dancing flames. The thing swayed back and forth, lumbering nearer the hearth. It was going to burn her alive.

Abruptly the fireplace pivoted, revealing a passageway. The animated chair lurched through the opening, then the fireplace swung shut. The chair walked through stifling blackness as Jadis did her best to swallow the panic that clawed at her throat. The thing must be some sort of wood golem, she realized—a construction of dead material granted life by dark enchantment. Who had forged the golem? Was it Azalin? Or some other being of power? Jadis suspected she would discover the truth soon enough. The chair moved on, twisting right and left, its rhythmic groaning echoing eerily off stone walls she could not see in the darkness. This was some sort of labyrinth. Soon Jadis's bearings were hopelessly lost. The silver cords bit painfully into her flesh as the chair heaved ceaselessly up and down, like a piece of flotsam adrift on a black, roiling sea.

The chair lurched to a halt. Jadis felt the wooden arms and silver cords release her limbs, then she sprang to her feet. A crimson radiance erupted, pushing back the darkness. She found herself standing before a dais of black porphyry. On the dais was a throne, and upon the throne sat a figure clad in a robe the color of dried blood.

Swallowing her fear, she bowed deeply. "My king," she murmured. "How may your Kargat serve you?"

"As you always have, my Jadis," replied the thunderous voice of the man who sat upon the throne. "With your loyalty and your adoration."

"Of course, my king."

Jadis had glimpsed Azalin before, on the occasion of his rare public appearances—each time concealed by heavy robes as now—but never before had she been so close to him. She could feel power and majesty radiating from him in hot, dizzying waves.

"One of my provincial barons has grown overly willful," Azalin said from the shadows of his heavy cowl. "I have learned that he has concocted some plot to usurp my power."

"Then he is a fool, my king, for none could dare dream to defeat you."

Chill laughter drifted down from the throne. "How truly you speak, my Jadis. Still, futile as they may be, I wish you to discover his plans and find a way to twist them to my own purposes. Let his impudent treachery serve me before I crush him in punishment."

"With pleasure I will serve you, my king."

"I know your loyalty, my Jadis. Details of the mission will be delivered to you."

The figure rose from the throne, then moved down the steps of the dais with unnatural slowness. His robe hung eerily motionless as he moved. Jadis could smell the sour scent of fear in her own sweat.

"Tell me, Jadis," Azalin whispered, though the sound of it roared in her brain. "Would you care to gaze more closely upon your king?"

She forced herself to take in a shuddering breath. "If you think it necessary, Your Majesty."

The robed figure nodded. "I do. You have risen high in my favor. There is a way for you to rise further yet, if you are strong enough. You have served me well with your mind, my Jadis. Would you care to serve me with your body as well?"

A sickly scent lingered in her nostrils, like the odor of rotting meat. "Show me, my king."

The heavy robe fell to the floor.

Jadis bit her lip fiercely to stifle a cry. Dimly, she noticed the metallic taste of blood spreading across her tongue. The man who stood before her was not alive, at least not in any usual sense of the word. He was a lich. His withered flesh clung to a skeletal body. Here and there a patch of leathery skin had peeled away to reveal livid bone. The simple kirtle he wore only accentuated the horror of his cadaverous body, as did the silver and gold rings that encircled his bony arms. Scraggly tatters of rotting gray hair framed the shriveled skull mask of his face. Most horrifying of all were the searing sparks of crimson flame that danced in the dark recesses of his empty eye sockets. They burned fiercely into Jadis's soul.

"Tell me truthfully, Jadis," Azalin croaked. "What do you see before you?"

She swallowed the sick taste in her mouth. "I see a king whose power is great enough to defeat even Death itself!"

"Oh, my lovely one!" The lich king reached out a skeletal hand, trailing tatters of dry-parchment skin, to caress the smoothness of her breast. "Ah, rapture!" he hissed. "To feel again the firmness of living flesh."

Jadis did not shrink from his undead touch.

"I am yours, my king," she whispered.

* * * * *

The man in the lion's mask prowled through the throng of gyrating dancers. Perhaps it was that he had not drunk as much of the crimson wine as had the other nobles. Perhaps it was that his will was stronger than most. Whatever the reason, the fierce desire that ached in his chest would not allow itself to be slaked on any common pleasure. Again and again he pushed away others who pressed themselves against him. There was one he did want, and only one. The darkly beautiful woman in the emerald gown. Searching for her, he stalked his way through the undulating sea of masked revelers. He *would* have her. Viscount Culdaine was accustomed to getting what he wanted.

His pulse quickened. There she was! He watched as she emerged from behind an iron door. Her dusky skin seemed strangely pale now, but that only made her lovelier yet. Culdaine pushed his way toward her, pursuing as she drifted down a dimly lit corridor. She cast a look over her shoulder, and a small, secret smile touched the corners of her deep red lips. Culdaine bared white teeth in a wolfish expression. She had only been toying with him before. Now she wanted him, even as he wanted her. He watched as she vanished through a doorway, giving him one more languid look. Moments later he pushed through the door after her, shutting it behind him.

The room was dark, though a single ray of moonlight spilled through a high window, illuminating a rumpled heap. Culdaine knelt and saw that it was a cast-off gown of green silk. Reaching down, he picked up a black mask with cat's eyes. A soft noise sounded behind him. Feeling his passion stir, Culdaine stood and turned around. There, in the shadows, he saw her moving sensuously toward him.

"My lady," he whispered, his voice throbbing. "Come to me. . . ."

Without warning, a bestial shape leapt from the shadows. Eyes flashed like green fire. Fangs glowed in the moonlight, growing longer even as Culdaine watched in terror. The sinuous beast fell upon him, knocking him forcefully to the floor. He screamed as sickle claws raked deep into his belly, spilling his guts out across the floor. His cry of agony was quickly silenced as the fanged maw clamped on to his throat, closing with crushing force. Blood gushed forth in a hot, dark fountain. Culdaine's hands beat feebly for a moment against muscled flesh covered by dark, glossy fur, then fell limply to the cold floor. The eyes behind his mask stared blankly upward, no longer filled with desire, but instead empty with death.

Uttering a low growl of pleasure, the werepanther began to feed upon her prey.

*   *   *   *   *

"There goes another one, Your Grace," Pock chirped merrily.

The little gnome was perched on the back of a chair, watching out the window of Baron Caidin's private chamber as, in the courtyard below, a headless corpse toppled off the scaffold to the muddy ground. As always, the impish gnome was clad in miniature imitation of the baron, from his crimson long coat trimmed with golden brocade to his blue velvet breeches. A few wisps of white hair flew wildly around an otherwise bald head that seemed too big for his scrawny body.

"Let's see," Pock went on. "So far this week that makes—" he counted his fingers, then held up both hands, fingers splayed "—three!"

Baron Caidin paused in his pacing to glare at the gnomish knave. "You mean ten, Pock. You're holding up *ten* fingers."

The gnome frowned. "Whatever, Your Grace."

Caidin gritted his teeth in annoyance, but there

was no point in correcting Pock. It was not for his brains that Caidin tolerated the foolish gnome. Castellan Domeck had caught Pock several years ago picking the pockets of petty nobles in Caidin's court. Normally a thief was beheaded without question, but Caidin had sensed that he might put the crafty gnome to good use. He had been right. These last years, Pock's big eyes and pointed ears had uncovered many interesting secrets and conspiracies whispered by Caidin's vain and ever-scheming courtiers.

"Ten this week, Pock. Twelve last week, and nine the week before that." Caidin moved to the window, watching as servants tossed the corpse and its detached head into a cart and hauled them away. "But it isn't enough." The baron turned from the grisly sight just as the keep's bells began to toll a funeral dirge. His lip curled back from his teeth in disgust.

"Wort!" he said sourly. "No doubt he's aping about his blasted belfry like an animal." He turned on the gnome. "Remind me to have you flogged for telling Domeck and Sirraun that Wort is my half brother."

"Er, what if I happen to accidentally forget to remind you?" Pock gulped.

Caidin grinned wolfishly. "Why, then I'll have you flogged for forgetting."

The knave nervously scratched his wrinkled head while he tried to decide if there was any sequence of events which *wouldn't* result in his getting flogged.

Caidin sat at his cluttered desk, absently fidgeting with a jeweled stiletto. He wondered if he should finally have Wort killed. The hunchback's appearance in the Grand Hall yesterday had been utterly embarrassing. Few in the keep remembered the deformed half brother of the baron's childhood. Caidin wanted to keep it that way. His eyes grew distant as an unbidden memory surfaced in his mind.

They had been children together. Even then Caidin had been tall and strong, and at all boyish things—riding horses, shooting arrows, convincing girls to skulk with him into the stable's loft—he far surpassed the other boys of the Old Baron's court. The keep's children looked to him as a natural leader, a role he gladly accepted. Yet there was one child Caidin always wished would not follow him.

"Wait for me, Brother!" Wort would call out, hobbling after Caidin and the other boys as they set off to buy plum pasties in the village or to go catch toads in the bogs. The others would laugh, making fun of the ungainly little boy who always tripped and fell in his haste to catch up. Caidin would only cross his arms and stare with silent disapproval. The stunted boy with the twisted spine became the butt of all Caidin's worst jokes. Hardly a day went by that Wort did not find horse dung between the covers of his bed, or worms in his bowl of stew. Nothing seemed to deter him. Blithely, a smile constantly upon his homely face, he continued to follow after his handsome brother. Even then, Caidin did not truly hate Wort. Not yet. That came later, one day on the edge of the sheer precipice west of the village.

The cliff was called Morrged's Leap, after a spurned lover who, legend held, threw himself to a bloody death on the jagged rocks a thousand feet below, and whose shade was said to haunt the place. Caidin and some of the keep's older boys had gone to the precipice one spring afternoon, daring each other to teeter on the precarious edge. As usual Wort followed, his hunched chest racked with exertion. A dark thought occurred to Caidin then. Perhaps here was his opportunity to be rid of his troublesome brother at last. Wort was so clumsy. If he fell, it would seem an accident. So Caidin balanced boldly on the edge of the cliff, taunting his brother.

"Come, Wort, I thought you wanted to follow me," he jeered. "Or are you too much of a coward?"

"Caidin, you mustn't!" Wort shouted in terror.

"You *are* a coward, Wort. I should have—"

That was when the rock beneath his heel gave way. The others screamed and stepped back as Caidin slid over the edge of the precipice. Desperately, he grabbed for a handhold, but the rock crumbled beneath his fingers. A strong hand clamped about his wrist, catching him. Caidin looked up in shock. It was Wort.

"I've got you, Brother," the hunchback said determinedly. "I won't let you fall."

With surprising strength, Wort hauled Caidin up over the cliff's edge to safety.

"Are you all right, Brother?"

Caidin only glared at Wort. Now he owed his life to the wretched hunchback.

"I hate you," he snarled.

"I'd sort of gathered that," Pock quipped from his chair-back perch. "Barons don't usually flog the people they like."

With a start, Caidin realized he must have uttered the old words aloud. The stiletto quivered before him, embedded deeply in the desk. Slowly he unclenched his fingers from its hilt.

"I don't mean *you,* you maggot," he snapped. Caidin reconsidered. "Of course, I *do* hate you, Pock. I'm just thinking of someone else right now."

Caidin sighed. Tempting as they were, he knew he must discard all thoughts of having the hunchback murdered at the moment. In his mind, he could still hear the terrible secret that the Old Baron, gray and withered on his deathbed, had whispered in his ear. As long as the hunchback kept to the solitude of his precious bell tower, the dark truth would be safe.

A sharp rapping came at the chamber's door. In a purple flash, Pock leapt from his chair and hid behind a heavy curtain where he could spy unseen.

"Enter," Caidin commanded. The unnaturally thin form of his lord inquisitor drifted into the chamber.

"You called for me, Your Grace?"

"Yes, Sirraun." Caidin pulled the stiletto from the desk. "I want you to increase the pace of the inquisition. It is taking too long. You must bring me more traitors."

A curious look crossed Sirraun's jaundiced visage. "Indeed, Your Grace. I hasten to obey. As you know, it is my sole purpose to see the conspiracy against you shattered."

Caidin slammed a fist against the desk. Parchment scrolls tumbled onto the floor. "Blast the conspiracy, Sirraun! You know as well as I that it does not exist. Of course there are peasants in the village who despise me. As well they should, for I have no qualms in using them for my own gain." His voice became an intense whisper. "But I need more bodies, Sirraun. If I am truly to challenge Azalin, I must have more bodies." He bore down on the lord inquisitor. "And so I must have more 'traitors.' Get them for me, Sirraun. I don't care how you do it. But do it, and fast!"

Sirraun gazed at Caidin for a silent moment. Slowly, a sharp smile cut across his thin lips. "With the greatest of pleasure, Your Grace." Bowing deeply, the lord inquisitor retreated from the chamber.

"How come you never flog *him,* Your Grace?" Pock complained, stepping from behind the curtain.

Caidin ignored his knave. *Soon, Azalin,* he thought with satisfaction. *Soon all that is yours will be mine.*

 **THREE**

"They think they know fear when they gaze upon me. . . ."

Roaring flames consumed the heap of leather-bound books in the fireplace. Shadows danced on the walls of the bell tower chamber, like dying phantoms writhing in the violent orange light.

"I will show them *real* fear. . . ."

With gnarled hands, Wort tore apart another book and heaved it onto the fire. The burning mound settled under its own weight, letting out a serpent's hiss. Searing heat blistered Wort's face, but he did not care. Handsome princes and brave knights—heroes he could never be, stories he could never live. Let all the books burn. Suddenly the flames made him think of the ashwife who had fallen in her haste to get away from him. He relived how her hands smoked and her face bubbled. For years he had wallowed in guilt from that day. Yet it had been her own fault, he told himself now. Perhaps she deserved to be burned. Perhaps they all did.

"They have mocked me for the last time," he croaked hoarsely. "I will show them that a monster is not an object of ridicule, but one of terror. I will show them all. Even Caidin." A murderous glint lit his eyes. "No . . . *especially* Caidin. Caidin who has had everything while I . . . I have had *this*." He clawed at his twisted face.

What a fool he had been! Oh, what a loathsome, laughable idiot! Now Wort saw everything clearly. *He* had not asked for this wretched, twisted body. *He* was the one who deserved pity. They were cruel and heartless, all of them—the villagers, the servants in the keep, the nobles of the baron's court. They deserved a monster, and he would give them one.

"But how?"

He stalked toward the slit of the chamber's lone window. Leaning heavily on the cracked window ledge, he glared at the folk that scurried like rats in the courtyard below.

"If only I could make them know what it is like to be an object of fear, Oratio," he whispered to a pigeon perched on the ledge. He picked up the bird, stroking the purple feathers of its throat. "Then I would know justice."

Perhaps the idea that came to him then was a phantasm of his fevered brain, brought on by the acrid smoke and heat of the fire. Whatever the genesis, Wort suddenly knew what to do.

"The darkling!" he realized. "Yes, I must go to the dungeon. The darkling will show me the way." He bared his jagged yellow teeth. "I will have justice!"

A sharp popping sound echoed off the walls. Startled, Wort looked down at the gory remnants of the pigeon in his hands. Blood matted the iridescent feathers of its limp neck, and its once-bright eyes stared now like dull stones.

"Oratio . . ." Wort gasped, blinking back burning tears. "What have I done?"

Peculiar thoughts crept into the turmoil of his brain. *Leave the thing, Wort. It is far too late now.* He dropped the pigeon to the floor. Wort gathered his black cloak around his tortured body. He did not bother to wipe the blood from his hands. Let it mark him.

"Farewell, Oratio," he whispered grimly.

*   *   *   *   *

Wort moved through the dank passageway deep in the bowels of Nartok Keep. The air was oppressive here, as if all the ponderous weight of the fortress pressed down ruthlessly from above. Rancid-smelling torches burned in crude iron sconces at irregular intervals, giving off more smoke than light. Dark slime dripped down cracked walls to pool on the stone floor, like ooze from some festering disease. Screams of agony and moans of suffering echoed in the distance. Wort's bulbous eyes gleamed in the torchlight, flicking nervously left and right. He clutched a small rusted knife, scrounged from beneath the rotting straw that covered the floor of his chamber in the bell tower.

Crude laughter drifted from ahead. Cautiously, Wort edged his way along the wall until he came to an archway that opened into a side chamber. Holding his breath, he peered through. In the small room beyond, three forms clad in shabby blue uniforms crouched on the floor, gathered around a circle drawn in chalk. Dungeon guards. Shaped like men, their flesh was a sickly green hue. Their bloated heads seemed too large for their bodies, and their eyes glowed like hot coals. Wort had read of such creatures. They were goblyns—pathetic humans who had been transformed by dark magic.

"Darkness grant me luck," one of the goblyns growled. He shook a wooden cup, and a dozen yellowed knucklebones tumbled into the circle.

"Blast you, Gordek!" another goblyn swore.

"You sold your soul to the cursed darkling, didn't you?" the third hissed accusingly.

"Fools," Gordek gloated. "You will never best me at Seven Bones." He reached to scoop up a pile of coins next to the circle, then froze. One of the knucklebones slithered away. Another followed suit. Suddenly all of the knucklebones started to twitch and scuttle across the floor like living things.

"So that's your secret, is it, Gordek?" one goblyn snarled.

"You're using golem bones to cheat us!" cried the other.

Gordek bared his needle teeth in a grin, then lunged for the coins. With bestial howls, the other two goblyns fell upon him. Green blood flowed as the three tore at each other with fang and claw. Wort took advantage of the distraction. Averting his eyes from the struggle, he scurried past the opening and continued down the corridor. Soon the walls gave way to corroded bars of steel. Chains clinked as shadows stirred in the cells. Scabrous arms reached out, clutching in vain at Wort's cloak as he moved past.

"Help me." The gasping whispers came from all directions. "Please, help me."

"No," he choked. "No, I cannot. I . . . I am sorry."

Wort hurried on. He glimpsed an iron door at the far end of the passageway, set apart from the other cells. He hobbled to the door. The portal was locked, but in the stone wall beside it was a small opening through which a bowl—or a spear point—might be slid. Awkwardly, Wort knelt on the slimy floor and peered into the opening. Beyond was absolute blackness.

"Vistana," Wort whispered. "Vistana, are you in there?"

For a long moment there was no reply. Then a voice like a rusting hinge spoke from beyond.

"Give . . . me . . . light."

Wort backed away from the opening and stood up. A torch guttered in a nearby iron bracket. With a painful effort, he managed to reach the torch. He bent down and slipped it into the hole. Something beyond grabbed the torch and dragged it through.

"Ah, light . . ." the cracked voice beyond the wall whispered. "Beautiful, yes. But oh, it hurts so to look upon."

Wort squinted one bulging eye and peered through the narrow opening. In the wavering light of the torch he could see a cramped, filthy chamber. Black water pooled on the floor, and eyeless insects hung on the walls. Huddled in the room's center, clutching the torch, were the wretched remains of a man. Rags clung wetly to his spiderlike limbs, and his skin was withered and mottled like rotten fruit. His sunken face was twisted into an expression that was part anguish and part weird mirth, while his colorless eyes glowed like moons in the darkness, staring with blind intensity. They were the eyes of one who had gazed too long upon things no man should see. While the goblyns had been frightening, the darkling was a thing of genuine horror. Wort could smell rank corruption radiating from him like the overwhelming stench of a decomposing corpse.

Swallowing hard, Wort dared to speak. "I have come . . . I have come to—"

"I know why you have come," the shriveled man spat, turning his disconcerting gaze toward the opening. "I am still Vistana. They cast me out for what I have seen, but they cannot change what I am!"

Wort knew it was perilous even to speak to a darkling. It was said their words alone were enough to cast a listener under a spell. All darklings were Vistani—or at least, all had been so at one time. Each had committed some nefarious crime for which the gypsies had branded him an outcast. Cut off from his people, the darkling descended deeper into evil, until he was utterly consumed by it. Though corrupted, darklings retained their Vistana power of gazing into the future. This darkling had been captured by the baron some months ago. Wort had watched from his bell tower as two of Caidin's knights had hauled the wretched Vistana to the iron gate that led to the dungeons.

"If you know why I have come, darkling, then you already know what you're going to tell me."

"Oh, no, not yet." The darkling jammed the end of the torch into a crack and scurried on all fours toward the opening. "For that, I must have your hand."

Reluctantly, Wort slipped his left hand through the slit. He shuddered as stick-thin fingers brushed his palm.

"Stained with blood, you are," the darkling hissed. Wort resisted the impulse to pull his hand away. "Your soul is twisted, as is your body. Only one thing can heal it."

"Vengeance," Wort snarled.

The darkling did not reply. It did not matter. That was the one thing Wort already knew.

"Tell me, Vistana," he demanded. "How am I to gain my revenge against Caidin and all the others who have despised me?"

The darkling spoke again in a wheedling voice. "Two leagues east of the village, a path leads northward from the main road. It is overgrown and difficult to see, but you will know it by the old stone watcher that stands nearby. Follow the path until you reach the ruins of an ancient cathedral. Within, you will find the means to gain your vengeance."

"How will I know what to look for in the cathedral?"

Shrill laughter raised the hair on the back of Wort's thick neck. Quickly he snatched his hand back.

"Oh, you will know."

The darkling fell silent. Peering again through the crack, Wort saw that the man had crawled to the far wall. He sat now, clasping his gaunt arms about his bony knees.

"I don't know how I can repay you for your help," Wort said finally.

The darkling did not answer for a long time. "Gain your vengeance. That will be payment enough."

Trembling, Wort backed away from the hole. He gripped his heavy cloak more tightly about himself and hobbled down the passageway—quickly, lest the dungeon's guards discover him.

*   *   *   *   *

In the foul cell, the darkling rocked back and forth in the flickering light of the dying torch.

"First the stone, now the bell." Queer laughter racked his withered body. "Oh, what dark mayhem I have wrought!"

A memory flitted into the darkling's crazed mind— a memory of all the smooth, lovely necks he had broken with his bare hands. How sweet it was to squeeze and squeeze until finally he felt bones snap . . . until the others had discovered who it was that was murdering their sons and daughters. They had cast him out, thinking that by doing so he could cause them no more harm. What fools they were!

"Now the stone is free," he chortled. "Soon the bell will be, too. Then they will be sorry. Then all the Vistani will be sorry!"

A bloated beetled scuttled across his bare foot. With uncanny swiftness, the darkling snaked out a hand and grabbed the insect. Dark splotches marked its pale carapace, forming the shape of a grinning skull. The insect wriggled violently, then shot a stream of dark liquid from between gnashing mandibles. The fluid struck the floor. It sizzled and smoked, carving a pock mark into the hard stone. The darkling took care not to let any of the fluid touch him. One drop of a skull beetle's venom caused one's flesh to start decomposing, and there was no antidote. In minutes, the victim was reduced to a pile of putrid ooze. Despite their poison, the darkling found skull beetles to be quite . . . delicious. One by one, he picked off the insect's legs and popped them, still wriggling, into his mouth.

*   *   *   *   *

The cold autumn wind whistled mournfully through the tangle of dry witchgrass that grew to either side of the road east of the village. Wort bounced on the bench of a rickety wagon harnessed to a dun-colored donkey. It had been curiously easy to steal the cart and donkey from the keep's livery. The stablemaster was called away at just the right moment, and the stableboy was asleep in the hayloft. It was almost as if some unseen hand were guiding Wort. However, now that he had stolen it, convincing the slow-moving donkey to keep up a good pace was not such a simple task.

"Come along, beast," Wort pleaded, giving the reins a shake. The donkey planted its hooves firmly in the mud, laying back its ears and rolling its eyes. "Please, beast. We haven't all day." Wort glanced up at the sky. The sun was invisible behind leaden clouds, but he knew it was past midday. Sighing, he clumsily climbed down from the wagon's bench and picked his way through the mud to stand before the donkey. "Now, beast," he said wearily. "Your legs are stronger than mine. Won't you bear me to the cathedral out of kindness?"

The donkey gave him a flat, sullen stare.

"I didn't think so," Wort grumbled. He pulled something out of a pocket. "Then will you do it for an apple?"

The animal's ears perked up as Wort held out a wrinkled fruit. It snuffled the apple briefly, then crunched it to pulp with big, yellow teeth.

"Now, there's more where that came from, beast." The donkey let out an excited snort. Wort hobbled back to the wagon and clambered onto the bench. "But first, the cathedral!"

The beast launched into a merry trot. Wort couldn't help but grin. It was a good thing he had stolen the stableboy's lunch as well as the cart.

After a time, the sound of thunder rumbled on the air. Wort glanced up nervously, wondering if it was going to rain. The rumbling drew nearer. Abruptly he realized it was not thunder at all, but the staccato hoofbeats of a horse. Over a low rise, horse and rider came into view. A massive white charger galloped swiftly toward him, mud spraying from its hooves. On the stallion's back rode a man with long golden hair, clad in the blue livery of one of the baron's knights.

"Out of my way, peasant!" the knight ordered in a booming voice. "I ride with a message for the baron!"

Wort pulled on the reins, trying to veer the donkey to the side of the road. The beast's hooves slipped in the mud, and the wagon slid sideways, blocking the road. Wort cringed as the charger reared onto its hind legs, skidding to a violent halt. The knight glared at Wort.

"I said out of my way, you wretched piece of filth." Rage contorted the knight's handsome, square-jawed face.

"I . . . I'm sorry, my lord," Wort gasped, cowering inside his concealing cloak.

"I did not give you leave to speak!" the knight said imperiously. He drew the saber at his hip and, with casual strength, struck Wort with the flat of the blade. Crying out in pain, Wort tumbled into the mud.

"Let that teach you to heed your betters."

The knight let out a harsh laugh, then spurred his charger past the wagon. Horse and rider galloped down the road toward Nartok Keep. Struggling to free himself from the tangles of his muddy cloak, Wort hauled himself slowly to his feet. He gripped his throbbing shoulder, staring hatefully after the golden-haired knight.

"Why must those who have everything be so cruel to those who have nothing?" Wort whispered bitterly. The only answer was the low moaning of the wind. He climbed into the wagon, and the craft lurched into motion once more.

Soon the road plunged into a copse of beech and ash trees, their branches already bare with the advent of autumn. A coarse cry from above pierced the still air, and a dark blur flew scant inches over Wort's head. The thing sped by and alighted on a stump. A crow. Wort had the disturbing sensation that it was staring at him. He reined the donkey to a halt. It was not a stump that the bird perched upon, but a statue. Long years of wind and rain had worn it almost beyond recognition, yet something about the statue made Wort think of ancient and neglected majesty.

Wort gasped as moisture trickled like tears from the dark pits of its eyes. The statue's stone arm was moving, beckoning to him. The crow spread its wings, flapping away through the trees. Trembling, Wort tried to calm himself.

"Don't be a fool, Wort," he muttered. "Statues can't move. It was a trick of the shadows. That's all."

He forced himself to look again at the statue. This time it did not stir. Then he noticed a faint track leading into the trees.

"Of course, beast," Wort whispered to the donkey. "This must be the stone watcher the darkling spoke of." The animal pricked its long ears. Its nostrils flared, as if it caught some disturbing scent.

"Come along, beast. We have a bargain."

Reluctantly, the donkey plodded down the overgrown track. Creaking in protest, the wagon rattled behind. The path was deeply rutted, and the trees closed in threateningly from either side. It looked as if no one had come this way in years. Wort tried not to wonder why.

The air was growing thick and purple as the barren trees gave way and the cathedral at last hove into view. The structure looked as if it had been abandoned centuries earlier. One wall had collapsed into dark rubble, and much of the roof had fallen in, leaving spindly stone buttresses to curve overhead, like the exposed ribs of some gigantic rotting beast. Grotesque stone gargoyles leered down from high ledges, water dribbling like dark saliva from their rain-spout mouths. Wort guided the wagon through the dim archway that led into the cathedral, its doors long ago reduced to splinters. The donkey pranced skittishly as the wagon ground to a halt. Wort climbed down.

Outside, the westering sun had broken through the dark clouds on the horizon. Now its light streamed through intricate stained-glass windows that were oddly intact. The radiance fell upon the floor like a scattering of fiery jewels. Here and there, nettles pushed up through piles of rubble, and more beast-faced gargoyles grinned down at Wort from high ledges. Their dull stone eyes seemed to follow him disconcertingly wherever he moved. He shivered, trying his best to ignore them as he cautiously began exploring the ruin.

"How am I to search for something when I don't even know what it is?" he muttered in exasperation.

The gloomy atmosphere seemed to stifle his words. He came to a pile of rocks near one crumbling wall. Atop the heap, leaning at a precarious angle, was a horned gargoyle hewn of dark stone. With no better idea of what to do, Wort picked through the jumble of rocks. He pulled a stone from the pile, then heaved it down in disgust. This was futile.

Motion above caught his eye. He jerked his head up, his eyes bulging in fear. The stone gargoyle atop the pile had shifted position, leaning sinisterly forward. Its muscled arms reached out toward Wort, its toothy maw gaping hungrily. Suddenly the gargoyle dived forward. With a cry, Wort scrambled back as the gargoyle tumbled downward. It shattered as it struck the hard floor, chunks of stone rolling in all directions. Wort gasped as the thing's head came to a stop at his feet. The frozen visage snarled up at him.

Abruptly Wort let out a nervous laugh. Nothing to be afraid of—just an old, falling-apart statue. Shaking his head, he turned from the broken gargoyle and continued his exploration of the cathedral. After poking around the rubble, he made his way up crumbling steps to the nave. The crimson light of the stained-glass windows filled the air with a thick miasma. Wort noticed a strange mound in the center of the nave. A rotting tapestry, fallen from above, shrouded the peculiar pile. Somehow the shape beneath the musty cloth seemed oddly familiar. Curious, Wort reached out and tugged at the tapestry. The rotting cloth tore to shreds in his hands, filling the air with dust. The object beneath shone in the scarlet light.

It was a bell.

Hardly daring to breathe, Wort reached out to touch the smooth surface of the bell resting on the marble altar. He had never before seen a thing of such beauty. Its smooth surface was flawless, glowing with a rich luster in the half-light, hinting at the wondrous sound it would have if it were rung. Flowing runes were engraved about the rim. Wort did not know what they signified, but they surely added to the glorious beauty of the thing.

"This has to be what the darkling said I would find," Wort murmured softly. "But how can a bell help me gain my vengeance?" He did not know, but whether it could help him or not, he had to have the wondrous bell for his own.

Maneuvering the bell onto the cart was an arduous task. Though only as large as the circumference of Wort's arms, the solid bronze bell was ponderously heavy. He found several wooden planks in the back of the wagon, and with them fashioned a sort of ramp from the altar, down the nave's steps. After much straining and heaving, he managed to push the heavy bell down the makeshift wooden ramp and into the wagon. He used some old rags to muffle the clapper, and then bound the bell securely in place with a length of rope. Wort stroked the bell with satisfaction. Just then the crimson glow faded from the stained-glass windows. Outside the sun had set.

"Let's be on our way, beast," Wort said to the donkey as he started to climb into the wagon.

Once again, movement caught the corner of his eye. Wort craned his neck, gazing upward. One of the stone gargoyles high above seemed to move.

"Why, it's just another loose statue," Wort grumbled to himself.

Another gargoyle stirred on its stone perch, stretching its dark wings as though waking from a long sleep. Wide-eyed, Wort spun around. He watched raptly as gargoyle after gargoyle began to come awake. The statues flexed powerful arms and extended sickle-shaped talons. Their movements were stiff and slow at first, but gradually they began to grow more fluid. Doglike muzzles curled back from fanged maws, making hungry, bestial grins.

Their wings began to beat more swiftly. Wort knew he had only moments before the gargoyles woke fully. In panic, he jerked his head from side to side, searching in desperation for some place he might hide. Then he saw a row of stone sarcophagi deep in the nave. The lid of one sarcophagus was askew. Without thinking, Wort rushed to the stone coffin and dived inside. With the strength of terror, he gripped the stone lid and hauled it into place, sealing himself inside. Outside, the sound of wings swelled the air.

After a moment, Wort realized that he was not alone in the suffocating darkness of the coffin. In the twilight that filtered through a crack in the side of the sarcophagus he glimpsed the mummified corpse that lay next to him. Rotten velvet and tarnished jewels draped the thing's leathery flesh, but nothing could hide the cruel hand of decay. Eyeballs, which dangled like gray raisins in the corpse's eye sockets, seemed to stare at Wort. Strands of musty hair, dry and brittle as old silk, brushed against his face. He squirmed to move away from the mummy, but the motion only brought its bony arms down upon him. The sweet scent of rot filled his lungs.

Outside the sarcophagus, snarls and grunts echoed around the cathedral. Wort heard the terrified braying of the donkey and the clattering of its hooves on the stone floor. Abruptly, the animal's terrible screams ended. Moments later came the hideous music of popping bones and ripping flesh, followed by the sounds of feeding. All too quickly the noise of the terrifying feast ceased. Growls of hunger rent the air once more. A clicking sound approached the sarcophagus—sharp claws on cold stone. Wort froze. Something was stalking outside. Through the crack in the sarcophagus, he glimpsed muscles that rippled fluidly beneath scaly skin and a reptilian tail flicking sinuously, its spiked tip dripping blood.

At last the creature outside the sarcophagus moved on. Wort shuddered. The mummy's shriveled fingers gently caressed his cheek. He clenched his jaw to keep from screaming. Surely he must be going mad. Yes, better it was to lose himself in the dark pit of madness than to believe that statues could somehow, by some dread enchantment, come to life at the setting of the sun—that gargoyles hewn of stone could feast on living flesh and thirst for warm blood.

Again and again that night Wort heard the chilling approach of claws on stone. Each time he held his breath, waiting for the lid of the coffin to be heaved aside, waiting to gaze upon one of the hideous beasts, waiting to feel long talons slice deep into his throat. Once, he saw a glowing green eye peer through the crack in the sarcophagus. Wort caught a glimpse of unspeakable malevolence in the eye—a malevolence so vast and ancient that he thought it would sunder his mind. Then the baleful eye was gone.

All night long, Wort lay stiffly in the suffocating darkness of the coffin, listening to the bestial howls outside while the ancient cadaver encircled him in a cold embrace. One by one he counted his frenzied heartbeats, praying for the dawn.

 **FOUR**

The red-haired youth sat with his back against the ancient oak tree, his eyes dreamy behind gold-rimmed spectacles. He absently twirled a white quill pen, frowning in thought. Suddenly, inspiration lit up his freckled face, and he bent to scribble fiercely on a crisp sheaf of parchment. He leaned back, reading over the lines he had scrawled. The youth's name was Robart, and he fancied himself a poet. Of course, presently he was merely the assistant to Master Demaris, the village scribe. Robart spent most of his time hunched over a small writing desk in the back of Demaris's dim shop, recopying boring old tomes, legal contracts, and other tedious documents until his eyes blurred and his hand cramped.

"Why don't we spend more time making copies of romances, Master Demaris?" he had once eagerly asked his employer. "Or adventure stories. Or love songs. Or . . . or *poetry*." He couldn't help but sigh as he breathed that auspicious word. "I imagine such things would bring in far more revenue than all these dreadfully dull histories you have me copy."

Demaris regarded Robart sharply with his one good eye. "Romances?" he spat. "Poetry?" Before Robart's face, he shook a hand, its fingers permanently curled from decades of clutching a pen. "Why, those are rubbish, lad! Fancy and foolishness! You would do well to put such things out of your head entirely. Keep your mind firmly fixed on practical matters. Otherwise you'll never succeed in this world!"

Robart had never mentioned the subject to Demaris again, but he did not give up his dreams. One day he was going to be the most famous poet in all of Darkon. All the greatest nobles would invite him to their courts to read his work—perhaps even the king himself. Then let Master Demaris try to tell him poetry was foolishness!

The snapping of a dry twig startled Robart from his reverie. He leapt to his feet, hastily smoothing his green coat and yellow breeches. The clothes were of the same style he had heard was all the rage in the city of Il Aluk, but they were cheaply made and a bit too short for his long, gangly frame.

"Who's there?" he called out nervously. He knew wild beasts were said to prowl the moors. Would they venture this close to the village? Perhaps, if they were hungry enough.

Without warning, a gray blur leapt from behind the oak tree and fell upon Robart, knocking him backward to the damp turf. He gasped in shock, fumbling to straighten his spectacles.

"Alys!" he exclaimed in surprise and relief.

On top of him was a pretty young woman with mouse-brown hair and bright eyes, clad in a gray homespun dress.

"Did I frighten you, my love?" she asked impishly.

He gently but forcibly extricated himself from her entangling limbs and sat up. "Of course not!"

She leaned on an elbow, gazing up at him mischievously. "Really?" She reached out and gripped his wrist, feeling his racing pulse. "Am I to assume that it's your excitement at seeing me that makes your heart beat so quickly?"

"Yes," he said defiantly, "you may." He bent over her then and silenced her mirth with kisses.

For a time, the two lovers sat together beneath the ancient tree. Before them, the countryside rolled to the distant horizon in patchwork waves of heath, grove, and stone-walled fields. Late afternoon sunlight spilled heavy as gold across the land. Somewhere doves were singing their mournful evening song.

Alys pointed to the dark stump of the half-finished tower looming in the distance. "What do you suppose that building really is?"

"I don't know," he answered with a shrug. "I suppose it is the pet project of one of the neighboring lords."

"Really? That's not what I think." Alys rested her chin on a fist, gazing at the jagged spire speculatively. "No one ever goes near the tower. Yet every night it seems to grow a little higher. I think . . . I think that it's some kind of magic."

Robart felt a chill creep up his spine. "Magic? But it can't be magic, Alys." He swallowed hard. "Can it?"

Alys gave him a mysterious look. "You know, I have half a mind to stay up tonight, camp out here, and watch what happens. The moon is nearly full. There'll be enough light."

Robart gaped at her. "No, Alys. You mustn't even consider it. It's too dangerous to be out on the moor at night." He licked his lips slowly. "There are wild beasts aprowl, you know."

"So? I'm not afraid."

"Please, Alys!" An edge of desperation crept into Robart's voice. "You mustn't stay here tonight!"

She scowled in annoyance. "Oh, all right. If you're going to be such a worrywart, I won't." She sighed, glancing once more at the tower. After a while she grudgingly let herself be consoled by more kisses. Finally, as the sun sank toward the dark line of the horizon, she pushed herself from Robart's embrace.

"I had better go home now, Robart."

Robart nodded reluctantly. It would be disaster if Alys's parents learned of their secret trysts. Alys's father was one of the most respected farmers in the village, and he would never approve of Robart and Alys's budding romance. Her father considered reading and writing frivolous pursuits, and he expected Alys to marry some farmer like himself one day.

"Will I see you tomorrow, Alys?" Robart asked hopefully.

"Perhaps," she replied. "If you're lucky," she added naughtily, vanishing from sight.

Robart gathered pen and parchment into a battered leather satchel and headed down the hill toward the village. Though the sun had only just set, shutters were already drawn against the night. Robart trudged through the churned mud of the streets, cold water seeping through his fashionable but impractical boots. Soon he reached the dilapidated boarding house where he rented a cramped attic garret for a silver penny a week. He opened the peeling-paint door and stepped into the dim squalor beyond.

"Good evening, Mistress Varsa," he said, nodding to the proprietress of the house, who sat behind a worm-eaten desk. A rancid candle provided the solitary light in the drafty entry hall.

"You're late, Robart," she replied in a surly voice. Mistress Varsa was a sour-faced woman, clad as usual in a shabby velvet dress that was far too snug for her expansive figure. "I was about to lock the door. And you know I open it for no one after dark. Not even the baron himself should he come knocking."

Robart ducked his head, biting his tongue to keep

from commenting on the unlikelihood of such an esteemed visitor coming to this rat's haven. "Of course, Mistress Varsa." He hastened past her and dashed up a rickety flight of steps.

"And don't dare pretend that you've forgotten the rent is due!" her shrill voice called behind him.

"Hideous old witch," Robart mumbled under his breath. He made his way down a murky corridor. Reaching the door of his tiny cubicle, he saw that the padlock he had fastened to the latch hung open. No doubt Mistress Varsa had called in a locksmith so she could snoop about his room. Muttering curses, he opened the door.

Inside the cramped cell stood two men. Robart's mouth opened in shock. The men were clad in the blue uniforms of the baron's knights, both armed with curved sabers. Robart saw that sheaves of parchment were scattered about the floor. His poems. Anger flared hotly in his brain.

"Hey there, what do you think you're doing?"

One of the knights stepped forward, his gloved hand resting comfortably on the hilt of his saber. "By the order of Lord Inquisitor Sirraun, you are under arrest."

Robart's face blanched. "Under arrest?" He slowly backed away, his poems suddenly forgotten. "What for?"

The knight advanced on him menacingly. "For high treason against His Grace, the baron."

"No!" Robart gasped. He turned to flee down the corridor, but the two knights struck him forcefully from behind. He cried out as they twisted his arms cruelly behind his back.

"You're coming with us, traitor." Ignoring his protests, the knights dragged Robart roughly down the stairs.

"Mistress Varsa!" he cried out as they reached the entry hall. "Help me!"

The sour-faced woman stood before the knights. "You said I would get my rent first," she demanded of one of them.

"Out of our way, hag." The knight pushed her aside.

"Curse you!" she shrieked, shaking a fist after the two knights. They shoved Robart through the door and out into the street.

"What's happening?" he sobbed in terror, but neither man answered as they dragged him into the cold night.

*   *   *   *   *

"Please, you must . . . believe me. . ."

Distant screams drifted on the fetid air, mixed with the sounds of clanking chains.

"I am innocent. . . ."

Robart hung limply by his shackled wrists, dangling between two stone columns. His shoulders ached with dull fire. He licked his parched lips, tasting sweat and blood.

"I am very disappointed in you, Robart," a sibilant voice said. "I fear that is the wrong answer."

Painfully, Robart opened his swollen eyes to gaze upon the sinister mien of the man who had brutally introduced himself as Lord Inquisitor Sirraun.

"I beg you," Robart gasped hoarsely. Even speaking was agony. "I have told you . . . the truth. I am . . . innocent."

Sirraun picked up a wooden box. "No, Robart. You are mistaken. You see, no one is truly innocent. Everyone conceals some dark secret in his heart. Sadly, the methods I am forced to adopt to discover those secrets are somewhat crude." The lipless gash of his mouth parted in an evil smile. "But they are, I have found, almost invariably effective."

Opening the box, Sirraun drew out a large silver ring covered with spidery runes. It looked like a circlet a king might wear around his head.

"You must wonder what this is," Sirraun said. "I confess, I do not truly know. But it is a most intriguing object."

He picked up a wooden staff and slowly slipped the ring over its tip. Strangely, the tip of the staff disappeared. After a moment Sirraun lifted the silver circlet from the staff. Robart gaped. The end of the staff was blackened and charred.

"I cannot be certain," Sirraun explained coolly, "but I suspect the ring is a gateway to another realm of existence—another world, if you will. It seems to be a world filled with fire." He approached the young man. "Searing fire." He moved the ring toward one of Robart's manacled hands.

"Please," Robart choked, staring at the ring fearfully. "I've told you everything I know."

"Oh, we have only just begun to explore the depths of your depravity," Sirraun cooed. "You see, we know you to be a reader of books. Books are dangerous things. They lead to ideas, which in turn lead to questions, which in the end, of course, lead to treachery. I think you will be amazed, Robart, at the crimes and sins to which you will find yourself confessing."

The ring hovered closer. Robart let out a wordless cry of terror.

"Enough, Sirraun!" a deep voice cut through the air. "I grow weary of your dramatics." A figure robed and hooded in rich purple stepped from an alcove. "I do not have all night to watch you satisfy your pathetic cravings for sadistic entertainment."

Poison filled the lord inquisitor's black eyes, but he responded with a sharp nod, placing the ring back in its box. "As you wish."

"Things are always as I wish." The robed man approached the prisoner.

Hope flared in Robart's heart. "Have you come to set me free?"

"In a way," the other replied. He held up a polished black stone. The robed man whispered a dissonant word, and a faint crimson light flickered to life inside the stone. The light began to throb, slowly at first, then faster. Abruptly Robart realized that the stone's pulsating rhythm was matching the cadence of his own frantically beating heart.

"What . . . what is it?" he gasped.

"Watch," the robed man replied.

A ray of crimson light arced from the stone, striking Robart in the chest. The young man screamed as crystalline pain pierced him. His back arched, and his hands clenched themselves into rigid claws. The ray of magical light flared, changing from angry red to shimmering green. Now the light seemed to stream outward from Robart's chest, rebounding into the dark stone. Suddenly the pain that racked Robart subsided. His body went limp. As the green light drained into the stone, he felt himself growing colder and colder. His skin turned sickly gray, and deep shadows appeared beneath his staring eyes. He shuddered one last time as the emerald ray of light vanished. The stone went dark. Carefully, the robed man stored the stone in a pocket.

"Please," Robart whispered. It seemed strangely difficult to move his jaw and tongue. He was unbearably cold. "Please . . . don't kill me."

"But don't you see, Robart?" Laughter emanated from within the purple hood. "You're already dead."

Robart stared in disbelief.

"Can't you feel it?" the other went on with eerie calmness. "You are no longer breathing, Robart. Listen. Your heart has fallen still."

"No . . ." Robart croaked. He tried to struggle, to free himself from his shackles, but his movements were feeble, jerky. "It's hard . . . to move . . . so cold."

"Ah, yes," the robed man said dispassionately. "The stiffness of rigor mortis is already setting in."

Robert could only move his lips wordlessly. Gradually his twitching stopped. The robed man reached out a hand and gently shut the apprentice's eyes

"Rest in peace, Robart," he whispered mockingly.

Darkness shrouded the young man. A cry of madness welled up inside him, rending his soul to shreds, but he could not give voice to it.

Dead men, Robart realized dimly, cannot scream.

*   *   *   *   *

Baron Caidin pushed back the purple hood of his robe. He was beginning to enjoy watching the stone drain the life-forces of its victims.

"You might have given me more time with him, Your Grace." Sirraun's voice was resentful. He ran a hand fondly over a machine fashioned of iron bars, leather straps, and sharp spikes—one of the many nameless engines of torture that filled the dank room far below Nartok Keep.

Caidin fixed his lord inquisitor with a disgusted look. "I couldn't care less whether or not you have the chance to satisfy your perverse pleasures, Sirraun. I'm a busy man."

He stalked around the slumped corpse of the young man. "He must be beheaded for treason in the courtyard like the others. We must keep up the ruse of the inquisition. I cannot allow Azalin to learn the real reason I need these bodies. When will he be strong enough to walk up the steps of the scaffold?"

Sirraun peered at the corpse. Already dark blood

was pooling beneath the pale skin. "They can usually move again in a day or two, after the rigor mortis fades. But I prefer to keep them chained up then. They are quite dangerous at that point, for they are in the midst of going utterly mad. It is better to wait a few more days. Once their brains begin to decay they are much easier to control."

Caidin nodded. "Very well. In the meantime . . ."

"Yes, I know—find more traitors." Sirraun finished. He bowed solemnly. "With pleasure, Your Grace." The lord inquisitor backed away, disappearing into the shadows.

Alone with the cadaver, Caidin drew out the dark stone once more. It was quiescent now, but he knew that the life-force of the young scribe—like that of all the other villagers falsely arrested for treachery— had been absorbed by the stone. The Soulstone was more powerful than he had ever hoped it would be.

Caidin had stumbled upon a reference to the Soulstone years earlier, in an ancient, forgotten tome in the keep's library. The notion of an object that siphoned the spirits of living men had excited him, and right away he had realized that such a thing could prove the key to great power. He had searched for more information about the stone but had found only tantalizing hints and clues. Interest grew into obsession, and for years he searched in vain for the Soulstone.

Then at last, in the ruins of a forgotten fortress, he found the darkling. In truth, it had been more as if the darkling found him. Regardless, it was the twisted Vistana who finally revealed the hiding place of the Soulstone: an underwater cave along the Vuchar River. For his help, Caidin had rewarded the darkling with imprisonment. From time to time, the baron descended into the dungeon to ask the evil Vistana questions about the stone, doing less so of late as he grew to understand the Soulstone's powers more and more. He supposed he should have the darkling killed soon.

"Just a few more lives," Caidin told the silent corpse. "A score or two, no more. Then I will finally have the power I need to confront the king." He turned on a heel and strode from the inquisition chamber, leaving behind the hideous iron contraptions and the stench of fear. Other matters required his attention.

An hour later found Caidin standing in the candlelit splendor of Nartok Keep's Grand Hall. His black hair and beard shone with perfumed oil, and his scarlet kneecoat was trimmed with gold braid. With graceful strength, he rested a white-gloved hand on the hilt of the decorative saber dangling at his side.

"So, tell me again, Domeck, who is this lady I'm suddenly playing host to?"

"She's a traveling noble from Il Aluk, Your Grace," the stout, gray-haired man replied in his gruff voice. "A duchess, I believe. I gather she recently inherited an estate some leagues north of here, and she's come to examine the property. Apparently there's a problem with the legalities of the transaction—missing papers or some such nonsense. She's hoping to indulge Your Grace's hospitality while the matter is sorted out."

"And perhaps His Grace will indulge the lady's hospitality as well," a mischievous voice piped up wickedly. Pock appeared from behind a marble column, clad in comical imitation of the baron. The small, purple-skinned gnome capered about in a naughtily suggestive dance.

"Be still, you maggot," Caidin hissed as the gilded doors of the Grand Hall started to open. Pock dashed back behind the stone column. Caidin leaned his head toward the castellan. "Quick—what is she called?"

"Her name," Domeck replied quietly, "is Lady Jadis."

A pair of pages with powdered faces and rouged cheeks pushed open the tall gilded doors. A woman drifted into the hall, her gown of emerald silk whispering against the smooth marble floor. Her jet-black hair was coiled intricately atop her head, and a single large pearl hung from a golden strand that encircled her graceful neck. Her skin had the tone of burnished copper, and her eyes glittered with green-gold light.

Caidin swore an oath under his breath. "You didn't tell me she was so beautiful, Domeck," he whispered.

"Your Grace didn't ask," Pock quipped from his hiding place. Caidin bit his lip to keep from cursing.

"Your Grace didn't ask—what?" the woman inquired in a lilting voice as she approached.

Caidin smiled, displaying pointed canines. He made a mental note to box the foolish gnome's ears. A heady scent emanated from Lady Jadis, like the sweet fragrance of exotic spices. "I would be honored by the lady's company at table." He kissed her hand, lingering over it just a heartbeat longer than etiquette required.

"I must thank you for your kindness in taking me in," the duchess said warmly. "I trust that my affairs will be resolved soon, so that I will not overstay my welcome."

Caidin's oiled mustache curled in a devilish smile. "Oh, I fear there is little chance of that." He moved to a golden table. "Wine, my lady?"

"Please."

He filled two crystal goblets with pale wine and turned to hand one to her. Abruptly his eyes flashed in anger. Pock stood behind the lady, puckering up his purple face and hugging himself in a mockery of a passionate embrace.

"Is something amiss?" Jadis asked.

"Not at all," Caidin replied smoothly. He gently gripped the lady's elbow and steered her away. In the process he found the opportunity to plant a firm kick on Pock's hindquarters. The gnome let out a squeal.

"Did you hear something?" Jadis asked. Caidin could not stop her from looking over her shoulder. Fortunately, Pock had already vanished behind the column.

"I didn't hear a thing," Caidin said pleasantly.

The two spoke for a time, sipping their wine and exchanging formalities while the castellan stood apart at a respectful distance. When she turned her head Caidin couldn't help running his eyes desirously over her supple neck and bare shoulders. Finally, he suggested they make their way to the dining hall. He downed his wine in a single gulp. Jadis nodded her acquiescence. Just then the gilded doors flew open. The pages hastily scrambled out of the way as a man with long golden hair stomped into the room.

"Your Grace, there you are," the man said breathlessly. Caidin noticed that his blue knight's uniform was spattered with mud. "I've been searching for you all evening, but no one I asked knew where you were."

Caidin gave him a sour look. "It never occurred to you, Logris, that if I had wished to be found I would have told people where to find me?"

The knight only stared at him in bewilderment.

Caidin sighed deeply. "I was attending to business, Logris," he said wearily. Was it his imagination, or did his knights grow more stupid with each passing year? "As I am doing now."

Logris bowed sweepingly. "Forgive me, Your Grace, but I have urgent news I must tell you." He cast a sideways look at the Lady Jadis. "Er, in private, Your Grace."

The baron suppressed a groan. Logris was a loyal knight, but a trifle overeager. Caidin supposed the only way to be rid of him—and to continue the beguiling game of seduction with the lady—was to hear Logris's message.

Caidin turned toward Jadis. "Forgive me, my lady. . . ."

"Think nothing of it, Your Grace." She touched his hand enticingly. "I will await you in the dining hall."

Domeck volunteered to escort her. Caidin wistfully watched the emerald-gowned noblewoman as she and the castellan left the Grand Hall. When the golden doors had closed, he turned on the knight. "This had better be important, Logris."

Ten minutes later, after listening with increasing interest to Logris's report, Caidin dismissed the knight. He poured himself another glass of wine.

"What a fool," he murmured.

"You shouldn't say such things about yourself, baron," Pock teased, scampering out of his hiding place.

Caidin scowled in annoyance. "I wasn't talking about myself, Pock. I was referring to King Azalin." He drank the glass of wine. "Didn't you hear Logris's report? He just came from Il Aluk. One of my agents there learned that Azalin has sent a Kargat spy to Nartok Keep."

"It isn't me, I swear!" Pock squeaked, falling to his knees.

"Get up, Pock!" Caidin snapped. "You're the one person I know would never betray me. You haven't the brains for it."

"Why thank you, Your Grace." Pock beamed.

Caidin gazed into the crystal goblet thoughtfully. "No, I think I can guess who it is that serves the Wizard King—someone who unexpectedly and quite conveniently arrived at the keep only today." He cast a murderous look at the doors of the Grand Hall, then advanced on the gnome. "I want you to keep an eye on the Lady Jadis, Pock."

"Begging your pardon, baron, but I would rather keep a hand on her." The gnome winked slyly.

"Pock!" Caidin growled threateningly.

The gnome scampered backward in alarm. "An eye it is, Your Grace!" he chirped, then scurried quickly from the hall.

"So, Azalin, you have sent one of your foul Kargat to spy on me," Caidin said aloud. He hurled the crystal goblet at the wall. "But I am one step ahead of you." Broken glass crackled beneath the heel of his boot as he strode from the hall. He did not want to be late in joining the Lady Jadis for dinner.

 **FIVE**

All through the endless night, Wort lay inside the ancient stone sarcophagus, the withered arms of the mummified corpse cradling him like those of a lover. Outside the coffin, howls echoed around the ruined cathedral. Wort cringed at terrible crashes and inhuman screams of rage. Could it be that the creatures out there were fighting each other? He wondered what they would do if they discovered his hiding place. Would the gargoyles battle each other to see which got the honor of tearing his throat out? Or would they simply begin to feed upon his living flesh?

He slipped into a dark delirium. The ravenous snarls, the scratching of claws, the dry-paper touch of the corpse—all of it wove itself into one endless nightmare.

Silence.

Dim realization crept into Wort's numb brain. Tomblike silence had descended over the cathedral. His eyes fluttered open. Faint golden light spilled through the crack in the side of the sarcophagus, illuminating his grisly companion. At last his mind grasped the import of these things. Dawn. Somehow he had lived to see the morning.

With the dull grating of stone on stone, the ponderous lid of the sarcophagus slid to one side, crashing to the floor. Wort climbed from the coffin, struggling to free himself from the clutches of the mummy. Its bony fingers held him tightly, as if unwilling to let him return to the realm of the living. With a violent jerk he twisted free of the thing's grasp. The skeleton's arms snapped like dry kindling as it sank back into the coffin.

Wort spun, gazed upward. He breathed a relieved sigh. The gargoyles had returned to their high ledges, lifeless statues once more. Shivering, he made his way to the wagon. The bell shone richly in the morning light, apparently undisturbed. At least that was something. He moved around to the front of the cart and clamped a hand to his mouth to keep from gagging.

There was little left of the donkey. The leather straps of the harness had been cleanly snapped. Splinters of bone and tufts of fur swam in blood that pooled thickly on the stones. Wort saw one gory stump of bone ending in a hoof.

"Now what am I to do?" he choked.

He could not stay in this accursed place, nor could he leave the bell behind. It was the key to everything. There was only one solution. Carefully, he picked up the broken harness and tried to shake the blood off of it. Winding the straps around his chest, he tied them tightly. He leaned into the harness. The cart did not budge. Grunting, he pulled harder. His face twisted into a horrible mask. The powerful muscles of his humped shoulders writhed beneath the coarse brown fabric of his tunic. Slowly the wagon began to inch forward.

As the cart gained momentum the pulling grew easier, but just barely. The leather straps bit painfully into Wort's flesh. With agonizing slowness, cart and bell moved through the open entrance of the cathe-

dral and into the blinding daylight. Sweat streamed
freely down Wort's brow, matting his shaggy hair. His
hunched back burned. Trying his best to ignore the
pain, he hauled the wagon down the overgrown
track. Gradually the skeletal trees closed in behind
him, blotting out the foreboding hulk of the ruined
cathedral.

If his hours in the coffin had been a nightmare,
then pulling the wagon to Nartok Keep was waking
torture. Wort's progress down the forest track was
agonizingly slow. Deep ruts continually caught the
wheels of the wagon, jerking him to a halt. Roots
tripped his aching feet, and thorny nettles tore his
threadbare breeches to strips, tracing angry red
weals across his shins. Fire ran up and down his
twisted spine in searing waves. More than once he
decided he could bear the agony no longer. Yet each
time he was on the verge of giving up, a voice whispered in his ear. He could not understand the words
the voice spoke, but they were oddly encouraging all
the same, and they gave him the spark of willpower
he needed to go on. Wort kept pulling.

He rounded a bend in the track and suddenly
found himself brought up short. Lying across the
path was a dead tree. In life it must have been a king
of the forest. The tree's knotted trunk was as thick as
the span of Wort's arms. During the night it had
finally lost its long battle against rot and had fallen
across the track. Wort stared dejectedly at the tree.
He could scramble over the trunk easily enough, but
no amount of will would get the cart over the obstacle. Nor could he drag the cart around it. The forest
was too thick here, the trees too close together. The
bell could go no farther.

Wort made a halfhearted attempt at pushing the
huge tree out of the road, but it was futile. Panting in
exhaustion, he collapsed onto a rock. He buried his

face in his hands as an air of gloom descended over him. It seemed he was not destined to have his vengeance after all. He should have known. Fate had never shown him any favor in the past. Why now?

A queer rustling noise intruded on his dark reverie. Dread pricking his skin, Wort glanced to one side to see insects stream out of the forest. There were hundreds of them. Thousands. Rivers of black-carapaced beetles, fire-red ants, and eyeless worms crawled on the ground, forming a thick, writhing carpet. Rapidly the insects swarmed over the fallen tree. In moments the massive trunk was no longer visible beneath the undulating shroud of bugs. More scuttled from the woods, and more. Worms slithered across Wort's feet, leaving behind trails of slime, but he did not shrink away. Revulsion froze him to the spot.

A weird buzzing noise filled the air along with a cloud of fine dust. The swarm of insects was chewing apart the rotting wood. With growing speed the chittering mass sank to the ground. Then, as if responding to some unheard signal, the insects began to stream once more into the woods. In moments the last of the vermin wriggled away, disappearing into the leaf litter that had spawned them. All that was left of the dead tree was a scattering of rotting splinters. The path was clear.

Wort rose to his feet. Bloated beetles squished wetly beneath his foot. Gagging, he approached the cart. Almost reluctantly he reached out and stroked the cool surface of the bell. Again peculiar thoughts drifted into his mind.

I wish to be free, Wort. I will do anything to be free once more.

He snatched his hand back. Could the bell have . . . ? No, he did not want to know. The path was clear now. That was all that mattered. As he turned from the bell, he felt a warm sensation rush over

him, so strong and delicious that it nearly overwhelmed him in a wave of dark pleasure. It was a
feeling of . . . gratitude. As suddenly as it had come,
the feeling disappeared. For a moment, Wort weakly
gripped the side of the cart, then gathered his
strength.

"You're imagining things, Wort," he muttered to
himself. "Now keep moving, or it'll be your own
funeral the bells toll next."

Strapping himself into the harness once more, he
struggled onward. Soon, he was again engulfed by
the throbbing miasma of pain. It was well after midday when he finally reached the stone watcher, the
timeworn statue that marked the path. He paused to
wrap himself once more in his dark cloak. From here
on it was best to remain concealed.

Though the rutted forest track had been nearly
impassable, the deep mud of the road seemed
worse. Time and again his feet slipped beneath him,
sending him plunging headlong into the stinking
muck. Every few hundred yards the cart bogged
down in the quagmire, and he was forced to kneel in
the slime, digging with his bare hands to try to free
the wheels. Several times riders galloped by, the
beating hooves of their mounts spraying him with
sludge. Not one even bothered to slow down as they
passed the hunched man struggling with the heavy
wagon. Wort slipped into a waking dream, drifting in
a twilight world of pain. How wonderful it would be,
he thought, to let go of the burning agony and allow
himself to sink down into cool darkness. Yet the distant music of bells continued to pull him onward.

Abruptly a new sound cut through the thick fog
that shrouded his mind.

"Are you simple, peasant?" a voice barked. "I said,
what's your business at the keep?"

Wort shook his head, blinking in dull amazement.

He stood before the great wooden gates of Nartok Keep. Ruddy light gleamed off the steel breastplate of the guard who stood before him. It was sunset. Yet it seemed impossible that he had completed the journey in one day. Or *had* it been just one day? Distance or time—or maybe both—had been strangely distorted during the course of his journey. Wort shivered, his mind dizzy.

The guard's eyes narrowed in suspicion as he peered into the shadows of Wort's hood.

Wort licked his parched lips. "A bell," he croaked. "I've brought a new bell for the keep."

"Who ordered it?" the guard demanded.

Wort blurted the first name that drifted to his brain. "Baron Caidin did."

The grizzled soldier let out a snort. "You're a liar. The baron does not trouble himself with such mundane matters. Let me see your face, peasant."

Wort hesitated. Slowly he raised his hands to the cowl that hid his visage. "As you wish." He lowered the dark hood.

"By the Master of the Gray Kingdom!" the guard swore, stumbling back in horror. Wort's visage, always homely, was now hideously contorted with exertion. Hastily, the guard made the sign against the Evil Eye. Before, such a reaction would have caused Wort sadness. Now he felt only a strange satisfaction at the revulsion in the other's eyes. He took a lurching step toward the guard, the heavy wagon creaking behind him.

"Let me pass, or I will curse you," he hissed.

The guard shook his head. "I . . . I can't. . . ." His hand fluttered weakly to the hilt of his short sword.

Wort raised a gnarled hand and pointed it at the guard. He grinned evilly. "Then let this be your curse. . . ."

"No, wait!" the guard cried. "Please! The castellan

will flay my hide if he finds out, but . . . "He swallowed hard, then stepped to the side of the gate. "I'll . . . I'll let you through."

Laughter rumbled deep in Wort's chest. "Wise choice," he whispered. A new feeling washed over him. Fear was a formidable weapon. Once more he seemed to feel a sensation of power radiating from the bell. Slowly, his whole body trembling with exhaustion, he dragged the cart into the courtyard of the keep. The guard only watched, the whites of his eyes shining, as he muttered over and over a charm his grandmother had once taught him to ward off curses.

*   *   *   *   *

It was midnight.

The cold light of the horned moon spilled through the iron gratings that covered the belfry's arched windows. Rows of sleeping pigeons lined high ledges, their heads tucked under their wings, glowing eerily in the pale illumination. Like some great, deformed bird himself, Wort perched atop the maze of thick wooden rafters that supported the bells.

"Almost done, my friends," Wort whispered. Several birds ruffled their feathers, then sank back into slumber. Wort finished threading the end of a stout rope through an iron pulley. Below him the rope disappeared through the trapdoor in the belfry's floor. His pulse quickened.

Earlier, as night had mantled Nartok Keep, Wort had managed to push the swathed bulk of the bronze bell from the back of the wagon through the door of his tower. After hiding the cart behind the keep's stable, he had stumbled back to the tower and collapsed in exhaustion. For a time he had slept like one dead, but a vision had gradually invaded his sleeping mind, glowing with brilliant incandescence. Then he had woken, knowing he could wait—*it* could wait—no longer.

Wort tightly gripped the end of the rope in thick-fingered hands. "Now it is my turn to fly, my friends." He leapt off the rafter.

His ragged cloak fluttering like black wings, Wort dropped down through the trapdoor. The rope whistled as it went through the pulley above, going taut as his weight began to lift the object tethered to the other end. Wort dropped through another trapdoor, and another, continuing his descent into darkness. A bulky shape appeared from below and rushed past him, upward. In moments, the bell vanished above Wort's head.

At last Wort's feet touched the ground. Quickly he lashed the rope to an iron ring in the floor, then lumbered up the tower's narrow spiral staircase until he reached the belfry once more. Gasping for breath, he craned his neck to gaze at the bell dangling above his head.

"There it is, my friends!" He clapped his hands together. "By my soul, it is beautiful."

The bell hung from one of the belfry's rafters. Moonlight dripped like water off its smooth surface, flowing into the runes carved along its lip. Wort clambered up a rickety ladder and busied himself with securing the bell to its moorings. Only when he was certain that everything was right did he carefully remove the rags that muffled the clapper. He climbed back down. Waves of emotion seemed to radiate from the bell. It was almost as if the thing were . . . satisfied.

"Now," he breathed. Trembling, he reached out and gripped the rope that hung from the bronze bell. "To hear its voice at last. . . ."

With strong arms, he tugged the rope. The bell

tilted. The clapper swung, striking metal. A single
note rang out. Startled pigeons erupted in a flurry of
gleaming white wings. At first the tolling was deep, a
thrumming so resonant and low Wort felt more than
heard it. Quickly it grew, cresting into a clear, thunderous noise that seemed to surge through him,
casting him adrift on the terrible beauty of its music.
Gradually, the noise faded. Wort blinked, like one
waking from a dream.

"It is glorious," he uttered in awe. He reached out
to pull the rope again. Abruptly he froze.

In the center of the belfry a patch of shadowy air
began to swirl. It seemed to Wort he was gazing at a
gray curtain billowing in a cold breeze, or at the surface of a languid pool of shimmering water. A sheen
of fear-sweat formed on his brow. The acrid scent of
lightning tingled in his nose. Dark shapes appeared
within the seething sphere of twilight. Gradually the
shapes grew more defined, taking on shape and substance. Then, like corpses rising from the murky
depths of a lake to bob on the storm-swept surface,
three figures drifted out of the roiling tendrils of mist.

"Who . . . who are you?" Wort whispered, backing
away. The shadowy forms were shaped like men, but
they were swathed in black robes and seemed fashioned of thick smoke rather than cloth. The three
vaporous forms hovered before Wort, floating slowly
up and down, buoyed by an unseen wind. One of the
dim figures raised an arm to point at Wort.

"We are the spirits of the bell," the figure spoke in
a reverberating voice. "You have called to us, mortal."

Wort shook his head dumbly. His heart thumped
wildly in his chest. "I?"

"Yes," answered another of the robed forms. "The
tolling of the Bell of Doom summons us, for we are
bound to it."

"But . . . but for what reason do you come?" Wort dared to ask.

"To kill," the three dark spirits answered as one. The single word echoed about the belfry, growing in volume until it was a deafening chorus. *Kill. Kill. KILL!*

Wort fell to his knees, pressing his hands over his ears. Finally the dreadful din faded.

"But why?" he cried out in terror.

"It is the bell's curse," one of the spirits spoke.

"Each time the bell is rung, someone *must* die," intoned another.

"That is the price to be paid for our blood," said the last of the spirits. "Blood that long ago was mixed with molten metal, so that silver would bind with bronze and forge a bell like none before."

Despite his fear, hope flared in Wort's heart. The darkling had spoken truth. Here indeed was the means to his vengeance.

"Who . . . who will you kill then?" Wort whispered.

The three spirits drifted menacingly toward him.

"You, bellringer. . . ."

Wort held his arms outstretched before him. Curse the darkling! Was this all a final, cruel joke?

"I beg you!" Wort moaned, groveling in the rotting straw before the hovering spirits. "Please, spare me!"

"We cannot alter the curse. The bell has been rung. Someone must die. . . ."

Despite his fear, a calculating thought occurred to Wort. "Must it . . . must it be *me* that you kill?" he asked slyly. "Tell me, spirits. Is there not some way that another may die in my stead?"

For a long moment the dark forms were silent. "There is a way. . . ."

"I knew it!" Wort exclaimed.

"But we must have a token," the spirits went on. "Something that belongs to the one we are to kill."

Wort's mind raced. "A . . . a token?" But what did he have that belonged to another? He could think of nothing. He felt hope slipping away like sand in an hourglass.

"Come, bellringer." The voices of the spirits blended in dark harmony. "It is time." They reached their long arms toward him.

Suddenly Wort remembered. "Wait!"

The spirits paused as Wort searched his tunic, sticking his hands into his pockets, pawing in panic. Then he found it. He pulled an object from his pocket and held it out. It was a glove.

"Here, take it!" he hissed. "It is not mine. Kill him, not me."

The three spirits nodded serenely. "It shall be so."

Wort gaped as the glove vanished from his hand. Looking up, he saw that the spirits had also vanished. He slumped to the floor. "Alive, Wort," he muttered to himself with weak laughter. "You're still alive." Shivering uncontrollably, he stared upward at the sinister shape of the bell.

*   *   *   *   *

Castellan Domeck walked through the silent armory. This was his favorite chamber in the keep. Nothing else could comfort him or free his mind as much as being surrounded by all the familiar trappings of war. Torchlight gleamed off rows of curved sabers and racks of steel-tipped spears. Oiled suits of mail hung on wooden stands while shields, axes, and spiked iron maces adorned the stone walls. Here in this chamber lay the real defenses of Nartok Keep. All of Sirraun's scheming and strategizing could not turn an attacking army away from the keep's walls. But these weapons could.

With a quill pen he made a notation in the small

leather-bound journal he carried. Despite the lateness of the hour, Domeck planned to work until he
had inventoried every weapon and every piece of
armor. The castellan required little sleep these days
anyway. He supposed it was just another sign of
aging. However, Domeck was far from ready to
spend the rest of his days sitting by the fire in the
kitchen with the keep's toothless uncles and aunties.
Beneath his blue uniform, his compact frame was
hard with muscle. He bristled with the energy of a
man ten or twenty years younger. Only in his heart
of hearts did he sometimes feel tired, defeated, worried.

"I just need once more to face an enemy with a
sword in my hand," the castellan told himself. "To
see my blade sliding through his guts. That would
make me feel young again."

Domeck found himself hoping, as he often did, for
a good battle—perhaps with one of the neighboring
barons. He knew there was nothing more pitiful than
an old warrior without a war to fight. Sighing, he
continued his counting.

"Odd," he murmured. "I didn't notice that before."

The castellan bent down to retrieve an object on
the floor, then stood again. It was a leather glove.
Puzzled, he realized it was the glove he had lost in
the courtyard some days before, when that wretched
hunchback had begged for his help. What was it
doing here? After a moment Domeck shrugged. It
was a good glove. He tucked it into his belt and
moved on. A faint clinking sound brought him to a
halt once more. He cocked his head, listening. There
it was again—a metallic clinking. Slowly he turned
around.

An empty chain-mail hauberk dragged itself
across the floor toward him like a sinuous, metallic
snake. Sparks of sizzling green light danced on the

mail coat's metal links. Domeck stared in numb astonishment. Other pieces of armor were moving toward him as well, all of their own volition. A burnished breastplate fell off a wooden stand and clattered to the floor. Jerking and shuddering, it dragged itself after the hauberk. Steel gauntlets scuttled like metal spiders. Propelled by an unseen hand, a wooden shield rolled toward the hauberk. Greaves, chausses, and spurs slithered after. As the pieces of armor converged, tendrils of green incandescence sprang from the hauberk, coiling about them. Engulfed in sizzling emerald fire, the pieces of armor rose slowly into the air, assembling themselves into a headless, man-shaped form.

"This cannot be," Domeck gasped.

The motley suit of armor walked haltingly toward him, dripping emerald fire. In moments, dozens of pieces of armor forged themselves into two other metallic forms. All three converged on the castellan, glimmering green. Domeck was no coward. Once he had faced a dozen footmen alone and had not so much as trembled as he systematically hacked them down. Now, however, his knees shook, and cold arms seemed to clamp tightly around his chest. Yes, Domeck thought, this must be what fear feels like.

A chain rattled behind him. He turned just in time to see a mace fly off the wall. The castellan ducked to avoid the murderous spikes. A moment later an axe jumped off the wall, then a warhammer and an iron flail. Spinning like a drunken dancer, Domeck narrowly managed to dodge them all. He glanced over his shoulder. The glowing suits of armor were closing in. A heavy oaken shield flew through the air to strike him in the chest. He tumbled to the floor, gasping.

"What . . . what is happening?" he choked, struggling to his feet. Domeck had never fled a battle in his life, but now he fixed his eyes on the doorway, thinking he might yet be able to flee.

A buzzing like the sound of insects filled the air then. Domeck felt a hot stinging sensation in his leg and looked down to see an arrow embedded in his thigh. Jerking his head up, he watched as scores of arrows flung themselves from a shelf, streaking through the air toward him. One grazed a fiery trail across his cheek. He grunted in pain as another arrow bit into his shoulder. With a cry, he dived behind a tall wooden rack laden with sabers and spears. Arrows pinged brightly as they bounced off steel.

Gritting his teeth, Domeck pulled himself to his feet. The scent of blood filled his nostrils. The pain in his leg and shoulder cleared his mind. Anger burned away his fear. His battle instincts took control.

"Come on, you bastards," he snarled at the three shimmering suits of mail. "You want a fight? I'll give you a fight!" He snatched a wickedly curved saber from the rack and waved it before him. His lips pulled back from his teeth in a fierce grin. This was what it felt like to be alive! One of the hollow suits of armor reached toward him. The thing was clumsy, opening itself to a slashing attack. Domeck spun inside and swung his the saber fiercely, striking the thing's breastplate.

"Take that!" he shouted. His blow was strong enough to cleave a man in two. That was his mistake, for there was no body within the armor.

In a burst of molten green fire, the suit of armor exploded. The strength of the castellan's swing spun him wildly around. He stumbled, fought to catch himself, then careened backward, crashing into the rack of weapons. Domeck tumbled to the floor. The wooden rack teetered precariously above him. For a second he thought it would hold. Then, slowly, it tipped toward him. A score of glittering sabers plummeted downward. Insane laughter welled up in

Domeck's chest. Only yesterday he had given orders for all the weapons in the armory to be sharpened.

Laughter transformed into a short-lived scream as a dozen blades plunged deep into his body.

*   *   *   *   *

Wort watched in shock as something dropped from the darkness of the bell and onto the moldering straw. He hobbled toward the thing and picked it up. It was a leather glove, dark and sticky with blood.

Suddenly the bells above him began to ring deafeningly. They rocked wildly back and forth in a cacophony, guided by some invisible hand as they tolled the death of the castellan. All except the newest bell—the bell from the cathedral—which hung still and silent. Wort stared down at the bloody glove clutched in his gnarled hands. Then, low at first, but growing in strength, his own laughter rang out in time with the frenzied music of the bells.

 **SIX**

Mika gazed through the window of the ramshackle coach as it rattled down the earthen road. Outside, the somber landscape crept slowly by. Forested ridges, shadowed dells, dark-watered lakes—all seemed to brood under the leaden sky. From time to time Mika glimpsed a crumbling ruin that loomed forbiddingly upon a hill in the distance, like an ancient sentinel keeping watch over the land. She sighed deeply, trying to shake off a presentiment of gloom. Mika had guessed the country would be different from the bustle and splendor of the city. In truth she found the landscape magnificent. She had just not imagined it would be so vast and desolate.

Perhaps it was just as well. It was not as if she were journeying from Il Aluk on holiday. She had heard that there were few doctors in the provincial villages and had decided to travel to the hinterlands of Darkon to judge the opportunities for herself. The truth was, in Il Aluk she had found it harder and harder to forge a living as a doctor. In the city, men became doctors while women were permitted to become, at best, midwives. Most people held only scorn and mistrust for woman physicians. She could only hope that village folk would be too glad to have a doctor in their midst to bother with similar prejudices. Gazing now at the countryside, Mika could believe that in a dreary land such as this there would be many who would need her healing skills.

She bit her lip to keep from crying out as the coach jounced across a particularly deep rut. She glanced at the other two passengers who sat on the hard wooden seat across from her. One was a rotund man, a merchant of some sort with ample jowls and muttonchop sideburns, stuffed tightly into a food-stained waistcoat. His eyes were shut, but Mika knew he was only feigning sleep. Next to him was a younger man, too weak-chinned and pasty to be handsome, clad in the gaudy finery of a minor lord. For the past hour he had been fidgeting with an ornate snuffbox. His face bore a peculiar mix of apprehension and longing.

That morning, when the three passengers had climbed into the coach in front of the dismal road-side inn where Mika had spent the night, the merchant had gazed at the other two with wary eyes.

"I suppose you're in league with highwaymen," he had grumbled darkly at the young lord. He turned his mistrustful glare toward Mika. "Or you. There's always one."

Mika and the nobleman had only stared.

"Well, you'll not have my valuables," the merchant had growled. "Remember this—if one of you tries to pull a knife on me, I'll be ready."

Clutching a bulky leather satchel, the rotund man had climbed into the coach and had not uttered a word since. As they had followed the merchant into the rickety coach, the nobleman had thrown Mika a wan smile she supposed was meant to be conspiratorial and friendly. She had shivered, thinking she had also caught lust in his dull eyes.

Now she learned her instincts were right. With a furtive glance, the nobleman moved to her bench and sidled close to her, exuding an odor that was part sickly sweet perfume and part old sweat. He held up the silver snuffbox. The lid was decorated with a grotesque face—a woman with snakes for hair. "This was a gift from King Azalin himself," the nobleman pronounced pompously. "I am high in his favor, you know."

He tapped the snuffbox, and suddenly the face of the woman lifted its silver eyelids, revealing glittering ruby eyes. The snakes sprouting from her head writhed silently. The lid popped open of its own accord, and a tendril of glowing crimson smoke rose from the box. The nobleman hesitated. A look that might have been fear flickered across his pasty face. Hastily he held the box beneath his nose and inhaled, breathing in the glowing smoke. For a moment, a crimson gleam flickered in his eyes, but then it vanished, leaving his gaze even duller than before, sated. The fear was gone.

He held the snuffbox out toward her. "Care for some, my lady?"

Mika recoiled from it. "No thank you," she choked, eyeing the writhing silver snakes. She had heard King Azalin often presented his courtiers with enchanted gifts. She had also heard that these gifts exacted a dark toll on those who accepted them.

The nobleman shrugged. He greedily breathed more crimson smoke, then closed the box. The face shut its silver-lidded eyes once more. He jerked his head toward the merchant. "Come, let us enjoy each other's touch while the old man sleeps." His rouged lips parted in a lewd smile, revealing yellow teeth, as he reached out to caress her cheek.

A minute later the petty lord was regarding Mika from the opposite bench, an abhorrent expression on his features. "I think you've broken it," he whined pitifully, rubbing his hand.

"No, it is only a bruise, not a break," Mika replied crisply. "However, I would be happy to demonstrate the difference to you, if you'd like."

The nobleman's powdered face blanched even further. Nervously, he breathed more glowing smoke from the snuffbox. Then, taking a cue from the merchant, he pretended to fall asleep so as to retreat from conversation. Mika was not exactly devastated.

Turning away from her traveling companions, she gazed once more out the window. For a moment she caught a reflection of herself in the glass. She was a pretty woman. Her cheekbones were high and slender beneath eyes that were the pale purple of wild larkspur. Despite her beauty, there was a hardness about her—in the firm set of her jaw, in the dark severity of her simple woolen dress, and in the manner in which her thick golden hair was pulled tightly back from her forehead. Mika downplayed her prettiness. Skillful hands, not beauty, healed the sick. She had learned that lesson five years earlier when she had watched a man with kindly eyes and a girl with hair as golden as her own being laid in the cold earth. The Crimson Death had stolen into countless homes, rich and poor alike, in Il Aluk that winter. Why Geordin and Lia had succumbed and she had survived she would never know. They had left the world, and she lived on. That was all. It was cruel, and lonely, and true.

"I miss you, my loves," she whispered softly, reaching up to grip a gold locket that hung about her throat. If only she had been a doctor then. . . . But it was only after she had lost both husband and child that, ignoring the disapproval of others, she had entered the university in Il Aluk and began her studies to become a doctor. It was too late to save Geordin and Lia, but there were many others whom she might yet heal.

The wagon shuddered to a halt, jolting Mika out of her reverie. The coach's door opened, and the ruddy face of the coachman poked through.

"This is your stop, milady. The village of Nartok. The Black Boar is just to your left. You can find lodging there."

"Thank you," she murmured, climbing out of the coach.

Her traveling companions shot her looks of good riddance and hastily pulled the door shut. The coachman had already set her luggage on the muddy street—one modest satchel of personal items and the black leather bag that carried her doctor's tools. He climbed back up to the driver's bench and clucked to the four swaybacked horses. The coach rattled away, leaving her alone.

Mika picked up her bags and drew a deep breath. The village's half-timbered buildings might have looked quaint, except they were grimy with soot and sagged wearily along the sludge-filled open sewer that passed for a thoroughfare. Grim-faced villagers clad in dull gray clothes hurried by without giving her so much as a glance. Nearby, hanging before a dilapidated three-story building, she saw a peeling wooden sign that might have had a piglike shape if she squinted just right. She supposed that was the Black Boar.

"Well," Mika said briskly to herself. "Here I am."

With a sigh, she began picking her way through the muck toward the inn.

That evening, when she asked the proprietor of the Black Boar if she might set up her practice at the inn, he adamantly refused. "I'll not have a crowd of sick peasants filling up my common room and keeping away customers!" he snapped.

Glancing around, Mika imagined there was little chance of that. The dingy common room was empty save for a single old man who hunkered in a corner, nursing the same mug of watered-down ale he had been drinking for hours.

She regarded the innkeeper. Everything about the middle-aged man suggested a miserly nature, from his threadbare clothes to the emaciated frame on which they hung, as on a scarecrow. Mika decided to try a gambit. "As you wish," she said with a sigh. "It truly is a shame, though." She looked about longingly. "This is such an ideal place."

The innkeeper's eyes narrowed suspiciously. "How so?"

"Sometimes patients must wait to see me," Mika explained nonchalantly. "When they do, they often grow so very thirsty and hungry. It would have been nice if they could tarry at an inn, where they might purchase refreshments." She shook her head firmly, as if resigned to his answer. "But no, I'll bother you no more about it. I'll begin searching for—"

With sudden animation, the innkeeper interrupted her. "I'll not hear of it, milady! I've been terribly thoughtless. You *must* set up your practice here. I insist. You can use the private dining chamber behind the common room." He began leading her away by the elbow. "After all," he fawned, "it's for the good of the village."

She could almost see him counting the stacks of coins in his mind. "Of course," she murmured softly. "For the good of the village."

The next day, neatly lettered notices had appeared around the village, proclaiming that a traveling physician was now in residence at the Black Boar. While this announcement was remarkable enough, curiosity was heightened as rumors spread that this was no ordinary doctor but in fact *a lady from the city*. No one could imagine why such a lady would want to journey all the way to a provincial barony

like Nartok, stranger still, by herself. By midmorning
the common room of the Black Boar was crowded
with curious villagers, all hoping to steal a look this
most unusual character.

In the cramped dining chamber, Mika made certain all her things were in order. Her doctor's tools
lay neatly arranged on a white cloth. There was a tin
cone for listening to heartbeats, a small silver hammer for testing reflexes, and other mysterious
objects. She had scrubbed every surface in the room
as best she could, wiping away the dust and mold,
and she had polished the grime off the lone window
to let in as much daylight as possible. Taking a deep
breath, she smoothed her white apron and opened
the door. A sea of eyes filled the common room,
staring at her. A small gasp escaped her lips. She
had not expected so many to be waiting. She
reminded herself that this was just what she had
journeyed here for, then stepped forward, donning
her best smile.

"I'm glad you all could come," she began, wincing
at the faint trembling in her voice. She tried to ignore
it, and pressed forward. "My name is Mika. I am the
new doctor." Silence. She cleared her throat nervously. "Well then. Who . . . who is to be first?"

No one moved. The crowd continued to stare at
her, as if they expected her to suddenly transform
herself into a toad, or vanish in a puff of smoke.

"Come now," she said gently, realizing that most of
these people had probably never laid eyes on a doctor before. "Surely there must be someone who
needs my care today, someone with an aching joint,
or a fever, or the gout. Really, I don't bite."

The crowd parted as an ancient woman shuffled
forward. Her back was bent beneath her dark shawl,
and her skin looked as tough as leather. She led a
child by the hand, a thin girl of seven or eight winters

with golden hair and large blue eyes.

Mika sighed with relief. "What can I help you with today?"

" 'Tisn't me, milady," the old woman said in a cracked voice. " 'Tis my grandchild here. She's simple, she is. Her head isn't all there. Do you think you can help her, milady?"

Mika knelt to study the girl's face. The child continued to stare raptly. "Hello," Mika said. "What's your name?"

"Oh, she won't answer you," the old woman said sadly. "Kaila has never spoken a word in her life, I fear."

"Is that so?" A thought occurred to Mika. She stood and walked behind the girl, then clapped her hands together loudly. The old woman jumped, but the girl did not shift her intense, blank gaze. This was not the first time Mika had seen a situation such as this. She turned to the old woman.

"Your granddaughter isn't simple. She's deaf."

"Deaf?"

"That's right. I'm afraid she cannot hear."

"Is it a curse?" the old woman asked fearfully.

"Of course not," Mika said emphatically. She knelt again, placing her hands gently on the girl's shoulders. "You aren't stupid at all, are you Kaila? No, I imagine just the opposite."

Mika smiled warmly. Suddenly the girl smiled back, the expression lighting up her thin face. Carefully, Mika made a gesture with her hands, then motioned for Kaila to do likewise. The small girl hesitated. Then, slowly and deliberately, she copied Mika's gesture. Mika nodded reassuringly and formed the gesture again, then drew the child close in an embrace. For a second, she remembered what it had been like to hold her own golden-haired Lia.

"What was that you just taught her?" the old

woman asked, distrustful. "Was it a spell?" A murmur ran through the onlookers.

Mika shook her head fiercely as she stood. "Not at all. It's a way of talking with the hands. Some say the hand-speak was devised by alchemists long ago, so they could trade their secret formulae without fear of being overheard. All I know is that those who cannot hear have found the hand-speak to be a great boon. I just showed Kaila how to say 'hello.' Would you like it if I taught you some of the hand-speak?"

The old woman gasped in wonder. "You mean I . . . I could learn to talk to Kaila?"

"Yes. I'll need to learn a bit more first, but I have a book that will help. We can start tomorrow, if you'd like."

"Aye, indeed!" the old woman replied. "Thank you, milady!" She bent down to hug the girl. "My, Kaila. Finally I shall be able to tell you that I love you."

As the old woman and child made their way back through the crowd Mika could not help but beam. Maybe this wasn't such a terrible place after all. "Well," she said, holding out her arms. "Who's next?"

Villagers stumbled over each other in the rush to be next.

*   *   *   *   *

With feline grace, Jadis strolled into the Grand Hall of Nartok Keep. The airy hall was filled with minor lords and petty nobles, all bedecked in frills, jewels, and gaudy finery, tittering and whispering among themselves like a flock of colorful, vain, and mindless birds. The baron was holding court today. The courtiers were waiting in the hall, hoping to be summoned into the baron's private antechamber to present him with a self-serving petition or ask some

favor. A disarmingly absent smile coiled about
Jadis's smoke-ruby lips, concealing her disdain. She
despised them all. However, it was custom for a visit-
ing lady to attend court affairs. She had to keep up
her ruse.

Gasps rose from a group of courtiers clustered
around a performing harlequin. A garish red smile
was painted across the clown's blotchy white face.
The harlequin was some sort of illusionist, for a trio
of shimmering colored balls hovered above his outstretched hands. Suddenly each of the spheres of
light flashed brilliantly, and in their place three simi-
larly hued doves winged into the air before vanishing
in puffs of mist. The onlookers applauded enthusias-
tically as the harlequin capered about, bowing.

Jadis watched contemptuously. "Simple entertain-
ments for simple minds, love," she murmured softly
to herself. She gazed down at her long fingernails
and wondered what the courtiers would think if they
witnessed a *real* transformation. It was tempting. . . .

From their constant whispering and sideways
glances, she knew the nobles of Baron Caidin's court
considered her quite the enigma. As anywhere else,
here the baron's supercilious nobles were constantly
caught up in their petty intrigues and silly scheming,
each trying to rise to the top of their meaningless
pecking order. Now all were attempting to determine
where Jadis fit in. Should they scorn her as an infe-
rior attempting to gain stature at the expense of others? Or should they fawn at her feet to bolster their
own position?

Of course, the truth of Jadis's nature went far
beyond anything their little minds could possibly
dream up. If she were only to whisper the word *Kargat,* half the courtiers would faint dead away and the
others would soil their fancy garments. Not so Baron
Caidin. Without doubt, the baron knew that she

belonged to King Azalin's secret webwork of spies. It was she herself who had supplied the information to the baron's agent in Il Aluk. As a result, Caidin would imagine he had the upper hand in this game. And in his overconfidence he was bound to make mistakes.

While she had more instinct than evidence, Jadis was certain Caidin's plot to usurp the throne from King Azalin was somehow linked to his inquisition. Through seemingly innocent questions and eaves-dropped conversations, she had come to the conclu-sion that Caidin's inquisition was a complete fraud. Villagers were arrested, tortured, and executed hap-hazardly. No effort was made to uncover any ring-leaders or to determine the scope of any overarching plots. That left Jadis with an intriguing question. If there was no treachery in Nartok, why go to such effort to fabricate the illusion that there was?

And what of the tower on the moor? The court was filled with whispers about the strange spire—how it had appeared one night without warning, as if it had sprung from the soil like some dark mushroom. Surely it was no coincidence that the foundation of the mysterious tower had appeared mere days before Azalin learned of Caidin's intent to usurp the throne of Darkon. Yet what was the connection between the tower and the inquisition? Jadis did not know the answer to that question—yet. She made a mental note to herself. The tower was definitely worth investigating. First, however, it was time to pay a visit to some of Caidin's "guests" in the inqui-sition chamber below the keep. Who better to answer questions about the baron's false inquisition than the victims imprisoned by it?

Deciding she had spent enough time in the Grand Hall to maintain her front, Jadis departed, ignoring the whispers and surreptitious glances that trailed her. She made her way through winding corridors and down twisting staircases until she reached the dim archway that led to the keep's dungeon. As always, a pair of armed guards stood to either side. She chewed a lip delicately with pearl-white teeth. She hadn't quite decided what to do about the guards. No doubt they would find it odd for a lady to express an interest in touring the dungeon.

So as not to arouse suspicion, she strolled casually past the guarded archway, though not before letting her eyes linger over the guards. Neither was particularly handsome, but both had youth and muscular physiques in their favor.

"Now, now, love." She whispered an admonishment to herself. "Let's not mix business with pleasure."

She smiled seductively at the two young guards, savoring the crimson rising in their cheeks, then continued on. Slipping into an antechamber, she paused to consider her options. She could dispose of the guards simply enough, but that would be a messy solution and would no doubt alert Caidin to her activities. She tapped a cheek thoughtfully.

Then she espied it. High in one wall of the dusty antechamber was a hidden opening. She approached the wall, running a finger over its rough-hewn surface. These stones were darker than those of the chamber's other three walls, and seemingly much older. Like any fortress, Nartok Keep had been built in dozens of stages over several centuries. It was clear this had once been an outside wall. That meant the opening concealed an outdated ventilation shaft. In which case it almost certainly connected with the sewers below the keep—and the dungeon.

The opening was at least a dozen feet off the ground, but that posed no great problem. Making certain no one was around, Jadis shut the door of the antechamber. Slipping out of her silken gown, she hid the garment beneath a pile of rat-gnawed sacks. She shivered in her nakedness, but in moments she would be warm enough.

Jadis shut her eyes and tilted her head back. For a heartbeat she stood as still as a statue. Suddenly her coppery skin began to undulate. Dark fur sprang out on the back of her arms, her legs, her neck, and quickly spread to cover her entire body. As fluidly as if made of clay, her hands and feet lengthened and her limbs grew shorter. Her back stretched sinuously. A tail coiled out behind her, flicking and lashing like a black serpent. Gracefully, she crouched on all fours.

The woman Jadis was gone. In her place was a black werepanther.

Jadis extended her claws and bared canine teeth gleaming like white daggers. It felt good to don her cat form once more. As with so many things, she owed the Kargat for discovering that she had been born with the blood of a werepanther surging through her veins. She would never forget the day an older Kargat, a grizzled wereboar, had helped her undergo her first glorious transformation. She had instantly fallen in love with the grace and power of her panther form, a love that had only deepened over time.

With easy strength, Jadis sprang into the high opening. She padded swiftly down the shaft. The blackness was no barrier to her green-gold eyes. She found herself in a labyrinth of ventilation shafts, many sloping down at odd angles. Guided by her sensitive nose, she followed the scents of damp rot and fungus, traveling deeper below the keep. Finally she leapt from the mouth of a tunnel into a dingy corridor. Moans of agony drifted on the air, along with the rank stench of blood and fear. The dungeon.

Clinging to the shadows, she padded down the passageway. She came to a huge iron door set within a stone archway. The scent of fear was stronger here. Instinct told her that beyond the door lay the inquisition chamber.

Jadis froze at the metallic sound of a lock turning. Her black fur blended seamlessly with the shadows. She watched with werepanther eyes as the iron door swung open. Two men clad in the livery of the keep's guard stepped into the corridor carrying a stretcher. On the stretcher was a young woman, her face a shroud of agony. She was quite obviously dead. Behind the guards came a gaunt man clad in tight-fitting black. Jadis recognized him as the Lord Inquisitor Sirraun.

"Shackle her in the cell with the others," he ordered the two men. "We'll execute them all in three days' time."

The guards nodded, disappearing down the corridor with their grisly burden. Sirraun locked the door with an iron key, then vanished into the gloom. Jadis waited until the shuffling sound of his footsteps faded before padding from her hiding place. Interest glittered in her eyes. Why had Sirraun ordered a dead body shackled? Stranger still, why behead a corpse? Curious, she approached the door.

Sirraun had locked the portal, but sometimes a talon was better than any key. Jadis's body contorted once more, but this time the transformation stopped halfway. In the dimness she might almost have appeared a normal woman, at least from the waist up. But flickering torchlight illuminated traits that were far from human—black fur, pointed ears, and a sharp-toothed smile. She stretched out a finger, extending a gleaming talon toward the keyhole.

Jadis's flesh was not the only substance capable of transformation. Without warning, the stone arch that surrounded the iron door began to twist and flow, forming itself into the shape of a huge maw.

Fangs of rock formed beneath curling basalt lips.
The gigantic stone mouth trembled with a deep rumbling sound almost like laughter. With terrible speed
the fanged maw snapped shut. Jadis sprang back
barely in time to avoid getting chewed to ribbons.
Even so, a knife-sharp fang traced a hot line across
her leg as she tumbled to the floor. The huge stone
mouth opened and closed hungrily several times,
teeth gnashing. Hastily, Jadis scrambled away. As
she did, the stone mouth undulated, reshaping itself
into a mundane-seeming archway once more.

   With calculating eyes, Jadis regarded the portal.
The enchanted stone mouth was a formidable
defense. She was more interested than ever in what
lay beyond the door. It had to be important. Bending
her supple neck, she licked the wound on her leg
with a pink tongue. Her form flowed once more. The
lithe shape of a werepanther disappeared into the
darkness.

*   *   *   *   *

   From his cramped hiding place inside an empty
barrel, Pock peered through a knothole at what
appeared to be a black panther dropped from an
opening in the far wall to land silently on the stone
floor. Earlier, he had pursued the sultry Lady Jadis as
the baron had ordered. He had followed her into this
room only to find she had vanished. Hoping she might
return, he had hidden inside the barrel to wait. Soon
he had all but forgotten about his mission. Once the
barrel had been filled with wine, and its wood still
exuded an intoxicating aroma. Pock's purple head
was spinning. He speculated whether this was the first
time anyone had ever *smelled* himself drunk.

   The sight of the black panther quickly sobered his
dizzy little brain. Pock wondered how the large wild

cat had found its way into the fortress. More importantly, he wondered if panthers had a taste for gnome meat.

As he watched in trepidation, the black panther padded across the room. Suddenly the creature's body blurred, molding itself into a new shape. Pock blinked. When he opened his eyes again the black panther was gone. In its place was a beautiful, naked woman with coppery skin. The Lady Jadis.

"I *must* be drunk!" Pock murmured to himself, though rubbing his eyes did not make her disappear.

He watched as the lady retrieved her gown from beneath a pile of old sacks and hastily slipped it on. She moved softly to the door and was gone. Pock waited until he was certain the coast was clear, then tumbled out of the barrel.

"Pretty kitty," he mumbled lasciviously as he tottered toward the door. "I wonder if she would like to be my personal pet. . . ."

He swayed groggily on his feet, grinning foolishly, as he made his way through the keep. Something told him the baron was going to be very interested in this.

 **SEVEN**

"I tell you, it ain't right, Cray."

"I hear you, Rillam."

"Teaching deaf children to speak wizard-talk with their hands! It's *unnatural,* it is."

Two men stood in the mud outside the Black Boar, speaking in low voices. A few other villagers had gathered around them. All wore the drab, threadbare garb of farmers and workmen.

"What's more, she isn't afraid of sick people," Rillam went on in a disgusted voice. He was a burly man with a piggish nose. It was clear from their attentive posture that the others regarded him as a leader of sorts. "Why, she put her hands right on Arn the Beggar's clubfoot without so much as a shiver! Now, I ask you—why would a pretty young woman in her right mind even want to look at cripples and lepers, let alone touch them?" Rillam rubbed his stubbly chin, his beady eyes speculative. "You know what I think?"

Curious whispers ran around the huddled knot of villagers.

"I think that just maybe she's a—" Rillam paused dramatically "—a *witch.*"

Gasps ran around the circle. A dozen hands fluttered in the sign against the Evil Eye.

"A witch?" a young man said tremblingly.

"That's right," Rillam said with a nasty grin. "And you all know what we do with witches. . . ."

Murmurs of assent ran through the small throng.

*   *   *   *   *

There was no moon that night. A thick fog had rolled off the moor to shroud the sleeping village in soft folds of darkness. Nothing stirred on the empty streets. The stray dogs that roamed the village square by day had sought out abandoned basements and forgotten shacks in which to cringe, as if even mere animals knew enough not to wander about the barony of Nartok after the sun had set. The mist swirled. A hunched figure lurched awkwardly out of the inky mouth of an alleyway between two shabby buildings. The streets were not entirely empty after all.

Wort limped silently down the narrow village street. He clutched his black cloak tightly around himself, keeping to the murk and shadows. He felt a strange giddiness. As a child he had lived in terror of the monsters said to stalk the night. No more.

"Now *I* am the monster," Wort whispered gleefully.

The thought left him strangely elated. No longer did the fear he instilled in others cause him regret. Fear was power. He knew that now. It was a truth he had embraced when Castellan Domeck's bloodied glove had fallen from the magical bell. He wasn't certain where the dark realization had come from. Perhaps it was the voice that had been whispering to him of late—the voice he was beginning to think issued from the bell itself. It did not matter. Everything was crystal-clear to him now. The folk of Nartok had branded him a monster. Caidin had deemed him one. By acting as a monster he would gain his revenge against them all for the suffering they had inflicted on him.

He came to a run-down building on the edge of the

village. In contrast to the silent dwellings around it, this structure's grimy windows flickered with light, and coarse laughter drifted on the air. A weather-beaten sign hung above the peeling door. Wort could just make out the lettering in the cast-off light of the windows. The Wolf's Head Tavern, the sign proclaimed. Below these words, as if further explanation were somehow needed, was the crudely drawn head of a wolf, severed at the neck and dripping gore. Wort noted the sound of angry voices, followed by the clinking of pewter mugs and more laughter. Uncoiling his bent back, he craned his neck and peered through one of the glowing windows.

In the dingy room beyond, a half dozen men sat around a knife-scarred wooden table, drinking and gambling with dice. By their unbuttoned blue coats and the sword belts and sabers slung over the backs of their chairs, they were knights of the baron, but their drunken behavior was anything but knightly. A plump tavern maid sloshed ale into dented tankards. One of the knights snaked an arm around her waist. She slapped his hand and wriggled away, though not before treating the man to a fatuous smile.

"Where is he, my friends?" Wort whispered, as though the pigeons in the keep's bell tower could somehow hear him. "I heard him speaking down in the courtyard today, telling his companions he would come to this place tonight. But where—"

Another man stepped into view. Like the others, he wore the blue livery of a knight. He was a handsome man with long golden hair. Smiling lustily, he swept the barmaid into his arms. She shrieked but made only a perfunctory effort to free herself from his grasp.

"There he is," Wort breathed. Hatred glittered in his bulbous blue eyes. He recognized the knight as the one who had almost trampled him with his charger on the muddy road outside the village. The barmaid gazed rapturously at the handsome man, dull-witted adoration shining on her plump face.

"She thinks you magnificent now, Sir Knight," Wort seethed quietly. "But soon you will know what it is to be an object of loathing. Just like me."

Wort turned from the window and slunk toward a blocky shape behind the tavern. He pushed open a wooden door and slipped inside. The loamy scent of horses filled his nostrils. He rummaged in the pocket of his cloak and pulled out a small object. It was a metal cylinder fashioned in the shape of a candle. Wort's brow furrowed in concentration. Suddenly a flickering flame sprang into being on the tip of the cylinder. Golden light illuminated the interior of the stable. Wort had discovered the silver candle some years ago in the forgotten storeroom in the keep, along with the enchanted book and the tapestry of the angel. Quite by accident he had learned that if he held the candle and imagined it was lit, a flame would appear on its tip. No matter how long it burned, the flame would never go out until he imagined that the silver candle had been extinguished.

Wort lumbered past stalls of sleeping horses until he found a white charger chomping drowsily at its feedbag. This was the one—the horse that belonged to the golden-haired knight who had almost ridden him down. Wort unbuckled one of the beast's saddle-bags. He pulled another object from the pocket of his cloak. It was a leather glove, stained with blood. Wort stuffed the glove deep into the saddlebag. Yes—this was what the voice had told him he must do. He refastened the buckle. Sinking down on the hay, he rested for a moment. The steep trek down from the keep was tiring for his malformed legs.

"You don't mind if I share your stall for a minute or two, do you, my friend?" Wort asked the horse. The beast only continued its placid chewing. "No, I thought not." Wort's eyes fluttered shut as he leaned back against the wall. "You know, my friend, I warrant you'll soon have a new master. . . ."

Somewhere a rooster crowed. Wort's eyes drifted open. Dim gray light filtered through chinks in the stable's walls. Suddenly he sat up in cold dread. He must have fallen asleep! He leapt to his feet, then froze.

A man's voice chortled outside the stable. "Looks like your purse is lighter than it was yesterday, Logris, while mine seems strangely heavier. You never were lucky at dice."

"At least I'm lucky at love, Adaric," another man replied jovially. "That's a game your dice won't help you win."

Panic seized Wort. He recognized the second voice. It was the golden-haired knight! Quickly he searched for some means of escape. The stable door rattled as someone undid the latch. With growing dread, Wort realized there was no other way out. In desperation, he dived into a pile of hay and hastily tossed handfuls of dusty grass over himself.

Light flooded the stable. Trading more good-natured slurs, the two knights entered. Wort cringed inside the pile of hay, not daring to breathe. The knights seemed to move with maddening slowness. Finally they led their steeds outside. Wort heard the clattering of hooves fade away. He crawled out of the haystack, but his relief was quickly replaced by new apprehension. He still had to traverse the village and the steep road up to the keep—without the mantle of darkness—before he reached the safety of his bell tower.

"You are a fool, Wort," he grumbled to himself.

There was nothing else he could do. Swathing himself tightly in his voluminous cloak, he left the stable, hoping that this time the villagers would not see him for what he really was. He kept mostly to dank alleys. Though the crimson orb of the sun had risen above the horizon, the shadowed paths he tread seldom saw its rays. Wort picked his way through fetid heaps of garbage and gurgling rivulets of filthy water. Rats scurried back and forth across the way, chittering hungrily. Once, protruding from a pile of refuse, he saw a human hand. Swallowing hard, he hurried on.

The alley dead-ended.

Wort muttered a curse under his breath. Then a thought struck him. Looking up, he saw that the buildings here were roofed with tiles, not thatch. Using his powerful arms, he pulled himself up a rough stone wall to one of the rooftops. Used to high places, he moved more easily along the roof, stooping to stay low. He saw villagers trudging through the streets below, but their cheerless gazes were all bent toward the ground. None saw the hunchback creeping along the rooftops above. Ahead, Wort thought he caught a glimpse of another alley leading toward the village's edge. He kept moving.

That was when he saw her. Transfixed, Wort halted, peering down at a woman who walked below. Despite her dark dress and the severe knot into which she had bound her pale hair, she was beautiful. Though delicate, her face was curiously strong, like the visage of an exquisite porcelain doll. Most wonderful were her eyes. Even from above Wort noted that they were the rare, deep violet of a winter night. Impossibly, she somehow maintained an air of dignity and grace as she picked her way through the squelching muck of the street, carrying a black leather satchel.

"It's her," he murmured in wonder. "The angel."

A vision descended before his mind's eye, of the

time-darkened tapestry he had discovered in the ancient storeroom, and the radiant angel floating in the midnight garden, her violet eyes swollen with love. The angel of the tapestry was there before him—or at least a living woman so kindred that there could be little difference between the two. She had the same calm beauty, the same shining hair, the same deep violet eyes. Wort moved along the rooftops above, following her like a shadow in the sky.

"My angel," he whispered. "I've found my angel."

*   *   *   *   *

Mika struggled down the lane, valiantly trying to hold the hem of her dress out of the muck, all the while curling her toes in her shoes to keep the leather from being sucked off her feet as she made slow progress.

"Apparently they don't have stones enough in the provinces to cobble these streets," she murmured wryly to herself. "Though with all the rocks the coach ran over on the journey here, I would have thought they could have found a few."

She was on her way to visit a village woman who was due to give birth shortly, to make certain all was well. Since her arrival in the village of Nartok several days before, Mika had found herself almost constantly occupied with the stream of villagers that poured through the door of the Black Boar complaining of all manner of maladies. It was exactly what she had hoped for. At last she had come upon people who were grateful for her skills, not dismissive of them because she was a woman.

Mika rounded a corner. She stopped short to avoid running headlong into a villager, a man wearing a grubby brown farmer's tunic.

"Excuse me," she said breathlessly.

The man only regarded her with a flat stare. He did not move out of the way. Mika thought this curious, but she supposed she could just as easily go around him. She turned to do so.

This time a red-faced woman blocked her way. Mika's heart skipped a beat. "I'm sorry," she blurted out. Hastily she turned to her left, only to find a toothless man with rheumy eyes standing before her. Spinning around, she saw that a dozen villagers ringed her in all directions.

She swallowed hard. "Do you . . . do you need healing?" She held her chin high, trying to keep the trembling from her voice. "If so, please come to the Black Boar this afternoon. I'll be happy to attend to you there."

Steeling her will, she tried to set off down the street. She quickly came up against a wall of villagers who wouldn't budge.

"No, thank you, milady," a rough voice said behind her. "No one of us wants healing . . . leastwise, not from a witch."

Gasping, Mika turned around. A burly man with close-set eyes had pushed his way to the front of the small throng. He grinned, but not in any expression of humor.

"Please, let me be on my way," Mika said hoarsely.

The burly peasant shook his head regretfully. "But how can we let you go, milady, knowing that you'll just place more folk under your spells?"

"Spells?" she echoed in confusion.

"That's right, milady."

"Tell her about the ones we know she's enchanted, Rillam," the red-faced woman said accusingly. "Tell her about Clampsy Atwell and Darci Grayheather."

"Oh, I'm sure she knows about them well enough," the man called Rillam replied, looming over Mika. "I'm sure she knows that the night after she gave old

Clampsy a potion to fix his palsy, his wife found him outside on all fours, baying at the moon like a hound. And I'm certain she knows that since she cured Darci's fever, three times shepherds have caught Darci stealing into their flocks, cutting sheep with a knife and sucking out blood. 'Tis abominable, it is."

"Indeed?" Mika said sharply, suddenly angry. "And do you know what I find abominable? That a grown man has nothing better to do then frighten folk by telling children's stories." She turned to the others. "This is nonsense. You've seen what I do at the inn. I heal people. That is my business and that's all I do."

Rillam nodded grimly. "Aye, you do. But the price for healing folk is their souls, isn't it, witch?"

"No!" Mika said emphatically.

"Don't lie to us, witch!" Rillam snarled. "We know you're in league with the Powers of Darkness. Look at your eyes. They give it away!"

Mika's outrage began to turn to fear. "My . . . my eyes?"

"Aye," Rillam accused. "I've never seen anyone with purple eyes before. No one has. But a witch always has a mark that makes her different from other people. It's the curse of magic."

The knot of villagers tightened about her. Mika saw that some held lengths of rope, and others smoking torches. Murder glinted in their eyes.

"Please," she said weakly. "Please, you must believe me. . . ."

Rillam's dark gaze bore into her. The mirthless smile he wore broadened.

"Burn her," was all he said.

Mika screamed as the crowd closed in on her.

"Burn the witch," they chanted gleefully. "Burn her. *Burn the witch!*"

Suddenly the sun was blotted out as a hulking shadow leapt down from above to land in the midst of the crowd. The villagers cried out, scattering in fear.

"A daemon!" someone shouted. "The witch has summoned a daemon to protect her!"

"No," the figure swathed in black snarled, standing before the paralyzed doctor. "She did not summon me here." The daemon pointed an accusing finger at the crowd. "You did!"

The villagers screamed in terror.

* * * * *

Rage burned hotly in Wort's mind. How dare these wretches threaten an angel? *They* were the ones in league with Darkness, not she. The villagers backed away, all except a burly farmer who stood his ground.

"Begone from our village, daemon." The peasant's voice was bold, but Wort could see trepidation glittering in his eyes. "Find yourself another witch. We are going to burn this one."

"You are wrong," Wort hissed. "It is you who shall burn. All of you." He pulled the magical silver candle from his pocket and focused his fury upon it. This time it was no dancing flame that appeared on its tip, but a shaft of blazing fire. Blistering heat radiated from the column of flame. "Come to me!" he shouted, holding out his weirdly elongated arms in a mocking gesture of love. "I am yours, folk of Nartok. You created me. And all of you are *mine!* We shall burn in the Abyss together!"

With a chorus of shrieks, the villagers fled in all directions. The burly farmer hesitated just a moment. Wort lunged at him, waving the magical torch. The peasant let out a yelp and turned to dash after the others, soon outpacing them. Wort watched in satisfaction. It was just as the voice had hinted it would be. He had never known such strength before, such mastery of others. Fear was indeed power.

He put the blazing candle out and placed it back in his pocket. "I owe you my thanks," a voice spoke behind him.

Wort whirled around to find himself gazing into the face of the angelic woman. She was still pale from fright, but stood before him straight and calm.

"Why are you here?" he whispered in shock. "Why did you not flee with the others?"

The suggestion of a frown touched her smooth brow. "I owe you my life. They're the ones I would have fled. Not you."

"You would be wise to flee me," he snapped. Strangely, he found he was the one shaking with fear. He reached up and pushed back the hood of his cloak. "I am a monster."

He saw many feelings flicker through her violet eyes—surprise, interest, even pity—but fear was not among them. "Who told you that?" Her voice seemed almost angry.

"The villagers told me," he growled ferociously. "And they are right!"

"No," she said firmly. There was steel in her voice. "No, they are not. You are no monster."

The confidence his power over the villagers had given him now drained from Wort. He took a step backward.

"Do you not fear me?" he demanded.

She shook her head calmly. "I do not."

Alarm flooded Wort's chest. What was wrong with this woman? Could she not see what he was?

"Well you should!" he cried fiercely.

Before she could reply, he turned and bolted into the dark mouth of an alley. He heard her voice calling behind him, but he shut the words out of his mind. It was not for him to listen to the voice of an angel. He lumbered down the alley, leaving the village far behind.

*   *   *   *   *

Baron Caidin paced up and down the length of the Grand Hall, fury darkening his handsome face. Pock scurried behind his master, short legs pumping frantically to match speed with the baron's swift stride.

"What do you mean you found nothing that indicates the Lady Jadis murdered Castellan Domeck, Pock?" Caidin rumbled.

"Forgive me, Your Grace," the gnome sniveled. "I meant to say that I *didn't* find anything that *did* indicate the lady murdered the castellan."

Caidin came to a halt, whirling around to glare at his gnomish knave. "That's the same thing, you dolt."

Flailing his arms wildly to keep from careening into the baron's shins, Pock skidded to a stop. "Oh," he gulped. "Then I suppose I was right the first time."

"As usual, Pock," Caidin said acidly, "your stupidity utterly astounds me."

Pock doffed his feathered cap and bowed deeply. "Indeed. Sometimes I astound myself, Your Grace."

"I can only imagine," the baron replied dryly. He resumed his pacing as Pock trotted eagerly after him. Sunset's crimson light streamed through tall windows, spilling across a mural that dominated the far wall—an intricate painting depicting fat cherubs drifting on fleecy clouds. The scene might have been serene and idyllic, but the scarlet sunset lent a lurid cast to the painting. The cherubs seemed to leer. Their lush smiles were too knowing and sensual for their childlike faces, and the clouds they languished upon were tinged with crimson, as if stained by blood.

"What can she have forgotten to hide, Pock?" Caidin mused. "There must be something the Lady Jadis failed to consider, something that will show she murdered the castellan. If I had proof of her guilt I could simply execute her, and Azalin would not dare raise a hand against me."

Pock's purple face wrinkled in puzzlement. "There's one thing I don't understand, Your Grace."

"Really, Pock? Are you certain there's only one thing you don't understand?"

The gnome went on blithely. "How do you know it *was* the Lady Jadis who killed Castellan Domeck?"

Caidin threw his arms up in the air. Sometimes he didn't know why he wasted his breath. "She's Kargat, Pock. Of course she killed Domeck."

Pock shrugged. "If you say so. I just wonder why a Kargat spy would go to all the trouble of setting up a dozen sabers to do the trick." He pranced about foolishly, making catlike slashing motions.

Abruptly Caidin halted, frowning. "I hate to say this—believe me, I do—but you might be right, Pock."

The gnome beamed smugly.

"It doesn't make sense," Caidin went on. "If Jadis is a werecat, why wouldn't she simply—"

The ornate, gilded doors of the Grand Hall flew open, and the gaunt figure of the Lord Inquisitor drifted in, followed by two guards hauling a young man between them.

"Forgive the interruption, Your Grace," Sirraun said as he approached.

"I will if it's worth forgiving," Caidin replied darkly.

The lord inquisitor bowed solemnly, then gestured to the young man held by the guards. "This man is the squire of Sir Logris—one of your knights, Your Grace."

"And?" Caidin inquired in a bored tone.

"Show the baron what you found, squire," Sirraun commanded. The guards shoved the young man forward. He fell to his knees, terror and awe written plainly across his simple-minded face.

"Well, what is it, you dunce?" an annoyed Caidin demanded.

"I-I'm sorry, Your Grace," the squire stuttered. He fumbled with something in his pocket. "I-I found this when I was emptying my master's saddlebags this morning. It s-seemed a trifle strange to me, so I showed it to my captain, wh-who then brought me to Lord S-Sirraun. . . ."

The squire held the object out toward the baron. Caidin drew in a sharp breath. It was a bloodstained glove. He took the glove from the shaking squire and gazed thoughtfully at the intricate letter *D*, embroidered in gold thread.

"Take him away," Caidin said with a disdainful wave of his hand. The two guards grabbed the wide-eyed squire and dragged him from the hall.

"So," Caidin said after a long moment. "It seems there is treachery in my keep after all."

Pock clapped his hands together. "Oh, joy!" he cried, capering about ecstatically. "There's going to be an execution, isn't there, Your Grace? I simply *adore* executions!"

A sharp smile sliced across Sirraun's cadaverous face. "If you like them so much, my good gnome, perhaps I can arrange a personal execution for you."

"Really?" Pock gasped.

"Enough," Caidin warned. "Sirraun, I want you to bring Sir Logris to me."

The lord inquisitor gave him a speculative look. "Shall I first render him a little more . . . cooperative, Your Grace?"

"If you must, Sirraun," Caidin replied wearily. "But I want him alive when he gets here. And sane."

"Of course, Your Grace." Sirraun bowed obsequiously and drifted from the hall.

When the lord inquisitor was gone, Caidin clenched his hands into fists. "Here I have been waging a false inquisition simply to gain bodies, and all the time it seems that there truly are some who would dare plot against me. I swear, Pock, by all the blackest oaths, I despise traitors."

The gnome thought about this for a moment. Finally he patted the baron's hand reassuringly. "That's all right, Your Grace. I imagine they must despise you as well."

Nimbly, the gnome scrambled away before Caidin could wring his purple neck.

* * * * *

Wort peered through the iron grating high in the belfry. In the courtyard below, a cold, drizzling rain fell on a crowd gathered in front of the scaffold. Kneeling before the bloodstained block was a man with long golden hair.

"You must believe me!" the knight cried out. A slash of crimson paint marked his blue uniform—the sign of a condemned murderer. "I am innocent!" The half-moon blade rose slowly into the air above him.

A chorus of jeers and hisses came from the throng. All knew the charge. The bloody glove of the murdered castellan had been found in the knight's saddlebag. It was more than enough to prove his guilt. "Murderer!" they shouted as they hurled handfuls of mud at the knight. "Beast!" Tears streamed down his cheeks, mixing with the rain and dirt.

In the bell tower above, Wort whispered in satisfaction, "Now you know what it is like to be reviled, my good, handsome knight. Just like me." He turned and hurried to the ropes dangling from the rafters above.

A moment later he heard the sound of a blade cleaving bone and gristle before biting deep into wood. Wort pulled on the ropes. The bells rang out in their glorious voices, tolling a dirge for the newly dead man. Except for the one bell—which remained silent.

"Don't you worry, my friends," Wort whispered to the pigeons that fluttered all about. "I will ring it again soon enough."

Dark mirth bubbled out of him as the bells tolled their dire music.

PART II

The Angel
in the Darkness

 **EIGHT**

Rain.

It lashed against the pockmarked walls of Nartok Keep, beating down in its gradual, ceaseless, and inexorable drive to wear away the ancient stones. Again and again, livid green forks of lightning pierced the jet-black night sky. Thunder rumbled mournfully in the wake of the violent flashes, shaking the very bones of the fortress. It was as if the elements sought to tear down this vast construction men had raised in their arrogance. High on a wall, Wort edged his way along a narrow ledge fifty feet above the dark abyss of the courtyard. He pressed his body close to the wall, his fingers scrabbling against rain-slick stone in a vain effort to find handholds. His cloak clung to his skin, drenched and heavy with rain. Howling gusts of wind buffeted him as he inched along the precarious ledge. More than once the crumbling stone gave way beneath him, nearly sending him plummeting before he caught himself.

"Almost there, my friends," he whispered through clenched teeth. "Almost there."

At last Wort reached the glowing square of a window. An overhanging stone arch afforded some protection from the wrath of the storm. He huddled on the sill and peered through the window's diamond-shaped panes of beveled glass. Inside was a chamber bathed in warm candlelight, decorated in rose-pink silk and peacock-blue velvet. A lady's room. She sat at a gilded dressing table, gazing into a glass mirror. Even from behind, Wort could see that she was very beautiful. The lady wore only a gauzy night robe that left bare the creamy skin of her shoulders. With smooth strokes she drew an ivory-handled brush through thick, cinnamon-colored hair. After a moment the woman set down the brush and stood. As she did, he caught a glimpse of her fine-featured face in the mirror.

Wort rubbed his gnarled hands together gleefully. He had come to the right window. He knew the lady. Often of late, when gazing down from his belfry, he had seen her draped over the arm of Baron Caidin as the two strolled through the courtyard below. Her name was Sabrinda. The Contessa Sabrinda. All in the keep knew her to be Caidin's favorite lover, at least for the time being.

As it had with growing frequency, a dry voice whispered in his mind. *Excellent, Wort. This is just the one you need . . . one who is close to your loathsome brother.* A brief shudder of pleasure coursed through his body, then receded.

The contessa approached a mahogany wardrobe. She opened the wardrobe's doors and ran her hands sensually over the silken gowns within. She selected one of crimson and draped it over the back of a chair to be ready for the morning. Stretching her arms languorously, she gave a delicate yawn.

"That's it, my sweet," Wort hummed like a lullaby. "Go to sleep now. It is late."

The contessa climbed into a bed draped with sheer curtains, then snuffed out the candles on the nightstand. Darkness stole into the room on padded feet.

Wort crouched on the cold windowsill as the storm raged on, waiting for the contessa to fall asleep. It was midnight when he pushed gently against the window. It swung silently open. Wort crept inside accompanied by a gust of rain. Quickly he shut the window, then paused. After a moment he heard it— the soft sound of deep, even breathing. Navigating by chaotic flashes of lightning, he lumbered across the chamber toward the contessa's dressing table.

What to take? he wondered. He supposed it did not matter, as long as it *belonged* to her. Picking up the ivory brush, he pulled off several long strands of red-brown hair. He wound them into a small lock and tucked it carefully in a pocket. He turned to hobble back toward the open window.

Something stirred softly behind him.

"Caidin?" a voice asked dreamily.

Panic jabbed at Wort's brain. In dread, he turned around. Behind the gauzy curtains that covered the bed the contessa stretched sleepily.

"Caidin, my love—is that you?"

Almost without thinking, he spoke in a low, husky voice. "Yes, love." He winced, waiting for her to cry out in alarm. She did not.

"Come to me, Caidin," she whispered, eyes closed. "Touch me."

Slowly he reached out a hand. Through the sheer silk he stroked her shoulder gently with a gnarled finger.

"Mmm . . ." she murmured drowsily.

After a moment her breathing slowed as she descended into sleep once more. Wort shuddered in relief. A giddy thought crossed his mind. In the darkness we are no different, my brother! He turned to make his escape before she woke again.

He froze at the rattling of a doorknob. The chamber door was opening! There was no time to think.

Wort saw that the mahogany wardrobe was ajar. Hastily he plunged inside, concealing himself behind perfumed gowns. He watched through a hazy curtain of lace and brocade as a broad-shouldered man holding a single candle slipped into the chamber. Wort's lip curled back from his yellow teeth. Baron Caidin blew out the candle and pushed past the sheer curtains into the contessa's bed. Soon soft sounds of pleasure drifted across the room. Wort did not dare attempt to creep to the window. Caidin would surely hear his footsteps. He could only hope the baron would eventually leave after the contessa fell asleep once more. Wort leaned against the back of the wardrobe to wait.

The wooden panel behind him gave way. Wort barely stifled a cry as he rolled backward through the opening. Struggling to right himself, he felt rough stone all around him. He was in some sort of tunnel. Realization dawned on him. This must be one of the secret passages that, from his explorations, he knew riddled Nartok Keep, many long forgotten. He wondered if the contessa even knew of its existence. Probably not, he decided. Thick cobwebs hung across the entrance, suggesting no one had come this way in years. There was no telling where the secret passage led, but Wort decided he had to find out.

Carefully, he slid the wooden panel back into place, sealing himself in the secret passage. He stood up in the narrow space, drew the magical silver candle from his pocket, and concentrated his mental energy. A small flame flared to life on its tip, illuminating the rough-hewn tunnel. Gripping the candle, he moved swiftly down the passage. The tunnel led downward, twisting and doubling back on itself until Wort lost all sense of direction. The blackness seemed to press menacingly from all around. Perhaps he should go back. Better to risk discovery in the contessa's chamber than to lose himself in this endless labyrinth beneath the keep. Wort turned around—and froze.

Drifting toward him was a cloud of silvery mist. It glowed against the darkness, swirling and billowing like a miniature storm cloud. It floated closer. Wort backed away, but the cloud quickly closed the gap, as if with malevolent intelligence it sensed his readiness to bolt. Wort turned to run down the tunnel.

He was far too slow. With a rushing sound, the glowing cloud of mist engulfed him. Chill tingling pricked his skin as he was lifted into the air. Wort clamped his mouth shut, holding his breath to keep from breathing in the clammy mist. He kicked and clawed at the silvery vapor, but it was as if he moved through thick ooze. His struggling had no effect. Finally he could resist the burning of his lungs no longer. He took in a shuddering lungful of the glowing gas. Numbness descended over his body, paralyzing him. The cloud began to drift down the tunnel, carrying Wort with it. Beyond the gaseous veil he had the impression of stone walls slipping by, illuminated by the mist's eerie phosphorescence. Whatever this cloud was, it was taking him somewhere—somewhere far below the keep. For what purpose he dared not consider.

At last the cloud of mist halted. As quickly as it had engulfed Wort, it let him go, dissipating on the dark air. Sensation flooded back into his numb limbs just in time to let him feel pain when he crashed to the hard floor. The silver candle clattered to the stones also, its magical flame casting a small circle of golden light. Groaning, Wort pulled himself to his knees.

There were at least a dozen of them—shadowed forms standing just beyond reach of the candlelight. Wort could not make out who they were. Or what. He caught outlines that were manlike in shape, and others that were . . . something else.

"Look what your mist elemental caught, Ghurr," a slurred voice spoke.

"What do you think, Ghurr?" bubbled another. "Is he Clan Krillek or Clan Borrash?"

A growling voice spoke then. "Why don't we find out, Clan Ghurran?"

Wort cringed inside his cloak as one of the figures—the one called Ghurr—stepped into the circle of light. He was not entirely human. He had the torso of a powerful man, but also goatlike legs that ended in sharp talons instead of hooves. One of his arms was human, but the other was a glistening tentacle, covered with suction cups. Instead of a mouth, he had the recurved beak of a vulture. His crimson eyes glowed with evil intelligence.

Other creatures lurched into the circle of light. A legless elf woman with arms ending in crablike pincers slithered on a slime-covered pad like a gigantic slug. A green-skinned halfling with hissing snakes for arms peered with gigantic frog eyes. A man with hundreds of insect legs sprouting from his body wriggled on the floor like a huge centipede. There were dozens of the creatures. A few seemed strong and powerful like Ghurr. Most moved clumsily, as if in constant agony. Some were little more than shapeless heaps of quivering flesh. Ghurr uncoiled his sinuous tentacle-arm and jerked back the hood of Wort's cloak. Hisses and growls came from all around.

"This is no Broken One!" a creature shrieked.

"He is an Overling!" screeched another in revulsion.

The elf woman clicked her pincers. "We must kill him, Ghurr. You know the Overlings fear us. If he tells the other humans about us, they will seek us out and destroy us!"

"No!" Wort cried out, his bulging eyes almost as wide as the froglike orbs of the halfling. "I won't tell anyone about you. Don't you see? I know what it is liked to be loathed by others. I am a monster, too."

Ghurr's growling laughter echoed eerily. "You? A monster? No, Overling." With his tentacle he pointed to the centipede-man. "This is monstrous." He turned to the legless elf. "And this." His tentacle coiled sadly, almost lovingly around a bubbling pile of flesh. Wort could make out two eyeballs swimming in the shapeless mass, gazing up at Ghurr in adoration. "And especially this," Ghurr said with sorrow and rage. "Look carefully, Overling. These are real monsters. Any one of us would trade his body for yours in a moment."

Wort shook his head, gasping for words. "How . . . how . . . ?"

"How did we become this way?" Ghurr paced a slow circle around Wort, his talons scraping against the stone floor. "We are the Broken Ones. But we were not always like this. Once we were whole and beautiful—elves and dwarfs, humans and halflings. Then we were captured by the Nightmage."

"The Nightmage?" Wort gulped.

"Yes. Three centuries ago he dwelt in this keep, a wizard more powerful than any this land has ever seen. He forged many objects of power." He pointed to the glowing silver candle. "That is one of them. There are hundreds of such enchanted artifacts lost throughout the keep. The Nightmage conducted experiments as well—magical experiments involving living beings and animals." Ghurr gestured to the others and himself. "We are the failed results of those experiments. And I tell you, there were many more failures than successes. The Nightmage kept us alive to study us. Finally we rose up against him."

"I tore his throat out myself!" the elf woman said hatefully, her crab-claws snapping.

Ghurr went on. "We thought his death would

release us. We were wrong. The magic that transmuted our bodies kept us alive, as it does even now. We retreated beneath the keep, to dwell here in the darkness. But if the Overlings learned of our existence, they would not tolerate us." His cold tentacle brushed Wort's cheek. "So we must kill you."

Wort shook his head, stunned by Ghurr's dark tale. "Please," he gasped. "Please, I won't tell anyone. . . ."

Ghurr's eyes glowed murderously. "I know," he whispered. His tentacled arm coiled around Wort's throat and began to tighten. Wort's hands scrabbled uselessly against the slimy tentacle. Bright sparks flared in his brain as he fought vainly for breath. So this is how my life ends, he thought giddily, at the hands of another monster. The tentacle squeezed tighter.

Suddenly green light exploded from above. Ghurr jerked his head up as the other Broken Ones cried out. The tentacle slipped from Wort's neck. He slumped weakly to the floor, gasping. In the emerald incandescence he could see that they were in the center of a huge cavern. A score of misshapen forms lurched and shambled across the cave—more Broken Ones.

"It is Clan Krillek!" the elf woman shouted. "They are attacking!"

"Clan . . . Krillek?" Wort choked in confusion.

"Not all the Broken Ones follow me," Ghurr snarled. "Some serve Borr, and these ones follow Krill. They have come to try to steal our territory from us. But they will not find it so easily done." His eyes flashed hotly. "I will deal with you when we are done with the Krillek, Overling."

Ghurr pushed Wort aside and lunged toward the advancing Krillek. The rest of Clan Ghurran hobbled, slithered, and crawled after him. With shrieks of hatred, the two clans of monsters clashed. Ghurr's tentacle wrapped around a lizard-scaled woman and squeezed until his opponent snapped in two. Blood spurted in a gory fountain. The elf woman's pincers closed on a beetle-man's insectile arm and sliced it cleanly off. Yellow ichor oozed from the stump as the beetle-man waved it in agony. One of the Krilleks, a dwarf with a boar's head, skewered the centipede-man on his long tusks. Suddenly the dwarf screamed. The shapeless blob of flesh with the staring eyes had landed on the back of his neck. From the center of the blob, a tube like a mosquito's mouth plunged into the dwarf's skull and began to suck out his brains. And that was only the beginning.

Somehow, Wort managed to tear his gaze away from the grisly melee. Then he spotted something. Nearby was another opening in the wall of the cavern. He did not hesitate. Grabbing the silver candle, he lunged. Without stopping to see if any of the creatures pursued him, he raced down the narrow passage as fast as his bowed legs allowed. Snarls of rage and squeals of agony echoed after him. Leaving the Broken Ones to their bloody struggle for dominion of the underdark, he raced on.

*　*　*　*　*

It was morning when Wort finally stumbled out of a filthy storm drain into the courtyard of the keep. He breathed the cold air in relief. For a time he had feared he would never find his way out of the labyrinth below. Then the now-familiar voice began to whisper in his mind, telling him where to turn and which passages to take. He had encountered no more of the Broken Ones. Though they had meant to kill him, Wort found he almost pitied the creatures. He was like them. He dwelt alone, hiding his monstrous appearance. Soon, he vowed, he would never have to hide again. He moved stealthily toward the bell tower.

When Wort stepped into his high chamber, he instantly knew something was awry. Crouching warily, he gazed about the dingy room. Nothing seemed out of place. It was the pigeons that gave it away. They fluttered about in agitation, calling out querulously in their sweet, stupid voices.

"What is it, my friends?" he whispered, moving slowly into the room. "What has happened?"

He heard a squeak in the floorboards above. There was someone up in the belfry. *His* belfry!

Murder glinted in his bulbous eyes. How dare someone trespass upon his private demesne? Casting off his cloak, he sprang onto the wooden ladder and scrambled nimbly upward like a malformed ape. He burst through the trapdoor and crouched on the floor of the belfry, long arms before him, ready to grapple the intruder and snap his spine like a willow sapling. What he saw plunged a cold spike into his heart.

"I wouldn't touch that if I were you," he said grimly.

Before him, an expression of shock etched across her pale visage, the violet-eyed angel-woman froze, in the act of reaching for the rope that hung from the cursed bell.

"I-I'm sorry," she gasped, snatching her hand back. "I only wanted to hear the sound of the bell."

"Believe my words," he croaked, taking a step toward her. "You would not wish to hear the voice of that bell. Any other bell, perhaps. But not that one."

She nodded, unconsciously backing away from him. Wort noticed this with satisfaction. Perhaps she was afraid of him after all. As well she should be.

"Why have you come here?" he asked accusingly.

The woman visibly steeled her shoulders, lifting her chin high. "I wanted to speak to you after you frightened that mob away in the village, but I didn't know how to find you. Then I heard folk talking of someone who lived in the bell tower of Nartok Keep. They said it was a . . . "

"A monster," Wort finished for her. "That's what they said, isn't it? That in the bell tower there lived— a monster."

She nodded gravely. "Yes."

Wort lurched closer. "So you put two and two together and thought you would come to get another glimpse of this hideous creature, is that it?"

The woman retreated farther, only to find herself backed up against one of the belfry's arched windows. "No," she breathed.

"Then you came in search of some perverse thrill, yes?" Wort demanded sinisterly. "Or perhaps you came to examine the monster, to make a study of it. I've heard talk. They say that you're a doctor." He indicated his twisted body. "Perhaps you find my horrible form . . . fascinating."

Sudden fire replaced the alarm in her purple eyes. "No," she said fiercely. "That's not it at all. I came here . . ." deliberately, she took a step nearer him ". . . I came here to thank you." She reached out and touched his gnarled hand in a gesture of gratitude.

Wort snatched his hand back, clutching it as if it had been burned. Now he was the one retreating. "This is my tower," he snarled. "You have no business here. Get out!"

The woman sighed. "As you wish. I was wrong to have come here without invitation. Again, I only wanted to thank you." She moved to the trapdoor.

As she bent to descend the ladder, the dappled sunlight spilling through the belfry's windows alighted like glowing sparks upon her skin and hair. Once again, Wort was struck by her resemblance to the radiant angel in the long-forgotten tapestry—the angel whose night-deep violet eyes were so full of compassion he had once dared to believe they might hold enough even for him.

"Wait," he said hoarsely.

The woman looked up expectantly.

He frowned. Now that he had her attention, he did not know what to say. He swallowed hard. "Why . . . why bother to thank me? Why do you even care?"

Straightening, she fixed him with a direct expression. "I know what it is to be mocked, you know. I myself have been an object of laughter, and scorn, and now—as you yourself have witnessed—even of fear." She walked slowly to a window, gazing through the intricate wrought iron at the keep's soaring towers.

"People fear the unfamiliar," she went on. "I think it's because it makes them realize that the world is greater and far more complex than they could ever possibly understand. That makes them feel vulnerable, and terribly, terribly small." She turned around, a rueful smile touching her lips. "In the city of Il Aluk, they feared a woman bold enough to become a doctor. Here in Nartok it is a man who is . . . shaped differently than others."

Wort realized he was shivering. Was this woman in truth an angel? He ran a hand through disheveled hair and across a face marked by deep lines—lines that made him seem far older than the man of three-and-thirty years he was.

"Do you truly not fear me?" he whispered in amazement.

She returned his gaze unflinchingly. "No, I do not."

For a moment they gazed at each other in silence. At last the woman spoke with mock chagrin. "You know, I've utterly forgotten my manners. My name is Mika."

He swallowed hard before managing to find the words to reply. "I am . . . I am called Wort."

"Wort." She repeated the word. "I am glad I came here today, Wort."

Mika smiled warmly. Hesitantly, Wort returned the expression. It was more grimace than smile, but it did not seem to disturb her. Suddenly she reached out to touch the hump that contorted his shoulders into their unnatural shape.

"You know, I *am* a doctor," she said softly. "Perhaps I could help you."

The warmth drained from Wort's chest. "Help me?"

She nodded nervously. "I might be able to . . . operate on your back. To make you appear normal."

Fury blazed to life in his eyes. The happiness he had felt only a moment ago now seemed a cruel lifetime away. Mika took a step back and gasped.

"Ah, then you *do* find me hideous," he said ominously. "Of course, I should have known. You are a doctor. It is your compulsion to seek out the diseased. Is that not so?"

Mika shook her head, her jaw working soundlessly.

"Tell me, do you wish to perform some kind of dissection on me?" Wort went on coldly. "I've heard doctors favor such experiments. Perhaps you can make a fascinating study of my deformities, or perform operations on me that you have only dared to try on animals." His voice built to a roar. "Then your brilliance will win you accolades from your counterparts in the city, and you will be scorned no more, but heralded as a great scientist—as one who transformed a monster into a man! Is that it?"

"No, Wort," she whispered sorrowfully. "You're wrong. I only want to help."

"If you want to help, then you can leave me alone!" he thundered. "I do not need your pity, doctor. Nor do I need your healing ability. Go!"

Quickly she moved to the ladder, but before descending she turned to give him one last pointed look. "I will go because you have asked me to," she said quietly. "But know this, Wort. I do not go out of fear." She disappeared through the trapdoor.

Howling in rage, Wort slammed the trapdoor shut.

"She is no angel!" he shouted, clenching his hands into fists. "She thinks me a monster; she is no different from the others." Wort lumbered to the bell ropes. "Yes, I will be healed someday—someday soon—my way!"

He pulled something from the pocket of his tunic. It was the cinnamon-brown lock of the contessa's hair. He tied it about the rope of the cursed bell, then tugged fiercely. The vast tolling of the bell shook the stones around him. As Wort had witnessed once before, the dimness before him roiled like an angry sea. Three black-robed figures surfaced in the darkling air. They drifted smokelike above the floor. This time, however, Wort was not afraid.

"You have summoned us, bellringer." The three spirits spoke in echoing unison.

"There is your token." Wort pointed to the lock of hair. "Take it. Take it and fulfill your curse!"

The three spirits bowed solemnly. "It will be so." Like mist before a wind, the apparitions dissolved. The lock of hair faded with them. A voice whispered in Wort's mind. *There are no such things as angels. . . .*

* * * * *

The Contessa Sabrinda stretched languorously on the satin sheets of her bed, clad only in a diaphanous nightgown.

"Farewell, my love," she murmured.

Baron Caidin leered licentiously at her as he finished buckling on his sword belt. He leaned over her, and she felt his moist breath in her ear. "Farewell," he whispered.

Sabrinda closed her eyes, listening to her lover's

bootsteps retreating from the room. She drowsed for a time in contentment. Then she roused herself from her bed to make her preparations for the morrow. She opened her wardrobe and chose a gown of dove-gray silk with silver brocade, laying it carefully over the back of a velvet chair. She turned to sit at her gilded dressing table, rhythmically brushing her hair with her favorite ivory-handled hairbrush. She paused in midstroke.

"That's odd." Setting down her brush, she reached out to pick up a lock of hair on the dressing table— her own hair by its length and color—which had been braided into a ring. Her frown of puzzlement gave way to a wicked smile. "I suppose this is a token left by my lover," she mused. She slipped it onto a finger. Soon Caidin would be thusly wrapped around her finger as well. Then, one night she would whisper casually into his ear that he should grant a fiefdom to one of his knights—a Sir Beacham by name—and surely the baron would comply.

"Then I can stop pretending to love the loathsome man," she crooned to herself, "and you and I can be together forever, my beloved Beacham." Smiling at her own genius, she reached down to pick up the brush.

Sabrinda froze, staring at the mirror before her. In its reflection she saw the gray dress that she had laid out rise into the air, stretching its empty sleeves toward her. Gasping in horror, the contessa stood and whirled around. Fluttering, as if wafted by some unseen wind, the silk gown drifted toward her.

"Get away from me!" she shrieked, hurling the brush at the animated gown. The dress floated nearer. Its sleeves coiled smoothly around Sabrinda's neck. Screaming, she fought against the gown, feeling its delicate fabric ripping beneath her fingers. Stumbling backward, she fell against the dressing table. There was a sharp crash of breaking glass as she felt something hot slice across the back of her head. Rolling to the floor, she grunted like a trapped animal, clawing at the gown. In moments the dress was reduced to tatters of silk that twitched strangely upon the floor. Sabrinda reached up and touched her head. Her hand come away streaked with blood. She struggled dizzily to her feet, and whirled around. A new wave of fear washed through her.

"No. . . ."

She tried to cry out, but her throat constricted, choking her voice to a whisper. From the open wardrobe, gown after gown was drifting out. As if propelled by a cyclone, the gowns swirled around the contessa, inexorably closing in on her. This time she did scream, the sound ripping forcefully from her lungs, but it was muffled by a mouthful of cool silk. The dresses clung to her tightly, encircling her arms, her legs, her throat, pressing themselves against her face. She struggled frantically, rending material and tearing brocade with clawing hands, but to no avail— soon she became tangled in the writhing gowns. She tumbled to the floor. The dresses piled on top of her in a soft but excruciatingly heavy mound. Choking, she clawed at her face. She could not breathe. Her lungs burned.

Gradually, the contessa's struggling grew feeble. It was so dark, and so warm. Sabrinda's last thought was of her beloved Beacham, and how they were going to spend eternity together. Then everything went black as the gowns smothered her with their silken softness.

*   *   *   *   *

Wort looked up as a lock of cinnamon-colored hair fell from inside the cursed bell. Abruptly, swinging wildly of their own accord, the other bells began to ring out a deafening dirge. Wort scrambled across the moldering straw to snatch up the lock of hair. It was wet and sticky with blood.

"Yes," he whispered exultantly, letting the throbbing music of the bells swell his soul as he clutched the lock of hair. "I will be healed *my* way!"

 **NINE**

It was after midnight. Alys opened her eyes with a start to see the quicksilver light of the moon pouring through the window of her attic bedroom. The cottage was silent. She sat up in bed, wondering what it was that had woken her. In her hands she cradled a small box filled with letters and poems Robart had written her. She must have cried herself to sleep, after she had argued with her father once again.

"We are a respectable family, Alys," he had thundered. "I will suffer no more talk of traitors in this house! Do you understand?"

"Robart was no traitor!" she had cried defiantly. Ignoring his shouts, she had climbed to the attic and had flung herself on her bed, sobbing and hugging the box of letters.

Now she carefully set down the wooden box. As if drawn by some irresistible force, she padded to the window. The cottage stood on the edge of the village, facing the fields her father owned and tilled. Beyond the fields was the rippling sea of shadows that was the moor. In the distance, looming atop a rise far out on the heath, she could just make out the jagged stump of the mysterious half-finished tower. Shivering, Alys moved from the window and traded the gray homespun dress she yet wore for a nightgown. As she turned to climb back into her bed, her gaze once more roved outside the window.

"It cannot be!" she whispered.

She raised a hand to the open circle of her mouth. Then, without thinking, she threw open the window and climbed out. Quickly, as she had so often as a child, she scrambled down the ivy-covered trellis. Her nightgown flowing behind her like pale wings, she ran barefoot across the barren late-autumn fields.

There! Up ahead. She had not imagined it. Impossible hope flooding her chest, she ran after a tall, lanky figure who marched steadily toward the open moor. In the brilliant moonlight she had caught a familiar glimpse of red hair. She laughed for joy, not knowing how it could be possible, only that it was, must be.

"Robart!" she cried as she neared the figure of the man. "Oh, Robart, somehow it *is* you!"

Alys threw her arms wide as the young man turned to greet her. A frown creased her forehead. Did he not recognize her? He shambled forward listlessly.

"Robart, it's me!" she shouted. "Alys!" There was a strange, earthy scent on the air. "What's wrong? Are you hurt?"

As Robart neared her, moonlight stroked his face. Crumbs of moist dirt and bits of mold clung to his tattered clothes and bloated flesh. A dirt-caked wound, sewn together with crude stitches, ran all the way around his neck. One of his familiar green eyes stared at her blindly, but the other had fallen from its socket and dangled at the end of its nerve like a putrid grape. The stench of rot radiated from his body in choking waves. Shaking her head in mute terror, Alys tried to back away. Her legs wouldn't move. He reached his arms toward her.

"My love," he groaned in a slurred voice, as

writhing worms dropped from his mouth. Alys felt his spongy flesh press against her own as his arms closed about her in the hideous mockery of an embrace.

A scream of utter madness rent the chill night air. Then the moor was silent, save for the haunting calls of owls.

*   *   *   *   *

"Alys!"

The cries rang out across the rolling heath, drifting with the gray mist that swirled along the ground.

"Alys, where are you!"

A stout peasant man stumbled across the moor, calling hoarsely. His wife trudged after him, her broad face swollen from weeping.

"It is my fault, Marga," the man said despondently. "I drove her away."

"I won't listen to such foolishness, Hannis," she reproached him wearily. He seemed not to hear her.

Urgent shouts pierced the leaden fog. "They've found her!" Hannis exclaimed.

The two broke into a dead run. They burst through a bank of mist to find several villagers gathered around a pale heap slumped at the base of a skeletal tree. Only after a stunned moment did Hannis realize indeed it was his daughter. He knelt down.

"Alys?"

Gently, he reached out and lifted the young woman's chin. He heard Marga's stifled cry behind him. Alys stared with blank eyes, her skin as gray and clammy as the mist. Bits of moss and earth were tangled through her hair; her nightgown was filthy and tattered. After a moment Hannis realized she was muttering something under her breath, a weird, sing-song rhyme:

"Where is my love?
Far under the earth—
Crowned by the worms
The mold gives birth.

"Who is my love?
The scion of Death—
Whose kisses drown me
With sweet, cold breath."

"Why it's . . . it's a poem!" Marga choked.

"Alys!" Hannis said fiercely. He shook the young woman's shoulders in desperation. "Alys, wake up. *Please.*"

The young woman only rocked back and forth, clutching her knees to her chest as she stared blindly with mindless eyes. And hummed.

"Where is my love?
Far under the earth . . ."

*   *   *   *   *

In the dank shadows of the inquisition chamber, Sirraun gave the iron wheel one more turn for good measure. The peasant man strapped into the machinery of pain let out a high-pitched scream. Sirraun nodded in satisfaction. He had created this particular instrument of torture himself. It was a complex device, with myriad wheels and levers, designed to bend the limbs of the client into agonizing contortions. It was one of the lord inquisitor's idiosyncracies that he never referred to the prisoners on whom he tested his machines as *victims.* The word seemed to imply some sort of malicious intent on his part, when in truth he bore them none. Pain was simply his craft, and one in which he took great pride. Sirraun preferred to call his subjects *clients*. They in turn never called him anything. They simply screamed.

"Excellent," Sirraun said, running his bony fingers over the peasant's sweat-slickened brow. His "client" today was a young man with a broad chest and strong limbs. A perfect subject. The peasant moved his lips, but only a few feeble whimpers managed to issue from his mouth. "No, do not speak," Sirraun admonished gently. "Do not try to fight it. Just feel the pain."

The man stared in mute horror. Abruptly his eyes rolled into his head. Sirraun sighed. Now he would have to wait until the man regained consciousness to continue the fun. He made some minor adjustments to the apparatus, then strode out of the inquisition chamber. As he locked the iron door something caught his eye. Wedged in a crack in the stone archway of the door was a dark and glossy tuft of black fur. He pulled it out to examine it. Interest sparked in Sirraun's eyes.

"It looks as if someone has tried to visit my inquisition chamber unannounced," he murmured. "A perilous mistake."

Sirraun stroked the archway with a slender hand. For a moment the stones quivered, then were still. He had discovered the magical doorway by accident some years ago. Since then he had trained the ancient artifact to recognize his presence—his and no other's. Sirraun tucked the fur into the pocket of his close-fitting tunic, then headed swiftly down the corridor.

"Are you certain she didn't gain entrance to the inquisition chamber, Sirraun?" Caidin demanded a short while later. The baron paced the length of his richly appointed private chamber, regal in his perfectly tailored coat of blue and crimson.

Pock marched behind his master, his purple face screwed up in comic imitation of the baron's angry mien. The knave wore a coat to match the baron's, along with a ridiculously ruffled shirt. "Yes, Sirraun," Pock mimicked in his piping voice. "Are you certain?" The gnome stuck his purple tongue out at the lord inquisitor, popping it back into his mouth before the baron noticed.

Sirraun fixed the gnome with a sharp look. Not for the first time did it occur to him that it would be very interesting to test some of his inventions on a client the diminutive size of a gnome.

"I am quite certain, Your Grace," Sirraun answered. "Yet we must not underestimate the resources of the Kargat. It may be only a matter of time before Jadis finds a way past the obstacles that surround the inquisition chamber."

Caidin struck his palm with a fist. "Then create *new* obstacles, Sirraun."

"Yes, Sirraun—new obstacles," Pock proclaimed pompously. He struck his own palm, then shook his fingers frantically, hopping about in exaggerated pain.

"I want you to delay her investigation as long as possible," Caidin went on. "By the time the Lady Jadis learns my plans, I want it to be far too late for her to do anything to stop me."

An idea occurred to Sirraun. There was a fascinating experiment he had wanted to try for some time. Now might be the perfect chance. "There is something I could arrange, Your Grace. However, it would require several . . . bodies, immediately. Can you spare some 'traitors,' Your Grace?"

Caidin considered this. He had used the Soulstone to drain the life essences of dozens more prisoners these last days. The magical stone had greedily drunk in the souls of its victims, and now it was nearly full. Soon it would contain all the life energy he required to defeat Azalin. After a moment, he nodded. "Very well, Sirraun. Take what you need."

"Excellent, Your Grace."

"If you need bodies, Sirraun, why not use Contessa Sabrinda's?" Pock chirped helpfully. "I imagine it's still quite fresh."

Caidin's visage darkened. "Pock!"

Sirraun raised a speculative eyebrow. "Of what does the knave speak, Your Grace?"

Caidin gritted the words between clenched teeth. "The poor contessa was found dead in her chamber this morning."

"It seems she suffered a fatal loss of good fashion sense," Pock chortled wickedly, "when she tried to put on all her gowns at once." He puffed up his face foolishly, bugging out his big eyes as if he was smothering.

"That will do, Pock!" Caidin thundered.

"Thank you, Your Grace," the gnome replied with a sweeping bow, like an actor after a bravura performance.

"I am sorry for your loss, Your Grace," Sirraun said diplomatically.

Caidin shrugged noncommittally. "If you need her body for your plans, it's yours. It's of no use to me any more."

Sirraun nodded gravely, the gesture concealing a satisfied smile. For the experiment he intended to perform, the fresher the corpses the better. Something told the lord inquisitor this was going to be his greatest triumph yet.

"Thank you, Your Grace," he said with genuine sincerity.

*   *   *   *   *

In the courtyard of Nartok Keep, Caidin climbed into a waiting carriage. He had decided to make a tour of the village. It was never a good idea to wait too long between appearances below the tor. The peasants might lose their fear of him. He could not bear that.

"Mind if I come along, Your Grace?" a voice squeaked. Pock scrambled nimbly into the carriage. The gnome perched on the bench opposite the baron, his frilly attire making him look like a peculiar purple bird. "If you wish, you can abuse me in public to show everyone how ruthless you are."

"An excellent idea, Pock," Caidin mused with an evil smile. "You do have your uses."

The gnome grinned broadly. "I enjoy being used, Your Grace."

"I know, Pock. That's why I tolerate you."

The driver cracked his whip. The carriage rolled through the gates of the keep and careened wildly down the winding road. Rounding a sharp bend, it bore down on a group of peasants. They were clad in grimy rags, stooped under heavy bundles of firewood. With cries of alarm the peasants flung themselves out of the path of the hurtling craft. The horses did not even slow as the carriage rattled by. Caidin glanced back through the carriage's window and saw the peasants shouting and running after the vehicle.

"Animals," he spat in disgust.

Soon the conveyance rolled into the village, slowing so the baron could survey his domain.

"Everyone appears to be rather well fed, Pock." He stroked his oiled beard thoughtfully. "I must not be taxing them enough. Make a note to double their tithes at harvest time."

With a plumed pen, the gnome scribbled merrily on a piece of parchment. "Of course, Your Grace."

A sudden commotion erupted outside the carriage.

"Your Grace!" a haggard voice shouted. "Please, Your Grace!"

Caidin looked out the window and saw that one of the ragged peasants they had passed earlier now ran alongside the carriage. He was pointing frantically to the craft's wheels.

"What now?" Caidin muttered angrily. He pounded on the ceiling, signaling the driver to stop. Flinging open the door, he stepped out. A huddled mass of villagers scurried backward, cringing fearfully. Quaking, the peasant man stepped forward.

"Well, vermin, what is it?" Caidin snapped.

With a shaking hand, the peasant pointed at the wheels of the carriage. Caidin turned and saw that a gray mass of tattered rags was wound about one of the axles. Only after a moment did he realize it was a trampled human body.

"It . . . it is my son, Your Grace," the man choked.

Caidin clenched a fist. "Then I expect you to remove the sorry trash from my carriage!"

The man scrambled forward with several other peasants. A minute later he stumbled down the muddy street, weeping and bearing a limp gray bundle in his arms. Caidin watched with a bored expression, then turned to sweep through the village as peasants scurried out of his path. How like a flock of mindless sheep they all were. He sheared taxes from them like wool, and slaughtered them when he required their carcasses. If it were not for these benefits he would gladly raze the village to the ground, permanently removing the dismal eyesore that it was from the land.

An hour later Caidin's tour of the village was done. As he made his way back to the gilded carriage, he noticed numerous mute, terrified faces peering at him from dim windows and doorways. It appeared he had accomplished what he had come here for.

"Pock, assist me!" he barked, pointing to a deep mud puddle before the carriage's steps.

"Yes, Your Grace!" The gnome scurried forward and bent down to spread his crimson cloak gallantly over the puddle.

Ignoring the proffered cloak, Caidin gave Pock a rough push. Arms flailing wildly, the gnome plunged face-first into the foul-smelling muck. Using Pock's back as a stepping stone, the baron climbed with great dignity into the carriage. The driver cracked his whip above the ears of the horses, and the carriage lurched into motion. Pock sprang onto the craft's running board, clutching the door's handle to keep from falling and being crushed under the spinning wheels. He managed to boost himself up and inside. They were nearly to the edge of the village when Caidin banged a the roof of the carriage, signaling the driver to halt.

"Pock, who is that?" Caidin whispered intently, leaning to peer out the window of the carriage. A woman clad in a plain black dress walked down the street carrying a leather satchel. Even from a distance, the rare violet hue of her eyes was visible.

"Her name is Mika," Pock informed his master. "She arrived in the village some days ago. Folk say that she's a doctor."

"Is that so?" Caidin mused, a hungry expression on his face. "She is quite beautiful, this doctor."

Pock shrugged, apparently unimpressed. "I suppose so, if you like high cheekbones, full lips, and perfect skin."

Caidin shot him a black look.

"Er, which I'm assuming you do," the gnome added hastily.

As the two watched, the golden-haired woman disappeared through the doorway of the Black Boar. Caidin knocked again on the ceiling, and the carriage rocked once more into motion.

"Perhaps I should invite the good doctor up to the

keep for dinner tonight, Pock." Caidin's eyes glittered speculatively. "I really should give her a formal . . . welcome to my barony. After all, I wouldn't want her to think I have been neglecting my duties as a good neighbor."

The gnome let out a round of bubbling laughter. " 'Good neighbor?' That's a rich one, Your Grace!"

Caidin glowered dangerously. "I wasn't joking, you maggot."

Pock hastily shed his grin. "Er, I knew that."

* * * * *

Clad in an elaborate gown of lavender silk, Mika stepped into the Grand Hall of Nartok Keep. Everywhere she looked there was light, refracted by the myriad crystals of a dozen chandeliers. It shimmered off silver plates and spun glass goblets and gilded wood. The people who filled the room were even more brilliant than the furnishings. Silk and velvet of a hundred different shades glowed richly. Jewels glittered against bare throats, ears, and fingers. Ornamental swords and daggers gleamed as if they had been polished with diamonds.

"It's beautiful," she whispered softly.

"Do you truly think so?" a man's voice asked behind her.

She whirled in surprise, silk rustling, to find an unusually handsome man standing behind her. He was regally clad in a blue coat with silver buttons, gray breeches, and boots as black as his hair and neatly trimmed beard. Realizing this must be Baron Caidin, Mika hastily attempted a curtsey.

"Good evening, Your Grace," she murmured.

"My lady." His voice was rich and deep. "I am so glad you could come." He took Mika's hand, kissing it gently. The warmth of his lips against her skin sent a shiver up her spine. She snatched her hand back. It felt as if all eyes were on her.

"Pay no attention to them, my lady." The baron gestured subtly toward the nobles of his court who milled around the vast hall, casting surreptitious looks in Mika's direction. "I'm afraid that all of them find you utterly mysterious and fascinating."

"Oh?" There was a faint quaver in her voice. "I find that hard to imagine, Your Grace."

"It is your skill as a doctor, my lady. You see, they aren't accustomed to ladies—or gentlemen, for that matter—who make their way through the world by doing something useful. Being nobles, they aren't required to be of much use."

Mika found herself laughing. Perhaps this wouldn't be as difficult as she feared. Still, she could not imagine why the baron had thought to invite her to his keep. Perhaps it was simply that nobles took sick like everyone else, and thus he wished to make her acquaintance.

"If they think me interesting, then I'm certain they'll be sorely disappointed, Your Grace," she said ironically. "I'm afraid I'm one of the very dullest of people." Suddenly she remembered her manners. "I must thank you for the gown, Your Grace. It is . . . er . . . quite lovely."

In vain, she attempted to smooth down the silk gown, but the wide hoops beneath the skirt only sprang back, puffing the dress out to absurd dimensions. Mika had the distinct notion that she looked like an overstuffed chair. But the gown had come to the inn along with the baron's surprising invitation. It would have been an insult not to wear it for the occasion.

His eyes glittered. "It suits you well, my lady."

Her cheeks flushed, and for this she scolded herself silently. It was an idle compliment, Mika, and nothing more! "Thank you, Your Grace," she said aloud. "You know, you have a beautiful voice. It makes me think of horns."

His smile revealed uncommonly white teeth. "How nice of you to say so."

The courtiers were edging toward the long table that dominated the center of the hall. It was time for the feast to begin. The baron guided Mika to a place halfway down the table. Nodding his leave, he moved to take a seat at the head.

Mika felt distinctly out of place among the ranks of viscounts, duchesses, and other nobles. Before her was a dizzying array of gold forks, silver bowls of scented water, and curious utensils whose purpose she couldn't begin to fathom. Unsure what behavior court etiquette dictated, she surreptitiously observed the nobles around her, attempting to mimic their actions. More than a few disapproving frowns and mocking glances indicated she was less than successful.

A silver pitcher poured wine into the crystal goblet before her. She turned to thank the servant, then gaped in astonishment. No one was holding the pitcher. It hovered in midair above her glass, red wine streaming from its spout. The liquid filled the glass to the brim, then overflowed onto the table.

A nearby nobleman in a rancid-smelling wig glared at her. "You're supposed to tell it *when*," he said curtly as if she were a simpleton.

"When!" Mika said hastily.

Immediately the silver pitcher stopped pouring and floated to the next empty glass. None of the courtiers paid any attention. Apparently flying pitchers are commonplace here, Mika thought wryly. She allowed herself a nervous laugh as she sopped up spilled wine with her napkin.

"Would you be so kind as to pass the saltcellar?" a plump woman to her left asked.

Mika reached for an ivory saltcellar carved in the shape of a spider. It scurried nimbly beyond her grasp. She bit her tongue to keep from crying out in alarm. Given the flying pitcher, no doubt a walking saltcellar was to be expected. The ivory spider scuttled behind a bowl of plums. Forming a strategy, Mika picked up a fork in her left hand and carefully prodded behind the bowl. The ivory spider dashed from its hiding place, and she deftly snatched it up in her right hand. She passed the wriggling saltcellar to the waiting woman.

"Thank you, my dear."

"You're welcome," Mika said with a forced smile.

At the foot of the table, two servants set down a ponderous serving dish. They lifted the silver lid, and the woman to Mika's left clapped her plump hands.

"Roast partridges!" she exclaimed. "My favorite!" She picked up knife and fork expectantly.

Mika was wondering how the roasted birds were to be served when her question was answered for her. One of the steaming partridges leapt off the silver platter and began hobbling down the table on crisp legs covered with curly roasting papers. Its roasted compatriots followed behind. In moments a line of headless cooked partridges were marching jerkily down either side of the table and plopping themselves onto empty plates. One of the roasted birds scuttled onto Mika's dish. It twitched several times, then lay still. She stared at it, wondering if it would be polite to stab it a few times to make certain it was ready to eat. The nobles around her fell on the feast, meanwhile, tearing into the birds and gobbling meat, wiping greasy fingers on silk and velvet. Mika picked unenthusiastically at the partridge and the rest of the food placed before her. She found everything to be lavishly prepared, exquisite to behold, and utterly tasteless.

After a time her thoughts drifted to her encounter with Wort the day before. The man in the bell tower was a riddle to her. It had been brave of him, even noble, to protect her from the mob of villagers. Yet when she had hinted that she might be able to heal his back, he had grown so terribly defensive. Mika sighed. She was suddenly struck by the contrast between the opulence of the Grand Hall and the bleakness of Wort's tower home. It made her feel strangely guilty. Despite his rage yesterday—maybe even because of it—she wanted more than ever to help him. Nartok's mysterious bellringer seemed so lonely, and loneliness was something she understood. But did she dare visit his tower again? Mika almost wished she were there now. Wort's face might be homely, but the garishly rouged and powdered visages laughing all around her suddenly seemed far uglier.

Finally the magical feast was over. As the courtiers drifted from the hall, Baron Caidin bade Mika farewell.

"You see, Your Grace?" she said with a wavering smile. "I warned you that I was terribly dull."

"Indeed, my lady." He raised a single dark eyebrow. "And when will I have the pleasure of your tedious company again?"

Mika felt a pang of worry in her heart. The light in his eyes suddenly seemed so . . . feral.

"I'm not certain. . . ."

"But I am, my lady. Return to the keep tomorrow." He reached out and took her hand. "Say yes. . . ." He pressed his lips against her upturned palm.

A shiver ran up her arm. That was exactly the way Geordin used to kiss her hand. With a choking sound, she pulled away.

"Please, don't!" she gasped.

Caidin looked up in surprise. His face seemed now

more daemonic than handsome. He reached for her.

"No, don't come any closer." In panic she backed away, gripping the golden locket about her throat. "Don't you see? It's too soon. My husband is . . . ."

Caidin's emerald eyes bore into hers. "Your husband is what, my lady?"

Mika gaped at him. Her lips could not form the words. Pulling the lavender gown up above her ankles, she turned and fled the hall.

* * * * *

Caidin paced before the blazing fireplace in his private chamber, a glass of wine held loosely in his hand, his coat unbuttoned.

"I don't understand it, Pock," he said furiously. "Before she ran off, she looked at me as if I were some sort of monster. How could she possibly resist me? No one is as handsome as I."

"You'll never seduce the good doctor, Your Grace," the gnome snorted, lounging on his back before the roaring blaze. "She's still faithful to her dead husband, you know. You'd sooner melt a glacier with your kisses."

The baron grinned devilishly. "Oh, my kiss can melt things far greater than glaciers, Pock."

"Really, Your Grace?" the gnome piped. "You know, my toes *are* rather cold at the moment. . . ."

The baron ignored him. "I will light a fire in her such as she has never known. I will win her love, Pock. Or if nothing else . . . her lust." Tilting his head back, he drained the glass of wine, then ran a tongue across his crimson-stained lips. "I am not about to let a dead man best me."

 **TEN**

Jadis threw open the window's shutters. Cold air and honey-thick sunlight poured into her chamber, but like a dark rip in the fabric of the sky, an ominous blackness hung high above. Rapidly it grew, blotting out the light, until it alighted on the stone ledge, filling the arch of the window with its sooty presence. It was a raven. A jeweled medallion hung about its throat, indicating the great bird was a lord among its kind.

Jadis curtsied deeply before the onyx-feathered raven. "Welcome, messenger of Azalin."

The raven nodded its sleek head, eyes sparkling like bits of smoked glass. "Greetings, Velvet-Claw," it croaked.

"I did not expect you to return until tomorrow, Goreon," Jadis said. "As ever, your feathers are as dark and swift as the midnight gale."

In truth, she had known the bird would return that day. However, Azalin's ravens were proud and ancient creatures—some had served him for centuries. It did no harm to flatter them. Two days before, Goreon had arrived to take word of Jadis's progress back to the Wizard King. In her report, she had made an unusual request. Now she would learn if it had been granted.

"I bring a message from our undying master, Velvet-Claw," Goreon said in his grating voice. "And a token."

Jadis saw that the raven gripped something in one claw. She held out a hand, and the bird let the token fall into her palm. It was a tiny golden case, sealed with a circle of wax into which had been pressed the image of Azalin's personal intaglio—the Fiery Eye.

"That is the token," said the raven. "And the message is this: 'Open the box, and fear not the bite of stone, my Jadis.' "

A smile coiled sinuously about Jadis's lips. She clasped the golden box tightly. "Thank you, Goreon."

The bird cocked its head, staring at her with one unblinking eye. "Azalin favors you, Kargat. You know this?"

"Yes." Jadis's smile deepened. "I do."

A coarse sound emanated from the bird's throat. It might almost have been laughter. "You are bold, Velvet-Claw. I like that. Thus I will give you a warning. Remember, as in all our master touches, there is Death in his love."

A frown creased the dusky skin of Jadis's brow. "You're wrong, Goreon," she said coolly. "I have known his touch. As you can see, I am very much alive."

The raven ruffled its shadowy feathers. "Do not presume to know what I see." It stretched its onyx wings. "May Darkness preserve you, Velvet-Claw."

Jadis nodded in reply. Like the shadow of a cloud passing across the sun, the raven was gone. Light and air streamed once more through the window. Jadis ran the back of her hand thoughtfully under her chin. It was time to pay the inquisition chamber another visit.

Soon a werepanther padded through the eternal night of the dungeon, muscles rippling smoothly beneath a glossy black pelt. Often, as a child, Jadis had cursed her parents, though she remembered them only dimly. All she knew was that they had abandoned her, leaving her to scrape a wretched existence in the dangerous back alleys of Il Aluk with a gang of street urchins. It had been a grim existence—living in the filth of abandoned basements, searching for bits of rotting food in heaps of refuse, daring to pick pockets for the local thieves' guild even though getting caught would have meant losing a hand. Even the stray dogs had it better. At least their mangy coats kept them warm in the frigid depths of winter.

In all likelihood her parents had not truly abandoned her, but simply died of the Crimson Death, leaving her an orphan. All the lonely, bitter child knew was that her parents had left her alone in life, and for that she had despised them. Yet there were some wounds time did heal. Nowadays Jadis regarded her unknown parents with more gratitude. At least one of them had possessed the lycanthropic blood type that she had inherited—the blood lineage that made her a natural werecat and allowed her to reshape her body whenever she desired into her cherished panther form.

Jadis stalked silently down a murky passageway until she reached the iron door of the inquisition chamber. Her flesh began remolding itself into a new shape. Her dark pelt rippled fluidly as muscles writhed and twisted beneath her skin. Limbs lengthened, her tail shrank to a stump, and her face melted into that of a woman's, though it retained pointed ears and daggerlike teeth. In moments the transformation was complete. Still covered with glossy fur, Jadis stood upright on bent hind legs. Her powerfully muscled arms ended in human hands with retractable talons. This was her manther form—half-panther, half-woman. Aesthetically it was not her favorite, but sometimes it was useful to have fingers instead of paws, yet still possess the fangs of the cat.

Jadis lifted the small golden box that hung now from a fine chain about her neck. Inside the box was a counterspell Azalin had prepared for her to break the warding enchantment of the door. A sound stopped her as she approached the portal. At first it was faint—a wet, smacking noise, like that made by the village women when they beat their dull gray clothes on the dull gray rocks beside the dull gray river on wash day. But the noise grew louder, and the reek of rotten meat filled the air. Jadis's eyes narrowed in alarm as the source of the noise came into view. It seemed Sirraun had arranged a new obstacle for her to conquer.

Three forms shambled out of the corridor's gloom. The creatures that moved spasmodically toward Jadis were grotesque mockeries of the human form, like beings seen through the warped glass of a nightmare. Each had been formed of pieces hacked from many different corpses. The crude stitches that held the mismatched body parts together were plainly visible. These were flesh golems—creatures forged of dead bodies and animated by dark alchemy.

Jadis crouched, extending her claws, as the flesh golems drew near. One was shaped like a normal man except that his face bore no mouth. His body, however, was covered with mouths. They were everywhere, gaping open on his neck, his torso, his legs—even snapping hungrily at the ends of his arms. The mouths gnashed, moaned, and drooled green spittle.

Another golem lurched clumsily forward. Its body was forged of two human torsos fused together. The abomination walked on four legs, and instead of arms, three more legs were crudely sewn to each of its shoulders. The golem's multiple legs kicked violently in all directions.

Behind these two came the most hideous of the three—a madly staring human head supported by eight writhing arms attached to the stump of its neck. It scuttled along the floor like a huge spider, an impossibly long tongue hanging from its mouth. Jadis was neither coward nor weakling, but the sight and stench of the flesh golems sent waves of revulsion shooting through her.

The golems moved fast as they fell upon her. An arm ending in a slavering mouth snapped at Jadis's face. Snarling, she slashed with her claws. There was a wet, ripping sound, and the arm went spinning into the darkness. Whirling, Jadis barely dodged a series of powerful kicks from the flailing legs of the second golem. Abruptly a cry of pain and surprise escaped her lips. The spider-golem was grappling her leg while its head gnawed at her flesh. She grabbed the golem and ripped it from her leg to heave it at the wall. Head hit stone with a gurgling *thunk!* and slid to the floor. One of the thing's arms had ripped free and still held her in a clammy grip. With a sound of disgust Jadis shook her leg. The arm fell to the floor where it flopped wetly like a dying fish.

The spider-golem had gotten up and was scuttling toward her again. Jadis backed away as the three golems closed in on her. Her blows seemed to have little effect on them. Again she lashed out with her razor-sharp claws, tearing open the abdomen of the many-mouthed golem. Guts spilled out, and Jadis gagged. Even its writhing entrails ended in snapping, sharp-toothed mouths. Suddenly she realized she had made an error. She had backed away in the direction of the inquisition chamber's door. She glanced over her shoulder and saw the basalt archway rippling, molding itself into the giant fanged maw that guarded the door.

A desperate idea came to her. Jadis tensed her powerful legs and sprang upward in a high, arcing leap. She somersaulted over the golems and landed on her feet behind them. Jerking her head up, she was just in time to see the momentum of the three flesh golems carry them into the gigantic maw. The huge mouth closed, sinking jagged stone teeth into dead flesh. The stone maw chewed fiercely on its grisly repast. The golems writhed mindlessly as bones popped and flesh tore. In moments all that was left of the creatures were quivering gobbets of putrid meat. The stone mouth gave a satisfied belch.

"My, we were hungry, weren't we?" Jadis laughed, though with a slightly manic edge. Clutching the small golden box, she picked her way carefully through the slimy remains of the golems toward the giant maw. Its stone lips quivered around stalactite teeth, sensing the nearness of more flesh. Jadis broke the wax seal on the box. There was a small crimson flash, and the acrid scent of lightning drifted on the air. Unassisted by her touch, the tiny hinged lid opened. Inside she saw a small amount of silvery powder. Raising the box higher, Jadis blew. A cloud billowed forth to engulf the enchanted stone mouth. Each of the countless motes of dust flared brightly like a tiny star. Their brilliant radiance tore the darkness to shreds, then dimmed. Jadis blinked. When her vision cleared, she saw that the stone mouth had hardened and was frozen solid. It was animate no more. King Azalin's counterspell had worked.

"You are indeed a great magician, my king," she murmured in admiration.

Moments later, still in her manther form, Jadis prowled through the dank inquisition chamber. What she found puzzled her. She saw all the predictable paraphernalia for causing pain—shackles, stretching racks, iron maidens—and more than a few of the instruments of torture still bore pathetic victims. But there was nothing else, nothing that would require the room's defensive measures.

"Why go to so much trouble to keep me out of here?" Jadis wondered to herself. Was it simply a false trail to waste her time? If so, then Caidin was more clever than she had given him credit for. With a growl, she turned to leave the inquisition chamber.

Jadis halted. One of the prisoners—a man whose limbs had been distorted to grotesque dimensions in a nameless contraption of steel and leather—seemed to be staring at her. Fascinated, Jadis approached. At first she thought he must still be alive. As she drew near, she realized that this was not the case. Blood pooled darkly beneath his pallid skin, and she could smell the first hint of decay emanating from his flesh. Yet he gazed at her with a sort of supernatural awareness.

"You can *see* me, can't you?" she said softly, leaning over the man.

"Must go. . . . He says . . . I must go. . . ."

Jadis raised an eyebrow. Now this was interesting. Though hideous, the flesh golems had been unremarkable. Every other Vistana in the bazaar of Il Aluk knew the charm that made a dead chicken's heart twitch across a piece of cloth and trace in blood the name of an onlooker's true love. But this— a dead man who was somehow still sentient—this was astounding. She bent closer. She had barely been able to hear his croaking words. Of course, it was probably difficult to talk if you couldn't breathe.

"Where must you go?" she asked intently.

The man twitched, his eyes staring widely. Though conscious, he was clearly insane. No doubt his brain was beginning to rot like the rest of him.

"He says . . . go . . . go to . . ."

"Where?" Jadis hissed.

"Tower. . . . " The man's blue lips formed the word almost soundlessly. "Go to . . . the tower. . . ."

The cadaver's twitching turned into violent convulsions. Jadis backed away, thinking. What tower could the dead prisoner mean? Her eyes flashed. An image came to mind of the forbidding, half-finished tower that loomed west of the village—the tower whose mysterious presence no one could seem to explain.

Suddenly shadows seemed to swirl about her body, molding it into a new shape. The black werepanther padded swiftly out of the chamber, leaving the dungeon's prisoners to their mad dreams of death.

*   *   *   *   *

It was all too easy.

Wort slipped the bloodied lock of cinnamon-colored hair between the pages of the book. Carefully, he set the tome back down on the circular table littered with scrolls, quill pens, and inkpots. Turning, he hobbled across the cluttered chamber that belonged to Lord Inquisitor Sirraun and opened the window. Nimbly, he climbed through.

Outside, dead vines clung to the stone wall. Wort clambered onto the vines. Some distance below him the wall met the sheer edge of the tor. From there it was five hundred feet down to the jagged heap of talus at the base of the crag. Wort was not afraid. The voice had told him he would be safe, and he believed it. Craning his neck, he peered through the window.

A short time later the door opened, and a boy dressed in a brown robe entered. Wort had never seen the boy before, but he recognized him all the same. The lad was Sirraun's assistant—he worked copying books and missives for the lord inquisitor. Wort knew this because the voice had told him. The voice of the bell whispered in his mind more and more each day.

The boy sat at the table and picked up a pen. He dipped it in an inkpot, then opened a book to begin copying. When the young scribe turned the page, he paused. Setting down his pen, he picked up something from between the pages of his book. Frowning, he studied it for a moment. Suddenly his eyes widened. Clutching the object, the boy dashed from the room.

Wort chuckled softly. He climbed down the vines to an open drainpipe. A thin stream of dark water poured from the wide mouth of the pipe. Wort climbed inside and soon waded through foul, knee-deep water. Crimson-eyed rats chittered angrily at the invasion. Following the whispered instructions of a voice only he could hear, Wort made his way through the sewers toward his bell tower.

At dawn the next day, as the bloody light of the rising sun dripped down the dark walls of Nartok Keep, the bells rang out, tolling another execution. A head rolled from the chopping block and fell into a gore-stained basket, staring upward with a wide-eyed expression of surprise and terror. Until a moment ago, when the magical half-moon blade had flashed and descended, the head had belonged to the Lord Inquisitor Sirraun. Now it belonged to the crows.

All in the keep had heard the dark story. Sirraun's young scribe had discovered a bloody lock of hair belonging to Caidin's unfortunate lover, the Contessa Sabrinda, in the lord inquisitor's study. In his rage at this apparent betrayal, the baron had refused to hear Sirraun's protestations of innocence. Despite Sirraun's years of service, Caidin had ordered his lord inquisitor clapped in irons and taken to the dungeon to await dawn—and death. Both had arrived on schedule.

High in the spindly bell tower, Wort let the bell ropes slip through his fingers as the last throbbing strains of the dirge washed through him. Everything had happened just as the voice had said it would.

"This is what it feels like to have power, Lisenne," Wort said softly to the mist-gray pigeon that perched upon his humped shoulder. "I've only just realized that, my friend, but it is so." A chuckle rumbled deep in his chest as he hobbled toward one of the belfry's windows. "Look at them—look at them down there, scurrying about like so many rats. They think they hold their own destinies in their hands. They are fools to believe so. It is I who control their fates. It is I who have the power to shape their lives—and to take those lives away. All of them. Even my brother Caidin." His eyes fluttered shut, and he drew in a sensuous breath. "I like this feeling, Lisenne. I like it very much. . . ."

He took the pigeon from his shoulder and tossed it into the air. "Go, Lisenne, join your companions." The creature winged away to a roost high in the belfry. "I must decide who will be next." While the pigeons cooed in their gentle voices, Wort busied himself with grisly plans.

It was late in the afternoon when a faint voice echoed from far below. "Hello?"

Wort jerked his head up at the sound of the distant call.

"Are you there, Wort?" Someone was ascending.

"She has come back!" he muttered under his breath with fury. And once again with impossible wonder: "She has come back!" Swiftly, he half climbed, half leapt into his chamber below the belfry.

"I would not have taken you for a common thief,"

he snarled as the violet-eyed doctor stepped from the spiral stairwell into the dingy room. "Do you often break into people's homes?"

Boldly, she took a step forward. "I am sorry. I knocked on the door, but you did not answer."

"Why have you come?" he demanded.

"To apologize," she said simply.

Those were not the words he had expected. She took advantage of his mute surprise to continue in an earnest voice. "You were right, you know. When I said I might be able to straighten your back, I wasn't really thinking of what you might want. I was only thinking that I was a doctor, and here before me was an affliction I might be able to cure." She shook her head fiercely. "I was wrong. What in truth stood before me was not an affliction, but a man. By expecting you wished healing, I made the gravest of mistakes. I assumed that there was something wrong with you."

Wort regarded her silently. Then his lips parted in a leering smile. "A pretty speech, Doctor," he said in a harsh voice. "No doubt a wretched hunchback should quiver with joy at being so lucky to hear such sweet words." He advanced on her. "Well, I tell you this, Doctor. It is an affliction! A *true* affliction." Spittle flew from his lips. "You claim to understand me, because you know what it is like to be loathed." Wort shook a heavy fist. "You understand nothing, Doctor. You—who have the beauty and grace of an angel— you have the audacity to cry your false tears and tell me that you know what it is like to be scorned. I laugh at you. Do not think for one moment that you are in any way like me. Look at *me*, Doctor!" He beat his shoulder furiously, pounding the misshapen hump that weighed so heavily upon his stooped shoulders. "This is loathing. This is hatred. This— this is true suffering!" Wort's raving echoed off the cold walls, then fell into silence.

Mika's eyes burned with anger hot enough to match Wort's. No—it was far hotter, a bonfire to his pitiful, guttering torch. "How dare you." Her words were quiet, even. They cut him like a knife. "How dare you claim to have a monopoly on misery." She roughly wiped tears from her pale cheeks. "I tell you this, Wort—it might as well be misery that fills each well in this kingdom rather than water, for sometimes it seems there is no man, no woman, no child who does not drink deeply of sorrow every day. A mother dies in childbirth. Her husband drinks a cup. A farmer is trampled by horses. His family passes the cup around. A nobleman loses his foot to gout. Let his cup be of silver then, though the drink is just as bitter. Disease races like a swarm of rats through the streets of a city—let all its people go to the well again and again, pulling up bucket after bucket of misery until their shoulders ache with the labor. Then let them drink down every drop of sorrow to slake their parched throats.

"You think I don't know true misery? Then reconsider. I drank a full cup from the well when my daughter died of the Crimson Death. I drank a deeper cup when my husband followed her to the grave a month later. Consider every time someone has scorned me for daring to be a doctor another sip I have suffered, and two for every poor soul I have tried to heal and failed. Pour it all into a pool together, and I will give you a lake of grief you would drown in, Wort, and in whose dark depths your body would never be found!"

She fell silent, as if the words had gushed out of her like wine from a broken barrel, and now the barrel was empty. Wort could only stare at her. It felt like someone had plunged a knife in his gut and was even now twisting it with abandon.

Once more the doctor spoke, though this time her voice was quiet, measured, and terribly distant. "If you think your suffering so much grander than anyone else's, Wort, then I will leave you to savor it."

Lifting the hem of her dark dress out of the moldy straw, she turned to go. Wort's heart lurched in his chest. Words issued raggedly from his throat. He himself listened in dull amazement, as if someone else were speaking.

"Please—don't go!"

Mika froze. She regarded him solemnly. "Why?"

"Because. . . ." He licked his lips slowly. Why did he wish her to stay? Why was there such a deep aching in his heart, a feeling that, if she were to disappear into the shadows of the stairwell, he would howl with madness, or lie down on the cold floor and die? "Because," he gasped at last, "because I am lonely, Mika. I am so terribly, terribly lonely."

Slowly she lifted a hand, reaching toward him. "I know you are, Wort." Her voice was as sweet and quavering as a nightingale's. "I am, too."

Trembling, he stepped toward her and clasped her small hand.

*   *   *   *   *

Wort peered through the iron grating, watching the fiery eye of the sun sink toward the horizon. The moor stretched as far as he could see, beautiful in its desolation. West of the village loomed the nameless tower. It was taller now than before. Yet even its ominous presence could not dampen the exhilarated fluttering of his heart.

For an hour, in the dappled light and shadow of the belfry, he and Mika had spoken as the pigeons fluttered around them like pale spirits. They had talked of simple things. He had asked her to describe what life in the far-off city of Il Aluk was like. Then he had listened angrily while she described the way others had scorned her for studying medicine at the university in Il Aluk, and had cried silent tears when she spoke in halting words of the Crimson Death, and the tragic loss of her husband and daughter.

She in turn had asked him how he knew which ropes to pull to form the clarion harmonics of the bells, which he was excited to explain to another for the first time. All the while he had marveled that such a wondrous creature would deign to be so close to him.

Finally, Mika had risen to go. But as she did so, she had said something to Wort that even now echoed in his mind. Gently, he stroked the pigeon that sat upon his outstretched arm, preening its iridescent feathers. "Did you hear her, Armond?" Wort whispered to the bird. "She said my voice was beautiful."

Wort could not help but laugh at this. How strange to think that anything about him might somehow be beautiful. Wort shook his head as he stroked the pigeon's smooth feathers. In the shadows above him, the last rays of the sun fell upon the bell forged of bronze, silver, and blood. Its rope dangled down, swinging gently in the faint breath of air that blew through the windows, as if to beckon *Come, ring me. . . .*

ELEVEN

The dying man's screams echoed eerily down the corridors of Nartok Keep.

"This way, milady. Please—we must hurry. I don't . . . I don't think he can hold out much longer."

Mika strode swiftly after a rag-clad serving boy with tousled red hair. In a white-knuckled hand she gripped her satchel of doctor's tools. The screams grew louder, rising and falling.

"Can you tell me what is wrong with your uncle?" she asked the boy gravely.

He cast a white-faced look at her over his shoulder. "You'll see, milady."

Mika clutched the hem of her dark dress up above her ankles, breaking into a trot to keep up. A quarter of an hour before, the boy had burst into the Black Boar, explaining breathlessly that his uncle, a manservant at the keep, was ill. Mika had grabbed her black satchel and rushed outside to the carriage Baron Caidin had sent in which to take her up the tor. Whatever she thought of the baron, it seemed he took an admirable interest in his servants.

"In here, milady!"

The boy led the way through a squalid warren of servants' quarters to a dingy room. A cloying odor hung on the air, so thick it was almost palpable. On a rude cot, a gray-haired man writhed beneath a blanket, shivering despite the fire roaring in a stone fireplace only a few feet away. Several servants clustered around the cot, staring with frightened eyes.

Mika entered with an air of authority. "All right everyone, step back," she said briskly. "Somebody bring candles—I'll need more light." The servants scurried to obey her requests. "How long has the patient been like this?"

"Since he was bitten this morning, milady," a young maidservant replied nervously.

"Bitten?"

The red-haired boy nodded. "It was an insect, milady."

"I see." Mika approached the cot. The man gazed up at her, agony contorting his pallid face.

"Please," he gasped. "Please help me."

"Don't be afraid," Mika said reassuringly. "It will be all right. I promise."

She pulled down the threadbare blanket, then clamped a hand to her mouth to keep from gagging. The man's right arm was bloated to hideous proportions and covered with purple-black splotches. Even as she watched, the dark splotches inched their way onto his shoulder and chest. Mika steeled her will. This was not the first time she had faced a terrifying illness, nor would it be the last.

She began by making notes to herself about his condition. "The patient's right arm appears to be in an advanced stage of gangrene. Infection is spreading rapidly. Immediate amputation is the only—"

All at once, the manservant's arm dissolved into a puddle of thick slime. Letting out a bubbling cry, he arched his back, raising his body off the cot. Blood gushed from his mouth in a hot, dark fountain, splattering Mika's dress. He slumped back down, his eyes glazed with terror.

"Please . . ." His words gurgled wetly in his throat.
"I don't want to die. . . ."

Choking back fear, Mika turned to the others who
stared in horror. "What sort of insect stung him?" she
demanded.

"I . . . I don't know," the red-haired boy gulped.
"But . . . but uncle caught it after it bit him."

He picked up a jar and held it toward Mika. Inside a
pale beetle scrabbled at the glass. Dark blotches
marked its waxy carapace, suggesting a grinning
human skull. The beetle gnashed sharp mandibles, as
if trying to bite through the glass. Without hesitating,
Mika snatched the jar from the boy's hand and hurled it
into the roaring fireplace. Glass shattered. The beetle
scuttled over the hot coals, emitting a piercing shriek.
Abruptly it exploded in a puff of noxious green smoke.

"A skull beetle," Mika breathed in revulsion.

The young maidservant cried out. "Milady!"

Mika whirled around. The man on the cot con-
vulsed violently. As his arm did a moment earlier,
with a wet sound his body collapsed into a shapeless
mass of quivering yellow jelly. His face remained
whole only long enough for him to let out a scream
of pure agony. Then it too dissolved into thick fluid.
Unaffected by the beetle's venom, two staring eyeballs floated atop the putrid puddle of slime.

Mika barely fought back the urge to vomit. Many
of the others were not as successful. "Burn it," she
choked. "Burn everything. And whatever you do
don't . . . don't let any of it touch your skin."

She did not need to instruct the trembling servants
twice.

* * * * *

Later, Mika stepped tentatively into the glittering
Grand Hall of Nartok Keep. This time she was clad in

a gown of indigo velvet. Baron Caidin spun on a heel to gaze at her, his hand resting elegantly on the hilt of the ornamental saber at his side. Outside the tall windows, purple twilight was drifting down from the sky.

"Ah, yes," the baron said with a wolfish smile. "That gown is better, my lady. Wouldn't you say?"

"It is, Your Grace. Thank you for lending it to me." Her voice was almost a gasp. The dress's bead-encrusted bodice squeezed her chest cruelly, making it difficult to fill her lungs. The thick velvet weighed down on her. She had the distinct sensation that she was not wearing the gown, but rather was imprisoned in it.

"I am sorry about your patient," the baron said gravely. "But I am glad that I could see you before you left the keep. I would not have had you returning to the village without my personal thanks. Oh—I am afraid my servants had to burn your other dress."

Mika only nodded. No amount of cleaning would have removed the bloodstains from it.

"You can keep this gown, of course."

An uncomfortable silence descended between them. Mika fumbled for words. "It was kind of you to send a carriage for me, Your Grace. I imagine few lords take such an interest in the welfare of their servants."

Caidin dismissed this comment with a casual wave of his hand. "It was nothing. I suppose I consider them my children, that's all. Wouldn't any man do the same if his child was ill?"

Mika smiled fleetingly at his words, wondering if she had perhaps misjudged the baron. Once again she was struck by how handsome he was. The blue coat he wore was less formal than the one she had seen before. It fell open to reveal a white shirt and crimson sash. He seemed as radiant as the nameless gods who appeared in the mosaic beneath his boots, floating in clouds above the scene of an ancient battle—naked deities with fierce eyes and sensual lips glowing in pagan majesty.

"Wine?" He proffered a silver goblet.

She accepted it with a murmur of thanks, taking a sip. The wine was cool and rich, tasting of cherries, cloves, and smoke. She looked up at him in surprise. "It's delicious, Your Grace."

"For you, my lady, only the finest."

His words startled her. Once again she thought she saw a hungry light glittering in his green eyes. Yet that was an utterly foolish notion. Caidin was a baron. He could have his pick of dozens of beautiful ladies of high birth. What could he possibly see in a vagabond healer whose blood was common to the last drop? Nothing, Mika told herself firmly. No doubt she had made an utter fool of herself two nights ago with her hasty departure after the feast. Surely she had misjudged his intentions.

Her certainty wavered as his gaze glided over her body like a caress. Hastily she swallowed more of the wine. "Did I ever tell you about my *husband*, Your Grace?" she blurted.

A bemused look flickered across his visage. "I don't recall asking, my lady."

She nodded jerkily, taking a few steps back. "His name was Geordin, and he was a tailor. Our daughter's name was Katalia, but I just called her Lia. We lived in a small flat in Il Aluk, overlooking the Vuchar River." Despite her nervousness, she smiled at the memory. "Oh, it wasn't much. Certainly nothing so grand as all this." She gestured around her. "But I planted geraniums in the box outside the window, and I used to love to look out and watch the gulls whirl and dive over the water." She sighed deeply. "We were happy there."

He poured more wine into her goblet from a crystal decanter. "Why do you say *were*, Mika?"

Just three whispered words escaped her lips, yet they explained everything. "The Crimson Death." She gulped down more of the wine. Its sweet aroma permeated her head, dulling her remembered sadness.

"I am sorry," he said quietly. "But remember, Mika—time will one day heal your hurting."

"No," she choked. "No, I don't want this wound to heal. Because . . . because then . . ."

Strong hands gripped her shoulders, trying to still her shaking. She tried to pull away, but the baron would not let her.

"Because then it might mean you no longer love him?" Caidin finished for her. "Is that what you think?"

She nodded.

"Look at me, Mika." Reluctantly, she let his powerful hands turn her around. "I would never presume to take away the sorrow of your past. But won't you let me grant you some joy—now, here, tonight?"

She shook her head in confusion. She felt dizzy—the wine, of course. She should not have drunk so much. It was difficult to think.

"I . . . I don't . . ."

His hands squeezed her tightly. She could feel the warmth radiating from him. By her soul, he was a handsome man.

"Please, Mika."

Geordin! she cried silently. What am I to do? Yet it was another voice that seemed to speak the faint words that fell from her lips. "Perhaps, Your Grace. For just a short while . . ."

The baron's dark mustache curled in a smile. He lifted her off her feet, whirling her around. The silver cup slipped from her fingers and clattered to the floor. Dimly, she heard lilting music. Holding her around the waist, Caidin whisked her about in a whirling dance. It was like a delirious dream. Mika's senses were filled with the sweet strains of the music, the rustling of her velvet gown, and his body brushing against hers. It felt as if she were slipping beneath the surface of a lake, only the water was so wonderfully warm that she had to believe that drowning would be a pleasure.

A dull glint caught her eye. As they spun by, Mika saw that it was the silver goblet she had dropped on the floor. Red wine spilled from it, pooling like blood. Suddenly the wine evaporated, as if absorbed into the floor, and she glimpsed the images in the mosaic as they began to move.

Two shining armies marched toward each other across a green landscape. The serene, cruel-eyed gods floating in the clouds directed the creatures below like pieces on a gameboard. The mosaic armies clashed, swords gleaming. Chips of red-ochre stained the verdant landscape. The gory images shocked Mika to her senses. With all her strength, she pushed herself away from the baron, gasping for air.

Caidin watched her with a perplexed expression. "What is wrong, my lady?"

"Nothing, Your Grace. I . . . I only . . ." In desperation, she searched for something—anything— to say. "I only wanted to ask you something."

He took a step toward her. "If you require anything, my lady, you have only to request it."

"In the keep's bell tower, there's a hunchback." Trying to make it look as if she were not backing away, she edged to one of the tall windows. Her own ghostly image gazed back at her from the darkened glass.

"Yes?" the baron said impatiently.

"He rings the bells," Mika went on breathlessly. She had to talk fast. It was her only defense. "I was wondering if you might be able to help him some-

how, Your Grace. You see, he's all alone. And so very
sad." The baron's pale image loomed behind hers in
the window.

"You should not go to the bell tower, my lady," he
said gravely.

The word leapt from her lips. "Why?"

"The hunchback you speak of—he is very *dangerous*. He is a violent man, perhaps even mad. You put
yourself at peril just to go near him." She saw hatred
glitter in the eyes of his reflection.

"Are you certain?" Mika said, suddenly unsure of
herself. "He is . . . I mean, he *seemed* . . ."

"You must not go near the tower again, my lady."
His voice was stern, like a father speaking to a child.
"I implore you."

Mika only nodded dumbly. She had run out of
words. Disturbing thoughts coursed through her
mind. Could Wort truly be dangerous? He was so
sad, so pitiful, and almost dear in the way he
befriended the pigeons in the belfry. Yet, she knew he
was also capable of rage. She had witnessed it herself. Still, she could not believe that he would ever
harm her.

"Come, let us dance more," Caidin said, reaching
out to take her hand.

Quickly, she turned away. "I'm sorry, Your Grace,
but I must go. Please forgive me. I have patients to
see early on the morrow."

Without waiting for his reply, she picked up the
hem of her gown and rushed from the Grand Hall,
back to the village, and the inn, and the familiar
safety of loneliness.

* * * * *

As he often did when he was upset, Baron Caidin
decided to make goblyns.

Dark water dripped down stone walls. Against one wall of the dungeon chamber leaned an iron sarcophagus. Carved into its lid was the grotesque effigy of a man with a dog's head, lips pulled back from a wrinkled muzzle in a malevolent snarl. The sarcophagus was an intriguing artifact. Caidin had come upon it during his long search for the Soulstone. While not as powerful as the stone, it certainly had its uses. Clad in a robe of executioner's black, Caidin approached the coffin. Grunting, he threw back the heavy lid. Inside was empty darkness.

"Bring in the prisoner, Pock!" he commanded.

A peasant man clad in a ragged brown tunic stumbled through the doorway behind the Baron, hands and feet hobbled by iron chains. Pock followed, clad in a dark robe that was Caidin's in miniature. The little gnome wielded a curved dagger that was long enough to serve him as a sword.

"Move along!" Pock commanded, waving the sharp dagger at the peasant. The man lurched forward as quickly as he could to avoid the slashing blade. Displaying small, sharp teeth in a nasty grin, Pock skipped after him.

"Enough of your antics, Pock," Caidin barked. He turned on the peasant. "You—into the coffin."

"Please, my lord!" the man wailed fearfully. "I didn't do anything wrong!"

"So?" Caidin said disinterestedly.

When Pock jabbed his knife at the peasant, the man quickly scurried into the sarcophagus, huddling fearfully.

"What . . . what's going to happen to me?" he whispered.

"Oh, you'll see," Caidin replied with a mocking laugh.

He slammed the sarcophagus shut, sealing the man within. Crimson light glimmered to life in the eyes of the dog-headed effigy carved into the lid. There was a desperate scrabbling sound on the inside of the sarcophagus, followed by muffled moans of pain. The eyes flashed brightly, then went dark. Slowly, Caidin opened the lid.

The form that stumbled out wore the peasant's brown tunic, but it was not human. The creature's skin was dusky green; its limbs were twisted and knotted with muscle. The thing's bloated head seemed too large for its body, and most of it was taken up by a maw filled with needle-sharp teeth. The newly created monster's eyes glowed dull red.

The goblyn groveled at Caidin's boots. "Master!" it hissed fawningly. "How can I serve you?"

"Go find the others like you, vermin," Caidin crooned. "Soon, I will tell you all what you must do." Bobbing its bloated head, the goblyn scurried from the chamber.

Caidin allowed himself a low chuckle. It was always diverting to create goblyns, and the mindless creatures usually proved useful as well. Caidin had a particular purpose in mind for these latest creations. Now that he was without a lord inquisitor, he would have to devise imaginative ways to detain the Lady Jadis in her investigations.

The revelation of Sirraun's betrayal had disturbed Caidin more than he cared to admit. He had begun the false inquisition simply as a way to collect lives for the Soulstone. Now he wondered if perhaps he should conduct a true inquisition throughout his fiefdom. Twice now he had caught men whose loyalty he had not questioned murdering people in his court. Perhaps there was genuine treachery afoot in Nartok. What was more, the game of cat and mouse he was playing with the Kargat was beginning truly to annoy him.

"If only I could simply murder Jadis and be done

with it," Caidin whispered savagely. Though the thought was tempting, he knew he dared not try anything so overt.

Caidin worked late into the night, using the sarcophagus to transform a half dozen more fearful peasants into slavering goblyns. When that was done, he felt a little better, but not much. Pock could not help observing the baron's glum sigh.

"What's wrong, Your Grace?" Pock asked querulously. "Usually creating goblyns puts you in a cheerful mood."

"I don't understand it, Pock," Caidin grumbled. "How could Mika resist me a second time?"

No woman had ever scorned Caidin once, let alone twice. More humiliating yet, he had been forced to stoop to an elaborate ruse to lure her to the keep in the first place. It was he who had placed the skull beetle—a gift from the darkling—in the manservant's chamber. Goodwill had been the furthest thing from his mind when he sent the carriage to the village to fetch Mika. Despite all his efforts to seduce the healer, still she had resisted him. Even more disturbing, he had learned that she had somehow met and befriended Wort. If the Old Baron's secret was ever revealed and Wort's existence made known, Caidin would be ruined.

"I still don't see why you're so determined to seduce the good doctor, Your Grace." Pock threaded his arms through a pair of iron rings bolted to the wall. He hung lazily between them, small pointed shoes kicking. "You could have any noble lady in the keep—or nobleman, for that matter—without having to go to all the bother of corrupting them. They've already all been corrupted for you. Wouldn't that be far simpler?"

"You just answered your own question, Pock."

"I did?" Pock's bald purple head wrinkled in confusion. "I must be even smarter than I thought."

"You said it yourself, Pock. The 'good' doctor." Caidin stroked his smooth black beard. "That's exactly what Mika is—kind, ingenuous, and so very innocent. That makes her all the more tempting."

"What if she resists you again, Your Grace?"

"I won't allow her to. She *will* submit, Pock." Caidin clenched a fist. "In the end, no one can resist me."

"Actually, I can, Your Grace," the gnome chirped. "You see, I have a fondness for purple complexions, and your face is only purple when you're mad. Er, just like it is now." Pock swallowed hard. "Come to think of it, purple doesn't really suit you, Your Grace."

"Is that so?" Caidin growled dangerously.

"No offense intended, Your Grace!" Pock gulped.

"Oh, none taken, Pock." Caidin's voice was as hard and sharp as cut glass. "Believe me."

* * * * *

Thunder rolled ominously across the leaden sky as Jadis pushed through the rusting iron gate and stepped into the graveyard. Stinging nettles scratched at her ankles. Dry witchgrass rattled in the wind. Everywhere tombstones lurched at odd angles, some cracked and fallen over, others sunk deeply into the damp earth. Here the folk of Nartok buried their dead—and here they forgot them.

The gnome Caidin had sent to spy on her was proving to be a nuisance, but Jadis had managed to lead Pock astray with a false trail. No doubt the little cretin was even now huddled inside a festering heap of refuse as was his wont, keeping watch on the alley in the village where she had led him to believe she was to meet with a secret messenger. Meanwhile, she had things to investigate here.

In the dungeon, she had confirmed her suspicion that Caidin's inquisition was simply a false front. Whatever his ulterior motive, it had something to do with the prisoners in the inquisition chamber—prisoners who, though dead, somehow retained a supernatural sentience. She had come to the cemetery hoping for more clues.

Jadis continued on, moving with catlike grace even though she was in human form. She reached a place where the graves were fresh. Nearby were several empty ones, yawning like dark maws, waiting for their occupants. Jadis doubted they would have to wait for long. Clutching a dark shawl around her shoulders against the chill wind, she went from grave to grave examining them. Nothing seemed out of the ordinary, but she did get the sense that Nartok employed two different gravediggers—one much more conscientious about his job than the other. Some of the graves were covered with neat mounds of damp earth, while others looked to have been filled in with careless shovelfuls of loose dirt.

"Wait a moment, love," Jadis whispered. Quickly, she bent down to read the epitaphs scratched into the wooden markers. A thrill coursed through her.

"Now, isn't that interesting. . . ."

There was a curious distinction between the epitaphs of the two types of graves. All of the neatly packed graves belonged to people who had died recently of mundane causes—a man who was kicked by a horse, an old woman who had long been ill, a husband stabbed by a jealous wife. The denizens of the graves covered with the oddly churned earth all shared a common fate. Each had been found guilty of treachery by the inquisition and had been executed.

Jadis tapped a cheek thoughtfully. What if there weren't two gravediggers after all? What if the graves had been neatly filled at first, but those belonging to the victims of Caidin's inquisition had been subsequently unearthed? But why?

Jadis's green-gold eyes flashed. Perhaps it wasn't that somebody had dug up the graves. Perhaps the corpses themselves had risen from their resting places. After all, she had seen the way the dead man had twitched in the inquisition chamber.

The first cold, heavy drops of rain began to splatter against the dirt of the freshly dug graves. Jadis decided to return to the keep to contemplate what she had learned. Shivering, she turned to make her way back to the gate. Suddenly the earth gave way beneath her. She had stepped too close to an open grave! Jadis threw her arms out, flailing to keep her balance, but with a cry she fell into the dark pit.

Jadis landed hard, the wind rushing out of her in a grunt of pain. Dirt rained down from above. Struggling, she tried to gain her feet, but she had become tangled in her shawl and soft gray dress. More earth tumbled down on her. The walls of the pit were collapsing, burying her alive. Pawing savagely at the damp earth, Jadis managed to gain her footing. She tried to scramble up the wall of the pit, but something tugged at her ankle, holding her back. She looked down, sick fear washing through her. A pale, waxy hand was looped around her ankle, pulling her down. Her hands scrabbled uselessly against the crumbling earth. The wall gave way and she fell. She screamed, but dirt filled her mouth, muffling the sound.

Gradually, the falling earth dwindled, then stopped. Everything went still. After a frozen moment, Jadis realized that she could move. She sat up, the loose dirt running off her in rivulets. In dread, she looked at the cadaverous hand that gripped her ankle. After a shocked moment slightly manic laughter rippled through her.

"Now, that's not like you, love," she whispered, "to let your imagination get the better of you."

For it was not a hand that clutched her ankle, but simply a tree root sticking up from the bottom of the grave. Jadis extricated her ankle from the root. Then, carefully, she pulled herself out of the pit. Lightning tore a rent in the sky, releasing at last the violent fury of the storm. Breathing a relieved sigh, Jadis hurried from the cemetery, leaving the empty grave for someone who needed it more than she.

 # TWELVE

The peasant family huddled together in the cold before their rude cottage, staring in fear as the uniformed knights ransacked the meager hovel. Kraikus, lord of the exchequer of Nartok, watched with an air of gratification from the vantage of his steed. He was a small, ratlike man with darting eyes and a pointed nose that was prone to twitching, especially when loot was nearby.

"You, there!" Kraikus shouted to one of his officers. "Make certain you look to see if they've buried anything beneath the floor. I wouldn't put it past this refuse to try to hide their valuables."

A minute later the knight stepped out of the cottage. "You were right, my lord. I found this buried in a corner of the dirt floor." He held aloft a bowl of beaten bronze. It looked very old and was no doubt a treasure passed down from generation to generation.

"Throw it on the pile with the rest," Kraikus ordered in his wheedling voice. He eyed the heap of iron pans, clay pots, and cheap knives. It wasn't much, but altogether it should bring a silver penny in the market, perhaps two.

"It really isn't enough," the treasurer snapped, glaring at the cowering peasants. "However, in my graciousness I will consider this heap of garbage as payment of your taxes. At least for this year."

Untangling himself from the clutches of his wife and children, the peasant man stepped forward and bowed deeply before the treasurer. "Thank you, milord," he said fearfully. "You're very kind. And I swear to you—we won't ever try to hide anything from you again!"

"Oh, I know you won't, my good man." Kraikus's lips curled in an unsavory smile. "That's because you'll have nothing left to hide."

The peasant man's jaw dropped as Kraikus turned to his officers, issuing the command.

"Torch the place."

Several of the knights lit pitch-soaked torches and tossed them onto the dry thatch roof of the cottage. Kraikus looked on in satisfaction, crimson flames reflected in his dark eyes. Then he whirled his mount around, leaving behind the roar of the fire and wails of loss and anguish.

Midnight found Kraikus in the treasury of Nartok Keep, happily counting the revenues of the day's collection. Here, ten-foot-thick walls of stone guarded Nartok's hoard of gold, silver, and other treasure. Only two people in all the fiefdom had keys to the chamber's massive iron door—the lord of the exchequer and the baron himself. As was his custom, Kraikus had locked himself inside the treasury while he toiled. There was nothing that irritated him more than a distraction that caused him to lose count.

Muttering numbers under his breath, Kraikus piled coins into neat stacks on the counting table before him, pausing now and again to scratch a few ciphers on a sheaf of parchment with a quill pen. For a moment he halted, yawning deeply. Tax-collecting was wearisome work—what with the plundering and burning, and all those screaming peasants. However, he was determined not to sleep until he had counted the day's haul down to the last copper half penny. He scribbled some more ciphers and, noticing his inkwell was running low, opened the drawer where he kept his inkpots. A murmur of surprise escaped his lips.

"So that's where I put you," he exclaimed. In the center of the drawer was a large gold coin. The coin was obviously old, its engraved surface worn smooth. It was the first gold coin Kraikus had ever counted, which he had kept as a fond memento. Often he held it in one hand, stroking it with a thumb, when he was worried or deep in thought. A few days before he had been terribly distressed, believing he had lost the precious coin. Now here it was. Kraikus should have known. He was not one for misplacing money. Grinning to himself, he picked up the coin.

It hopped out of his grasp.

Kraikus let out a small cry. As if it had a life of its own, the coin jumped onto the desktop. It rolled a short way, then spun to a stop. Kraikus gaped at it a moment, then shook his head. What was he thinking? Coins couldn't roll of their own volition. He had dropped it, that was all. Once again, he reached for the coin.

This time, before he even had touched its smooth surface, the coin leapt upward. It hovered for a moment, flashing brightly as it spun in midair. Kraikus was entranced by its beauty. Suddenly the coin dropped to the floor and rolled toward a locked chest. As the coin approached, the lock sprang open and the lid lifted slowly upward. The gold coin hopped neatly inside. A heartbeat later a brilliant radiance began to emanate from within the chest. The silver-gold glow pulsated, slowly at first, then with increasing speed.

Drawn by the hypnotic light, Kraikus rose from his chair and walked slowly toward the chest. He knelt before it, peering inside. Cool light played across his ratlike face. Inside the chest, the gold coin lay atop a pile of copper pieces, glowing brilliantly. Even as he watched, the glow spread out to the surrounding coins and seemed to infuse them. Each shone brightly for a moment, then dimmed. Kraikus drew in a sharp breath. The copper coins had been transmuted to silver and gold!

Wondrous realization struck him. "I'll be rich," he whispered greedily. "Richer than Baron Caidin. Richer than King Azalin." His nose twitched fiercely. "I'll be surrounded by gold!" He reached into the chest to pick up his magical coin.

The lid slammed down with a violent *boom!*

Kraikus stumbled backward, then slowly lifted his right arm. The wrist was cut off in a ragged stump. The splintered ends of two bones gleamed white against torn flesh. Blood spurted out in arcs of liquid crimson. Kraikus stared numbly at the gory stump, too shocked to feel pain. He jerked his head up to see the lid of the chest open again, like a dark, hungry mouth. The chest rose into the air and floated toward him with sinister deliberation.

"No," Kraikus choked. "Stay away from me. . . ."

He lurched to his feet and stumbled backward, clutching the stump of his wrist. Blood pumped through his fingers. The chest drifted closer. It tilted forward. Something tumbled out, falling to the floor with a wet *plop!* It was his own hand, still clutching the glowing coin. Kraikus retreated. He was starting to feel the pain in his wrist now—sharp, exquisite, soul-tearing. His shriek rose to the high-vaulted ceiling.

"Get away!"

There was a creaking noise behind him. Madly,

Kraikus glanced over his shoulder to see another trunk behind him with its lid opening. The other chest was almost upon him. Kraikus fell back in revulsion, his heel slipping in the blood that slicked the stone floor. Flailing, he tumbled backward into the open trunk. The other chest tipped. A glittering shower of silver and gold cascaded down on the treasurer. It was raining coins. A burst of manic laughter escaped him.

"Surrounded by gold!" he shrieked.

Coins piled heavily on top of Kraikus, filling the trunk, crushing him with their terrible weight. A piercing pain spread throughout his body. He could feel his chest collapsing. Kraikus's last thought was of how cool all the coins felt against his skin, how wonderfully smooth. Then, along with the clinking of gold and silver, came the percussion of popping bones. The lid of the trunk slammed down, sealing Nartok's treasurer and all his precious coins inside.

* * * * *

In the moonlight that filtered into the belfry, Wort watched as a small object fell from the inside of the cursed bell. He greedily snatched the thing up from the moldy straw. It was a gold coin, sticky with blood.

The tower's bells swung wildly back and forth, tolling the death of Nartok's treasurer. Wort grinned in dark satisfaction. He bore no particular enmity toward Kraikus—that is, no more and no less than he bore toward all the folk of Nartok. It had simply been good fortune (or had it? he wondered, gazing up at the silent, cursed bell) that, while prowling about the keep, he had seen the coin fall from the treasurer's pocket. Sensing it would make a perfect token for the Bell of Doom, he had retrieved the coin.

Abruptly, the frenzied tolling stopped. Quiet mantled the bell tower once more.

"It has begun, my friends," Wort whispered excitedly to the pigeons that fluttered about him. "My final vengeance. But what now? What action do I take next?" He squatted down on the rotting straw to ponder his next move.

There was a harsh squawk, followed by a soft *thud!* Wort's head snapped up. He stared at the gray shape of the pigeon that had dropped to the floor in front of him. Its neck was bent at an unnatural angle, broken. A second pigeon fell beside the first, and a third. Both stared with dull, lifeless eyes, their necks violently wrenched. Wort looked up in shock. A dozen pigeons whirled slowly in the air above him, but not under the power of their own wings. Each was frozen, its beak gaping and silent. One by one the dead birds dropped to the floor.

"My friends . . ." Wort gasped in anguish.

He reached out toward the poor broken birds, then suddenly hesitated. The pigeons lay in a pattern. Their gray bodies and splayed wings formed the shapes of letters, spelling out a word: MORE.

"But how . . . ?" Wort did not need to finish his question. His gaze rose to the cursed bell. Suddenly his sorrow was replaced by exultation.

"Of course," he whispered excitedly, leaping to his feet. "It is a message. If I am to gain vengeance against Caidin, one token will not do." He gripped the blood-stained coin tightly. Gradually, a dark plan unfurled in his mind.

Wort scrambled down the ladder to his chamber below the belfry and opened the trunk next to his pallet. He drew out a small wooden box and set the bloody coin carefully inside. Then he returned the box to its place. Cackling to himself, he curled up on his musty pallet and went over things in his feverish mind. He was not certain which thoughts were his own and which were whispered by the dry, ancient voice. Nor did he care. At last he drifted into the dark waters of sleep.

Wort woke with the dawn and made his way downstairs to find, as he did on every third day, the basket of brown bread and jug of water that were left outside the door of his tower. Taking these back up to his chamber, he broke his fast, sharing some of the crumbs with the surviving pigeons that clustered around him.

"Do you think she will come today, my friends?" he asked the mist-gray birds. He was answered with a soft chorus. "Truly? Well, I hope that you're right. I find . . . I find that I am lonely when she is not here."

Wort closed his eyes for a moment, picturing the pale oval of the doctor's face, glowing like the angel who drifted in the ancient tapestry. Sometimes Wort did not see Mika for several days, and then, just when he had given up hope of her ever returning, he would once more hear the gentle rapping at the tower's door. Rushing down, he would find Mika waiting, and she would explain with grave eyes that she'd been detained by a bad outbreak of fever in the village, or that she had just had to attend to a village woman going through a long, difficult birth.

Happily, there were also times when Mika managed to come several days in a row. Often she brought things with her—flowers to brighten his dismal chamber, or honey cakes, or a gameboard with carved wooden pieces to play Castles and Kings. Wort had never played the game before, but Mika seemed to draw upon an endless reservoir of patience as she explained the complex rules to him.

It was midday this time when he heard a faint rapping echoing up from below.

"She's here!" Wort exclaimed, jumping to his feet.

In vain, he tried to smooth down his matted brown hair and brush bits of straw from his threadbare brown tunic. He flung open the trapdoor in the center of the floor, threw down the length of rope coiled next to the opening, and clambered down to the bottom of the bell tower. In one swift motion, he sprang from the rope and opened the door.

Mika gasped in surprise, holding a hand to her breast. Then she laughed. "I'm happy to see you, too, Wort." She was clad in a dress of thick gray wool. She had thrown a heavy sky blue cloak over her shoulders against the autumn chill. She carried a straw basket in her arms.

"Please, come in, doctor," Wort said, attempting a clumsy bow. His grin was a trifle mischievous. "I've been practicing my opening gambits in Castles and Kings. I think you might not find me so easy to beat today!"

Mika arched a single eyebrow. "Is that so? Well, I'm afraid you'll have to wait until another day to embarrass me. Today we're going on a picnic in the woods."

Wort stared at her. He had never been on a picnic before. In fact, he had no idea what a picnic involved, but he grinned at Mika all the same.

"I'll need my cloak," he said gruffly. He hobbled quickly upstairs to the belfry and grabbed the garment, but as he turned to head back down, he paused. The cursed bell brooded darkly among the rafters. A strong feeling of . . . *disapproval* seemed to radiate from it.

"Why shouldn't I go?" Wort whispered angrily. "What's the harm in it?"

The dry voice echoed in his mind. *Monsters do not walk with angels.*

"I don't have to listen to you," he snarled. "You are not my master!" The voice repeated its message, but

Wort clamped his hands to his ears and dashed back down the stairs.

"What's wrong, Wort?" Mika asked, concern clouding her violet eyes. "Were you arguing with someone up there?"

He shook his head. "No," he said hoarsely. "Let's go."

That afternoon found them walking together through a grove not far from the keep. The trees were bare with the lateness of the year, and the ground was a crisp, crackling carpet of russet, crimson, and dark sienna.

"This looks like a good spot for lunch," said Mika when they reached the mossy bank of a brook. The jagged stump of a dead tree stood beside the brook. Only a few dark, twisted branches still clung to the gnarled, moss-covered trunk. "What an interesting old tree. I bet once it was the tallest tree in the forest." She started to set down the straw basket.

Wort shook his head, suddenly feeling uneasy. "No, not here," he whispered. "This is a sad place. Can we go somewhere else?"

Mika regarded him with serious eyes. "Of course, Wort."

They wound up in the center of a small glade. Mika pulled bread, cheese, dried fruit, and a clay jug of wine from the basket. As they ate, Wort was once again amazed that one so fair as she would deign to be friends with one as monstrous as himself. It was like a miracle. Of course, weren't angels accustomed to performing miracles?

After they had eaten, Mika coaxed chattering gray squirrels into plucking raisins from her hand. Then she made Wort give it a try. His big, clumsy hand shaking, he held out a palm full of dried fruit. A squirrel approached tentatively through rustling leaves. The creature regarded Wort with bright eyes, then scurried forward to snatch a raisin from his hand before hopping away.

"It . . . it didn't fear me!" Wort said in amazement.

"Why should it, Wort?" Mika asked, puzzled.

Wort almost spoke the words. *Because I have killed, Doctor.* He shook his head and said nothing.

For a time, Mika took her basket and collected herbs useful for her healing craft while Wort explored among the trees. In a small hollow he was surprised to discover a flower blooming despite the lateness of the season. He did not know its name, but its petals were the same dusky lavender as Mika's eyes. Thinking it would give her joy, he reached down to pluck the bloom. Then he cried out in sudden pain.

Mika rushed toward him. "Wort, what is it?"

Shaking his hand, he dropped the flower. He could see a long thorn protruding from its stem, wet with blood. "The flower. It . . . it pricked me."

"Here, let me see."

Gently, Mika took his hand and turned it over. Blood welled up freely from a deep puncture. She examined it critically, then took several of the leaves she had gathered and crushed them into a ball. She held the fragrant compress against Wort's wound. Instantly the fiery pain vanished. From the pocket of her dress, Mika pulled out a pale purple handkerchief and deftly bound it around his hand with a neat knot. "That should do the trick."

Wort flexed his fingers. "Thank you, my lady," he said in a low, shy voice.

Mika frowned at this. Suddenly a flicker of realization crossed her face. "That's where I've heard it before," she said.

"What?" he asked in trepidation.

"Your voice, Wort. I've told you that your voice is beautiful, and it is. But I've also had the strange feeling that I've heard a voice just like it somewhere before. I only just now realized where." She studied his features carefully, then nodded. "Yes. Now that I take a closer look, the resemblance is clear." The doctor took a deep breath. "You are Baron Caidin's brother, aren't you Wort?"

Slowly, almost painfully, he nodded. "How is it that you know my brother?" he asked warily.

She turned away with a shrug. "Oh, we've met briefly once or twice." The doctor turned to face him. There was a sadness in her eyes. "*Wort* . . . it hardly seems like the name of a baron's son."

"They say . . . they say my mother called me Worren when I was a baby. She didn't live very long after my birth." Anger tinged his voice as he dredged up the dark memories. "You see, something went wrong the night I was born. She ripped deep inside, and I . . . I came out misshapen. The midwife thought me cursed because I was not formed right. She wanted to put me outside in the cold to die. My mother forced the Old Baron to swear I would not be killed. He gave her his word . . . and then she died."

"She was a courageous woman, your mother," Mika said firmly. "Was she the Old Baron's wife?"

Wort shook his head. "No, my mother was his mistress. Caidin was born about the same time I was, to the baroness—though she too died in childbirth. Caidin was the Old Baron's legitimate heir, while I . . . I was his bastard." Wort had never told this tale to anyone before. The words seemed to gush out of him.

"After my mother died, no one wanted to care for me. But though I knew he despised me—despised the fact that his offspring could be so terribly deformed—the Old Baron was a man of some honor, and he did not forget the fact that his blood ran in my veins. He saw to it that I was cared for, though mostly by servants who were threatened with death if they neglected their jobs. As long as I can remember, I was called not Worren, but Wort." He shrugged as if none of this mattered anymore. "I suppose it's a good name for a hunchback."

He went on glumly. "When we were children, everyone adored Caidin. How could they not? Even then he was strong and handsome and smart. I loved him just as much as the others. Probably more. As for myself . . . well, you can imagine how the other children regarded me. In the end, I found it was better to keep to the tower, with my pigeons, and my bells." Wort fell silent.

Finally Mika spoke softly. "Worren. I like that name. It's gentle—just like you."

Wort shook his head. What could he say? That she was indeed an angel he had no doubt. Slowly, she reached out to touch his shoulder.

"Wort, I know that once I made you angry by saying that I could . . . help you. But I want you to know something. You don't have to live with your affliction forever."

He cringed, but this time he did not lash out at her. There was too much compassion in her voice.

The doctor went on earnestly. "More than once I've operated to correct clubfoot. I don't think this is so very different." He felt her fingers running lightly over his humped shoulder. "There seem to be extra spurs of bone protruding from some of your vertebrae." Her hands followed the contorted curve of his spine. "Yes, that's it. And the ligaments along the right side are too short and too tight. I might be able to cut some of them to release the tension. It might take several operations. There would be some pain, and a fair amount of work afterward to stretch and lengthen the muscles. Nor do I think we could straighten your back entirely, but . . . "

Wort dared to breathe the words. "But what?"

"I think, with time, I could heal your back." Mika gripped his hand. "Let me help you . . . Worren."

Wort opened his mouth, but he truly did not know what to say. Quickly she pressed a finger to his lips, silencing him. "No, don't give me an answer. Just think about for a while." She leaned forward and fleetingly brushed her lips across his cheek in a kiss. After a moment she turned and picked up her basket. "I'm going to search for a few more herbs. Firespur berries should just be getting ripe by now."

As she wandered off among the trees, Wort gazed after her in mute shock. For a long time he sat numbly on the ground, like one struck by lightning. Could he truly be healed? Once again the words he had heard in the belfry drifted through his mind. *Monsters do not walk with angels. . . .*

"But what if she can do it?" he demanded angrily. "What if I can stand tall, like Caidin? What then?"

The voice whispered again in his brain, but was cut off as a scream shattered the air.

"Mika!" Wort gasped in alarm.

Leaping to his feet, he dashed through the trees. He ran stooped over, using his long arms as a second pair of legs, like some sort of beast. Another scream rang out but was cut short, muffled. Panting, Wort ran faster. Tearing through a tangle of brambles, he found himself on the edge of the small brook. The first thing he saw was Mika's straw basket on the ground. Bright red berries had spilled beside it, glistening like blood on the green moss. A creaking sound drew his gaze.

The dead tree beside the brook was moving. Its rough bark was twisted into a shape that suggested a grotesque human face. Two pits glowed with eerie green light like eyes, and a ragged hole in the trunk gaped like a huge maw, gnashing splintery teeth. Once this had been a living, evil, animate tree—a treant—but as it died it had not been willing to give up its carnivorous appetites. In undeath, it hungered more than ever for flesh and blood. Long ago Wort had read about an undead treant in one of his books—but then it had been only a story. This was all too real.

The treant bent its branches toward a struggling Mika. The doctor fought in vain against the dark roots that snaked out of the ground to entwine her. One had coiled about her mouth, stifling her cries. Another root wrapped itself about her arm. Its tip sank into her flesh. Her body went rigid as her flushed cheeks turned white. The thing was draining her blood.

With a wordless cry of rage, Wort leapt over the brook and threw himself at the tree. A branch-arm swatted him aside as easily as an insect. He landed hard on the ground, grunting in pain. Damp roots started to encircle his legs. Kicking fiercely, Wort scrambled out of their reach. He turned back to see Mika staring at him with terrified eyes. Her struggling grew weaker as the root continued to drain blood from her body. The treant's maw opened in a terrible grin.

Wort searched the pockets of his cloak frantically, then drew out an object—the magical candle. Focusing his anger, he created a shaft of searing fire that leapt from the tip of the candle. Roaring like an animal, Wort lunged at the animate tree, swinging the blazing candle like a fiery sword. The shaft of fire bit deep into one of the treant's branch-arms, cleaving it in two. The tree opened its ragged mouth in a scream of fury that seemed to vibrate through the earth. With the blazing candle, Wort hacked at the roots that gripped Mika. The treant screamed again as its roots released the doctor. Gasping, face deathly pale, she stumbled away and collapsed on the mossy ground.

"Mika!" Wort shouted, turning toward her.

One of the treant's gnarled arms struck him hard from behind. He fell forward, and the magic candle flew from his grip. Its flame went out as it struck the ground. Like a cold serpent, a thick root coiled about his body, holding him fast. Countless twig fingers brushed his face, scratching him. A weird creaking that might have been laughter emanated from the treant as it slowly lifted him toward the rotting hole of its mouth, ready to sink its splinter-teeth into his flesh.

Another soundless cry vibrated through the rotten wood, only this one was not fury, but agony. The root let Wort go, and he tumbled to the ground. He dragged himself to his knees just in time to see Mika pull the blazing shaft of the magical candle out of the undead tree. There was a grim expression on her ghostly face and a flinty light in her purple eyes.

Then Mika slumped weakly to the ground. The candle went out—but the undead treant still burned. Tongues of scarlet flame licked up its moss-covered bark. The ancient tree writhed violently. In moments it was engulfed in a pillar of roaring fire. It waved its branches wildly, then gradually grew still as a column of black smoke reached to the blue sky above.

Wort scrambled over to Mika, helping her sit up. "I'll be fine," she said hoarsely. Crimson still oozed slowly from the puncture wound in her arm. She cleaned it with a handful of dry leaves as Wort tore a strip from his cloak for a bandage. The two watched as the burning tree toppled over in a spray of sparks.

"It's dead," Wort whispered grimly. In his storybooks, the heroes had always been jubilant after they slew a beast. All he felt was sick. He helped Mika to her feet, and together the two walked slowly back toward Nartok Keep in the waning daylight.

 **THIRTEEN**

Pushing open the heavy door, Mika stepped into the dimness of the charnel house. Quickly she clutched a handkerchief to her face against the fetid stench of rot. Here, in this windowless stone building on the edge of the village, corpses were kept until the gravedigger could perform his job. Mika hung a burning oil lamp on the end of an iron chain. Its wavering light illuminated several forms lying upon stone slabs, draped in white burial shrouds, awaiting interment. These days Nartok's gravedigger had more business then he could easily accommodate.

Mika peered under each shroud until she found a body suitable for her purpose—a hale, middle-aged man who was fresher than most of the others. The crude stitches that held his severed head to his neck marked him as a traitor executed by the baron's inquisition. Mika set down her satchel and laid out her tools. She tied a handkerchief, which she had soaked in attar of roses, tightly around her face, although the rank scent of decay still filled her nose and lungs. At the university in Il Aluk she had spent long hours studying anatomy using the human cadavers that were always in great supply in the teeming city. That morning, when she had asked if there was a dead body which she could dissect, the gravedigger had looked at her strangely with his one good eye. Then she had offered him a gold coin for his trouble, and the look had turned from curiosity to greed. Clutching the coin in a dirty hand, he had led her to the charnel house.

Mika pulled back the white pall. The cadaver lay faceup on the stone slab, staring at her with dull eyes. She tried several times to shut his eyelids, but they kept springing back open, no doubt from rigor mortis.

"I do so hate working with someone staring at me," Mika murmured with a shivery laugh.

With a silver scalpel she made the first incision. After much cutting and sawing, she opened the cadaver's ribcage and removed the organs of his chest—his heart and lungs—which she set on the empty slab behind her. Now she could examine his spine from the ventrum, the belly side of his body. In a small leather-bound notebook she carefully sketched the anatomy of the bones, muscles, and nerves surrounding his spine. If she were to operate on Wort's hunchback, she had to learn such things. Otherwise she might make some dreadful mistake with her scalpel, perhaps paralyzing Wort, or even killing him.

After she finished her drawings, Mika turned the heavy cadaver over on the slab to examine it from the dorsum, the back side. Before continuing, she rested a moment. She pulled a flask of water from her satchel and took a few sips. She had still not recovered entirely from the attack by the animate tree in the forest two days before. Shivering, Mika sipped more water, then put the flask away. She turned to continue her dissection.

The cadaver stared up at her with lifeless eyes.

"That's odd," she said with a frown. "I thought I turned you over." Struggling with the heavy body, she turned the cadaver over on the slab and made an incision down the center of the back. Soon she was busily making more anatomical sketches in her notebook.

A faint sound echoed off the stone walls. Mika paused a moment, listening. Silence. She shrugged and continued sketching. The sound came again—a wet, slapping noise. Slowly, the small hairs on her neck prickling, she turned around. The dead man's heart was beating! She clutched her notebook with white-knuckled hands. The fist-shaped organ lurched across the stone slab, flopping like a dying fish, trailing dark blood.

Mika stared numbly. A choking sound escaped her throat. The smears of blood on the stone made by the beating heart formed letters, spelling out two words: HELP ME. There was a rustling sound behind her. Mika spun around. The cadaver lay faceup on the slab once more. His dull eyes stared at her with an expression of . . . anguish.

With a muffled cry, Mika snatched up her satchel and dashed to the door of the charnel house. She gripped the knob and pulled. It was locked. Mika screamed, pounding at the wood, her hands clenched. She could feel the dead man's eyes boring into her back. Suddenly the door swung open. Mika stumbled forward into fresh air and sunlight. She jerked the handkerchief from her face and took in deep, gasping breaths.

"Are you well, milady?" the gravedigger asked, squinting at her with his one eye.

She gazed back at the door of the charnel house. The cadaver she had been dissecting lay facedown on the slab. The heart was no longer moving. Any message it had traced on the stone was now just a smear of blood. Shuddering, she turned to the gravedigger.

"The door," she said breathlessly. "It was locked."

"I'm sorry, milady. I forgot to tell you that the door only opens from the outside."

Mika stared at him. "But why?"

The gravedigger fixed her with another peculiar look but did not answer. "Are you finished, milady?" he asked finally.

She nodded. "I am now." Clutching her notebook and satchel, she hastily set off down the street.

In the light and air of the day, Mika felt her fright lifting. Soon she wondered if she hadn't simply imagined it all. It would hardly be unusual after her and Wort's nightmarish encounter with the treant. Relieved by this thought, Mika walked swiftly. She did not want any of the villagers to see her leaving the charnel house. Since Wort had scared away the mob that had accused her of witchcraft, she had been able to practice her craft in peace in Nartok. She didn't want to give anyone cause for starting further dark rumors about her.

When Mika returned to the Black Boar, she found a patient waiting for her in the dingy chamber behind the common room. It was a middle-aged woman, clad in the plain brown dress of a farmer's wife. "Begging your forgiveness, milady," the woman said, standing nervously. "I don't mean to disturb you. . . ."

Mika smiled warmly, trying to put the woman at ease. "It's no bother." In truth, she was glad for something to take her mind off the grisly charnel house experience. She stepped into the chamber and set down her satchel. Only then did she notice the farmer's wife was not alone. In a chair in a dim corner sat a young woman. Mika stared in alarm, a hand unconsciously creeping to her breast. Something was terribly wrong with the young woman. Her face was pale and shadowed, and her eyes stared blankly forward—dark, unblinking, and utterly empty. Were it not for the slow, steady rise and fall of her chest, Mika might have thought her dead.

"I hope I've done the right thing in bringing my Alys here," the peasant woman said in a shaking voice. "Hannis—that's my husband, you see—Hannis wouldn't like it if he knew I'd come to see you. He says healers are all either charlatans or warlocks, each one worse than the other. Though I love him, sometimes half of what Hannis says is poppycock, and the rest is just plain nonsense."

Mika knelt down to examine the young woman's face. There was no movement, no expression—no indication that she saw or heard anything at all.

"Do you think . . . do you think you can help her, milady?"

"I hope so," Mika answered gravely. "But tell me, how did this happen?"

Soon Mika knew the whole, sad tale. The mother's name was Marga. She and her husband had woken one morning to find their daughter Alys missing and the window of her bedroom open. They had discovered Alys far out on the moor, shivering and staring with unseeing eyes. At first she had muttered things in a singsong voice. . . .

"Strange things, like dark, eerie poems," Marga said sorrowfully. "They chilled my blood, they did."

Gradually Alys had turned utterly silent. Now she seemed neither to hear nor see anything, as if trapped in a waking slumber.

"I believe your daughter is suffering from catatonia," Mika explained after she had finished her examinations. "I'm afraid it's a sort of madness, usually brought on by some awful shock."

"Madness?" Marga gasped. "Can you possibly heal her, milady?"

"I'm not certain. Sometimes such patients heal themselves." Mika took a deep breath. "And sometimes . . ." She faltered.

"Sometimes they stay this way forever," Marga finished in a whisper. "That's what you were going to say, isn't it?"

Mika could only nod. She went to a cabinet where she kept packets of herbs, jars of ointments, and other medicines. She returned with a small vial. "This might help your daughter. It is a distillation of mandrake root. I've used it before in cases of coma or sleeping sickness." Mika carefully poured some of the elixir into Alys's mouth.

Alys screamed.

The two woman stared in astonishment. Alys's blindly intent eyes were now focused on something only she could see. Horror twisted her ghost-white visage as her hands clenched into rigid claws. Despite the terror on her face, weird laughter bubbled out of her mouth. She began to chant in a queer, melodic voice:

"Where is my love?
Far under the earth—
Crowned by the worms
The mold gives birth.

"Who is my love?
The scion of Death—
Whose kisses drown me
With sweet, cold breath!"

"That's it!" Marga cried. "That's what she was saying when we found her. Over and over again. That's what she said. What do you think it means?"

Mika shook her head. Bracing herself, she knelt before the traumatized young woman. "Alys," she said softly. "Alys, can you hear me?"

"I see him." Alys's voice was at once whisper and

shriek. "I see him, out my window. He is walking to
. . . to the tower."

"Who, Alys?" Mika asked intently. "Who do you
see?"

"Yet how can it be him?" Alys went on eerily. "Oh,
but it is. That is all that matters. I run to him. Yes, I
run to him, to throw my arms around him. But . . ."
Her body began to shake violently. "What is wrong?
He is . . . he is so cold. And the smell—like the
damp, fetid earth." Her voice rose to a scream. "No!
Don't touch me! His kiss . . . his kiss is filled with
writhing worms!"

Mika gripped the young woman's shoulder fiercely.
"Who, Alys? Who is it you see?"

Alys's cry of anguish froze Mika's blood. "Oh,
Robart! What have they done to you?" The young
woman collapsed into Mika's arms, sobbing.

"Who . . . who is Robart?" Mika finally managed to
ask.

Marga's voice was so faint Mika had to strain to
hear it. "Robart was Alys's lover. He was executed by
the inquisition almost a week ago."

Mika swallowed the metallic taste of fear, trying to
grasp the implication of Marga's words. The sound of
murmuring brought her head around. Alys was
chanting the queer melody once more.

"Whose kisses drown me,
With sweet, cold breath. . . ."

* * * * *

Mika watched through the grimy window as the
peasant woman led her blankly staring daughter
away down the muddy street. There was little hope
Alys would ever recover her sanity. The imagined
sight of her dead lover—or perhaps real, Mika dared

to think after her strange experience in the charnel house—had struck too deep a blow to Alys's psyche. Mika had visited the asylum in Il Aluk more than once. There she had seen men and woman who, like Alys, had also witnessed things so unspeakable their minds were shattered. Lost Ones, they were called— lost, because they never found their sanity again.

Mika shivered, wishing there was someone there to hold her, to speak gentle words of comfort and help her forget the day's disturbing events. But there was no one. She felt utterly and completely alone. She lifted the golden locket that hung around her neck and opened the tiny latch. Inside was painted a portrait, small as a robin's egg, of a young man with kind brown eyes. Suddenly Mika found herself shaking—not with sorrow—but with anger.

"Why, my love?" she whispered bitterly. "Why did you leave me? How could you leave me alone in this dark and terrible world?"

Somehow she had always forgiven little Lia—she was just a child—but Geordin was her husband. He should have clung to life. But he had given up. Geordin had died, abandoning her.

Mika clutched the locket tightly, tears of rage streaming down her cheeks. "How could you be so cruel, Geordin?" she said hoarsely, choking on her words. "How dare you leave me alone like this?" She jerked the locket from around her neck. The gold chain snapped. At long last she spoke the words that burned inside her. "I . . . I hate you, Geordin!" she cried, hurling the locket across the room. "I hate you for leaving me alone!"

Sobbing, she collapsed into a chair, curling herself into ball like a small, frightened child.

An hour later, as the blood-red sun waned slowly on the western horizon, a courier entered the room to find Mika in that same position. He cleared his throat.

"Ahem."

Startled, Mika leapt to her feet, seeing that she was no longer alone. She roughly wiped the dampness from her pale cheeks.

"I am sorry to disturb you, my lady," the courier said with a half-bow. He was clad in a frilly suit of pale blue silk, and he wore a powdered wig.

"Not at all," she finally managed to voice the words.

The courier went on in a bored tone. "I am pleased to inform my lady that the baron has requested her presence at the keep this evening. A carriage awaits outside, and he has sent my lady this gift." He snapped his fingers, and a page with a powdered face and rouged lips scurried into the chamber carrying a puffy mound of satin the exact lavender hue of Mika's eyes. He plopped it down on the table. It was a gown.

"May I inform the baron that my lady will be accepting his invitation?"

Mika's lips started to form the word *No*. She didn't dare visit Caidin at the keep again. It would be tantamount to a rabbit paying the wolf a house-call. Abruptly she halted. Out of the corner of her eye she caught a dull glint of gold on the floor—the locket. Again a wave of bitter loneliness swept through her. The voice that spoke hardly seemed her own.

"Tell the baron I will gladly accept his invitation."

The courier bowed again, retreating from the room with the page.

"What have I done?" Mika whispered in a quavering voice, but it was too late. The courier had gone, and she was expected.

* * * * *

Twilight was wrapping its thick, gray mantle around the spires of Nartok Keep as Mika stepped from the carriage. The smooth satin of the gown felt almost delicious against her skin, and the thought that something the baron had chosen now touched her body so intimately made her feel vaguely wicked. The white-faced page led her through labyrinthine corridors, so that soon she became utterly lost. At last they stopped before an ornately carved door. Mika stepped through it and found herself in a chamber richly appointed with crystal, gold-threaded damask, and gilded wood. Baron Caidin rose from a divan of crushed velvet to greet her.

"My lady," he murmured in his rich voice. "You look ravishing."

He kissed her hand lingeringly. She started to snatch her hand away, then stopped. Why shouldn't she wish to be touched and caressed after so many years alone? The baron glanced up at her, surprise and delight apparent in his vivid green eyes. Gripping her hand, he led her deeper into the chamber. He poured her a glass of dark, ruby-colored wine. She gulped it down.

"More," she breathed, holding out the goblet.

He arched an eyebrow wonderingly, then complied. Greedily, she drained the glass. Warmth flowed through her, dulling the horrors of the day and the regrets of the past. At last she set the empty goblet down. The baron regarded her with a bemused expression. He wore only a pair of tight-fitting breeches and a loose white shirt unlaced at the collar. She could easily make out the muscular lines of his chest beneath the delicate material.

For a moment Mika wondered if she should leave. The baron was a dangerous enigma to her. On her last visit to the keep he had displayed great kindness for an ill servant. Yet this was the same man, she knew, who was waging a brutal inquisition in his fief-dom—an inquisition that had stolen the life of Alys's

lover and left her a Lost One with a shattered mind.
Then there was Wort. Why had Caidin warned her to
stay away from the bell tower? Did he truly believe
that his half brother might harm her? Or did he have
some other, darker motives she could not fathom?

Caidin gestured to a table set with gold and crystal. "I thought we could dine together, my lady."

Slowly she shook her head. "No, Your Grace."

He regarded her in puzzlement. "I'm sorry, my
lady?"

Satin rustling softly, she approached the baron. "I
am not hungry for dinner, Your Grace." She reached
out and ran a finger along the smooth line of his jaw.

His expression was one of total shock. He looked
almost like a small, startled boy whose secret
dreams had wonderfully and quite unexpectedly
come true. The baron's lips parted in a toothy grin.
Languidly, Mika shut her eyes. Strong hands moved
down the sides of her body, and warm, moist breath
caressed her neck. It had been so very long since
she had been touched this way.

"My beautiful doctor."

The voice filled her senses. For the space of a
heartbeat, Mika found herself trying to picture a
face—the face of a man with kind brown eyes. But
all she could envision was darkness. Reflexively, she
reached up to touch the gold locket that always
hung at her breast. Instead her fingers closed around
a warm, strong hand. Slowly she opened her eyes.

"Your Grace . . ."

Her words were willingly drowned in the passion of
his embrace.

*   *   *   *   *

In her private chamber, Jadis slipped out of her
customary green-gold gown to stand naked before a

full-length mirror. Tonight was the perfect night to pursue her investigations. She had managed to neutralize the troublesome little gnome by leaving a large jug of wine outside the door of his room. As she had expected, the little cretin had been unable to resist drinking it, and had fallen asleep, thanks to the small amount of powder Jadis had mixed into the wine. Nor did she expect any interference from Baron Caidin. She knew he was presently busy with his latest romantic quarry—the golden-haired doctor from the village. Why he had chosen her, Jadis did not know or care. The doctor was pretty enough in a pale, fragile way, but Jadis had always found innocence dreadfully uninteresting. Innocence was easily seduced, and then what was one left with? A clumsy amateur in the intricate art of desire. For that game Jadis preferred opponents with far more skill and experience.

Briefly, she admired her lithe, copper-skinned figure in the mirror. She was about to turn away when she noticed something that made her frown.

"What is this, love?"

She studied a single flaw that marked her otherwise perfect skin. It was a dark spot just beneath her left collarbone, some sort of bruise. She rubbed the spot, but there was no pain. After a moment of hesitation, she shrugged. No doubt she had hurt herself slightly in her explorations of the keep. But it was nothing to worry about.

Her form undulated, reshaping itself, and in seconds the black werepanther stalked to the chamber's open window and leapt outside.

Enjoying the graceful strength of her panther form, Jadis loped easily down the steep side of the crag upon which Nartok Keep perched. Night had fallen, but the sky was clear, and the moon was just rising above the horizon to cast its gauzy illumination over the land. Skirting around the village, she moved like a windswept shadow northward across the rolling heath. She saw no signs of activity as she went. No one dared travel about Nartok by night. Except for werecats, Jadis amended mirthfully.

Soon she reached a low hill rising above the moor, its crest surrounded by a rusting, spiked fence. The cemetery. Quickly she padded through the gate and made her way toward the graves. Using her sharp claws, she pulled herself up the trunk of a dead tree and curled in the hollow between two branches. Her eyes glowing in the darkness, she watched the graves below. Jadis did not know what she expected to see, but she had a strong feeling she would see something.

She did not have long to wait. A faint, scrabbling sound reached her sensitive ears. Moments later, the dirt covering dozens of the graves, those belonging to victims of Caidin's inquisition, began to churn. A pale hand broke through the surface of one. It clawed at the dirt. More hands broke through the damp soil. In moments dozens of clutching hands and pallid arms rose up from the earth as though this was not a cemetery but some sort of grisly, blossoming garden. The hands scratched at the soil, and slowly an army of corpses rose out of the ground. Mold covered their rotting flesh, and dirt clung to their lank hair and tattered clothes. The corpses began shambling forward. Zombies. Jadis's pink nose wrinkled at the stench of their bloated flesh.

Shuffling listlessly, the throng of zombies marched through the graveyard. All stared with blank eyes. Some dropped gobbets of flesh or even loose fingers or ears behind them as they passed. When the last had clambered from his grave and stumbled out the cemetery's gate, Jadis jumped from the tree. She stalked silently after the corpses as they moved down the side of the hill.

Jadis followed the gruesome cavalcade across the moor. Soon a dark shape hove into view. It was the mysterious tower, now almost complete. Jadis slunk around the spire, her fur blending seamlessly with the night, watching as the zombies converged on the vast stone construction. The animate corpses began pushing ponderous blocks of stone up wooden ramps and sliding them into place atop the tower.

The undead moved clumsily as they went about their mindless labor. Two zombies bearing armfuls of tools collided with each other. One stumbled away, oblivious to the chisel embedded in her forehead, while the other tried vainly to pull out the crowbar that skewered his torso. A zombie woman shuffling toward the tower stepped in a trough of wet mortar. She lurched to a halt, her leg stuck in the rapidly setting cement. The decomposing woman strained, trying to pull out her foot. With a ripping sound her entire leg tore free of her body. Blithely, the zombie woman hopped forward on her one remaining leg.

A dwarven zombie waved a flaccid arm toward the dirt-encrusted corpse of the man that guided a wooden crane. A ponderous block of stone hung from the end of the stout boom.

"Drop . . . here . . ." the dwarven zombie groaned.

He started to point to a nearby pile of stones, but his rotting hand chose that moment to fall off, landing at his feet. The dwarf stared dully at the hand twitching on the ground. Slowly, he looked up.

"Uh . . . oh . . ." he moaned.

The wooden crane swung into position. The block of stone dropped, crushing the dwarf to a gooey pulp beneath. Next to the block of stone lay the dwarf's still-pointing hand.

Worms dropped from the mouth of the zombie man controlling the crane as he smiled. "Right . . . on . . . target. . . ."

Jadis twitched her whiskers with satisfaction. Now she understood the purpose behind Caidin's false inquisition. He was executing supposed traitors simply as a means to gain corpses to transform into zombies—zombies who emerged from their graves each night to work on building this tower. Yet this begged a crucial question. Why was Caidin going to such elaborate lengths to build the tower?

Jadis's flesh rippled fluidly as her limbs lengthened and her dark fur vanished. Human once more, she scooped up handfuls of dirt and rubbed them over her naked body and through her hair. In moments she looked little different than the zombies. Slumping her shoulders and staring dully forward, Jadis shuffled toward the tower. The other zombies paid her no heed as they went about their mindless labor. She joined several who pushed a heavy block of stone up one of the wooden ramps. When they reached the top of the wall, she slipped away. The moonlight afforded a clear view of the construction.

So—it was a tower of war. Strong buttresses braced thick walls. Narrow windows slits were designed to make it easy to fire arrows at approaching targets. Overhanging ledges with holes created machicolations for dropping hot pitch onto enemies below. Jadis frowned. How would a tower of war in Nartok allow Caidin to defeat King Azalin in far-off Il Aluk? It was a riddle she could not solve. Having learned all she could for the moment, Jadis moved to the ramp to head back down.

"Stop . . ." a slurred voice croaked behind her.

Jadis froze, then slowly turned around, keeping her face expressionless. A zombie man lurched toward her, dropping stray bits of putrid flesh as he moved. Jadis swore silently. Even in this state of decay, the zombies Caidin had created were still surprisingly sentient!

"Where . . . you . . . go?" She could hardly make out the zombie's words. His mouth was filled with dirt and worms.

"Down," she mumbled thickly.

"No . . ." the zombie groaned. "Come . . . with . . . me."

Panic jabbed at Jadis's heart. Limply, she shook her head. "Down," she mumbled again.

The zombie advanced on her. A dozen more shambling corpses appeared out of the gloom behind him. If she changed into her werepanther form she could destroy perhaps half of them. That would not be enough.

"Why . . . you . . . disobey?" The zombie's slurred voice sounded suspicious. "Come!"

Jadis did not dare refuse a second time. Nodding stonily, she joined the others and shuffled after the zombie. He led them to the top of the wall.

"Must . . . carve . . . stone," he groaned. "Make . . . smooth."

While the zombie foreman watched, the other zombies clumsily picked up hammers and chisels and began chipping away at the stone blocks, squaring their edges so more blocks could be set on top of the wall. Jadis followed suit. She picked up a hammer and began chiseling away at the stone. Soon her hands were blistered, and her shoulders throbbed painfully. The zombies around her worked tirelessly, never ceasing. If she were to stop to rest, even for a moment, they would know she was not one of them.

"You can't fall asleep, love," she murmured hysterically under her breath. "No matter how lovely it sounds. If you fall asleep, they'll tear you to bits."

Biting her lip to stem the pain in her burning hands, desperately trying to shrug off her weariness, she kept chiseling. Eventually she drifted into a dark delirium, a waking nightmare filled with the endless clanking of steel on stone and the suffocating reek of rotten meat.

Suddenly Jadis looked up. The zombies were setting down their tools and shuffling away. Pearly light glowed on the distant horizon. It was almost dawn. Shuddering in relief, she set down her own hammer, stretching her throbbing shoulders.

"Back . . . to . . . coffins," a zombie moaned.

The zombies tottered down the wooden ramp to the ground and began lumbering back toward the cemetery. Jadis took the chance to slip away. Moments later the lithe werepanther loped across the moor, quickly leaving the gruesome procession of zombies behind. As she headed toward the keep in the misty gray light, a wry thought crossed Jadis's mind. Caidin ought to thank her for helping build his blasted tower.

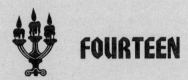# FOURTEEN

Wort parted a gauzy veil of cobwebs. It had been months since he had last come to the forgotten storeroom to gaze upon the ancient tapestry. His breath caught in his chest. He had forgotten how beautiful the angel was.

The weaving drooped upon the stone wall. At least a third of it had rotted away over the centuries, and the rest was stained dark by smoke and the passing of time. Once the scene must have been a sylvan glade in the golden light of the morning sun. Now it was a garden swathed in the shadows of dusk. Yet in the midst of all that murkiness drifted the angel. A single ray of sunlight slanted down from a high window, illuminating the pale oval of her face. Her violet eyes gazed out serenely, and her rosebud mouth bore the faintest trace of a smile that was dreamy, and knowing, and hinting ever-so-slightly of love.

"How can it be her?" Wort whispered in amazement. For centuries this tapestry had hung here. Yet somehow it *was* her. He reached out and carefully traced a gnarled finger over the angel's white-gowned form. "Mika," he sighed. Carefully, he reached up to lift the tapestry off the hooks that fastened it in place.

A short while later, Wort painstakingly hung the

tapestry on the wall of his chamber high in the bell tower. He stepped back, making certain it was not crooked. For a startled moment he almost thought the diaphanous shift the angel wore was fluttering. A thrill raced through him. Was the angel somehow coming to life? He sighed. It was only a draft blowing through chinks in the stone, stirring the tapestry.

"I am letting my imagination have its way with me, Lisenne," he said as a cloud-gray pigeon fluttered down to land on his outstretched hand. "She does seem very real though, doesn't she? Mika will be very surprised, I think. Don't you agree?"

The pigeon replied with an amiable coo. Wort tossed the bird into the air, and it winged away to roost in the rafters. Deciding it would be a good idea to practice his endgame in Castles and Kings in anticipation of the doctor's next visit, he turned to open the trunk by his pallet.

Wort froze, staring. The ancient tapestry was not the only new weaving in his chamber. Stretching across the room's narrow window was a spider web. Drops of moisture clung to the silken strands, glittering like diamond-fire in the light of the westering sun. The weaver of the web still clung to its creation. Above the spider, the perfect spiral of the web was broken by a pattern spelling out three words in pearlescent strands: RING IT, WORT.

He jerked his head up, gazing at the ceiling. He could feel it. The sensation poured from the belfry above like foul water dripping between floorboards. Disapproval.

Shaking, Wort knelt before the ironbound trunk and drew out a small wooden box. He opened the box and took out some tokens. Only one of the objects was stained with blood—the gold coin that had belonged to Nartok's treasurer. The other tokens were as yet untainted. Wort had stolen them over the

last week, prowling around the keep and village.
There was a belt belonging to the villager's tanner,
whom Wort had seen brutally beat a young apprentice for a trivial mistake. There was a hat he had
stolen from a drunken highwayman he found passed
out in a ditch beside the road. And there were two
shoes—a man's and a lady's—which he had pilfered
from a pair of adulterous courtiers who had ventured
into a grove for a wicked liaison.

There were more tokens besides—rings and
bracelets, knives and tools. The objects belonged to
peasants, craftsmen, and nobles. Despite their disparate classes, all the people to whom the tokens
belonged had one thing in common. Wort had
observed each of them to be cruel, or selfish, or
licentious, or brutal, or greedy.

A cold gust of wind whistled through the chamber.
Wort raised a hand before his face, blinking. Dust,
straw, and feathers whirled on the wind. Suddenly
the flotsam began clumping together in midair, coalescing into three shapes. In moments, three vague
forms outlined in moldering straw and stray feathers
floated before Wort. The wind brought a chorus of
angry voices to his ears.

Why have you not rung the bell?

Wort shrank away from the sinister forms. "I have
not summoned you!" he cried. "How can you be here
before me?"

These are but images, nothing more. The voices of
the spirits whispered on the wind. *Why have you not
rung the bell? You have many tokens. . . .*

"I'll ring it went I wish," Wort snarled. "Do you hear
me? When *I* wish it. Go back to your bell and wait!"

The wind rose to a howl. *We grow weary of waiting!*

Wort pressed his hands to his ears, trying to block
out the shrill voices. It was no use.

You are afraid, bellringer. Why? Why do you refuse

to ring the bell? Tell us!

Shuddering, Wort pointed to the tapestry.

Ah, it is the doctor! the voices on the wind hissed in understanding.

Wort let out an anguished groan, rocking back and forth on his knees. "Why, spirits? Why must she care so much what happens to me? Why could she not have left me alone after I helped her in the village? I could have killed them all by now. I would have the tokens I need to gain my vengeance! But I cannot. . . ."

Yes, Wort. You sense the truth. She would condemn you utterly for what you must do to make yourself whole. The voices surged dizzyingly through his brain. *That is why you must forget her. . . .*

"Forget her?" Wort choked. "How can I forget an angel? How can I forget that she wants to heal me?"

Perhaps she can heal your body, Wort. Only we can heal your soul. In the end, her love means nothing. . . .

Wort's heart leapt. "What did you say?" he gasped.

The wind rose to a deafening shriek. *Her love means nothing, Wort! Nothing!*

"Love?" Wort whispered the word as if speaking it for the first time. His eyes bulged. At last, it all made sense in his tortured brain—the way she had returned to the tower despite his violent outburst, the gentle words, the flowers she brought, her patience in teaching him new games, the hours spent talking in the dappled light of the belfry. Then there was that day in the woods, when she gently touched his shoulder, and then . . . yes, her soft lips brushing against his cheek. He had been too blind to realize it before. Now it was perfectly clear. He knew what he had to do.

Wort lurched to his knees, shaking his fist at the straw effigies. "Go back to your blasted bell!"

Why resist us, Wort? In the end, you will ring it again.

He pulled the magical silver candle from his pocket. Ignited by his rage, fire flared to life. "I said begone!"

Heed our words, Wort, you will—

Wort thrust the blazing candle at the three hovering forms. Straw and feathers burst into crimson flame. In moments the three figures were transformed into writhing columns of blazing fire. Turning, Wort slashed at the spider web in the window. Flames licked at the silken strands, consuming them, crisping the fat insect in the center. Cold wind whipped wildly about the chamber—mad, howling—then suddenly died. Dark cinders drifted to the floor—all that remained of the three effigies of the spirits. The silver candle sputtered.

Slowly, Wort picked up the box of tokens. He fingered the myriad objects. Suddenly he heaved the box into the trunk. He did not need them anymore.

"I must go to her, my friends," he whispered to the fluttering pigeons. "I must tell her that I finally understand!"

Wrapping his cloak around his twisted form, Wort dashed from the chamber, pausing only once to glance over his shoulder at the tapestry of the pale angel drifting through the darkened garden.

"I love you, too, Mika," he whispered. Then he vanished into the shadows of the bell tower's stairwell.

* * * * *

Wort found her sooner than he had hoped. He was lumbering through a small, little-used courtyard, making his way toward the keep's gates, when he heard the bright sound of laughter. A moment later the laughter came again, wafting over the top of a high stone wall. He recognized the clear, musical voice. It was Mika.

"What is she doing here at the keep, my friends?" he murmured to himself. Grinning, Wort flung himself against the wall and began pulling himself up its rough surface with powerful arms. If he fell, the hard cobbles below would almost certainly snap his neck. He did not care. Breathing hard, he heaved himself to the top of the wall.

On the opposite side lay the keep's garden. There were no flowers this late in the year, and the trees and hedges were dark and leafless, yet there was a stark beauty about it all the same. Then he saw her—as pale and radiant as the angel in the shadowed tapestry. She wore a gown he had never seen before, a flowing concoction of lavender silk that was in utter contrast to the plain dresses she usually favored. She had never looked so beautiful. Wort raised a hand to signal her and opened his mouth to call. Before he could do anything, however, a second figure stepped from behind a statue. Baron Caidin. He held his arms out, and Mika laughed again as she flung herself into his embrace.

Desperately Wort tried to look away. He could not. With dread he watched as Mika's fine-boned hands ran sensually across Caidin's broad back. The baron's green eyes glittered hungrily as he bent down, pressing his lips against hers. She did not resist him. Just the opposite. The golden-haired doctor leaned into Caidin's body—his strong, whole, handsome body—as the two kissed passionately again, and yet again.

At last Wort managed to turn his head. Going limp, he half slid, half fell down the face of the wall, crashing painfully to the paving stones. A hot wave of nausea surged through him. "I should have known," he croaked, his mouth filled with bile. "You've always had everything I can only dream of, my brother. Everything. While I have nothing."

That was not completely true. There was one thing Wort had that Caidin did not. The bell. Lurching to his feet, Wort hobbled across the empty courtyard, toward the looming spire of the bell tower.

When he burst into his high chamber, his cry of rage sent pigeons flapping in all directions. Wort did not care. He batted the birds viciously out of his path. They were hateful creatures anyway. They cared naught for him—they desired only the bread crumbs he fed them. When he spied the tapestry hanging on the wall, fury ignited in his brain. He grabbed fistfuls of the rotting material. With a terrible rending sound and a cloud of dust, the tapestry tore apart. Turning in disgust, Wort flung open the trunk and snatched up the box of tokens. He clambered up the ladder to the belfry. The cursed bell gleamed in the fading daylight, radiating an aura of gloating.

We knew you would come back, bellringer. . . .

"You were right," Wort snarled. "Her love means nothing. There is only one way I will ever be whole, and that is to have my revenge." He grasped the bell's rope in strong, twisted hands. "And I will have it—now!"

The air shook with the thunder of the bell.

* * * * *

Mika knocked again on the stout oaken door at the base of the bell tower, but still there was no answer.

"Perhaps he has gone out somewhere," she murmured. Suddenly from high above came the clarion sounds of a bell. Mika smiled. That was why Wort hadn't heard her knock. He was up in the belfry, with his bells and his pigeons.

"I suppose I shall just have to be rude and let myself in," she decided aloud.

Opening the door, Mika began making her way up the dim shaft of the tower's spiral staircase. She lifted the hem of her dress to keep from stumbling. She had traded the lavender gown Caidin had given her for her usual dress of dark wool. It had been difficult to wrest herself away from the baron. These last days it had felt as if she were caught in a sweet, burning dream. All she could think of were Caidin's brilliant eyes, and the fiery touch of his body. It was wrong—it had to be. Yet she could not help herself. Each time she decided to turn him away, it seemed as if he knew just where to find the wounds of her loneliness, rubbing words of passion into them like salt, until she almost cried out at her need to be held, and touched, and . . . desired. It was manipulative, and cruel, and so very delicious.

This afternoon, however, she had vowed to slip away from Caidin. She had not seen Wort in several days, and wanted to make certain he was well and to talk more about the operation she planned that would hopefully heal his back. Telling Caidin there was a sick person she needed to see—and indeed this was not entirely untrue—she had managed to convince him to let her go, at least for an hour. She knew that the baron thought his half brother mad and violence-prone, and that Caidin did not want her to visit him. Yet the baron did not seem to know Wort as the gentle-spirited person she did.

"Perhaps one day I can help Caidin see that his brother is truly a good man," Mika whispered. "Perhaps I could even help them become friends." The thought made her smile.

"Hello?" she called as she stepped into the dreary room where Wort made his home. Only the soft warbling of pigeons answered her. Again the ancient stones of the tower thrummed with the deep tolling of a bell. Something about the tone of the bell suddenly made her shiver. Shaking off the premonition, she moved toward the ladder that led to the belfry.

Mika paused. Something she had never seen before caught her eye. A tattered shape hung on one of the chamber's rough stone walls. Curious, she approached the wall. Reaching out, she stroked soft, frayed fabric.

"Why, it's a tapestry," she murmured. The fabric was rotten, and the weaving badly torn, almost shredded. Carefully, she lifted the tatters of cloth, holding them together to see what tableaux they might once have depicted.

A gasp escaped her lips. A serene face gazed back at her with deep violet eyes, the perfect reflection of her own. It was like staring into a dark, dusty mirror. A jagged rip ran right through the visage of the woman, like a livid wound. Mika let the ragged tatters fall. She backed away, clasping both hands to her mouth. She tried to blink away the disturbing image of the pale face—*her* face—brutally torn in two.

Again a thunder of bells sounded from above. Mika jumped, her heart rattling in her throat. This time the tolling was distinctly ominous. Filled with inexplicable dread, she craned her neck upward and gazed at the trapdoor in the ceiling. Almost without thinking, she moved to the rickety ladder. She ascended slowly, as if reeled in by some unseen force. She pushed the trapdoor open and peered through the crack. What she saw froze her blood.

Wort was pulling one last time on the rope hanging from a bronze bell, a maniacal grin on his twisted face. A patch of air before him began to roil like a miniature storm cloud. Smoky tendrils swirled together, coalescing into three amorphous blobs.

Gradually the black blobs took on shape and form.
The coils of mist vanished. Three dimly translucent
figures hovered before Wort, bobbing slowly up and
down like corpses floating on a midnight sea. Mika
bit her tongue to keep from screaming.

"Here, take them!" Wort snarled. He thrust a small
wooden box out toward the three dusky apparitions.
"Take them all, and do your work!"

The three spirits bowed as one. "It will be done,
bellringer." Their voices blended into chilling harmony. As the apparitions dissolved into the air, the
box in Wort's hands did the same. With a look of
hateful satisfaction, he nodded and began to sham-
ble across the floor, heading for the trapdoor.

Fear flooded Mika's brain. Dizzy at what she had
seen, she let the trapdoor snap shut and backed
down the ladder. In her fright she missed her footing.
Slipping from the ladder, she tumbled to the rotted
straw that covered the hard stone floor. The wind
rushed out of her painfully, and she lay paralyzed by
pain and terror. Only one thought thrummed through
her mind, as deafening as the noise of a bell.

What had Wort done?

*   *   *   *   *

As Wort turned away from the bell rope, he heard
something in his chamber below—a *thump!* followed
by a soft cry of pain. Rage flared in his chest. Someone had invaded his personal domain. Pulling up the
trapdoor by its iron ring, he clambered swiftly as an
ape down the ladder. He leapt to the floor and
crouched, staring with blazing eyes.

"I see you have come back, Doctor." His voice was
low, hoarse, dangerous.

Hastily, Mika scrambled to her feet. "Of course, I
have, Wort," she said breathlessly. She made a visi-

ble effort to compose herself. "I know it has been some days since I last came, but you know . . . you know how busy I am sometimes in the village. I came as soon as I could."

Weird laughter bubbled in his chest. "Oh, yes, doctor. I know very well about the things that occupy your time."

A frown cast a shadow across her forehead. "I'm afraid I don't know what you mean."

"Truly? Don't you?"

Worry shone in her eyes. "Are you well, Wort?"

"Oh, yes, Doctor. I am now." He took a menacing step toward her, leering. "So, as usual I see it is black wool for me—not the lavender silk you prefer to don for my brother."

The blood drained from her cheeks, leaving them as chalky as marble. "Wort, I . . . I . . . " She could not seem to find the right words.

"So, how long have you and Caidin been lovers?" he hissed accusingly. "Did it happen after the first time you came to my tower? Or before? Tell me, Doctor. Does the sight of his handsome face fill you with love? Or merely lust?"

Mika took a step away from him. "No, Wort. You don't understand—"

"On the contrary, Doctor, I understand perfectly." His voice was as cold as stone. "I understand that I have been an utter, laughable fool. You should be proud of yourself, you know, for you have deceived me completely. I confess, I truly thought you did wish to heal me."

She shook her head in dull astonishment. "What are you saying?"

"Come, Doctor, you can give up the role of ingenue. Though you play it well, you need it no longer." He spat the words. "I know why you were so anxious to operate on me. Oh, no doubt you have some degree of scientific curiosity. Like a cruel, inquisitive child pulling the wings off a fly, you wanted to see how much you could do to me before I died. But that would only have been an additional benefit to your true purpose."

A pigeon fluttered down to land on his shoulder. He took it in his gnarled hands, stroking it tenderly. "I suppose Caidin promised you some reward for your help," he went on viciously. "Or perhaps his attention is enough. It does not matter. Either way, you agreed to help him get rid of me. For so long, he has loathed the fact that I exist—a deformed bastard son of his father, the Old Baron. Yet he himself could not kill me outright. There are still a few in the keep who know we are half brothers. If he murdered me, people would be bound to talk. The secret would leak out. He could not bear that disgrace.

"But you, Doctor, gave him a unique opportunity." Wort's harsh glare stifled her protestations. "Caidin sent you to convince me that you could heal me through an operation. Only it is an operation I would never have survived, isn't it? Caidin would have exactly what he wanted. And no one would ever blame a good-hearted doctor who attempted to heal a hunchback—and lamentably failed—resulting in the wretch's demise." He took another menacing step toward her. "So, Doctor, have I told your story well?"

Her expression was not fear, but terrible sadness. "Please, Wort." She reached a hand out toward him. "I would never hurt you. You must believe that."

For a moment, Wort almost took her hand. It would have been so sweet to surrender into her arms. What healing balm could have better eased his agony? An image flashed through his mind. He saw that same fine-boned hand running passionately over Caidin's muscular back. Hot as lightning, fury flooded his heart.

"You had better go, Doctor." His voice was softly threatening.

"But why?" she asked with a gasp of alarm.

"Because I am a monster, my lady. And I will surely kill you if you do not." Slowly, deliberately, with the terrible strength of his thick fingers, he twisted the neck of the mist-gray pigeon he held in his hand. Its bones popped audibly. Blood sprayed, splattering Mika's pale, lovely face.

At last he saw it, blossoming in her eyes like a dark flower. Horror. Satisfaction welled up inside him. There was no more worry in her expression, no more sorrow, and no more love. There was only pure, sublime horror. At last, like all the others, she too saw him for the monster he surely was. With a wordless cry she turned to flee down the stairwell. Wort's mocking laughter echoed after her.

When she was gone, he scrambled up the ladder into the belfry. All at once the tower's bells began to swing back and forth, rocked by unseen hands, tolling out a tremendous dirge. In exultation Wort stood beneath the Bell of Doom, holding out his arms to catch the rain of bloodstained tokens.

PART III

Angel and Monster

 **FIFTEEN**

A murderer stalked the barony of Nartok.

By most accounts, Nartok's treasurer was the first to die. Few were sorrowful to see the merciless tax collector meet his end, but even fewer failed to shiver at the gory details of his demise—crushed to death by a chest heaped with gold. Next to go was the village tanner, a man known to tan the hides of his apprentices as readily as those of the animals whose skins he fashioned into leather. He was found dangling from a rafter in his shop, horror on his bloated face, hanged by the neck with the belt he had used to whip his errant helpers. Some whispered that perhaps the apprentices themselves had turned upon the man. As the days passed and the bodies were heaped higher and higher in the charnel house, such mundane theories were forgotten.

Each killing seemed stranger and more gruesome than the last. A pair of lovers were found in the woods, dark leaves clinging damply to their naked skin, bound together by the thorned vines that had strangled them. In the keep's kitchens, a scullery boy stirred one of the gigantic iron kettles hanging above the hearth only to see the bulging-eyed face of the kitchenwife bob to the surface. The sharp-tongued woman had been boiled alive in her own

foul stew. The village scribe, the acerbic Master
Demaris, was discovered in his shop one morning,
quill pens protruding from each of his eyes. His body
was covered with sheaves of parchment, and on
each, penned in the dark-rust ink of human blood,
was a hideous poem. The one he clutched in his stiff
hand was perhaps the worst of them all:

> We live out our lives the dreaming dead,
> All born to brief waking, to know and dread
> The ancient, cruel, voiceless call—
> Proclaiming our fate
> To lie swaddled again
> In the tomb's cold pall.

> Eternity breathes dark breath on our face,
> Whispering of earth and its damp embrace.
> We rise from the soil only to fall—
> Our souls to reap
> Then grind to meal
> Doom shall come for us all.

By day, folk huddled together in taverns, stables,
and smithies, whispering of the bizarre and grisly
deaths that plagued the fiefdom.

"Did you hear about the miller?"

The peasants gathered in the common room of the
Black Boar shook their heads fearfully, gazing at the
man who had spoken. He took a sip from his mug of
dark ale and wiped the foam from his bushy mustache.

"His brother found him this morning," the man
went on grimly. "Ground to bits on his own millstone,
he was." The others shuddered. "That makes thirteen so far. Thirteen murdered in the last week
alone. You know what I think? I think that it's a—" He
lowered his voice dramatically. "—a werewolf."

Another man snorted at this. "You're wrong, Rory. Everyone knows the killings have to do with the tower on the moor. It's the ghost of the murdered Vistana, it is. The gypsy is building the tower, and he's using the blood of the people he kills to mix the mortar." Gasps of shock went around the circle. All knew the tales concerning the mysterious tower—how the ring of stones had first appeared on the exact spot where a gypsy man had been robbed and stabbed to death, and how his spirit was said to haunt the accursed place.

"That's not what I heard," the brewer's wife countered. "I heard it's the monster that lives in the bell tower. Haven't you heard the bells ringing at odd and frequent hours of late?" This was greeted with murmurs of assent.

A beady-eyed man spoke then. "You are fools," he sniveled in a wheedling voice. "Have you all forgotten about the witch and her daemon?" He cast a fearful look at the door, behind which all knew the golden-haired healer saw her suffering patients.

The man with the bushy mustache frowned. "We've all heard enough of your witless talk, Cray. If the doctor's a witch, then you're a warlock. Besides, I still say it's a werewolf. . . ."

Every evening as the eye of the sun drowned in a sea of blood-red clouds, folk in the village shut themselves tightly inside their hovels. In the keep, courtiers and servants alike barred the doors of their chambers and lit candle after candle until their rooms were virtually ablaze. All stared with wide eyes until at long last they heard the dissonant chorus of cocks heralding the dawn, and shuddered with relief that they had lived through one more night. Then all would emerge fearfully from their hiding places to discover, as they knew they would, which of them had not been so fortunate. Even by day, now, the fiefdom seemed deathly quiet. No travelers came to the keep, no merchant wagons slogged through the muddy streets of the village, no gold changed hands, no goods were crafted, no dice were thrown in the dank back-street hideaways. Fear held Nartok utterly in its paralyzing grip.

Then at last came the dark discovery.

*   *   *   *   *

"Kill the fiend!"

The angry cries rose up the rocky slope of the tor from the village far below. Baron Caidin gripped the stone balustrade of the balcony outside his chamber with white-knuckled hands. He watched grimly as countless torches bobbed in the dusky half-light, streaming like a procession of fireflies up the twisting road that led to the massive gates.

"Kill the fiend!"

Caidin swore bitterly. For the hundredth time that day, he asked himself how this could be happening. His plans were so near completion. The tower was all but finished. He had pored over every detail of his grand design to wrest the kingdom of Darkon from Azalin's hands. He had considered every possibility and difficulty. Yet, in all his scheming, he had not planned on this.

"Kill the baron!"

The mob of villagers approached the stone walls of the keep, chanting their bloodthirsty chorus. "Kill the fiend! Kill the baron! Kill the fiend!" Some shook sharpened hoes and wooden pitchforks. Those who did not angrily gripped wooden clubs and heavy stones. They surged against the gates, crimson torchlight flickering in their eyes.

At last Caidin heard the sound he had been waiting for. Clear and stirring, a horn pierced the air, signaling a charge. With the clank of iron chains and the groan of wood, the ponderous gates of the keep swung open. A score of the baron's blue-coated knights thundered out astride galloping white coursers. The knights drew their curved sabers. Firelight glinted on the steel blades. The horses plunged into the mob.

Still chanting their violent refrain, the peasants raised their crude weapons. The knights spurred their horses through the crowd, crushing those unfortunate enough to fall beneath the hooves of their horses, hacking in all directions with their wickedly curved blades. The peasants clustered around each horse, jabbing upward with rusted spears and sharpened stakes. One of the knights screamed in agony, blood bubbling from his mouth, as a steel pitchfork plunged into his belly. He toppled out of the saddle and was trampled by the stamping hooves of his own horse. A rock struck another knight between the eyes, leaving a wet, crimson blossom on his forehead. He, too, fell to the ground, where a dozen peasants clubbed his quivering form while the mob cheered.

Eyeing their fallen comrades, the rest of the knights changed their tactics and formed two solid lines. They flanked the throng on two sides, slashing with their sabers. Untrained in the art of war, the peasants were no match for the organized onslaught. The chanting of the mob quickly changed to panicked screams. One peasant clutched his stomach, trying to keep his entrails from spilling to the ground. Another waved the severed stump of an arm, spraying the crowd with gore. A third futilely tried to close the gash in his neck as blood spurted in a crimson fountain. In moments the battle became a rout. The villagers dropped their torches and weapons. They turned to flee, dragging the dead and wounded with them. The knights let out a cry of victory. They sheathed their sabers and wheeled their mounts around, retreating into the keep's courtyard. The ponderous gates swung shut.

It was over. For now. Caidin knew the mob would return. Three evenings in a row the vengeful throng had approached the gates of the keep, and three times Caidin's men had repulsed them. Yet each night the mob was larger than the night before. More importantly, Caidin knew that whispers of suspicion had begun to circulate among his knights and servants. It was only a matter of time until his own followers turned against him. When that happened, all hope was lost.

Caidin did not know who had hidden the wooden box filled with bloodstained objects in his chamber. Whoever the interloper was, he was the true fiend, the agent of over a dozen macabre deaths in the keep and village. Each of the objects in the wooden box had belonged to one of the killer's victims. Each was an accusing finger of guilt. They had been found by a servant three days before in Caidin's own chamber.

Like any strong ruler, Caidin had always maintained a clever balance of terror in his fiefdom. The people had to fear him enough to obey his every command, but not so much that they would rebel. With the discovery of the incriminating objects, the folk of Nartok now believed their baron to be not only a cruel overlord, but the vilest and most heinous murderer of the time. The scales of fear had tipped wildly out of balance. The result was a violent uprising that could conceivably end in Caidin's own execution.

As night drowned the countryside in darkness, Caidin went to his private chamber. Pock lounged on a velvet chaise, clad in a ruffled shirt and a puffy coat of yellow satin that clashed with his purple skin. At least Caidin could be certain that the gnome would not turn against him. Who else would put up with the sniveling little maggot?

"I just thought of something, Your Grace," the gnome said, his bald head wrinkled in concentration.

"Please, Pock, I'm in no mood for jokes," Caidin replied acidly.

"None of this makes any sense," the gnome went on blithely. He scooped up a handful of blood-encrusted objects from the incriminating wooden box. "Why would someone go to so much trouble to frame you for a bunch of crimes you didn't commit, when there are so many other crimes that you actually did? It seems like it would be far simpler just to mention those to the peasantry to get their dander up." Pock chewed on his lower lip thoughtfully. "In fact, now that I think about it, Your Grace, it's truly a wonder that the people haven't risen up against you a long time ago."

"No, Pock," Caidin countered. "It's truly a wonder that I didn't wring your scrawny neck a long time ago."

The gnome gulped, dropping the bloodstained objects back into the box. "May wonders never cease, Your Grace!"

Caidin groaned, flopping down into a gilded chair. He did not have the energy to give his wretched little slave the drubbing he deserved. All his life, Caidin had lived in utter confidence of his power and superiority. He had never encountered a situation of which he did not feel he was the ultimate master. Now, for the first time, he felt a hint of uncertainty, perhaps—did he dare think it?—even vulnerability.

"I am lost, Pock," he said forlornly. "If the tower were complete, I would have nothing to fear from the most widespread rebellion. Indeed, a few nights more are all the zombies need to finish their task. But something tells me that I do not have even that long. Something tells me that a few more nights will find me dead." He covered his eyes with a many-ringed hand. "What am I to do, Pock?"

"Actually, Your Grace, I think I can suggest a solution."

Lowering his hand, Caidin shot the gnome a sour look. "It was a rhetorical question, Pock."

"You should have said so in the first place, Your Grace," the gnome complained. "The villagers seem to have their minds set on pounding a stake in your heart, stringing you up, and then burning you alive." The gnome frowned. "No, I suppose they would have to burn you alive *first,* then string you up. Hmmm . . . Of course, then there wouldn't be much left to—"

"Enough, Pock!" Caidin growled. "I get the point."

Pock clapped his hands together happily. "How terribly brilliant of you, Your Grace!" Caidin's face coloration approached that of the gnome's. Pock did not appear to notice. "Well," he went on, "my plan's actually very simple."

"What a surprise."

"If the villagers want to kill you because they're worried you're going to keep on murdering people, then why don't you just give them something *else* to worry about? Surely you can think of something dire enough to occupy their time—at least for a few days, until the tower is done. Then who cares what the peasants think. You can squash them all like bugs!" This last idea was apparently too much for the gnome, sending him into a histrionic fit of laughter. He fell backward on the chaise, kicking and rolling as his purple little body was racked with uncontrollable mirth. "Bugs!" he squealed gleefully once more.

Caidin ignored him. A sharp light brought the old flicker of life to his green eyes. He sat up straight in the chair. The familiar confidence returned. "Of course," he said in amazement. "It's perfect. Yet so simple it would take an idiot to see it. And no one is more idiotic that yourself, Pock."

"Why thank you, Your Grace!" the gnome snorted between giggles. "You're too kind!"

Caidin had already stalked from the chamber to begin giving the orders.

*   *   *   *   *

Mika stared out the grimy window of the inn's back room into the gray morning light. The question that had tormented her all night, and the three nights before that, still festered in her mind. How could she, a woman of healing, have known such exquisite pleasure in the arms of a villainous murderer? She clutched the gold locket that once more hung around her neck.

"Forgive me, my loves," she whispered. "I am so very sorry. Forgive me."

That was the worst of it. Were they here, Geordin and Lia *would* forgive her. She knew it as surely as she knew her own name. They would hold her in their arms and take her tears upon their own cheeks, and truly, absolutely forgive her.

"I do not deserve forgiveness, my loves," she whispered despairingly. Sighing, she turned away from the window.

She had not heard them come in.

Mika clamped a hand to her mouth, stifling a cry. Three women stood in the open doorway. That they were Vistani she knew from their garb—full white shirts, embroidered vests, skirts of brilliant, swirling colors. Over it all they wore so much jewelry that the sheer weight of it ought to have borne them to the ground. They glittered with copper bracelets, glass earrings, and beaded necklaces.

Despite their similar attire, the three women were markedly different from one another. One was barely more than a child, cheeks pink and bosom full with the first bloom of womanhood. A ring set with a large green stone sparkled on her hand. The second Vistana was of middle years, radiant in her maturity, the fine lines about her eyes and mouth accentuating her beauty. She, too, wore a ring with a shining stone. The third gypsy was ancient in aspect, a crone stooped over a twisted walking staff. About her wrinkled visage and wispy white hair there existed a faded, fragile beauty. Her ring bore a stone so black it seemed to absorb all light that strayed near its polished facets. Though the three women differed greatly in age and appearance, the same wise light shone in each of their eyes.

Forcibly, Mika regained her composure. She had heard many mysterious stories about the Vistani— how they traveled constantly in their gilded, brightly painted wagons, considering all the land their home; how they read hints of the future in the patterns of cards and the flight of birds; how they were said to be able to look at a man's palm and know his soul completely. Still, somehow she knew that the three gypsies meant her no harm.

She cleared her throat. "Can I . . . can I help you? Is one of you hurt?"

To Mika's surprise, it was the youngest of the three gypsies who stepped forward to answer. "No, Doctor. It is your own hurt that brought us here. It is *we* who would help *you*."

Mika found herself sinking down into a chair. "I see." These were the only words she could manage. What did these Vistani want with her?

The women entered the chamber, accompanied by the faint music of their clinking jewelry. Their radiance seemed to brighten the dingy room.

The middle-aged Vistana spoke next. "May we ask you something, Doctor?"

Mika nodded dumbly.

"We have learned that there is a hunchback who lives in the bell tower of Nartok Keep. You are familiar with him, are you not?"

Surprise flickered across Mika's face. "Yes, that's so. His name is Wort. How . . . how do you know of him?"

A cackle escaped from the lips of the eldest Vistana. "How do you know that the sun shall rise each morning, my child? How do you know that, after winter, spring will come again?"

Mika shook her head in puzzlement. "I suppose I just know."

The ancient gypsy nodded gravely, as if Mika had just uttered some profound truth.

"We believe your friend may be in terrible danger, Doctor," the youngest of the three spoke.

Mika thought of her last encounter with Wort and found that she was shaking. Her heart still held many feelings for the hunchback—sorrow, pity, even a degree of love. Now to that list had been added another—fear. For a moment, she remembered the way Wort had twisted the neck of the poor gray pigeon.

"He . . . he isn't my friend any longer," she replied at last.

The pretty Vistana arched a single eyebrow in curiosity. "Then he is in even greater danger," she replied solemnly.

"Tell us, Doctor," the middle-aged gypsy asked, "do you believe in evil?"

"I . . . I'm not . . . " Mika swallowed hard. She thought of all she had witnessed, long ago in Il Aluk, and now these last days. Finally she forced herself to say the word. "Yes."

The youngest of the three nodded. "You are right to believe so, Doctor. You see, long before there was light, there was darkness. Even now, night dwells in brooding jealousy of day, begrudging the hours when light touches the land darkness once possessed so completely. Darkness is very ancient, and very powerful, and it schemes ever for the time when it will rule the world once more."

"But what does this have to do with me?" Mika asked hoarsely. The Vistana's words terrified her.

"Nothing," the gypsy crone answered. "Or everything."

A slightly manic smile touched Mika's lips. "Well, that about covers all the possibilities."

"It does indeed," the young Vistana replied. She grew solemn once more. "There remain in this land many relics of the ancient time when darkness ruled the world, objects of terrible evil. We are fortunate, for most are lost, or at least hidden away so deeply they will never be found. Yet a perilous few are not so well concealed. From time to time, such a relic is unearthed, and then only woe can follow."

Mika shivered. "You believe Wort has one of these . . . these *relics?*"

The Vistani nodded. For a time they spoke while Mika listened. She learned the names of the three women—Karin was youngest and most forthright, Riandra motherly and questioning, and Varith the wizened crone who wrapped herself in mystery.

"Ages ago, in another land, there was an arrogant and foolish king," Karin began the horrible tale. "In his kingdom lived a great smith, and one day the king demanded that the smith forge for him a bell of bronze and silver. The smith told the king that these two metals would not mix, and that such a bell would crack the first time it was rung. Because of his pride, the king would not recant his request, ill-considered though it was. He commanded that the smith forge such a bell, and if it cracked when it was rung, the smith's eldest child would be killed. In anger and fear, the smith set to his impossible task. At first he despaired, but then—and how we will never know— dark knowledge came to him. He discovered a way to make molten bronze and silver bind.

"When at last he unveiled the bell, the king marveled at its beauty. The king commanded the smith to ring the instrument, and this was done. The bell's voice was pure and rich and like nothing those who looked on had ever heard. What was more, it did not crack.

"But the king's joy at this triumph was marred. As the bell rang out, the smith gleefully revealed how he had accomplished this impossible task. He had learned that there was one substance, and one alone, that would cause silver and bronze to bind, and that was human blood. 'Whose blood was spilled to forge this abomination?' the king asked in dread. The smith's laughter rang out as loud as the bell. 'That of your three sons,' he replied. 'It seemed fitting, since you would have gladly slain my child had I failed.'

"Before the king could call for the smith's death, the tolling of the bell faded, and suddenly the air darkened as three apparitions appeared. They were the spirits of the king's dead sons. The smith fell to his knees, begging for mercy, but as the others gazed on, the spirits tore his body apart. Then they vanished into the air once more. Forever after, it was the curse of the bell that, each time it was rung, someone was forced to pay for its music with his life."

After Karin finished, silence reigned for a spell. At last, Mika managed to ask the question whose answer she feared to learn. "What . . . what became of this bell?"

"The bell's history is long and tangled," Varith replied in a voice like a crow's. "Eventually it came to lie in a cathedral, a cathedral whose ruins yet stand in the forest east of here."

Riandra placed a motherly hand on Mika's shoulder. "Tell us, child. You have seen something in the bell tower, something that stirs fear in your heart even now. What was it?"

Mika could barely speak for her trembling. "I saw him. I saw Wort in the belfry. He had rung one of his bells, and he . . . he was talking to . . . them."

"Who, child? You must tell us!"

Mika drew in a ragged breath. "Three dark spirits. . . . "

As one, the three Vistani nodded grimly.

SIXTEEN

Baron Caidin paced the length of the Grand Hall, his thumb stroking the darkly mottled Soulstone. The stone was now filled with the life-forces of over a hundred villagers. It was ready—and in two days the tower would be ready as well. Then at last it would be time to set his plans in motion.

He paused to pour himself a glass of wine, setting the stone down on an ornately carved table. Suddenly a faint spark of emerald light sizzled around the stone and plunged into the wooden surface of the table. The table shook, scuttling a few inches across the marble floor before becoming still. Caidin snatched up the stone.

"I had better be more careful," he whispered in fascination. "The stone is so full it is nearly overflowing."

He slipped the stone into a pocket. Abruptly the gilded doors of the Grand Hall flew open. Caidin spun on a heel. Surprise played across his regal visage, followed by smug awareness.

"My lady," he said with a white-toothed smile.

Even in her woolen dress of drab gray, the golden-haired doctor looked radiant. "Your Grace," Mika said breathlessly, rushing toward him. "I must talk to you."

Interest flickered in Caidin's green eyes. "My lady, it is dangerous for you to have come here."

She shook her head fiercely. "I know it wasn't you who committed the murders, Your Grace. That's why I came." She took a deep breath. "I . . . I think I know a way for you to prove your innocence."

Caidin raised a dark eyebrow. This was a curious turn of events. He reached out and took her hands. "Tell me, my lady."

Abruptly she pulled away, showing her back to him. "First . . . first you must promise me something, Your Grace." Her shoulders were trembling.

The baron stroked his oiled beard. Was the naive doctor actually attempting to weave some little web of intrigue? Very well, he would play along with her little charade. "You have only to ask it, my lady," he said gravely.

Slowly she turned around, her gaze intent. "Then swear to this, Your Grace. No matter what I tell you, you will do nothing to harm Wort."

Caidin clenched his teeth to keep from cursing aloud the bastard's name. Evidently the doctor still pitied the wretched hunchback. Her expression was resolute. It was clear she would say nothing more without his promise.

"On my honor as a baron, I swear it, my lady," he lied with perfect conviction.

She nodded. "This morning, three Vistani came to visit me. . . ."

With growing interest, Caidin listened as Mika explained what the gypsies had revealed to her. At last she fell silent, her face pale.

"What . . . what are you going to do, Your Grace?" she asked finally.

"This," he replied. He drew her in close to his lean body and pressed his lips burningly against hers. Only for a fraction of a second did she resist, and then he knew that his corruption of the good doctor was almost complete. He swept her into his strong arms. She clung to him desperately, trembling like a small animal, as he bore her from the Grand Hall to his private chamber.

Later, as twilight gathered its purple mantle around the keep, Caidin sprawled among the tangled silk sheets of his bed. He held a crystal wine goblet upon his chest, its base cool against his bare skin. After hours in his embrace, Mika had left at last to return to the village before sundown. He pondered again what the doctor had told him. A bell that killed whenever it was rung—a fascinating relic, and Wort had been putting it to devious use. Now Caidin would use it against Wort. All these years he had not dared to kill his brother for fear that the Old Baron's secret would be revealed. Now, however, he could expose Wort as the fiend behind all the recent gruesome murders, and the folk of Nartok would kill the hunchback themselves. The Old Baron's secret would die with him.

"At last I'll be rid of you, Wort," Caidin crooned. He hurled the empty glass at the far wall. It struck a tapestry, then fell, shattering with a brilliant sound.

"Ouch!" came a muffled voice from behind the tapestry. "That hurt, Your Grace!"

Behind the weaving a strange lump slid to the floor, landing with a *thump!* A small purple form crawled from beneath the bottom edge of the tapestry on all spindly fours.

"Pock!" Caidin growled in annoyance.

"Your Grace!" Pock scrambled to his feet to offer a sweeping bow.

"Have you been spying on me again, you little maggot?"

"Of course not, Your Grace!" The gnome's pale eyes grew as big as saucers in a less-than-convincing display of innocence. "I didn't see a thing, I swear. I only just arrived through the secret passage. The Lady Jadis is on her way to your chamber. I thought you might like to know."

Caidin swallowed his annoyance. "Strange as it may seem, you are correct, Pock. You may go now."

"You're welcome, Your Grace!" Pock slipped nimbly behind the tapestry. "By the way," the gnome's muffled voice came from behind the thick cloth. "Did you know that you look like a cross-eyed werefish when you pucker up for a kiss?"

This time a heavy bronze urn struck the far wall, but the shape behind the tapestry had already disappeared into the secret passage. Caidin did his best to forget the impudent little gnome. He needed to have a cool head when he faced Jadis.

Rolling out of the tousled bed, he pulled on a pair of tight-fitting buckskin breeches. Caidin knew well enough that Jadis had learned about his troop of zombies building the tower on the moor. Even Pock was not dim-witted enough to drink the cask of wine Jadis had left outside his door. Given the gnome's considerable experience with the sodden condition, it had been simple for him to feign drunkenness. Then Pock had followed Jadis to the cemetery and the tower.

"She is crafty, Your Grace, this pretty little kitten," Pock had reported afterward with a lascivious grin.

"That 'pretty little kitten' is a werepanther, Pock," Caidin had replied flatly. "She could gut you with once swipe of her paw."

"I know!" the gnome had said excitedly. "Isn't she marvelous, Your Grace?"

Caidin reached for a shirt to pull over his bare torso, then paused. Why not let his appearance disarm her? The baron knew well that there were few—if any—men in the realm of Darkon handsomer than himself. He dropped the shirt.

A soft rap came at the chamber's door. Caidin moved toward the portal. As he did, he glimpsed a reflection of himself in one of the chamber's windows. The glass was ancient and warped, its surface flawed with imperfections, and the reflection gazing back at him seemed hideously distorted. One side of his torso was squat and compressed, the other stretched out to bizarre proportions. Worst of all was his face, a twisted mockery that looked more like one of the grotesque masks the villagers wore for the Festival of the Dead than any human visage.

The knock came again, more insistent this time. Shuddering, Caidin managed to break himself away from the strange image of himself in the glass. It was only a reflection. There was no threat in it. Taking a deep breath, he opened the door.

The Lady Jadis gazed speculatively at his naked chest. "Have I come at an inconvenient time, Your Grace?"

He smiled broadly. "Not at all, my lady. Won't you come in?"

With a murmur of acceptance and a whisper of golden silk, she stepped into the chamber. Caidin poured them each a glass of wine. The hairs on his neck prickled. He could feel her gaze running over his back. The Kargat spy was a cool-headed professional, but she was a woman as well. He smiled to himself. Turning back, he handed her one of the glasses of wine.

"Your Grace, I've come to express my dismay at the turn of events in your fiefdom. The rabble have shown themselves for the animals they are."

Caidin nodded gravely. "Thank you, my lady." In satisfaction he noticed a rapid throbbing in the hollow of her swanlike neck. "Despite these troubled times, you need not fear for your person. I will keep you under my watchful eye, my lady."

A smile fluttered about her smoke-red lips. "I'm certain you will, Your Grace." She sipped her wine delicately. "Of course, the affairs that beckoned me to your land are nearly in order. Soon they will reach their conclusion."

"Indeed. Does this mean you will soon be departing my barony?"

"I'm afraid it does, Your Grace," she said demurely.

Caidin scowled at this. He found himself suddenly annoyed with this game of cat and mouse. "Come, my lady, let us forgo this little charade," he said suggestively.

"Your Grace?"

"You feign astonishment very well, Jadis, but truly you must know that your performance is wasted on me."

"I see."

"I grow bored with this game. I will do you a favor, my lady, and save you precious time. Tell your master that I seek to sit upon his throne. Tell him that I have slain my own subjects under the guise of a false inquisition to create a legion of zombie slaves. Tell him that I have used them to raise a dark tower for a purpose known only to myself. Tell him all these things. It will do him no good."

Jadis smoothed her elaborately coifed black hair. "Very well, Your Grace. You wish to be candid. Then let us both be. You know as well as I that King Azalin could send an army here at a moment's notice, a force strong enough to take this keep apart stone by stone, and you with it. He suffers your machinations only so long as he is amused. As soon as that amusement wanes, he will cast you aside like a broken toy."

Caidin grinned. "And only then will Azalin realize that it is too late, that sometimes toys can turn against their masters, and that a tower in the provincial hinterlands can indeed challenge his great castle of Avernus in far-off Il Aluk."

Interest danced in her eyes. "I should thank you for the time you have just saved me in my investigation, Your Grace."

He bent his head toward her. "I can think of a way you might demonstrate your gratitude, my lady." He closed his eyes and felt her warm breath against his lips.

Suddenly four lines of searing fire traced themselves across his chest. Crying out in pain and surprise, Caidin stumbled backward. His bare chest bled from four parallel gouges. The wounds were not deep, but they did sting fiercely. Jadis flexed her hand, and for a disconcerting moment he thought her fingers ended in claws.

"Damn you to the Abyss!" he snarled, clutching at the scratch marks. Blood oozed through his fingers.

"I am sorry to be so cruel, Your Grace," she purred. "I thought it important for you to learn that one cannot always have everything one desires."

With sensual grace she drifted from the room. With burning eyes, Caidin watched her go, his breaths coming in short, painful gasps.

"You are wrong about that, Kargat," he spat. Yet for a troubling moment, he wondered if he had perhaps given away too much in his confidence. He quickly dismissed the thought. There was nothing Jadis could do to stop him now.

"Pock!" he bellowed. "Show yourself quickly, you wretch, or I'll pound your thick skull. I need you. Now!"

*   *   *   *   *

Jadis purred deeply.

She had concealed herself atop a high ledge outside the baron's chamber, the dark fur of her werepanther form blending perfectly with the surrounding shadows. Her little encounter with the baron had been quite intriguing. His overconfidence played right into her hands. Or her paws, as the case may be. Now all she had to do was wait to see what move he made next.

The door of the baron's chamber flew open. Caidin stepped out, clad now in a purple coat and gray breeches. He strode forcefully down the corridor. Jadis waited until he rounded a corner, then leapt to the floor. Silently, she padded after her quarry. She winced slightly as she moved, allowing herself a low growl of discomfort. The peculiar bruise below her left collarbone had grown larger over the last few days. It still did not hurt—in fact, it was oddly cold and numb—but it hampered her movements. She supposed she must have injured herself more seriously than she had thought.

Jadis kept out of Caidin's sight. She could easily trace his footsteps. Soon she rounded a corner and watched as Caidin entered the dark archway that led to the dungeon. Two blue-coated guards saluted him as he vanished into the darkness. This time there would be no circumventing the guards.

The first guard never knew what hit him. Jadis leapt from the shadows, striking him from the side. Her fanged maw clamped around his neck. She shook her head violently, and his spine snapped like dry kindling. He slumped to the floor. Tail twitching, she spun around. The other guard swore, staring with wide eyes as he fumbled to draw his saber. He was woefully slow. Jadis pounced, knocking him to the floor. He was a brawny man, but his struggling was useless against the muscular werepanther. She raked her hindpaws across his belly, spilling his guts onto the floor. Blood spurted out of his mouth. Almost casually she bared her fangs and tore his throat apart.

She paused to lick the blood from her paws—she hated it when they were sticky. Satisfied, she slipped through the archway, leaving behind the mutilated remains of the two men. She padded through the dim labyrinth of the dungeon, her eyes piercing the gloom like emerald lanterns. The last time she had tread these dank corridors they had echoed with screams and moans. Now they were filled with tomblike silence. Yet if Caidin had slain all the prisoners for his mysterious purposes, why had he ventured down here? Jadis was determined to find out.

It was the light of their eyes that gave them away.

She turned to see a dozen crimson sparks bobbing down a darkened side passage. Despite their ungainly bodies, the creatures moved so stealthily even her sensitive ears might not have warned her of their advance. With cries of bloodlust, a half dozen goblyns leapt from the mouth of the passage into the wavering light of a smoking torch. Rags that might once have been clothes draped their twisted bodies, and they clutched barbed spears in arms knotted with muscle. Their flesh was a sickly green, and their bulbous heads were dominated by grinning maws filled with needle-sharp teeth. Swiftly they surrounded the black werepanther, their crimson eyes glowing murderously.

Jadis scratched her claws against the stone floor, sharpening them. She tensed, waiting for the right moment. As one, the goblyns lunged for her. Uncoiling her powerful limbs, she leapt over them and landed gracefully, turning to see the goblyns crash into each other in the spot where she had crouched a moment before. Two of the creatures howled in agony and stumbled away, clutching the spears that protruded from their stomachs. Both fell to the floor, dead. The other goblyns untangled themselves and turned toward Jadis. They advanced more carefully this time. Goblyns were stupid, but they were not completely without cunning.

A goblyn lunged at her with its spear. Jadis leapt easily out of its path. Growling, she whirled quickly, only to have another spear jabbed in her face. She ducked it narrowly, then backed away. The long spears made it impossible to get close enough to slash at the goblyns with her claws. Her tail brushed the rough stones of the wall. She had little room to retreat. Grinning toothily, the four goblyns drew their spears back, ready for the plunge.

Jadis tensed her limbs as if to spring. Hastily, the goblyns waved their spears upward as though to strike at her underbelly. But it was a feint on her part. Staying low instead, Jadis charged, crashing into two of the goblyns. Their spears flew from their hands and clattered to the floor. She broke one creature's neck with a lazy swipe of a paw, then sank her teeth into the skull of the other, piercing its brain. Whirling, she saw the other two goblyns lunge. She sprang high. Landing atop the two goblyns, she bore them to the floor. They struggled desperately, trying to sink their sharp teeth into her flesh. She beat them to it, ripping out their throats with swift precision.

A heartbeat later it was over. Jadis sat back on her haunches, observing as the eyes of the goblyns flickered like dying coals, then went dark. She turned and slunk swiftly down the corridor, following Caidin's scent. Jadis's black-velvet ears twitched, homing in on a sound, a faint noise floating on the dank air. Voices. She quickened her pace. Suddenly she halted, shrinking into a dark alcove. A dozen paces away, an iron door swung open with a shriek of rusted hinges.

"That is truly all, darkling?" a low voice demanded. "I have only to place the Soulstone upon the altar to invoke its power?"

"That is truly all," a wheedling voice replied, raising the hackles on Jadis's back. There was a pause. "You need me no longer. Will you not release me?"

Laughter rang out on the foul air. "We shall see, darkling."

Baron Caidin stepped into the corridor, pulling the iron door securely shut. Jadis froze. Caidin strode past her hiding place. In moments he was gone. The dark air seemed to swirl and coil about the werepanther's form. Moments later a woman with coppery skin walked down the corridor, moving gracefully on bare feet. Jadis reached the iron door. She noticed a small opening in the wall low to the ground. Kneeling, she peered through the hole. Her eyes needed no torchlight to make out the squalid chamber beyond.

"Greetings, Velvet-Claw."

Jadis gasped at the high-pitched voice. "How do you know that name?" she asked warily.

"I know many things."

A form that might once have been a man scuttled into view. Jadis curled her lip in revulsion. Filthy tatters of cloth clung damply to skeletal limbs as dark and gray as ashes. His colorless eyes bulged, staring madly, as if he gazed upon some unseen world of nightmares. By the tarnished earring he still wore, she knew him to be a Vistana. Suddenly she remembered Caidin's words. He had referred to this creature as *darkling*. Jadis had heard of such beings—cast-out Vistani, pariahs of the gypsy clans, whose souls were willingly consumed by evil.

Jadis steeled her will. "Is that why you're here? Because you know certain things of value to Baron Caidin?"

Broken laughter grated against cold stone. "Of course, Velvet-Claw. Why else? I certainly do not stay here because I like the food." The cadaverous gypsy snaked out a bony arm and snatched up a mushroom-colored beetle. He popped the insect into his mouth and crunched down with alacrity.

Jadis swallowed her unease. "I have a bargain for you, darkling. You badly want your freedom, don't you?"

A wary yet intrigued grunt was her only reply.

"Here it is then. I have the power to free you from your cell. But first you must tell me what you and the baron were speaking of just a moment ago."

A silence ensued. Finally, the darkling spoke. "I cannot do that, Velvet-Claw. The truth I speak for Caidin is his truth. Your truth is something . . . different."

Jadis frowned. She had no time for riddles. "Then we have no bargain." She started to move away from the opening.

"Wait!" The gypsy went on in a hissing voice. "I cannot tell you what words I spoke for the baron. You see, I can barely remember them now that he is gone. That is the nature of the Sight. Yet I could tell you something else . . . something that would grant you the means to defeat him."

Jadis had little to lose. "Done."

After a long pause, the darkling spoke in an eerie, almost chantlike voice. "You must journey toward the dawning sun, Velvet-Claw. I see . . . I see the shadowed forest surrounding you. Do not fear—there is no creature here more fearsome than you. Venture onward. Then . . . ah, yes . . . then the trees part like a dark curtain. There it looms before you. The broken remnants of faith forgotten. Shattered dwelling of old gods . . . cursed gods so ancient they forgot their own names long ago. It is . . . it is a . . . *cathedral!*" There was a long silence. At last the darkling spoke again. Now his voice seemed hoarse and weary, as if he had just undergone some great exertion. "That is all the Sight will reveal to me, Velvet-Claw. You must journey to this ancient cathedral. I do not know what you will discover there—only that it will grant you the means to destroy Baron Caidin."

Jadis's eyes glittered suspiciously. "Is that it?"

"That is your truth, Velvet-Claw."

At last she nodded. "Then the bargain is complete."

She stretched out a hand, and suddenly sharp claws sprang from each of her fingertips. She slipped one of her talons into the door's rusted lock. It was time to fulfill her end of the deal.

A short while later, the werepanther leapt through the window of her private bedchamber. Onyx fur rippled, and in moments the woman Jadis stood in the cat's place. A strange thrill fluttered in her heart. Somehow, she sensed that the darkling had indeed spoken truthfully to her. Whatever this ancient cathedral was, she was certain she would find something of importance there. Humming to herself in satisfaction, she turned to pick up her gown of green silk from the bed. As she did, she caught a glimpse of her naked body in the silver mirror. A chill spike plunged deep into her heart.

"It cannot be, love," she whispered to herself in disbelief. "It cannot."

She reached out and tentatively touched the livid mark that darkened the flesh beneath her collarbone. It had grown even more, and now, quite clearly, had assumed a distinctly ominous shape— the shape of a skeletal hand.

*   *   *   *   *

The darkling cringed in the shadowed mouth of the slimy drainpipe, waiting for twilight to fall. His eyes had grown too used to darkness, and the light of day was painful in its brilliance. At last the burning eye of the sun sank beneath the distant horizon. Chill blue shadows mantled the countryside. The shriveled Vistana crawled from the drainpipe, picking his path down the rocky slope of the tor to the rolling plains below.

Cackling happily, he hobbled across the moor. How wondrous it was to be free again. He wondered where he should go, what he should do. There were so many more relics of darkness he had learned about, so many objects besides the stone and the bell that were capable of wreaking massive strife and woe, and glorious mayhem. He would see them all unearthed from their ancient tombs. That would show the others once and for all how foolish they had been to cast him out. But first, perhaps, he would find some throats. Yes, that was it—some smooth, lovely throats to snap and crush with his long, shriveled hands. That was what just what he needed to revive himself after such long confinement. His mirth bubbling weirdly, he pushed his ravaged body on, into the purple gloaming.

Suddenly the darkling paused. With a gasp he turned around. His pale eyes shone as round as moons in the dimness. "No," he croaked. "No, you cannot be here. I would have seen your coming long ago."

"That is not so, Accursed One." Three figures stepped from the cold gloom. "Your powers have diminished since you were banished from the clan. We blinded your Sight, so that you would not sense our coming."

The darkling shuddered violently. This could not be happening. He thought he was finally free! "Varith, Karin, Riandra—please, do not harm me. I will leave this domain, yes? I will go far away. You will never see me again!"

The Vistana women cast back the hoods of their cloaks, revealing three faces—one fresh and young, one full in bloom, one wrinkled by time. Sorrow and pity shone in their wise eyes.

"We cannot allow that, Accursed One. We cannot let you bring your darkness to another land, as you did to our clan. It must end here."

The darkling spun around, desperately searching for an escape, but the gypsies had surrounded him. He fell to his bony knees. "I beg you!" he pleaded piteously. "Let me be! I will try . . . I will try to live in the Light once more."

The eldest of the three gypsies clutched her walking staff tightly. "It is our wish, Accursed One, that you dwell in the Light as well. But it is too late for you to do so in this existence. It is far too late."

The jeweled rings each gypsy wore began to pulsate—one with leaf-green brilliance, one with dusky-blue radiance, one with midnight-purple darkness. Holding the glowing rings before them, the Vistani closed in.

The darkling's cry of primal agony rent the night. Abruptly it ended, its echo drifting through the rising mist. The three gypsies stepped back, sorrow and pity written across their disparate faces. The three jeweled rings were quiescent once more.

On the ground in their midst lay the darkling. A silver, rune-covered dagger protruded from his sunken chest. His frozen hand still clutched the knife, and his pale eyes stared upward, gazing no longer on nightmares, but simply on emptiness.

"Has he found an end?" Riandra asked in a chantlike voice.

"He has found an end," young Karin replied firmly.

Ancient Varith knelt and covered the darkling's pale eyes with two dark leaves. Slowly, leaning upon her staff, she rose. "He is Accursed no longer, but dwells now in the Light." Tears streamed freely down her wrinkled cheeks. "Fare thee well, Brinn. Fare thee well, child of Vistani."

Drifting tatters of mist coiled about the dead body of the darkling, concealing it in a damp gray shroud. A sharp wind blew the fog away. The corpse was gone. Karin bent to pick up the silver dagger. The knife glimmered dully in the half-light as she slipped it carefully into the leather sheath at her hip. Then the three women turned away, vanishing into the deepening night.

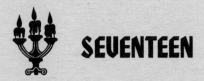

SEVENTEEN

Mika stood before the mirror in her chamber in the Black Boar, clad once more in the baron's gift—a gown of lavender silk. By this she knew she was defeated. Shame, sorrow, guilt—all these things seemed to evaporate like mist in the heat of her desire for Caidin. He owned her now, utterly. Mika loathed herself for this. Yet even worse, she still wanted Caidin—more than ever. Leaving the inn, she picked her way through the muck toward the gilded carriage that waited to deliver her into sweet imprisonment.

"Milady!" a voice called behind her. "Milady, please wait!"

Mika turned in surprise. A young woman dashed down the muddy street, coming to a breathless halt before her.

"Begging your pardon, milady, but it's my grandmama." Worry was written clearly across the peasant woman's flushed face. "She's terribly ill."

Slowly, Mika shook her head. "I'm . . . I'm sorry. I was—"

"Please, milady." The young woman rung her hands desperately. "Please, won't you come?"

Mika opened her mouth wordlessly, casting a look of longing at the waiting carriage. Finally, realizing that she could not turn the disconsolate young woman away, she nodded. Moments later, she followed the peasant woman—whose name was Lillen—through the main room of a neatly scrubbed cottage.

"She is in the back chamber, milady. This way. She barricaded the door, but Elgar—that's my husband, milady—Elgar removed the hinges. She was very adamant in her wish not to see a healer."

From the back room came the crash of something breaking, followed by a shrill cry. "Leave me be, Elgar! And put my door back on, do you hear?" A peasant man, so young his beard was little more than fuzz, dashed out of the room, ducking to avoid a small clay vase that flew through the open doorway. It hit the far wall and shattered.

The young man gave his wife a chagrined look. "It appears your grandmama is feeling better, Lillen."

"She certainly seems to have a strong arm," Mika noted dryly. Carefully, she peered into the back room.

"I see as usual my granddaughter has ignored my wishes."

Startled, Mika realized that what she had at first thought only to be a small heap of rumpled blankets on the bed by the window was in fact a tiny, shriveled woman. She blended well with the threadbare bedclothes. Only her eyes stood out. They were bright as polished stones, shining with sharp intelligence.

Mika cleared her throat. "You granddaughter has told me that you require a doctor."

The old woman snorted. "My granddaughter says all sorts of foolish things. I am sorry you made the trip here, milady, but I have no use for a doctor. I am dying, that's all."

"Grandmama!" Lillen gasped in protest, but a flick of the old woman's piercing eyes made her shut up.

Mika nodded gravely. "Do you mind if I come in for a moment all the same?"

The old woman threw up her arms in defeat. "Oh, very well." She glared at the young couple, who clutched each other in concern. "But you two stay out!"

As Elgar led a sobbing Lillen back to the main room, Mika sat on the edge of the bed and opened her black satchel. The old woman grudgingly revealed her name—Irsyla. After several minutes of silent examination Mika leaned back, her expression solemn.

"You *are* dying, Irsyla. But it is not from an illness. You're just very old, and your body is worn out."

"A fact of which I am well aware. But try telling that to those two young ninnies out there."

Mika laughed gently. "They only love you, you know."

Irsyla's expression softened. "I know, milady. I love them dearly as well. But I am tired. I have lived a long, good life. Now it is time for me to sleep."

Mika smiled warmly at her patient. "I'll leave some herbs for a tea your granddaughter can brew. It has no medicinal purposes that I know of, but it tastes nice, and it might make Lillen feel that she's doing something to help."

Irsyla reached out to grip her arm in thanks. It was then that Mika noticed that the old woman's hand was missing two of its fingers.

"How did this happen?" Mika asked with a doctor's curiosity, feeling the old woman's hand.

Irsyla snatched her arm back. "I do not think you wish to know that, milady." There was an ominous tone to the old woman's voice.

Mika looked up in surprise. "Why do you say that?"

Irsyla's eyes glittered sharply. "Why? Because you

wear a gown that belongs to him even now, milady. And I have seen you through my window, riding in the gilded carriage to his keep."

"Baron Caidin?" Mika's heart skipped a beat. "You mean the baron did this to you?"

The old woman slowly shook her head. "Not this baron, milady. The Old Baron."

"Tell me."

At last the old woman sighed. "I had thought to take the tale to my grave. I have never told it to anyone. Not even Lillen. But perhaps it is right that you hear it." Irsyla went on in a low voice. "In my younger days, I was the village's midwife. I helped the young come into this world, and to draw their first breaths. But all that ended more than thirty years ago."

"What happened?"

"It was a dark midwinter's night. Two of the Old Baron's knights barged through the door of my cottage to tell me I was needed at the keep. They hardly gave me a chance to gather my things before bundling me into a carriage and hauling me up the tor. There I discovered that, not one, but two women were caught in the throes of labor, sharing the same birthing chamber. One was the Old Baron's wife, the baroness. The other was his mistress, a beautiful woman by the name of Kylene, whom some whispered was a witch. The baroness delivered her child first. It was a son, and at this news the Old Baron was joyous. As I examined the child, I could see that it was not well formed. Its limbs were ill-proportioned, its spine curved. The Old Baron flew into a rage. He might have throttled the child there and then, but the baroness clutched the infant to her breast.

"Moments later, Kylene gave birth. Her child was also a son, but this infant was strong and bonny like his father. It was then that the Old Baron concocted a foul scheme. 'I will not have a cripple for an heir,' he

roared. 'Let my bastard be the misbegotten one.'
Ignoring the screams of the women, the Old Baron
tore the crying infants from each of their arms and
switched the two babes."

Mika's violet eyes went wide. "But didn't the
women tell people the truth about what was done?"

Irsyla shook her head grimly. "They never had the
opportunity. Neither woman lived out the night. The
Old Baron poisoned them both to keep his deed a
secret."

Mika stared in open horror.

"I was the only one alive who knew the truth,"
Irsyla went on. "But the Old Baron did not forget me.
The next day, two of his knights came upon me
unaware. They dragged me far into the snowy forest
and hurled me down into a deep crevice to die." A
toothless smile spread across her wrinkled visage.
"But I am clever, milady. Though my leg was broken,
I crawled along the bottom of the crevice until I
found an abandoned animal's den. There I survived
for many days, melting snow in my mouth for water,
and eating bitter winter herbs for nourishment. I lost
two of my fingers to frostbite, and nearly all my toes.
At last a woodcutter heard my calls, and others
came to haul me up from the crevice. After that I
lived far from here, in another village with my sister.
The Old Baron never believed anything but that the
midwife who knew the truth was dead in a forest pit.
When he died, I finally returned to Nartok to live with
my dear Lillen."

Mika shivered. "Then it is Caidin who is the bastard son, while the true heir to the barony is . . ."

Irsyla nodded grimly. "The hunchback in the bell
tower."

"Does . . . does Caidin know this?"

"What do you think, milady?"

Mika's mind reeled as she tried to comprehend

this new, astounding knowledge. Wort was the true baron, not Caidin! At last she understood the real source of Caidin's hatred for his half brother. What a fool she had been to think Caidin would help her save Wort from the power of the cursed bell. No doubt he would gladly see Wort die—and the secret of Caidin's own illegitimacy with him. Cold dread filled her chest, freezing her heart. It was up to her to save Wort now. She would have to do it alone. But how?

A voice whispered in Mika's mind. *The bell's history is long and tangled . . . it came to lie in a cathedral, a cathedral whose ruins yet stand in the forest east of here. . . .* She blinked in surprise, unsure whether the voice had been her own or that of some . . . other. It did not matter. Mika remembered what the three Vistani had said about the place where the bell had lain forgotten for long centuries. Perhaps she would find something there—some clue that would help her free Wort from the bell's enchantment.

"Irsyla," she said urgently. "Do you know of a ruin that lies to the east of here in the forest, the ruin of a cathedral?"

"I do, milady. It is an ill-fated place. You would do well to forget it."

Mika shook her head firmly. "I cannot. Please, Irsyla. Will you tell me how I can reach the ruins?"

The old woman studied Mika's earnest face for a long moment. At last, gripping Mika's arm tightly once more, she nodded.

*   *   *   *   *

"Calm yourself, love," Jadis whispered to herself. "This is no time to lose your wits. Not if you intend to stay alive."

Alone in her bedchamber, she studied her naked form in the mirror. Now there were dozens of the hand-shaped blotches all over her body. Some of them had merged into larger splotches of dark purple, ash gray, and livid green. None of the spots caused her pain. Instead, they were all disturbingly numb. She walked with a slight limp now, and the movement of her arms was clumsy. Then there was the smell. It was so faint that others might not have noticed it, but the odor was clear to her sensitive nose. It was the sweet, wet scent of decay.

Jadis peered over her shoulder to study the mottled blotches on her back. It was just as she feared. Each of the hand-shaped marks appeared in a spot where King Azalin had touched her flesh. A shiver coursed through her.

"Be brave, love." She tried to control her fear. "It is not too late. Not yet."

Cold air rushed into the chamber, accompanied by a rhythmic flapping sound. A shadow absorbed the morning light. She turned, hastily clutching a robe about her naked body, to see a huge raven alight on the windowsill. The ruby medallion at its throat glistened like wet blood.

"Goreon," she gasped.

"Greetings, Velvet-Claw." The raven cocked its head, staring at her. "I bring you news from our master in Avernus."

"What is it?" she snapped. "What does Azalin say?"

Goreon ruffled his ebony feathers. "He has heard your message, and his reply is this: 'Forgive me, my Jadis. I do sometimes forget the frailty of living flesh. Return to me, and I shall make your delicious body pure once more.' "

Jadis let out a deep breath of relief. "Then I must journey to Il Aluk at once."

"Wait," the raven croaked. "There is more."

Her blood froze in her veins.

"Our master also speaks thusly: 'But do not forget your duty, my Jadis. Do not return to Avernus before you have discovered Caidin's intentions. My love for you is nearly boundless. My wrath for servants who fail me *is* boundless.' "

Jadis could not suppress the shudder that racked her body.

Goreon's scaly claws scratched against the stone windowsill. "Did I not warn you, Velvet-Claw? There is death in all the Wizard King touches."

Rage flared in Jadis's brain. She grabbed a heavy silver candelabra and hurled it at the raven. "Begone with you, carrion-eater!" she snarled. The dark bird fluttered into the air, easily dodging the missile. "Tell Azalin that I am, as ever, his loyal Kargat. Tell him that he will have the knowledge he seeks. Now away with you!"

She launched a heavy book at the window, but the raven had already spread its night-cloud wings to rise into the azure sky. Gradually, she forced her anger to cool.

"That's more like it, love," she murmured. "Now finish what you came here for, and when you return to Il Aluk, Azalin will make you whole and beautiful again."

Her flesh began to ripple in transformation.

* * * * *

It was midafternoon when Mika reached the cathedral. The forest parted to either side of the rutted track like a dark curtain, revealing the brooding ruins. She slipped from the back of the sturdy pony Lillen's husband, Elgar, had given her at Irsyla's stern command. The beast let out a nervous snort.

"I know." Mika stroked the pony's gray-velvet muzzle reassuringly. "I feel it, too. It's as though something is watching over this place. A presence. Whatever it is, I don't think it wants us here." She tied the pony's reins to a tree branch. Fighting her trepidation, she walked slowly up the crumbling steps to the gaping doorway of the cathedral. The shadows swallowed her up as she stepped within.

The ruin looked to have been abandoned for centuries. Piles of rubble from the high-arched ceiling were heaped everywhere, and nettles pushed up through the cracked floor. Stone gargoyles leered down from high ledges, grins plastered on their weird mouths. A crimson miasma hung in the air, permeating the stones. The light came from stained-glass windows that seemed oddly out of place amid the decay and disintegration. They shone as brilliantly as they must have the day they were first raised into place, their myriad fragments of glass transformed into shards of sapphire, ruby, and emerald by the sunlight that poured through them. Three stained-glass windows high in the cathedral's nave captured Mika's attention. Slowly, she climbed the steps, gazing upward at the glowing windows. Each depicted a stern-faced knight clad in ornate, archaic armor, and bearing an antique broadsword. The mosaic had been fitted together so skillfully that the knights looked almost real—so real they seemed to follow her with eyes of smoked glass.

Shuddering, Mika forced her eyes away from the windows. She found herself staring at the broad slab of dark porphyry that must have served as the altar. Like everything in the cathedral, the altar was covered with a thick layer of dust—except in the center. Here, there was a perfectly round space where the stone shone glossily, a circle about as large as . . .

"Of course," she whispered excitedly. "This must

be where Wort discovered the bell."

Cautiously, she began to explore around the altar
and nave. After some time she could only sigh in
frustration. She found nothing save ancient spider-
webs and the small bones of rats and birds. She sat
down on a fallen chunk of stone, resting her chin on
a hand, wondering what she should do next.

That was when she saw them. They were almost
completely obscured by dust and mold. Only now
that the steep angle of sunlight cast deeper shadows
could she just glimpse them. There were letters
carved into the altar. She knelt, wiping away centuries of grime with her bare hands. At last she could
make out archaic-looking words incised into the
dark stone: *In its breaking will the curse be lifted.* . . .

"That's it," Mika murmured in realization. "That's
how to free Wort. The bell has to be broken."

Suddenly sure of what she had to do to, she gathered up her dress and turned to descend the steps. A
strange sound halted her. It was an oddly dissonant
chiming, like the tinkling of glass. The hairs on her
arms pricked up. She stared at the floor in front of
her. The glowing patches of colored illumination that
fell from above were swirling and flowing. Slowly,
Mika turned around, craning her neck upward.

The armored knights in the stained-glass windows
were moving. Like living creatures, they stretched
their arms and shrugged their shoulders, as if struggling to free themselves of their imprisoning restraint.
With a sound like breaking crystal, the knights
pulled themselves free of the lead outlines that held
them in place. They jumped to the floor. Slowly,
deliberately, holding their glass swords before them,
the stained-glass knights began to advance on Mika.
Their eyes glowed hotly as though the sun still illuminated them.

Mika tried to stumble backward, but her legs didn't

seem to work. One of the knights turned sideways, and she nearly lost sight of it—they were no thicker than window panes. Then the knight turned to face her once more, gnashing its glass teeth hatefully. All that escaped her throat was a low sound. She could not scream. The knights of glass bore down on her, raising their shardlike swords.

A ferocious snarl echoed around the cathedral. Like dark lightning, a shadow streaked from nowhere to crash into one of the glass knights. The knight stumbled, waving its sword wildly, then fell backward against the hard stone altar. With a deafening sound, the glass knight shattered into a thousand pieces of colored glass. Its eyes rolled across the floor like glowing marbles.

Mika could only watch, paralyzed with fear, as the two knights turned to face the creature that had attacked them. It was some sort of huge, black-furred beast with ivory fangs, slashing claws, and a twitching tail. Yet the creature was also vaguely human in shape, and walked on two crouched legs. Though the beast was powerfully muscled, it moved with clumsy, lurching motions, as if wounded.

The knights slashed at the beast, but it dodged their blows. It lunged again, shoving one of the knights forcefully against the other. The two stained-glass figures collided, exploding in splinters. A spray of shards rained to the floor with the din of a thousand chimes. The magical knights were no more.

The beast turned in Mika's direction, stalking slowly toward her.

"Please," Mika somehow managed to gasp through her constricted throat. "Please, make it swift." She squeezed her eyes shut.

Oddly, a woman's voice spoke. "I do not intend to kill you."

Mika's eyes fluttered open. Instead of a beast, a

naked woman stood before her. The woman's hair
was as dark and glossy as onyx, and her eyes glittered green and gold like a summer forest. Mika recognized the woman. The Lady Jadis. Dark blotches
covered her body, but before Mika could study them,
Jadis pulled a woolen dress from a small pack tied
around her waist. Swiftly, the dark-haired woman
donned the dress, concealing the strange bruises.

"My lady Jadis," Mika said breathlessly, trying to
adapt to this peculiar turn of events.

Jadis nodded deferentially. "My lady Mika."

Mika took a hesitant step forward. Whatever the
lady was—woman or beast—she was obviously
injured. "You're hurt, my lady. Will you let me examine you? Perhaps I could—"

Jadis's sultry laughter cut her off. "No, my good
doctor. Thank you. But I am afraid that you cannot
cure me. Only one being can, and he is far away
from this place."

"I see." Mika could think of nothing else to say.

"I had expected to find something of interest here,
Doctor," Jadis mused. "I had not expected it to be
you. Now, how does your presence here fit what is
going on?"

Mika shook her head. "I don't know what you
mean, my lady."

"No, of course you don't." Jadis lurched closer.
"Tell me, Doctor, if you will—why have you journeyed to this strange place?"

Mika hesitated, wondering just what she ought to
say. "I came to help a friend."

"Let me guess—the hunchback in the bell tower?"

Mika let out a small gasp. "How did you know?"

"Oh, you'd be surprised, Doctor, at the things I
know." Jadis smoothed her coal-dark hair. "You
must tell me, why should you care for a lonely
wretch everyone else despises? Is it simply your

inherent goodness that compels you to such perverse extremes?"

A frown touched Mika's brow. "You say much I don't pretend to understand, my lady. I will tell you this. There is no one in this fiefdom who deserves my help more than Wort. Indeed, there is no one who has been more wronged."

"How so?"

Mika gazed at her defiantly. Why not speak the truth? "Wort is the true Baron of Nartok."

"Is he?" Jadis purred with obvious fascination. She tapped her chin thoughtfully. "I'll tell you what, Doctor. I have some information concerning your lover, the good baron, which you might be eager to hear. Let us make a bargain. My secrets for yours. What do you say?"

Mika shivered. What sort of *information* could Jadis mean? There was only one way to find out. "Agreed," she whispered.

The two women spoke for a long time in the gloom of the cathedral. First Mika explained why she had come to the cathedral—to find some way to free Wort from the dark power of the cursed bell and to keep him from committing any more murders. Then she spoke of what she had learned about the unusual circumstances surrounding the births of Caidin and Wort.

When it was the other's turn, Mika found herself utterly hypnotized by Jadis's dark revelations. Jadis was a servant of King Azalin of Darkon himself, and had been sent to spy upon Caidin. Mika listened in growing horror as Jadis described in detail all the abominable actions Caidin had taken in his pursuit of the throne of Darkon—from the false inquisition in which hundreds of innocent people had been executed, to the building of the tower on the moor accomplished by his army of zombies.

This was the fiend who had held her in his arms. He had kissed her lips lingeringly again and again. Now the thought made Mika want to vomit.

At last Jadis was done with her tale. "Can we consider the bargain fulfilled, my lady?" she asked with a smile that was somehow both kind and wicked.

"Yes," Mika barely managed to choke out the word.

"Then I bid you farewell." In a surprising gesture, Jadis reached out and gripped Mika's hand warmly. "You may have saved my life after all."

Mika smiled wanly. "And you may have saved my soul."

As the shadows of afternoon lengthened further, the two women left the cavernous cathedral. Mika mounted the pony once more. The beast let out a frightened snort, and when she looked up Mika thought she saw a black shadow speed into the forest. In a heartbeat it was gone. She nudged the pony into a trot, starting the long journey back.

"How could I have loved such a fiend, my dear ones?" she whispered as she gripped the golden locket. Yet she had not really. The feelings Caidin had instilled in her had been anything but love. At least now she knew the truth. Not only was he a bastard, he was the monster as well. A resolved expression took her face. She was more determined than ever to help Wort.

Behind her, in the silent cathedral, the waning rays of the sun filtered across the dark stone altar. Gradually the angle of the light grew steeper, revealing another row of words carved into the ancient rock: . . . *and by its final tolling will the dead awaken.*

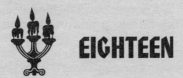

EIGHTEEN

In human form, Jadis roamed the corridors of Nartok Keep. Startled courtiers leapt out of her path, revulsion written across their faces. The high-necked dress she wore could no longer conceal the decay that ravaged her body. Livid blotches stained her hands and face, and her glossy hair was falling out in clumps. Walking was arduous now—it felt as if her legs were carved of wood. Her right arm was still functional, but the left dangled uselessly from her shoulder. Even breathing was difficult. She had to make a constant effort of it, forcing her lungs to fill with air and then expel it again in a rank cloud.

A maidservant screamed, dropping a tray of dishes. Wailing in fright, she dashed away down the corridor. Jadis did not notice or care. In minutes she would have the knowledge for which she had journeyed to Nartok. Then she would stumble into the carriage waiting outside the keep—the carriage that would bear her rapidly back to Il Aluk. She had only to stay alive in the meantime. When she reached Avernus, she knew, King Azalin would heal her decomposing body.

"You shall see, love," she whispered to herself. "You will be more beautiful than ever."

At last she reached the chamber where a terrified

servant had stuttered that she would find the baron.
She barged through the door. Beyond was a spacious sitting chamber. Its walls were lined with heavily laden bookshelves, but the other furnishings were
spare, limited to a pair of velvet chairs spaced some
distance apart. In one of these, Baron Caidin looked
up with a bemused expression.

"What? No polite knock, my lady? Have we surrendered all the niceties, then?"

Jadis curled her lip into a snarl. "As you said yourself, Caidin, this little charade has grown wearisome."

She hobbled into the chamber as a genuinely startled look crossed the baron's face. Strangely, this
gave her some satisfaction.

"What is wrong, Caidin?" she said in a slurred
voice. "Do you no longer find me desirable?"

His eyes narrowed in disgust as he regained his
composure. "I might, my lady, were I a vulture with a
taste for carrion."

Jadis glared at him hatefully.

"But please," he went on indulgently, "won't you
sit down?"

Caidin gestured for her to sit in the chair opposite
him, and this she did clumsily. As she sank down
into the velvet cushion, she had the distinct impression that the chair shifted beneath her.

"You seem oddly calm, Your Grace," she began
musingly.

"Oh? Why is that?"

"I would have thought that a baron who was about
to be executed by his own subjects might get a bit
more apprehensive. I understand the rabble plan on
assaulting the keep in force tonight. And in an effort
to save their precious, powdered necks, most of the
members of your court—ever the pragmatists, you
see—plan to join in the fun when the peasants clap

you in irons and drag you to the dungeon."

Caidin pressed his hands into a steeple shape before him. "Oh, I wouldn't be surprised if the peasants found themselves a bit too preoccupied for an uprising tonight."

Jadis licked her peeling lips. "Why is that?"

"Enough about myself," Caidin sidestepped smoothly. "What brings you to see me, my lady?"

Gathering her wits, Jadis proceeded carefully. "We're going to have a conversation, Your Grace, and it's going to go like this. You will tell me something I wish to know. Then I will tell you something that I am quite certain you yourself will very much wish to know.

"You see, I've learned some interesting details concerning your birth, Your Grace." Jadis allowed herself a caustic laugh. "But that title isn't really appropriate, is it?" Smugly, she noticed the flicker of alarm that passed over his countenance. "Perhaps you can tell me. What is the proper aristocratic term for *bastard?*"

Caidin's composed expression shattered. "How do you know that?" he hissed.

"It is unimportant. All that matters is that, somewhere on the edge of your fiefdom, a courier awaits a message from me. His instructions are such that if by sundown tonight he does not receive this message—and indeed it is a simple message, but a single word—this courier will ride hard to Il Aluk and deliver to a select set of nobles some very exciting news concerning Baron Caidin of Nartok."

Caidin gripped the arms of his chair in white-knuckled fury. Jadis shook with mirth. This was simply too wonderful.

"I will be ruined," he whispered hoarsely.

"Precisely, Your Grace. If word spreads among the nobility of Darkon that you are a bastard, you are finished. No noble will bend his knee to an illegitimate ruler. In their utter contempt, the nobility will never support you. I would give you two weeks on the throne before you were assassinated. Perhaps less."

"Very good, Jadis," Caidin said in open admiration. "Very, very good. You're right, of course. I would indeed like to know this one remarkable word that would stay the courier's spurs. And let me postulate as to what piece of information you wish to receive in return." He clenched his hand into a fist. "Could it be how I intend to depose Azalin in his castle of Avernus with a tower that presently stands in my fiefdom?"

"Your Grace can read my mind," Jadis replied with mock demureness.

"Very well, Jadis. I will tell you what I intend to do. In fact, I do not think it will help your master very much, even if you manage to survive long enough to deliver the news." He eyed the dark splotches on her hands.

"Get on with it," she snapped.

Soon her anger was replaced by fascination as she listened to the dark words the baron spoke. When he finished, Jadis could barely suppress a shudder. The fiendishness of Caidin's plan surprised even her. However, now she had what she had come for. She had to return to Il Aluk without delay. "You have fulfilled your end of the bargain, Caidin. Once I am outside the keep, I will fulfill mine." She started to push herself out of the velvet chair.

"I wouldn't do that if I were you, my lady."

Something in Caidin's voice made her hesitate.

"In fact, I think you would do well to stay seated in that chair and proceed to tell me just where I might find this courier of yours, and what word I must speak to him."

Jadis studied him with calculating eyes. "And

what, pray tell, would compel me to do that?"

Caidin stood and approached a small wooden shelf near the door. On it was a small object concealed by a black cloth.

"You see, my lady," he explained matter-of-factly, "the square of stone upon which your chair stands is sensitive to the weight that rests upon it. The slab is attached to a rope and pulley beneath the floor, which is in turn attached to the rod that supports this shelf. Should you leave the chair, the rope will move, and the support will be pulled out from under the shelf. As a result, the glass jar beneath this cloth will fall to the floor and shatter."

Jadis frowned. "I fail to see why a jar shattering should bother me."

"Oh, normally it shouldn't," Caidin concurred. "Except this is no ordinary jar, but is instead an enchanted prison for a most interesting creature."

He pulled away the dark cloth. Crimson flames danced and shimmered inside the glass jar. Jadis thought she glimpsed a tiny, humanlike being amid the flickering fire, but she could not be certain. The flames were too bright to gaze at directly.

"I found this peculiar item in a forgotten room deep below the keep," Caidin went on casually. "The creature within is a fire elemental. Oh, it looks small and harmless. Of course, it has been imprisoned for centuries. I imagine that, if it were released, it would be quite . . . annoyed."

Fear clawed at Jadis's throat. King Azalin sometimes summoned fire elementals to dispatch his enemies. When the magical creatures were finished there was little left of their victims but ashes.

"So you see, my lady, since the jar is out of your reach, and you couldn't possibly hope to catch it before it crashed to the floor and shattered, you would do well to obey me."

Jadis glared at him. What was she to do? Once he knew where to find the courier, what reason would he have to let her live?

"I will withdraw to allow you to consider your answer."

Before she could utter a word in protest, he backed from the room and shut the door. The lock made a grinding sound. Jadis swore a bitter oath. She was trapped.

* * * * *

In the corridor outside the sitting chamber, Caidin jerked aside a purple curtain. Perched on a wooden stool in the alcove beyond was his gnome lackey.

"Keep an eye on her, my faithful little worm," Caidin commanded.

"With pleasure, Your Grace!" Pock bent forward to peer through a small crevice in the stone. He recoiled in sudden surprise, making a nauseous sound. "Er, kitty isn't so very pretty anymore, is she?"

"No, she is not. But she is still dangerous, Pock. And clever. Make certain she does not escape. She has some knowledge that is . . . most important to me."

"Don't you worry, Your Grace," Pock chirped happily. "I'll watch her like a hog!"

A scowl crossed Caidin's face. "You mean *hawk,* don't you? The phrase is, 'Watch her like a hawk.' "

Pock's purple face wrinkled in puzzlement. He shrugged. "I hadn't thought of that, Your Grace, but I suppose I could give it a try."

The baron bit his tongue. What was the use? "Just keep an eye on her, Pock!"

"Aye, aye, Your Grace! I'll keep an eye on her just like a—"

Caidin pulled the curtain hastily shut. He did not

want to hear any more. There were other things to worry about besides Pock's stupidity. Turning, he strode purposefully down the corridor, his glossy black boots beating a sharp tattoo against the stone floor.

He had an uprising to crush.

*   *   *   *   *

Jadis's mind raced. There was no time to spare. With every passing moment, another part of her body ceased to function. She had to return to Il Aluk before it was too late.

"Keep breathing, love," she said hoarsely, willing her lungs to continue their laborious work. "Just keep breathing."

She gazed about the chamber, searching for anything that could help her. But she could see no way out of the trap.

"Wait a moment, love," she whispered thickly through numb lips. She had an idea.

As swiftly as her clumsy body allowed, she set to work. After much laborious contortion, she managed to shrug off her heavy woolen dress without taking her weight off the chair. To that she added her soft doeskin boots, and all her jewelry—gold rings, bracelets, even earrings. Every last ounce was crucial. She piled everything on the cushion beneath her. Then, with painstaking care, she began to inch her way out of the chair.

At first Jadis thought it was going to work. She made it far enough that only her right hand was resting on the chair. Then she heard a faint grating of stone on stone. Across the room, the wooden shelf tilted slightly. The fire elemental shimmered inside the magical jar. Desperately, she lunged back into the chair.

It had almost been enough. Almost. If only she could add a little more weight to the chair. It was a useless thought. There were no other objects in reach, and she had removed every last item of adornment from her body. There was nothing else she could leave behind on the chair.

"No, love. That's not true, now is it?" A thought flickered through her mind. It was such a ghastly thought that she almost laughed aloud. In dread, she realized that she was going to do it. What other choice did she have? It was either this, or death.

"Come now, love," she murmured reassuringly even as she shuddered. "It won't really hurt, now will it?"

Jadis looked at her left arm. The flesh was darkly bloated and utterly lifeless. She raised her right hand, focusing her willpower. Sharp talons sprang from the tips of her fingers. She swallowed the taste of fear. With slow, painstaking motions, she used the talons to rip the useless arm from her left shoulder.

It was easier than she would have thought, and indeed there was no pain. Again, she almost laughed aloud. Would not any wild animal caught in a trap chew off its limb just to gain freedom? The putrid flesh yielded easily to her sharp claws. Yellow liquid oozed from the appendage. In moments she reached the bone. Even dislocating the joint was not as hard as she feared. She used her talons as a lever. For a moment there was slight resistance. Then, with a wet *pop!* her arm fell free.

This time mad laughter did issue from her lips. "Oh, my king," she said exultantly. "What I suffer willingly for you!"

Setting the severed arm upon the dress, she carefully rose from the chair. This time the weight proved enough. The chair did not shift, the magical jar did not fall. She had escaped!

Lurching toward the doorway, she tried not to glance at the oozing stump of her left shoulder. Azalin's powers were great enough to defeat death itself. He would be able to heal her. Extending a sharp talon, she easily picked the door's lock. Opening the portal, she took a step toward freedom.

"Not so fast, nasty kitty!"

Jadis spun around. A block of stone in the wall swung open, and a small form tumbled through. It was Pock, the baron's cretinish gnome.

"You're not going anywhere!" the gnome squeaked. "Baron's orders!"

A feral smile twisted itself about Jadis's lips. "And I suppose you're going to stop me?"

Pock drew a laughably diminutive knife from his belt, his pale, bulging eyes blazing. "Good guess!"

Jadis's canine teeth lengthened into stilettolike fangs. She could tolerate this one distraction. It would be satisfying indeed to rend the wretched little gnome to bits. "Try then," she hissed.

With a cry, the gnome lunged at her. As he did, Jadis's form undulated, molding itself into her manther shape—half woman, half cat. With an almost casual motion, she slashed at the gnome with her right arm. The purple knave moved more nimbly than she had anticipated. He ducked under her swipe and stuck his little knife deep into her side. Fiery pain shot through her body. She screamed in rage and amazement. Howling with fury, Jadis grappled the gnome with her one good arm. Shrieking, Pock struggled fiercely, biting and scratching. She tensed her arm to break his neck. In a desperate attempt to free himself, the gnome gave one last furious kick.

The toe of his small black boot just brushed the wooden shelf upon which the magical jar rested.

Time seemed to distort. Both Jadis and Pock

watched in astonishment as, with terrible slowness, the jar slid over the edge of the shelf. Caught as they were in their violent embrace, neither could reach the thing before it fell. The jar struck the floor, shattering. For a fleeting moment the elemental flickered like a tiny, fiery dancer among the broken shards of glass. It was almost beautiful, Jadis thought dimly.

Then all at once the elemental grew. Confined by the magical prison no more, the brilliant creature expanded outward. Searing waves of fire radiated from its lithe form as it whirled and danced. In the space of a heartbeat the entire chamber was transformed into a blazing inferno. Books burst into puffs of flame. Velvet curtains went up like paper torches. The marble floor darkened and cracked. Blistering fire engulfed the woman and gnome as they clutched each other. Their screams rose in a shrill duet, but the sound was quickly drowned in the vast roar of the fiery sea as the elemental danced faster and faster.

*   *   *   *   *

The throng that massed at the base of the tor was far larger than any that had gathered previously. Torch smoke rose in the air. In every hand was gripped some object capable of wounding, maiming, or killing. To the rusted swords, scythes, and sharpened stakes had been added buckets of hot pitch and bottles of flammable naphtha. Only the very young and the very old had stayed behind in the village. Jubilant shouts rang out.

"The fiend won't stop us this time!"

"There are too many of us!"

"The baron's knights can't kill us all!"

The dark chant rose. "Kill the fiend! Kill the baron! Kill the fiend!" The crowd started up the twisting road to the keep.

The sound of thunder rumbled in the distance.
Peasants toward the rear of the mob turned to see if
storm clouds were approaching. Their screams
brought the rest of the throng to a halt. All spun
around, gazing in horror. It was not storm clouds that
appeared over the distant horizon, but dark, galloping horses. A score of riders thundered toward the
village, bearing red-hot sparks of light. Torches.

"Raiders!"

With cries of fear, the people turned their backs to
the keep, forgetting their rage of moments before,
and surged toward the village. The marauders raced
ahead of them. The dark horsemen moved swiftly
through the streets, thrusting blazing torches into
thatch roofs and tossing them into woodpiles stacked
against timber walls. Swiftly the raiders whirled their
mounts around and pounded away across the moor.
By the time the screaming peasants reached their
hovels, it was far too late. Countless pillars of scarlet
flame rose toward the leaden sky along with howls of
anguish.

The village was burning.

* * * * *

"Damn him to the Abyss."

With hate-filled eyes Wort peered through the belfry's rusted iron filigree. Columns of greasy black
smoke rose from village below. For the last five
evenings, Wort had watched in glee as angry mobs
marched up the road to the keep. The folk of Nartok
had forgotten all about the daemon in the bell tower.
It was the fiend in the Grand Hall they despised. Now
there would be no uprising. The mysterious raiders—
raiders Wort suspected were wearing coats of blue
beneath their concealing cloaks—had seen to that.

Wort's cry of anguish sent ghost-pale pigeons

winging in all directions. He gripped his lank brown hair in twisted hands, pulling it out in clumps. Madness assailed his brain. He could not bear this. After all he had done, after all the dark deeds he had dared to commit, he could not possibly bear this—that once again his brother Caidin had bested him.

"I should have let you fall, Caidin!" he cried wildly. "All those years ago at the cliff—I should have let you fall. I could have done so. I had the power, only I did not use it. What a fool I was to save you!" He sank to his knees, clutching his head as though it was going to burst. "I should have let you die, my brother!"

Suddenly, as though drawn by an unseen force, his gaze flickered upward to rest upon an object half brooding in shadow, half glowing in burnished light. The bell. His cries fell silent. The pigeons drifted to their myriad perches. All at once it came to him. He had wasted one opportunity long ago. Here before him was a second chance. He had been so caught up in the dementia of his desire to brand Caidin a monster that he had overlooked the obvious.

The dry voice whispered in his mind. *Ring it, Wort. . . .*

He hauled himself to his feet. Eerie laughter racked his misshapen chest. "Yes, my friends," he cackled. "Let the bell toll one last execution—that of my dear brother. Then at last I will have one thing, one precious thing that he does not—life!"

First he needed a token. Wort clambered down the ladder to his chamber below and threw open the lid of his trunk. He sifted through the ancient junk, then stood up with a gurgle of triumph. In his hand was a faded wooden soldier. In a moment of jealousy he had stolen the toy from his brother decades ago. For years Wort had been racked with guilt at this deplorable deed. Now he stroked the worn soldier fondly. Swiftly, he scrambled up the ladder to the belfry.

"The end has come, my friends," he chortled. He placed the wooden soldier carefully beneath the sinister bronze bell. "This token belonged to my brother, you see." Wort tightly gripped the rope that hung from the cursed bell. "Now the spirits of the Bell of Doom will do what I myself should have done long ago. They will take the token and kill Caidin!" He tensed his arms to pull.

"So, Wort," a darkly elegant voice spoke behind him. "That's how your intriguing bell works."

Wort jerked around, the rope slipping from his startled hands. Tall, handsome, and powerfully graceful, Caidin climbed through the trapdoor into the belfry. A pair of knights followed in his wake, the heavy iron shackles they bore clanking dully.

"No!" Wort cried in desperation, turning back to the bell rope.

"Don't let him ring it!" Caidin thundered.

Wort tried to grab the dangling cord, but a brutal impact from behind knocked him away. Another blow struck him forcefully from the side. He careened into the wall, his skull striking the stones with a resounding *crack!* By the time he shook his head clear, the knights had him. His arms were twisted cruelly behind his back, while hot pain shot up his hunched back. He fell to his knees. Cold iron clamped tightly around his wrists as the knights shackled him, looping the chains around a stout post. A look of smugness played on Caidin's face. More knights appeared through the trapdoor.

"Remove the bell," Caidin ordered the new arrivals. "Transport it to my tower on the moor. And take care that it does not make a sound as you move it!"

In minutes the knights had bundled the instrument carefully in wool and lowered it through the trapdoor. Wort could only stare in despair. It was over.

"Now, my brother," Caidin said after all the others had gone, stroking his bearded chin thoughtfully, "I am curious to try out this bell of yours. Thank you for so kindly showing me how it operates. I'll need a token, yes?"

In terror, Wort realized what his brother intended. He tried to scramble away, but the manacles bound him tightly to the wooden post. Quickly, Caidin searched the pockets of Wort's ratty tunic. After a moment he pulled out an object.

"Ah, yes . . . this filthy little handkerchief of yours should do nicely." Caidin shot Wort a satisfied smirk. "I'll place it on the bell, and once I ring it . . . well, I'm certain you know what will happen after that."

Wort gaped dumbly at the handkerchief in Caidin's hand. It was stained darkly with blood, but here and there remained a spot of its original color—lavender so pale it was almost white. It was the handkerchief Mika had used to bandage his hand that day in the woods that now seemed so long ago, when he had been pricked by the thorn. The object was not Wort's, but Mika's. If Caidin used it for a token when he rang the bell, the spirits would not come to kill Wort. Instead they would appear before—

Wort's mind reeled. Mika! Suddenly, in that one fractured moment, he realized a terrible truth. Whatever she had done, whatever she thought him now, what he believed her to be meant nothing. She was as far above him as the pale moon above the dark earth. She was and always would be—regardless of his fury, his hatred, or his sorrow—an angel.

Desperation etched his voice. "No, Caidin! You mustn't ring the bell with that! That handkerchief is—"

—is Mika's, he was going to finish, but the back of Caidin's gloved hand knocked him forcefully to the moldering straw, silencing him. Caidin moved to the trapdoor, but once on the ladder he paused.

"Farewell, my brother. As always, I am fortune's favorite, while you . . ."—cruel mirth danced in his eyes—"you are simply fate's bastard." Then he was gone.

Dizzily, Wort sat up and stared after the baron, a single thought resounding in his mind. "I cannot allow you to kill an angel, my brother."

His powerful arms flexed with uncanny strength, and iron began to groan.

NINETEEN

"Wort!"

Mika's cry reverberated upward through the dark shaft of Nartok Keep's bell tower.

"Wort, are you there?"

The plaintive echoes of her voice died slowly. The only reply was the soft rustling of countless pale wings. Clutching the mud-stained tatters of the lavender silk gown above her ankles, Mika stumbled desperately up the spire's twisting staircase.

What a fool she had been to believe that Caidin would honor his word. Yet how could she have known what a fiend the baron truly was? She had been caught under Caidin's dark spell as surely as Wort was bound in thrall by the enchantment of the cursed bell. Mika quickened her pace, daring to hope she had not come too late to save her friend.

In truth, she had almost not come at all. Not long after leaving the cathedral, her pony had slipped on the muddy edge of the forest track and plunged into a deep ravine. Mika had suffered only scratches and bruises, but the poor pony had broken its neck. On foot, she had stumbled along the marshy bottom of the ravine for hours before she had finally found a place where she could scramble up the treacherous slope. By then dusk had spread its sooty mantle over the forest. She had spent a cold, frightening night huddled at the base of a tree, pulling the moss and leaf litter over her for scant warmth. At dawn she had continued on her way. At last she had reached the forest's edge, finding herself not far from the village—or at least what remained of it. The village had been reduced to a smoking pile of ashes, but Mika had not stopped. She knew one thing only—she had to find Wort.

"Wort, it's Mika!" she called out as she burst into his chamber. He was not there. Without hesitating she clambered up the ladder into the belfry. It too was empty. After a moment she noticed that iron chains had been looped around a thick post. Kneeling, she examined the chains. They ended in heavy shackles, but the thick metal was twisted and broken, snapped by some awesome force. She stood as sick fear overwhelmed her.

The cursed bell was missing. Frantically, Mika searched the rafters to be sure. The place where it had hung was filled only with shadows.

Yet something here did not make sense. The only person who could have taken the bell was Caidin. But if it was Wort who had been shackled to the post, what had happened to him? Hope surged in her breast.

"Wort must still be alive! But where?"

Instinct told her that if she found Caidin, she would find Wort as well. Whatever fateful web entangled the lives of the two brothers had not unraveled yet.

Dashing from the tower, Mika ran recklessly through the keep, calling out for Wort and Caidin. As she did, servants and petty nobles alike gaped at her and leapt out of her path. She looked more like some specter risen from the grave than a living woman. Dark smudges stained her deathly pale face, and the shreds of her silken gown, stained with earth and blood, clung damply to her body. In minutes rumors spread through the keep. A White Lady

haunted the corridors, folk whispered, crying out for
Baron Caidin. All knew that when such an apparition
named a person, the person was doomed to die
before the following dawn. Soon Mika found herself
moving down empty corridors, through empty
chambers, and up empty stairways. The folk cowered in their chambers, fearing the White Lady.

Mika made her way to the Grand Hall, the armory,
and Caidin's private chambers. There was no sign of
Caidin or Wort in any of these places. Deciding to try
the dungeons, she turned down a new passageway.
Rounding a corner, she saw thick smoke sluggishly
oozing out of an open doorway. She slowed, wondering if were safe to pass by.

Mika was nearly upon it before she saw the thing. It
was a charred husk lying on the floor, half out of the
doorway, half in. Only after a long moment did she
realized what the shape was: a human body, blackened
beyond recognition. Clamping a hand to her mouth to
keep from gagging, she started to back away.

"Wait . . ."

The croaking voice was so faint she almost didn't
hear it. Then it came again.

"Wait . . . Mika . . ."

It was the burnt body. Somehow it was still alive.
Mika shook her head in wordless horror. She commanded her legs to run, but they remained, as if
rooted to the floor. The dark form stirred, reached
out a withered hand toward her. Impossibly, it
opened its eyes. They glistened feverishly in the
wasteland of the face, like two green-gold gems.
Mika knew those eyes.

"Lady Jadis," she choked, clutching the wall to
keep from reeling. "But how . . . how can . . . ?" She
could not bring herself to say the sickening words.
How can you possibly be alive?

Jadis answered the unspoken question in a parched

whisper. "There is . . . death in Azalin's touch. But there is also life . . . undying." Horribly, she smiled, her singed lips crumbling to reveal teeth like small white pearls. "You seek . . . your lover, Doctor?"

Numbly, as if against her will, Mika found herself kneeling, bending closer to hear the Kargat's words. The rank odor of burnt flesh filled her lungs.

"Shall we . . . make another . . . bargain? I will tell you . . . where to find . . . Caidin. Then you . . . must do what I . . . ask of you."

Mika could only nod.

"Look for the baron . . . in the tower he built. It is . . . with the tower that he . . . will assail Azalin." For a brief, agonizing time, Mika listened raptly as the burnt woman spoke, explaining in halting phrases Caidin's plan for using the tower on the moor to defeat Azalin. At last Jadis finished. She coughed weakly. Dark smoke issued from her ruined lips.

Mika started to stand. "I must go to the tower."

"Wait," Jadis hissed like a dying fire. "First you must . . . fulfill . . . our bargain."

"Yes, of course." Silently, with both pity and revulsion, she wondered what she could possibly do. "Shall I . . . shall I see to your wounds?"

Broken laughter shook the black husk on the floor. "No, you cannot . . . heal me, Doctor." The dry voice throbbed with sorrow. "My beauty has been . . . consumed. You cannot . . . give it back to me. No one . . . can."

"Then what do you want me to do?" Mika finally managed to whisper.

A burned hand reached out, its fingerbones like the talons of some dark bird.

"You know . . . Doctor. There is but . . . one thing."

At last Mika nodded. A sound of satisfaction escaped the withered form as it sank slowly back to the floor. Mika looked around until she saw what she needed. A pair of decorative sabers hung on the corridor's wall. She reached out and gripped one of the weapons. The hilt felt cool and smooth in her hand. She returned to the Kargat, steeling her will. Holding the saber tightly in both hands, she raised it above the burned woman.

Slowly, almost serenely, as though covered by dark cinders, the green-gold eyes closed.

"Forgive me," Mika whispered.

The saber glinted sharply as it descended.

*   *   *   *   *

Alone, Baron Caidin of Nartok stood in the highest chamber of his newly completed tower of war. His zombie slaves had performed their labor well. Everything about the dark spire spoke of strength and violence. Vaulted buttresses braced thick walls that would be able to withstand any attack. Slit-shaped windows would render the fiercest storm of arrows ineffectual. Not a single scrap of wood had been used in the construction, and thus not even a blazing inferno would be proof against it.

"The tower is invincible," Caidin said softly. He held up the darkly mottled Soulstone. "And this is the key to all its power."

Before him stood a low altar hewn of a single block of basalt. Weird symbols and arcane runes traced its surface, just as the darkling had described. In the center of the altar was a small depression, exactly the size of the stone. All he had to do was place the stone within the hollow. Then nothing would be able to stop him. The throne of Darkon would be his.

Once again, Caidin marveled at the ancient magic of the Soulstone. He had enjoyed using the stone to drain the life-forces of the victims of his false inquisition. The stone had transformed the hapless peasants into zombie slaves—but wondrous as that was, he had only begun to scratch the surface of the stone's potential. Now, trapped within the dark stone were hundreds of combined life-forces. With the proper ritual, those forces could be transferred to any inanimate object, granting it the ability to move and obey orders. That was the true greatness of the Soulstone.

"I wonder what the look will be on Azalin's face," Caidin mused with a self-satisfied smirk, "when he sees my living tower of war walk across the plains and stride right up to the walls of Avernus."

No army Azalin could raise would be able to block his way. The tower would crush them all beneath its ponderous weight. And that was only the beginning. Once he reached King Azalin's fortress, he would transfer the life-force from the tower to the stones of Avernus. The very walls of the castle would obey his commands. He could order the animate stones to attack Azalin's servants and imprison the king. Then all he had to do was pluck the crown from Azalin's head.

"I will turn Azalin's own fortress against him! His strongest defense will become his greatest weakness. And I will become king!"

Carefully, Caidin tucked the stone back into the pocket of his midnight-blue coat. He had a few extraneous affairs to tidy up before he set the wheels of his victory in motion. No doubt Jadis was even now desperately waiting for his return, so that she could tell him where he would find the courier, and therefore save her life—at least what was left of it.

Then there was Wort. Caidin's eyes rested upon the gleaming curve of the bell that hung above his head. The Bell of Doom. With its dark magic, he would be unbeatable. His tower was no longer simply a tower of war. It truly was a Tower of Doom.

Now, to test the bell and see for himself how its formidable curse worked. The rope dangled near the circular hole in the stone floor through which the bell had been raised. Caidin drew out the handkerchief he had taken from Wort and tied it to the rope. That way the three spirits would be certain not to mistake the token he offered them.

"Poor, Wort. I almost pity you. From the day we were born, I have always taken everything from you that I wanted—your noble blood, your humanity, your precious bell, and now . . . finally, your life." Reaching out strong hands, Caidin gripped the rope. "But if it is to be me or you in this game, Wort, then by all means—let it be you." Murder glinted in his emerald eyes. "Farewell, my brother!"

Suddenly the world seemed to spin around Caidin. It took his brain a moment to realize what was happening, and by then it was already too late. Struck by an unseen force, he found himself hurled backward, the rope slipping through his groping fingers. Pain exploded in his body as he struck the tower's stone wall. Dizzily, he blinked through the haze of pain to see a twisted face floating before him and grinning hideously.

"Come now, my brother," a voice spat. "Did you really think that the threads that bind us could be cut so easily?"

Only a single word escaped Caidin's lips, but in that word there resided a veritable ocean of disgust, hatred, and terror.

"Wort . . ."

*   *   *   *   *

Mika clutched the ghostly gray stallion's mane with freezing fingers as the beast thundered across the rolling heath. Skeletal trees and crumbling stone walls flashed past, but she only vaguely noticed these, as if they were part of some other person's murky dream. She rode directly into the wind, her pale hair streaming wildly behind her. In the distance, the dark tower drew her inexorably onward.

After leaving the charred husk that had once been the Lady Jadis—and that finally now lay lifeless, thanks to the sharp saber—Mika had made her way to the stable. There the stableboy had fled in fear at the sight of her.

"The White Lady!" he cried. "The White Lady has come for me!"

Mika did not know what this meant, nor did she care. She had grabbed the reins of the first saddled horse she came upon. Climbing into the high saddle, she had kicked the courser's flanks until it leapt into a gallop. Horse and rider had careened wildly down the road from the keep and out onto the open moor. Living for so many years in the city, Mika had little experience at the art of riding. At any moment the horse could stumble on the uneven turf, throwing her to the hard ground, injuring her, even snapping her neck. Still she prodded the horse, urging it to go faster yet.

As the land flew by, Mika reached up with one hand to grip the golden locket dangling about her throat. "Let it be that I come in time, my loves," she whispered. "Let it be that I can atone for the wicked deeds I have set in motion."

Though it was midday, the sky overhead was dark and heavy as iron, weighing oppressively on the barren countryside. Livid green lightning flickered behind the menacing clouds. It was as if the land itself were somehow aware of the terrible events that were unfolding upon it. Perhaps in a sense it was. What other explanation could there be for the evil

that plagued Nartok but that it rose like some noxious vapor from the very soil itself to infect all those
who were forced to dwell in its fumes.

The three Vistani women had spoken of an ancient
battle between Light and Dark. Mika did not believe
their words any longer. She could believe nothing
except that Dark had always reigned supreme in this
land, and that it always would.

"When this is over, I will leave this place, my
loves." Tears streamed coldly down her cheeks, tracing pale tracks through the dirt and grime. "I will
leave this cursed fiefdom far behind. Perhaps I will
even return to our little flat in the city, to our river,
and our white, white gulls."

Finally the dark walls of the tower rose up before
her. The stallion skidded to a halt. She unclenched
her stiff fingers from the creature's mane and half
climbed, half threw herself to the wet ground.
Numbly, she looped the stallion's reins about an iron
ring set into the wall of the tower. Turning, she stumbled to a shadowed archway. Mika paused only for
the space of a heartbeat, then plunged inside.

*   *   *   *   *

Wort pressed Caidin viciously against the stone
wall, his gnarled fingers clamped tightly around the
baron's neck. Caidin gripped Wort's wrists, attempting to force the hunchback away. Powered as they
were by the strength of rage, Wort's hands closed
about the baron's throat. Caidin's handsome visage
began to darken. His lips turned blue. Elation
flooded Wort's misshapen chest. How glorious, to
finally be robbing his brother of something instead of
the other way around.

"You see, Caidin," Wort jeered between clenched
teeth. "In the end your pretty face comes to nothing.

The worms will devour comely flesh as readily as ugly. Just so long as it is dead!"

Hoarse laughter escaped Caidin's lips. "You will not kill me, Wort."

"You think not?" Wort squeezed harder. Caidin's hands were growing tired. They could not hold Wort back much longer.

"No, you will not," Caidin gasped. His green eyes nearly bulged out of his skull, yet a mocking smile twisted his lips. "What are you without me, Wort? I . . . " He struggled desperately for breath. "I define you. I am day to your night. You cannot exist if I am gone. Without me, you are nothing!"

Caidin's words plunged an icy spike into Wort's chest. For a fleeting moment he wondered if this could possibly be true. For so long he had dwelt in awe of his brother, and then in jealousy, and then at last in loathing. Every day of his life, his feelings for Caidin had shaped him, molded him into what he was. What indeed would happen to him when Caidin was dead? Would he simply vanish, like a shadow on the wall when the candle that cast it was extinguished?

A dark seed of doubt crept into Wort's heart, and his hands relaxed ever so slightly. It was just the opening Caidin needed. The baron brought his knee up forcefully. Crying out in pain, Wort stumbled backward. Caidin did not wait to strike again. This time the baron's black boot caught Wort square on the chin. Wort spun around, a crimson arc of blood gushing from his mouth to splatter against the wall. Caidin advanced, digging his elbow into Wort's hunched shoulder. Wort cried out once more. Again and again, Caidin struck the hump on Wort's back, sending waves of paralyzing pain through him. At last Wort sank to his knees.

Caidin grinned in satisfaction. "Yes, you are noth-

ing without me, Brother. But I—I am everything without you." Swiftly he strode past Wort, reaching
toward the rope that hung down from the bell.

Fear made Wort forget his pain. "No!" he bellowed,
lunging forward. Caidin fell, his fingers brushing the
rope. Caidin grunted in pain as he struck the ground.
Wort fell on top of him. Grappling each other, the two
brothers rolled along the edge of the hole in the center of the chamber's floor. Propelled by Caidin's
fleeting touch, the bell rope swung lazily back and
forth over the pit.

"Do you delude yourself into thinking that if you
kill me you will become baron?" Caidin grunted as
his arms strained to pry Wort off of him.

"I don't know, Brother," Wort hissed. "Why don't I
find out?" He shoved a hand against Caidin's face,
pushing him backward over the edge of the
precipice.

"I already know what the folk of Nartok will do.
They will kill you like the monster you are!" Caidin
rolled over, carrying Wort with him, reversing their
positions. Now it was he who gritted his teeth,
attempting to push Wort over the edge.

"If I am a monster, it is because others have made
me so," Wort shouted. "But you, Caidin—you are a
monster by your own choosing!"

The two men froze. Caidin's harsh laughter echoed
coldly off the stone walls. Gazing flatly at his brother,
he spoke in a voice that oozed calm, terrible, unde-
niable logic. "Do you honestly think that makes any
difference whatsoever?"

In that fractured moment, Wort knew Caidin was
right. As different as the two brothers appeared, in
the end they were the same. A fiend was a fiend.
What did it matter how each had become such? All
that mattered was what each was. Wort and Caidin
stared at each other for a moment, caught in their

violent embrace. Like a pendulum, the bell rope
swung slowly across the pit toward the two brothers.

Caidin bared his teeth in a cruel grin. He reached
toward the rope. In panic, Wort kicked his feet
upward, propelling the baron over him, into the dark
hole. Caidin screamed as he dropped—but he did
not release his hold of Wort. Wort scrabbled fiercely
at the stone, but his fingers found no purchase. He
felt himself jerked over the edge by his brother's
weight. One of his flailing legs struck the bell rope.
The cord wrapped itself around his ankle. The two
brothers plummeted down into shadow.

With a snap, the rope tightened around Wort's
ankle. Above, a thunderous tone rang out. The Bell
of Doom. For a moment, Wort and Caidin dangled
precariously in midair, but their weight was too
much. The rope broke. They screamed as they
plunged into darkness. Then their screams were cut
short.

It took Wort several moments to realize that he
was alive. Pain pulsated through his entire body. He
blinked, finding that he could see. Faint gray light filtered through a narrow opening. He realized that he
did not lie on hard stone, but on something warmer,
softer. He heard a feeble groan beneath him. It was
Caidin.

Agonizingly, Wort dragged himself to his feet.
Caidin lay facedown. The baron groaned once more,
but he did not move. Wort craned his neck. He could
see now why he and Caidin were still alive. The
opening through which they had fallen was no more
than twenty feet above. They had not fallen all the
way to the bottom of the spire, but had instead
struck an intermediate landing.

Suddenly Wort heard a faint cry—high, clear, and
filled with horror. The sound came through the open
mouth of a spiral staircase. Wort's dizzy mind

cleared. He recognized the voice.

"Mika," he choked.

She must have come to the tower! Yet the Bell of Doom had tolled as he and Caidin had fallen, and it was Mika's handkerchief that had been tied to the rope. That meant—

The cry came again.

"Mika!" Wort shouted it this time. Leaving the motionless form of Caidin behind, he dashed down the stairway. In moments he burst through an arched portal onto the ground floor of the tower.

"Wort!" Mika called out desperately. "Help me!"

Clad in a tattered gown, terror written across her moon-pale face, Mika backed away from the three smoky apparitions that drifted toward her.

"Get away from her!" Wort thundered, stumbling forward to place himself between the three dark spirits and Mika.

Eerie laughter floated from the dark cowls that concealed the faces of the apparitions. "You cannot keep us from what is ours, bellringer."

As though Wort were immaterial, the spirits of the bell passed through him. He gasped as the ethereal substance passed through his flesh, turning his heart to ice. Frozen, he could only watch as the apparitions closed in on the doctor.

TWENTY

With a grunt, Caidin pulled himself to his knees. Deep in his chest, he could feel the broken ends of several ribs grating sickeningly against each other with each ragged breath he took. Clenching his teeth against the pain, he staggered to his feet. Wort was gone. The wretched hunchback had fled like the coward he was.

"The bell has been rung, my brother," Caidin said aloud between gritted teeth. "You can run from me, but you cannot run from the spirits of the bell." Laughter rumbled low in his chest. It hurt, but he did not care. A panicked thought occurred to him. Hastily, he checked the pocket of his coat to make certain the Soulstone had not been lost in the fall. His fingers found its reassuringly smooth surface. He smiled, walking stiffly toward the spiral staircase. It was time to finish things once and for all.

A scream echoed up from below. A moment later, an anguished voice bellowed, "Mika!"

With a rush of alarm, Caidin recognized both voices. Wort was still in the tower—and still alive! Somehow, the doctor was here as well. Was the hunchback assailing her? Swiftly, Caidin drew the knife at his hip—an ornamental blade, but nonetheless sharp and deadly.

"If the spirits of the bell will not kill you, Wort," he snarled, "I will do it myself."

Ignoring the grinding noise of his broken ribs, he dashed to the stairwell.

*   *   *   *   *

Wort turned with agonizing slowness. It was as if he moved, not through air, but chill mud. The ghostly apparitions had left a paralyzing numbness in his limbs. He could only watch with bulbous eyes as the three dark spirits surrounded the terrified doctor.

"The bell has been rung," one of the smoky forms intoned in its reverberating voice.

"The price for our blood must be paid," spoke another.

"Blood for blood," whispered the last. "That is the curse."

Shaking her head wordlessly, Mika backed up against a stone wall. There was nowhere to go. The spirits reached out their translucent arms.

"What is this?" a voice cried out.

Caidin burst out of the archway of the stairwell, a glittering knife clutched in his hand.

"It is him you are to slay!" Caidin pointed the knife at Wort. "Not the doctor. She is mine!"

"That is not so." The spirits' eerie susurration hissed from all directions. "The token has led us to this one. Her blood belongs to us."

Caidin lunged toward the spirits. But as one the three shadowed cowls of their robes turned toward him, and he froze in midstep. His emerald eyes bulged. He tried to move, but to no avail.

"Fear not. You can have her corpse when we are through."

The spirits turned toward the doctor. A strange calm descended over Mika's face. She braced her shoulders and raised her chin, as if facing a fate she no longer feared. Pressing her eyes shut, she gripped the gold locket at her throat.

"I am coming, my loves," she murmured. "Wait for me but a little longer." The spirits of the bell fell upon her, enfolding her in their darkness. The two brothers could only stare, tormented by their powerlessness. For the last time an image came to Wort of the shining angel floating in the twilight garden of the ancient tapestry. Now night had fallen, and it seemed there was no place in all its darkness for the radiance of angels.

A deafening shriek rent the air. It was a cry like none ever voiced by a living creature, a scream so vast and wounded that it pierced Wort to the quick, stripping away all the layers of his being to expose the naked soul.

Then, like dark tatters of mist blown before the winds of a gale, the three spirits spun away from their victim. Sparks of violet brilliance crackled about their dusky forms. As the humans watched in awe, the apparitions began to swirl wildly in the air above the doctor, as if caught by an invisible cyclone. Shreds of darkness tore away from their robes.

"No!" the spirits screeched. "It cannot be! Her heart is untainted by the least speck of darkness."

The cyclone whirled faster. More shreds of shadow ripped free. Their voices blended together to form a keening chorus.

"How can there dwell in this land one whose soul is truly pure? But we cannot harm her. It must be so!"

Their shrieks rose to a stentorian roar, shaking the foundation of the tower. The three onlookers clamped their hands to their ears, but still the dreadful voices of the apparitions flooded their senses, drowning out all other thoughts.

"The curse is broken!" the spirits wailed.

Purple magic sizzled around the apparitions, shredding the dark substance that formed them. The cowls of their robes ripped away. The mortals gaped in horror. The spirits did indeed have faces. Yet they were not the shriveled, cadaverous faces of death. They were the faces of children—pale and perfect, like porcelain dolls. In that moment Wort realized the horrible truth. He had known only part of the history of the bell before. Long ago, when ordered by the wicked king to do the impossible—to forge a bell of bronze and silver—the vengeful smith had used the blood of the king's three sons to make the two metals bind. Wort had always assumed that the three princes had been grown men at the time. Now he knew that was not so. The king's sons had been children. Yet the ancient malevolence that shone in the glowing eyes of the spirits was like none that had ever glimmered in the gaze of a mortal child.

The dark cyclone whirled impossibly fast, casting off violet sparks in a shimmering fountain. Suddenly it began to contract, as if it were a murky whirlpool draining into some distant, unknown space.

"Father, we come to you!"

With a clap of thunder, the dark funnel collapsed in on itself. The purple radiance vanished. The spirits were no more.

*   *   *   *   *

High in the dark tower of war, the bell forged of bronze and silver hung silently at the end of a thick iron chain. Suddenly it twitched. It was still for a brief moment. Abruptly it twitched again, more violently this time. Then, with a sound like lightning, the bell cracked. A dark fluid began to ooze from the jagged crevice. It quickened into a torrent running thickly down the side of the bell. Blood.

The groan of metal echoed on the dusky air. With a loud *snap!* a link broke in the heavy iron chain that supported the bell. The instrument lurched precariously, tilting to one side. Slowly, the link gave away. Like a stone cast into a dark pool, the bell plunged into the pit below.

*   *   *   *   *

"I don't need the bell to kill you, Wort," Caidin snarled. Violence shone in his eyes. His lips pulled back from his teeth in a rictus grin. For a moment, the baron looked more animal than man. He advanced on Wort, clutching the knife.

Wort scrambled backward. He looked wildly about for anything he might use as a weapon to defend himself. There was nothing. Frantically, he tried to gain his feet, but his numb legs would not support his weight. He fell back to the hard floor. Caidin loomed over him.

"You have not made this easy, my brother," Caidin hissed. Insane rage twisted his features. Now, the baron was anything but handsome. "But I enjoy challenges."

Caidin raised the knife. Wort lifted an arm futilely to ward off the blow. Mika's scream pierced the air.

"Die, Wort." The baron spat out the words.

The knife never descended. With a resounding crash, the stone ceiling high above gave way under some terrible, unseen force, bursting apart and crashing downward in a spray of jagged rubble and shards of broken rock. Through the breach plunged an object—dull, gleaming, ponderous. The bell.

There was only a split second to react. Wort heaved his body to one side, rolling out of the bell's path. Caidin jerked his head up, his eyes wide. Defiant laughter ripped itself from his chest.

"But I am to be—"

The baron's final word was lost in a deafening *clang!* as the bell crashed down upon him.

Wort covered his head with his hands, cringing as a cascade of falling stone pelted him. Gradually the rain of rubble dwindled. Like fading thunder, the final tolling of the bell rumbled into silence. Slowly, Wort shook off his shroud of rock dust and pebbles and staggered to his feet. He looked up to see Mika staring at him. The falling dust had left her paler yet, making her wide violet eyes seem almost impossibly luminous.

"Are you . . . are you hurt?" Wort managed to gasp.

Numbly, she shook her head. The same could not be said for Caidin. The lower half of his body lay crushed beneath the heavy bell. His hands were clenched into claws, and his green eyes bulged upward. Agony had twisted his face into a gruesome death mask. Wort slowly knelt beside the dead baron. With trembling fingers, he reached out and shut the staring eyes forever. He gazed at his hand, amazed at his own actions.

"You were wrong, my brother," he whispered. "See? You are gone, and yet I remain. Perhaps we were not bound together after all, you and I, save that both of us were monsters."

A shadow fell over him.

"He was the monster, Wort. Not you."

He looked up to see Mika. Her gown was a barely recognizable mass of tatters, her smooth skin was marked by red weals and dark bruises, and her face was smudged with dirt and tears. She was utterly beautiful. No matter what happened to her, no matter what she did, Mika would always be as beautiful as an angel. It was her nature. Just as it was his own nature to be . . . what he was.

"You're wrong, Mika," he replied hoarsely. Oddly, he felt a sort of peace. He knew what he was now, and in the full knowledge and acceptance of that truth there was a curious reassurance.

She started to protest, but he held up a hand, silencing her. Something had caught his eye. Next to the baron, amid the dull-gray rubble, was a stone unlike the others. It was so small that he might not have noticed it, save that it was darkly mottled and perfectly smooth. He could have sworn that he detected a shimmering aura of green light about it. He reached out and picked up the stone. It felt heavy and warm in his grip.

"What is this?" he wondered aloud.

"It must be the enchanted stone," Mika breathed.

He looked at her speculatively. "Enchanted? How so?"

Mika's gaze drifted to the hideous face of the baron. Quickly she looked away, swallowing hard. "It's called the Soulstone. The baron used it to drain the life-forces of his prisoners before he falsely executed them for treachery."

Wort looked at both stone and doctor in turn. "How do you know this?"

"There is . . ." With a shuddering breath, she corrected herself. "There *was* a spy in the keep, one of King Azalin's secret Kargat. Her name was the Lady Jadis. Caidin intended to attack the king with this tower. Jadis told me how he planned to do it. The stone . . . the stone was the key."

Wort rose, his brain working feverishly. Caidin had planned on attacking King Azalin with the stone? It must be powerful indeed. He clutched the thing tightly in his hand. Perhaps he could use this power to his own advantage somehow.

"Tell me more," he demanded.

With growing interest, Wort listened as she spoke of what she had learned from the dying Kargat—how Caidin had planned to use the life-force contained within the Soulstone to animate the tower, causing it to advance to the king's fortress of Avernus, crushing any army that stood in its way.

"But how did he intend to transfer the life-force within the stone into the tower?" Wort asked.

Mika shook her head. "I'm not certain. Jadis . . ." a frown creased the mask of dust and grime that covered her forehead. "Jadis mentioned something about an altar."

Wort snapped his fingers. "Yes! I saw it above, in the summit of the tower. There was a hollow in the altar, exactly the size of this." He gazed at the stone that rested in his palm. It was hard to believe that so much power resided within such a small object.

"It was a hideous plan." Mika shuddered, glancing one last time at the dead baron. "But now it will never come to pass. It is over, Wort." Her violet eyes met his own. "We are both free now." She held out a hand toward him.

Wort recoiled. "Don't touch me," he snapped, eyeing her warily.

Confusion flickered across her face. "What do you mean, Wort?" She took a hesitant step toward him.

He scrambled back over a pile of rubble. With sudden certainty, he knew that he must not let her lay a hand upon him. "Don't come any closer. I've seen . . . I've seen what your touch does to creatures of evil."

"What do you mean?" she gasped.

"You witnessed it yourself, Doctor. It happened when the dark spirits of the bell attempted to grasp you. Your innocence repelled them. Your radiance drove them back. Your very goodness destroyed them." He shook a misshapen fist at her. "I will not let you do the same to me."

"What about your back?" Mika said desperately. "I have studied the operation. I can heal you, Wort. I am certain of it. Please listen to me." She stumbled toward him, sobbing. "I can make you whole!"

His voice dripped venom. "I *am* whole."

Mika stared mutely.

"Though I despised him, I owe my brother this. He has made me see myself for what I am. Not for what I could have been, and not for what I might be—but for what I truly am." He raised weirdly long arms above his head in a gesture of exultation. "I am a creature of evil, Doctor. I am a being of utter darkness." His voice rose to a crescendo. "I—am—a—*monster!*"

He dropped his arms, jabbing a crooked finger at her. He uttered but a single, hoarse word. "Go."

Mika clenched her hands to either side of her head. "Please, Wort!"

He spat the word again. "Go."

Her voice rose. "I beg you, Wort—do not turn me away!" Trembling, she reached her arms out toward him. "I . . . I . . . ."

For a moment he almost thought she was going to say the words, *I love you.* Had she done so, those words might have wounded him, might have burrowed deep into his chest to pierce his heart, might have made him fall to his knees and, weeping like a child, cling to her as her cool hands soothed away his maddening fury.

Wort did not have the opportunity to find out. She fell silent as a forbidding new sound throbbed upon the air. At first it was a thrumming, so low that Wort felt it more than heard it, vibrating beneath his feet and deep inside his chest. It was as if some huge hand were drumming against the earth, beating out a tattoo. The sound grew rapidly louder. Wort lumbered to the door of the tower. After a moment's hesitation, Mika followed. Both stepped into the gloomy day outside.

At first Wort could see nothing in the misty air. Then his breath caught in his throat. Figures appeared out of the fog, lurching toward the tower. They came from all directions, more of them with each passing moment, walking slowly, clumsily toward him. Even before he caught the first fetid wisps of charnel house air, he knew what the figures were.

"Zombies," Wort croaked.

Still more of the creatures shambled out of the mist. The land itself shook with the weight of their footsteps. He heard a choking sound from Mika behind him, but he did not turn around. He could not tear his gaze from the sea of zombies. A spasm of realization passed through his body. There were actually some among the approaching undead whom he recognized.

There was Castellan Domeck, dirt clinging to the countless slashes that showed through his tattered uniform. And Contessa Sabrinda, clad in a worm-eaten gown, her face dark and swollen. There, too, was the bloodied form he knew to be Nartok's treasurer, and the dead-eyed tanner, and the two lovers, still hand in hand, their bodies pierced by a hundred thorns. All of the people he had murdered with the bell were there, risen from the grave, shuffling toward him. But there were hundreds of other zombies. Thousands. He could not possibly have slain them all.

One last time, the dark voice whispered mockingly in his mind. All whom the bell had ever slain, all who had paid the price of its curse, all who had ever died at its grisly tolling during the centuries of its existence, were climbing from their tombs to march upon the tower. They were coming for Wort. They were coming for vengeance.

"No," he whispered.

"Wort, what are they?" Mika cried shrilly.

"No," he said it again, louder this time. "I will not let them take me!"

The zombies stretched out their rotting arms as they drew nearer. Mika dashed toward the gray stallion tied next to the door. The beast snorted, staring with wild eyes at the approaching throng of undead. Unfastening the reins, Mika climbed into the saddle.

"Come on, Wort!" She gestured frantically for him to mount behind her. "We can outrun them! We'll be safe once we're away!"

"No. . . ." Dully, he shook his head. He could not take his eyes off the zombies. He could see hatred gleaming in their dead eyes, hatred and murder.

"Wort!" Mika cried plaintively. The frightened horse danced skittishly. Somehow she guided it toward him. "Please. Before it's too late. Come with me!"

Suddenly he knew what he had to do. His lips parted in a feral smile. He turned toward Mika. "You wish to help me, Doctor?" he growled. "You wish to save me? Very well, then!" He glanced at the zombies. They were closing in. "Let them follow you, not me!"

With a hand he struck the stallion's rump. The beast sprang into a gallop, its hooves pounding as it fled the tower. But the zombies approached from all directions. The horse could not avoid them. Mika screamed, holding on to the creature's mane in terror as it wheeled about.

Laughing, Wort dashed back into the tower. He knew the zombies would not possibly harm Mika— she was too innocent, too pure. But he hoped the doctor would occupy them long enough for him to do what he must. Gripping the Soulstone tightly, he clambered up the tower's steps. Chest heaving, he reached the top chamber. Lurching to the altar, he slapped the stone into the waiting hollow.

"Walk, tower!" he commanded. "Take me away from here!"

Green incandescence burst to life about the stone, engulfing it in a crackling sphere of magical fire. Wort stepped back in alarm, but the cool fire did not burn him. Suddenly tendrils of emerald magic sprouted from the shining stone to coil about the altar, tracing the arcane symbols in its surface until they too glowed with green fire. Slowly, the altar began to rise into the air. Like shimmering vines, more tendrils of magic snaked out from the floating altar, undulating across the floor of the chamber and traveling up the walls. The sizzling tendrils burrowed into the tower's stones like brilliant serpents. In moments the floor, the walls, the ceiling, the whole tower, was ablaze with crackling emerald magic. The acrid scent of lightning permeated the air.

Wort cowered as blazing bolts of energy arced back and forth across the chamber, accompanied by the roar of thunder. He was too slow. A crackling ray of magic plunged into his chest, passing completely through him. His body went stiff as the arc of magic that pierced his torso slowly lifted him off the floor. Frozen utterly still, flesh tingling as if pricked by a thousand cold needles, Wort hovered in midair next to the altar while countless bolts of green lightning sizzled back and forth across the chamber.

Abruptly the tendrils of emerald magic flared brilliantly. Wort squeezed his eyes shut, but it was no use. Green radiance flooded his brain. He was awash in a sea of liquid emerald fire. Then all went dim. Wort tumbled to the floor, rolling just in time to avoid being crushed by the altar as it did likewise. Slowly he dragged himself to his feet, panting for breath. All trace of the green magical energy was gone. For a panicked moment, Wort feared that the magic had failed.

That was when he felt the floor lurch beneath him. He almost fell, gripping the altar to steady himself. The tower shook again. A low groaning throbbed on the air. The floor began to rock up and down, almost like the heaving deck of a ship.

Carefully, Wort made his way to the narrow slit of a window. A howl of glee escaped him. Outside, the land moved steadily by. He peered downward and saw that the tower had raised itself upon two massive stone legs. These surged up and down, pounding the ground with terrible force as the tower strode swiftly across the moor. Wort clapped his hands together.

"I have done it!" he cried jubilantly. "I have—"

His words abruptly trailed off. Through the window he saw something that froze his blood. It was the sharp edge of a cliff. Before him lay Morrged's Leap. Wort knew the defile well. There, so long ago, he had saved Caidin's life. It was a thousand feet from the edge of the precipice to the sharp, jagged rocks below. And the tower was heading straight for it.

"Stop, tower!" Wort shouted. "Turn back!"

The rhythmic swaying drew the cliff closer.

"Halt!" Wort cried desperately. A thought struck him. The tower had responded before when he had gripped the stone. Perhaps he needed to do so again. With a flicker of hope, he turned toward the àltar.

He had not heard them climbing up the stairwell.

They shambled into the chamber in a ghastly flood. They had not wasted time on the doctor after all. The zombies. In seconds they surrounded him. He struggled fiercely as their clammy hands closed upon him. Rotting flesh tore in his fingers; his hands sank into their decomposing bodies. There were too many of them. They continued to spill from the stairwell in a rank, crushing tide. Hundreds of them.

"No!" Wort shrieked. "Don't you understand? The tower is heading for the cliff. We'll all be killed, you fools!"

Dark laughter bubbled from Wort's chest as the zombies sank their dirty claws into him. It was *he* who was the fool.

"Don't you see, Wort? They don't care. They're already dead!"

More twisted laughter escaped his lips as the zombies began to tear him apart.

*   *   *   *   *

Mika clutched the stallion's tangled mane, trying desperately to stay on the courser's back. The beast screamed as it whirled around, but in every direction its wild eyes saw the same horrible sight—hundreds of zombies. They shuffled by in varied states of decay. The stench that rose from them was so thick Mika thought it would drown her. Yet none of the animated corpses seemed to take note of her or the panicked horse. All shambled unceasingly toward the tower.

A terrible grating of stone on stone shook the air. Slowly, ponderously, the tower began to rise. Those zombies that had just been stepping through the doorway fell, striking the ground with wet thuds. Mika's amazement at this turn of events barely registered in her reeling mind. The stone spire rose higher into the air, revealing two massive pillars of stone beneath. Emerald lightning sizzled, coiling about the thick columns. Suddenly one of the gigantic columns lifted itself off the ground and swung forward. The tower tipped at a precarious angle. Mika screamed. It was falling!

The second column rose and swung forward, striking the ground with a *boom!* The tower moved forward. At last, realization pierced the fog that clouded Mika's mind. The spire was not raised upon two columns, but two massive legs hewn of stone. The ponderous stone legs moved forward. The massive construction lurched up and down as it began to move across the moor. The dark tower of war was walking.

Mindlessly, the zombies streamed after the moving spire. The weighty stone feet came down upon them, crushing dozens to an oozing pulp with every step. The other zombies seemed not to notice. They continued to swarm after the tower. Like a weird, armless giant of stone, the tower lumbered onward.

The gray stallion could not find passage through the roiling sea of undead. As if caught in a dark rapture, Mika watched the tower stride across the moor. It was almost . . . glorious. She did not notice the edge of the cliff until the tower was almost upon it. Then she clamped a hand to her mouth, unable to tear her eyes away from the grim spectacle. One stone leg stepped over the precipice. For a moment, the tower tottered precariously. Then slowly, almost majestically, the tower toppled over the cliff. For a long moment, the only sound was the low moan of the wind. Then a violent tremor shook the air.

Mad with fright, the stallion reared onto its hind legs. Mika grabbed at the creature's mane, but her fingers were torn loose. Like a rag doll, her body was hurled through the air. For a second it seemed as if she were flying. Then she struck the ground with violent force, fire exploding in her shoulder. A single thought, like the feeble flame of a dying candle, flickered through her brain. *I am coming, my loves.* Then all went dark.

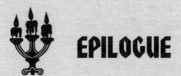

EPILOGUE

Purple twilight drifted down from the sky to settle gently over the Vistana camp. Countless lanterns flared to life, their golden light driving back the gathering gloom. Smoke rose from a dozen cookfires, thick with the rich scents of venison, pepper, and sage. Wild music drifted through the motley collection of painted wagons, as did bright laughter, the clinking of cups, and the rhythmic clapping of hands. Fires and lanterns were by no means the only warmth in the gypsy caravan.

In most of the realm of Darkon, the Vistani were regarded with mistrust and suspicion. They were rumored to be shiftless wanderers, dabblers in dark magic, thieves and swindlers all. Here, on the open moor, there were none to look askance at them. Here the gypsies were their own masters. The Vistani were an ancient people—perhaps as ancient as the land itself, some few and wise dared to whisper—and all the land was their home. So it had always been, and so, they believed, it would always be.

Near the edge of the camp, three gypsy women stood in the flickering shadows cast by a stone-ringed fire. The three women were very different in aspect, one being fresh and young, another at the midpoint of life, and the last a wizened crone. Each seemed to wear a mantle of wisdom about her shoulders, and each wore an ancient jeweled ring on a finger. Their names were Karin, Riandra, and Varith, and they were the sages of this gypsy clan. They spoke together in soft tones, apart from the others.

"Was the augury fully unveiled?" asked Riandra.

Young Karin nodded firmly. "It was. The cards spoke clearly, as did the crystals. The bell has cracked. Its curse has shattered. Darkness has lost this battle."

Varith's sigh was like the low voice of a winter wind. "You speak hastily, Karin. The bell is no more. Yet many other relics of Darkness remain to devour the Light." Her small eyes glittered sharply as she leaned upon her crooked staff. "The battle is far from over."

"Will it ever truly be over?" Riandra murmured wistfully.

Silence was the only answer as the three women gazed solemnly at one another.

Suddenly the wild music that drifted on the purple air halted. Shouts of surprise and joy rang out. As one, the three Vistana sages rushed to the center of the camp.

"Steffan is back!" someone called out excitedly.

As one, the folk of the clan dropped what they were doing and rushed to gather about a man who limped into the circle of the wagons. He was handsome, with coal-dark eyes and a long mustache. His colorful gypsy attire—billowing pants, embroidered shirt, and crimson sash—was torn and stained with mud, and a splint fashioned of willow saplings was lashed tightly to his left leg. Quickly a chair was brought for him, and a silver cup of spiced wine placed in his hand. With an exhausted sigh, he sank down into the chair.

"It is good to be with the clan once more." His grin

was tired but happy.

"Steffan, the Light shines upon us!" Karin said, her pretty face beaming as the three sages approached. "We feared that we had lost you."

Riandra nodded gravely. "What happened, Steffan?"

A dozen voices echoed the question. Ancient Varith silenced them with a sharp look.

"Shame! Can you not see the man has been through a dark ordeal? Let him be!"

Steffan held up a hand. "It is all right, Wise One. They are curious, that's all. Besides, I have good news." He reached into a pocket and drew out a small object. It was a darkly mottled stone.

"The Soulstone," Karin breathed. "You found it, Steffan!"

He nodded, then held the stone toward Varith. "Will you take it, Wise One? I find that I do not like to carry it on my person."

"Nor should you, for it is a thing of utter evil." Varith took the stone. Carefully, she wrapped it in a cloth of blue silk and spirited it away into a pocket of her skirt. "You have done well, Steffan. Now one less relic of darkness is loose in the land. I will keep it safe and hidden." She glanced at the other two sages. "Until we find a way to destroy it."

"What happened to your leg, Steffan?" Riandra asked then.

The gypsy man shook his head sheepishly. "I was so happy when I found the stone in the wreckage of the tower that I grew careless. As I was climbing back up the cliff face, I slipped and fell. My leg was broken. I thought . . . I thought that I would die." He shuddered at the memory. "But I didn't."

Karin knelt to examine the splint on his leg. "A skilled hand did this," she murmured. "Who helped you, Steffan?"

His eyes glittered. Finally he whispered the words. "It was the angel. . . ."

Gasps went around the circle. In these last weeks, all had heard the legend of the Angel of the Moor. Again and again, folk who had become lost or injured on the desolate heath told the identical tale. Just as hope had faded, a mysterious woman had appeared out of the swirling mists to help them. Without speaking a word, the angel had healed their wounds and guided them to safety before vanishing silently into the fog. Some people said she was hideously disfigured. Others said she was radiantly beautiful, as pale and ethereal as a ghost. All spoke of her eyes—haunting, mesmerizing eyes like violet flames.

Steffan went on. "Just when I was ready to let the crows take me, there she stood. She splinted my leg and gave me herbs to ease my pain. For three days she brought me food and water. Not once did she speak a word. Finally I was strong enough to try to walk again. As soon as she saw I could make it on my own, she vanished. I never even had the chance to thank her." He was silent for a moment. When he spoke again his voice was soft and low. "As long as I live, I will never forget her eyes." He shook his head in wonder. "An angel's eyes. . . ."

Karin, Riandra, and Varith exchanged knowing, sorrowful looks, but they said nothing.

Music and light drifted anew on the darkling air, filling the night with celebration.

*   *   *   *   *

She stood on the edge of a sheer precipice, glowing in the gauzy moonlight like a statue hewn of white marble. The wind whipped soft tatters of silk about her body like tendrils of lavender mist, and her golden hair streamed back from a face as round and pale as the rising moon. Injury had twisted one of her shoulders into a hideous hump, yet this imperfection only seemed to accentuate the ethereal beauty of her face. The woman gripped something that hung about her throat. Metal glinted in the moonlight. It was a golden locket. The woman stared madly into the night, as if her glowing violet eyes glimpsed something there that no other could see—something vast, and ancient, and eternally ravenous.

At last she turned and vanished into the gloom, leaving the darkness to its own designs.